Plateye

An African Spirit of Fear
Haunts Post-Colonial Georgia

Jennifer Allen Noyer

Jennifer Allen Noyer

Plain View Press
http://plainviewpress.net

1101 W. 34th Street, STE 404
Austin, TX 78705

ISBN: 978-1-63210-003-0
Library of Congress Control Number: 2014942677

This is a work of fiction. Names, characters, places, and incidents either are the product of the author's imagination or are used fictitiously. Any resemblance to events, locales, or actual persons—living or dead—is entirely coincidental.

Cover painting by Albert Noyer
Layout by Pam Knight

We Find Healing In Existing Reality
Plain View Press is a 36-year-old issue-based literary publishing house. Our books result from artistic collaboration between writers, artists, and editors. Over the years we have become a far-flung community of activists whose energies bring humanitarian enlightenment and hope to individuals and communities grappling with the major issues of our time—peace, justice, the environment, education and gender. This is a humane and highly creative group of people committed to art and social change. The poems, stories, essays, non-fiction explorations of major issues are significant evidence that despite the relentless violence of our time, there is hope and there is art to show the human face of it.

To the loving memory of my father James Allen

and to my husband Albert Noyer for all his support

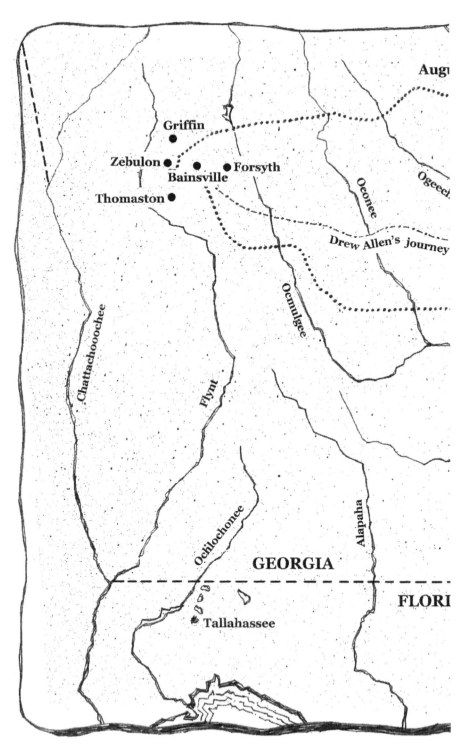

Map of South Carolina Post Revolutionary War

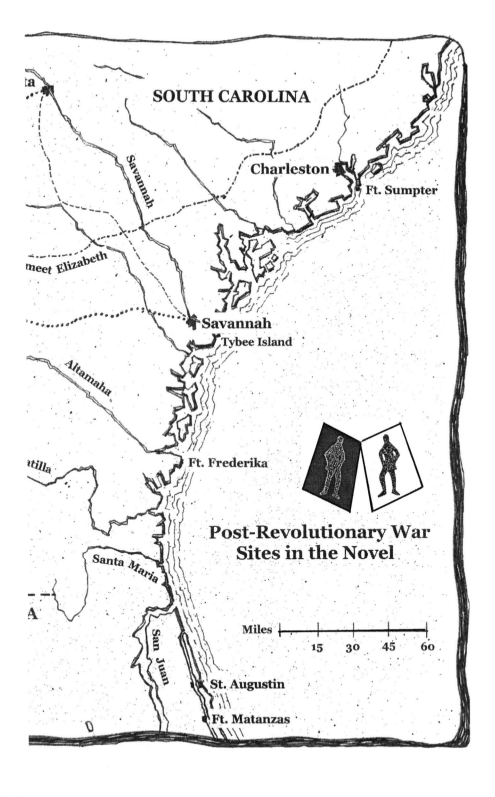

SOUTH CAROLINA

Charleston

Ft. Sumpter

Savannah

Savannah

meet Elizabeth

Tybee Island

Altamaha

tilla

Ft. Frederika

Post-Revolutionary War
Sites in the Novel

Santa Maria

Miles

15   30   45   60

San Juan

St. Augustin

Ft. Matanzas

Foreword

The mythical figure of Plateye, also spelled Platteye, floats through the folklore of the deep South in the United States as a kind of demon who searches out human weakness and terrifies the dreams of believers. While the black people of the Sea Islands off the coast of Georgia and South Carolina tell stories of Plateye's evil, the history of New Orleans reeks with steamy tales of voodoo and Plateye. In this novel, Plateye serves as a metaphor for the spiritual damage done to both white and black by the evil of slavery.

The novel's characters, living in the frontier lands of Georgia at the beginning of the 19th century, are all fictional, although the family name, Allen, was my own before marriage. Some of the childhood experiences of James Allen and his siblings are recorded in my family's written history, but have been rearranged to appear at different times than they originally occurred. When he was a boy, the real 20th century James Allen was indeed struck down with a mysterious paralysis, which lasted one year.

Old timers, some of whom were born in the 1860s, have written in the *History of Pike County Georgia: 1822–1989* that some white men in the communities there supported two families, one black and one white. The situation in this novel is a creative speculation that at times, someone might have taken his or her mixed race child and passed them off as white through motivations of love and the drive to have offspring. It is a device to explore the conflict between the forces of love and social rejection: fear and hatred in conflict with friendship and desire.

Jennifer Allen Noyer

Prologue

I had a dream, last night
That's troublin' me.
I had a dream
Last night
That's troublin' me

The voice rises from the kitchen and moves across the marsh and into the darkness. Its plaintive melody soars higher with each word at first, then finally sighs into the lower registers on the last three words. Old men and women sit alone in shadowed rooms in the heat of early evening, dreaming old dreams as the fading light sends long, low shafts across the floors.

Ghosts wander among the live oaks on this semi-deserted island in the Georgia wetlands. Spanish moss dips and sways above deserted trails. A small group of wild donkeys ceases to crop the long marsh grass as each one raises its head in silence. The moss flows in the wind over their heads, and they seem seized by a wandering spirit of the night.

Oh, I jus' lay down in ma bed,
Somethin' jump into ma head—
I had a dream—
Last night—
That's troublin' me.

The air seems to tremble as the last vibration dies. Outside, the thick tropical growth is backlit by reflected light on the marsh beyond.

Something seems to disturb the leaves on a path through the forest. The wind picks up a wraith, a ghostly memory of the African will-o'-the-wisp, a man-deceiver, a god called Plateye. It moves across ancient shell mounds like smoke, curling around sharp edges picked clean by Indian tongues five hundred years ago. It lingers, gestating, gaining mass from restless souls; Calibans whose dead eyes long to search the island once again for giant turtles, birds and deer.

Tiny frogs dart away sensing invisible feet. The time warp of imagination works in a space of frightening separation. Stronger now, the spirit stretches out to probe the thick jungle of palm, live oak, pine, and twisting vines. Old decaying trunks of trees, are rich with new parasitic life, feeding on ancient shell mounds. Like a morning swamp mist, the spirit's ghostly fingers probe the forest. It swirls around giant shapes draped with gray, air-breathing moss.

It bows to them: primeval totems—grotesque, frozen forever, monuments to lost gods, lost worlds.

Finally, man-made shapes appear. Squares and rectangles of cleared areas open to the remains of an old barn, a barracks for now-dead field hands, abandoned ruins of a main house. Feral pigs rut through fallen clumps of plaster made of mud and shells. All this is seen and understood as the silent being hovers, explores each crack and sends out tongues to lick the corners clean of all their secrets. Finally it comes to an end. Only palms and palmettos fringe the deep forest where island ends and sea begins. The sounds of growing land-things stop, and the long incline of white sand begins the descent into the waves.

A few brave skeletons remain there as bark scavenged by the constant wind. These trees challenged the sea and were wiped clean by it, twisted into agonized shapes, and left to remind the land of the great water.

Close by is a small patch of land with a little fence around it, half blown down. It is a different sort of clearing in the forest, with little mounds of dirt covered with bits of broken crockery. Old medicine bottles, a spoon sticking up out of the dirt, a broken goblet, and a doll's head adorn the small mounds. The spirit lingers here, spreads like a blanket over the burial ground. Some energy disturbs the grains of sand, vibrates there amongst old buried bones, awakes a sleeping memory of this ancient spirit. He glows like an earthbound moon, struggling to rise and join the orbit of his mother.

Who is this searching for a tenuous home?

Descendants of these African bones say little about him—only that he is very old, displaced from the old land when he pursued his people here as slaves.

Plateye lured, beguiled, and finally destroyed. In Africa, red flags on sandy beaches, smiling white faces, and glittering baubles drew the people from the forest's rim. Some on this new island have followed him with eager, loving eyes, into the swamp, only to become lost, drained of strength and warmth, to sink and die in the mud. Now dark faces turn their heads away and hide.

Plateye saw and knew white men too: he reached out to lead them on and on. Now he still may creep into the hearts of each generation to be reborn. White men followed Plateye to Savannah in search of instant wealth, mansions, and gardens. English debtors hoped to lie in perfumed splendor, while silk worms wove their fortunes and set them free. Pirates smelled old Plateye as they cruised around the mysterious marshy islands and crept into a sheltered harbor at night. Silk worms failed and sickness thrived, but men kept coming south.

Chapter 1 — Betrothed

Just before entering the house, Elizabeth Yarborough glanced at the shabbily dressed man coming along the dirt road. She thought, *November, and another one. The War of Independence has been over two months and General Washington surely is letting his men come back.*

A chill shook Elizabeth's body as she closed the door, canceling her red cheeks and bringing a blue-white pallor to her lips. "In this cold," she chastised herself, "I should have dressed warmer for that walk to the north field."

Thin, with a complexion so fair that the tiny blue vessels beneath the skin on her forehead were visible enough to cast an aura of frailty about her face. Light-blue eyes set deep in their sockets enhanced the lost, abandoned look of an ill child. Yet the woman's brilliant red-gold hair, curving over one delicate shoulder, belied her sickly demeanor and somehow suggested a source of vitality concealed within the skull underneath.

A knock sounded on the door as she hung her cloak on the peg by the kitchen window. *Is it that fellow?* When she half-opened the portal, fearful, a tall man stood outside, his feet swathed in dirty bandages instead of shoes. He wore splattered homespun pants under a soiled, leather-fringed jacket, and had pulled his broad-brimmed hat low over his brow. *Too ragged to be a Continental. Some Gypsy or wandering Indian, most like—*

Elizabeth drew back in horror when one of his feet blocked open the door and a large, bony hand reached forward to grasp her arm. She looked desperately around like a trapped animal and almost screamed. There was no one within two miles to hear her.

"M...move on, sir," she found the courage to order. "On with you now!" She flung an arm gesture in the direction of the road. "I have nothing here to share with beggars."

The stranger pulled his hand away and smiled. "Let me fetch wood and fix your shed," he offered in a voice barely more than a hoarse whisper. "A little ale and bread will do me quite well at first...and then, Elizabeth, we've much to do together."

"You...you know my name?" She drew back in disbelief. *This gaunt man in thread-bare clothes knows me.* The possibility shook her and a remembered quaver vibrated deep in her belly. The dark, uncut hair curled above a forehead grimed with dust from the road, and the man's black eyes were hooded beneath his brows. "D...Drew? Drew Allen?"

He nodded and the smile broadened. "Back from the war."

"Back from the war, are you? What do you want from me? You haven't sent a word in years! Years! Do you think I'll fall on you with tears and kisses, man?" Her hands trembled at her sides, curling into fists as she spoke.

"You want to strike me, Elizabeth! I don't blame you, but hear me out... please, sweet girl!"

Drew looked so forlorn and ragged that she turned abruptly, wiped a tear from her cheek, and muttered, "Come in. Come in then."

He followed her into the room that served both as small parlor and tiny kitchen. A large fireplace lay cold in the far wall with a high backed bench in front of it. Elizabeth hurried to the pile of wood that lay in an alcove next to the wide opening to the fire pit. "The fire has died. I was walking out by the river for too long. I must..."

She felt a restraining hand on her shoulder; Drew reached down in front of her and plucked four logs from the pile, then knelt to arrange them on the blackened bricks.

"Let me do this for you. Rest there on the bench." He turned his head to smile at her, and nodded as she sat down. As a small flame started to lick the starter twigs, then gradually climb toward the larger logs, Drew stood with his back to her and watched its progress. "If you only knew how many times I imagined a moment like this, standing near you in front of a home fire." He shook his head and came to sit beside her. Elizabeth inadvertently leaned slightly away from him, and shivered when he put his arm around her and tried to draw her towards him. He smiled again and gently withdrew his arm, leaning forward, both elbows resting on his knees.

"I'm so sorry, Drew. It is just that you seem strange. I need to understand many things about you." She saw hurt in his eyes as he turned to look at her. "You were gone for seven years! Other men stopped from time to time on their way to battles and told of the war to the north, but you never came. My sister began three years ago to pester me about you. Her husband swore I should accept new suitors. There were offers, you see." Elizabeth covered her face with her hands as tears threatened to flow. She gritted her teeth to choke back sobs. "I...don't know you anymore!" She felt his hand rest gently on her cheek, thumb caressing her lower lip, and almost moaned.

Then, raising her chin with his other hand, Drew murmured, "I want to know you, my dear—very, very much." He bent to lightly touch his lips to hers, then held her trembling in his arms as tears crept down his cheeks. "Here's a beginning then," he whispered and leaned his head to rest against the wooden backboard of the bench. "I came south from Virginia, here to North Carolina to gain a promise of marriage from you, Elizabeth."

"Marriage! Do you really think so? I'm an old maid now." She stood abruptly and stepped away from him. "Everyone laughs to see me working side by side with my sister and her husband. 'Look at the poor thing! She is fading like a September rose. That scoundrel from Virginia's gone to ground.' And I've kept spinning tales to stop their wicked tongues." Elizabeth turned and went to open the front door again. "I can't believe you now, isn't that pathetic? I almost wish you'd been killed. Go on, take your marriage promises with you!"

Drew had never seen this anger from his betrothed before. "At least listen, Elizabeth," he pleaded, "then throw me out if you must. I...I tried to send news, but was wounded twice and half out of my mind for weeks at a time. Each time I healed they sent me on to other battles."

She walked slowly back around the bench, her eyes taking in every detail of his body, seeing the gauntness anew, the stooped shoulders and bony wrists. Finally she sat beside him once more, and dropped her hands to her lap.

Drew sighed and leaned back before continuing, "That was in Seventeen seventy-seven. You were only sixteen years old then, but so sunny, filled with delight every time I smiled at you, and you looked to me like the perfect dream of a wife. I was perhaps hasty, but felt I had to have you for my own. You seemed willing, Elizabeth, and your father gave me your promise." He looked hard at her then. She could feel the intensity of him, but she remained silent. "When General Greene put out the call for men in the Carolinas, and Redcoats were said to be raiding farms and killing all, slave and freemen, I felt I had to enlist in the Continental Army. I thought any war would not last more than a few months, that surely the British would come to see how strong was our conviction to be free of them. Sometimes I came within forty miles of you here, but that was at least a two days ride from the camp." He stood and walked toward the fire, now roaring with flames licking almost too high against the firewall. "I have plans for us, Elizabeth. If you'll have me again, we'll go south to claim new land given me by General Washington. He gave grants to all of us who stayed with the army through to the end."

Elizabeth felt the power of the man, his strength and focus. She remembered the feel of his arms about her when they had danced at a local party years ago. Her muscles seemed to contract in pleasure at the memory of being lifted in his arms into a wagon that carried them across the meadow towards town to file papers for betrothal. She was still captive to his brooding charm, but fearful of the intensity of his desire now that he stood close. She had lived in dreams for too long.

❧❧

Weeks passed while Elizabeth watched Drew as he worked beside her brother-in-law, Charles Hilton. He was planning to expand the farm and build a large house for his family, complete with slave quarters along the edge of the forest. Hilton had invested recently in a shipping company allied to New England slave importers, and planned to avail himself of a large company of Negro workers for his vision of a fine plantation. Drew rode out with Hilton each morning, but Elizabeth saw that he grew more and more frustrated with the family projects.

One afternoon she begged her sister Candace to forgive her, but that she must walk out alone for a few hours. "I need to think quietly about a marriage with Drew Allen, for he grows impatient with me. I am still confused and a bit frightened by the man."

Candace shook her head impatiently, her tight blond curls bobbing above her brow. She grew weary of her sister's moods. Since she had waited this long, why not, for the good Lord's sake, go and settle with Drew. She'd not get many offers now, not at her age. Heavens, she was almost twenty-four years old, though she looked much younger, practically like a child at times. "I do declare, Elizabeth! Go on out to the river if it will help, but do make up your mind! Hilton's quite tired of all this back and forth with you and Drew!"

Elizabeth frowned and turned away from the house without a word to her sister. Wearing her long blue wool coat with the hood wrapped tightly to her face by a scarf, she strode over the near fields toward the large rocks at the foot of a flat-topped hill. She worked her way through brambles and thick bushes to her favorite plateau, a huge horizontal rock that protruded over the nearby river. It was a thinking spot, a place to imagine different lives in different worlds. She had come here often during the lonely years of waiting, imagining Drew as an elegant, slightly dangerous young lover, a tall guardian in a striking blue military jacket.

Elizabeth lay down on the browning grass, and leaned over the edge of the plateau to look down at the tiny beach. She had heard that this was the place where Indian children had tried to learn to fly many years ago. She thought of them as flocks of screaming crows dipping into the bordering trees, or flying into the wind over the cliff's edge. Phantom children, feathered now, daring to fly forever, and wondered, *Do tiny bones lie buried beneath the sand below?* A shadow fell across her hand that rested on the brim of the cliff. She turned her head abruptly and saw the tall figure above her. Without a word Drew kneeled with his legs on either side of her feet, and bent to encircle her chest with his arms and lift her back towards him. His breath was warm against her cheek. She sighed and turned to face him.

"I do love you, Drew!" she whispered and leaned her forehead against his chin.

"Then marry me soon, Elizabeth, for I cannot endure this longer."

Five months passed after a small, solemn wedding, The man and woman worked together as an efficient team, grooming the brother-in-law's land by day, side by side with his black workers, and warming each other in the small bedroom by night as the winter months wore on to an early southern spring. With shyness and sometimes a quiet anger, Elizabeth began a marriage seven years late. Drewry found himself holding back from her delicate type of beauty, but loved to watch her by the kitchen fire in the evenings as the light danced through her strawberry hair.

One night, as they lay side by side, like marble statues on top of a sepulcher, Drew rose on one elbow and looked down into his wife's face. "Are you asleep already, Elizabeth?" When she moved her head slightly from side to side, to indicate she was not, but kept her eyes tightly shut, he ventured, "I feel there is something that rests between us, a barrier I fear to touch. Do...do you love me yet? Or is there something that you are afraid to tell me?"

Elizabeth opened her eyes, but looked over his shoulder as she spoke. "Where were you all those years during the war that always kept you from me? Others returned after their time was up, but you stayed on and on. My sister thought me a fool to wait for such a man, while I dreamed of so many heroic battles that demanded your attention."

He caressed her hair, then bent to kiss her cheek. She pushed him away, "Answer me, Drew! Was I a fool, and where were those pretty ladies that follow the army and distract men like you?"

He rolled away from her. The air was cold in the early spring night, and he shivered as a draft from the open window swept across his chest and carried him back to the battle at Cowpens. *Aye, can ye wipe the cow shit from yer musket and give us a fight, Scottish trash?* yelled a blue-lipped boy from some city slum. The crude taunts of English soldiers were silenced with a thrust of a bayonet. How could he explain the seductive lure of the pack, the heart clutching siren's song of rifle fire and cannons belching into the night? And there was the sturdy girl indentured to the tavern keeper near Baltimore, who sneaked out one night, never to return, and followed him to Guilford Court House. But she left, building a hoard for her future with a host of lovers in the company.

"Drew, can you answer me?"

"I'm here, M'am. I've froze up north and buried men old enough to be my father, and young enough to be my baby brother. I want to love you, take you with me into the rich lands to the south of here. I'm a man now, Elizabeth, and I know I've been careless of my duty to you. Be with me now. Come, turn back. Let me see your eyes looking straight into mine for once!"

She reached to touch his cheek, and slowly turned to look up at his face. How could he have been so frightened of being a man before? Was she forbidding? Did she lack somehow? He was her first love, and she guessed he would be her only one. At twenty-four there was little chance of another. She was old to be starting out on the road of marriage.

Drew rose from the bed and searched in his pants that hung on a peg by the bed. When he found the papers, he lit the candle on the windowsill and bent to read once more the exciting promises listed in the letter. The Continental Congress of the United States, it said, was pleased to grant William Drewry Allen one hundred acres in Monroe County, Georgia in recognition of bravery in the line of duty in the Continental Army, North Carolina line. He handed it to Elizabeth. "Look there. Do you see the hand of General Washington himself? Here's proof of what I have been telling you for months."

Elizabeth read the letter slowly, thinking as she read, *Alone with this man in the wilderness! No family at all. Can he take their place? Does he really want me or just a white slave to help him with the new land and mother new children? Do I really love him? And yet—land of our own! No one to answer to, except him, of course. My own private places!* "Do you know me well enough Drew? I mean, we will be together, alone for years in the forest, with neighbors miles away..." Her voice broke, and she turned her head towards the feather pillow. "Can you love just me?"

Drew pulled her to him, and rolled her over his chest. "Aye, I'm yours. See, I'm in your power!" He grinned and lifted his head to kiss her lips.

Living on another man's land was not for Drewry Allen. North Carolina would do, but he looked farther south, to Savannah and the rich lands around the Georgia coast. Exotic tales of tropical fruit trees, a land of rich spices, even silk, and the excitement of discovering new territory! All of this stirred uneasy couples to pack a wagon for the trek that drew so many after the war.

Drew and Elizabeth loaded what furniture they had—plus whatever Candace insisted she take from their father's estate—on a wagon pulled by two horses and started south along the eastern slope of the Appalachian Mountains.

Chapter 2— Journey South

E ach night they stopped to make a simple camp next to the wagon, grateful for the now warm evenings as they looked up into the sky from their blanket rolls. In the mornings, Elizabeth noticed a growing unease and tension in Drew's face as he moved around gathering enough wood for a morning cook fire. By the time they had loaded up again and hitched the horses, he seemed to have regained his energy and quiet eagerness for the journey. But he began praying at night, kneeling by the camp fire. He alternated mumbling with eyes closed, and shooting furtive glances into the darkness before slipping under the blankets next to his wife.

"Your mighty close to Jesus these nights, my dear" she remarked one evening. "But why do you look so often into the dark trees?"

He turned wide, feverish, bloodshot eyes to her, took her face in his hands and turned it toward the black forest. "Do you see a light yonder, Elizabeth?"

She squinted as she tried to see beyond the black silhouettes of pine branches into the depths of the woods. The moon was barely visible with just the curved cusp of light sneaking out from behind a smoky cloud. She saw nothing. "You dream, husband."

"I think it is a sign. The Lord wants to lead us to our new place. He knows a better way out of this desert. Each night I pray for guidance, Elizabeth. It seems to take too long on this path, and it wanders in ways I don't see on the map Jonathon drew for us."

Elizabeth was amazed at the passion of what seemed a strange obsession in this man who laughed at the visions of spirit birds that flew through her dreams.

"What do you see, Drew?"

"A yonder light through the trees! It beckons me every night." He sagged against the wagon wheel. Looking down at the faint glimmer of the campfire he sighed. "It's not there now. It was, but now it's gone." He slid down to the ground, and with a slight shiver reached for her hand and kissed it before pulling the blanket back up over her shoulders and stretching out beside her. "I'm sorry, my dear. You must be right. The emptiness here it...it conjures!" He shook his head sharply. *Almost like a tic,* she thought. "Such strange sights— here, in my head." he murmured striking his temple with the heel of his hand.

"My dear, I'm so sorry for you." Elizabeth reached over to gently touch his face.

Yet each night Drewry swore he saw the light through the forest, ephemeral, yet strangely familiar. Some nights it appeared to be a blue-white moon, hung low, which lit a cleared path through the pines. Elizabeth began to dream of a different spirit. The dream birds, who became friendly visitors at her river hide-away in North Carolina, were replaced by a smiling face on a gray head. It bobbed like a giant cork on a stormy lake, forward and back, a reptilian tongue darting out of its mouth.

After a long day on the trail, around sundown they arrived at the foot of a mountain. The ground felt soft beneath their feet, as though recently watered by a spring shower. The trees at the edge of the woods were softly green with young leaves. The purplish tint of redbud glimmered from deep within the growth. With an unfamiliar sense of peace, they settled down for the evening. Two rivers met about fifty yards away; the Saluda joined the Congaree as it rushed toward the coast.

Elizabeth carried water to the campfire Drew had built, and began to mix a batch of stew in a great black pot brought from home. She broke up hardtack in boiling water that was softening salted pork. A plant with succulent leaves, like watercress, grew nearby that she remembered growing near the streams on the Wake County property. She added it for its slight lemon flavor, just as Drew returned with a fat rabbit he had killed. Within the hour they were able to eat their meal and then settle down for the night.

They were now somewhere in the middle of South Carolina, and had traveled about two hundred miles, with two hundred more to go before reaching Greene County, Georgia. The nights had grown warm by this time, and they fell asleep quickly as the shadows faded into total blackness.

Sometime in the night Elizabeth dreamed she heard a voice laughing somewhere in the forest. Then, an hour or so before dawn, she was shaken awake by Drew.

"Come quickly, woman!" he ordered brusquely. "We must pack up now and follow the Lord. I cannot deny him again! Look, He shows a way through to a safe and narrow crossing of yonder river. Come now! Look!" He pointed to a faint glimmer that even Elizabeth saw between the trees.

She felt haggard and weak, needing rest as never before in her life. A terrible fear gripped her as she saw the hot-eyed obsession in her husband's face. She had thought she was beginning to know him again, but this...this strong, sturdy man was trembling with such a wildness! "Go, if you must," she protested, "yet leave me be! I'll not step into that dark place! If you are right, and it is the Lord calling, I'm just not ready for Him."

He turned on her and growled, "How obstinate you are! You can rest tomorrow. I'll carry you." He stooped to pick her up, but she pushed him away and stumbled forward a few feet in the direction of the light.

"Leave! Go, Satan!" she screamed, and began to rock and keen.

Drew calmed immediately and went to her, pulling her shaking body to his chest.

"Shh, hush, I'll not go till morning. You'll feel better then."

Neither one truly had slept as the dawn slowly began to draw the silhouetted shapes of bushes, rocks, and trees around them. Drew sat by the morning cook fire, his black brows drawn together. *Brooding*, she thought a she packed their wooden bowls away on the wagon.

"Do ye know what we're up against, Elizabeth? You're frail and fearful to be crossing this wilderness with me."

She turned to see Drew standing next to the smoking remains of the fire, his expression one of desperate frustration. He pulled savagely on the brim of his hat and finally threw it to the ground. "Why in Hell did you wait for me so long? You've wound your way in, lady, and I can't seem to tear you out! I'm tangled with you now, it seems." Sometimes he felt like gasping for air when she lay beside him and longed to grasp her, shake her. It was hopeless, he admitted to himself. He loved her, and they would ignore these important calls and visions. They would travel the long way outlined by her earthbound, unimaginative father back in North Carolina.

"I love you, Drew. Indeed I really do, but sometimes I'm stronger than you." She smiled slyly. "Especially when it comes to all them ghostly lights in the forest." He turned away from her then and sat down abruptly on a rock next to the fire. She poured one more bucket of water on the remaining embers. After an awkward moment, Elizabeth stretched out her hand to draw him back, and whispered, "Where was yonder light in the forest?"

He gestured sullenly over his shoulder toward a depression at the northern edge of the clearing. Elizabeth walked over, picked up a rock at her feet, and threw it as far as she could in the same direction. Drew turned to see it fall heavily to ground. Together they watched with growing horror as the rock slowly sank in a hidden bog.

"The Lord's saved us from danger." Drew said quietly. After hitching the mules to the wagon, he walked carefully over the ground leading to a spot where the rock had disappeared. He tested each footstep gingerly with the sole of each foot before placing his weight, and then began to pace off the dimensions of the treacherous ground. It was almost eight feet long, and four wide. A thought shivered through his body: *Perfect for a double grave!*

Traveling almost fifteen miles each day, they finally reached Greene County twenty-six days after leaving the farm in Wake County, and then further west yet. They bought two hundred eighty acres there that were adjacent to their grant land, for five hundred dollars. The house they built was primitive, but was so well designed by Drew that it offered unlimited possibilities for expansion. The dwelling was made of logs, with two rooms divided by a central hall that extended from the front to a back porch. It lay in a gently sloping hollow at the edge of a wood. The land then dropped sharply to a creek. When Drew and Elizabeth first arrived, local Indians still shared the creek amicably with settlers.

Drew cleared his land and began to farm that first year. The same flow of energy that brought him so far from the "civilized" South worked in his favor, and the farm grew. In the front yard, he planted two cedar trees, one on each side of the front porch stairs. Settlers clung to symmetry in the wild new lands.

In the early mornings, a mist would swirl over newly cleared land, cradling felled trees where they lay. While the young settlers still slept, in preparation for the stupefying labor required for a first planting, the steamy strands formed shapes in the air: features slowly came together for a fanciful, willing eye to see. Drew rose early at dawn, but now it was Elizabeth, whose imagination caught the misty shapes as she stood in front of her house. Scratching sounds, the rush of frightened and hurrying clawed feet, could be fashioned by superstitious minds into savage spirits dashing through a haunted landscape, or creatures fleeing some apparition.

Elizabeth gradually came to fear this land.

Oh, jus' lay down in your bed,
I jus' jump into yo' head.
Dream, dream
Some nights—
It's me be troublin' you.

Chapter 3— Dilby

In 1764, James Hargreaves invented the first successful spinning machine, called the 'cotton jenny.' By the turn of the century, 20,000 jennies were in use in Lancashire, England. Cotton fabric became available in a great variety of patterns, costing the public a fraction of what had previously been paid. Since cotton would grow only in very warm climates, British merchants from Bristol and Liverpool began what became known as the Triangular Trade. They sailed to Africa with manufactured goods, which were exchanged there for Negroes. These were then taken, as slave labor, to the West Indies and the American colonies to be exchanged for supplies of raw cotton. The cotton was brought home to England and manufactured into dresses and household textiles.

Therefore another migration, this time involuntary, was proceeding from the docks of Savannah westward. African slaves, many of them Ibos, were thrust out of ships to work the new lands. Two groups met, and their destinies mingled. Each changed, but the relationship was to become a long and turbulent marriage.

A little Negro girl followed her father from the swampy coastal lands into the forests and rolling hills of central Georgia. She clung so tightly to his leg that prospective buyers preferred to take them both as a pair. The man looked fierce, but was controlled and exceedingly gentle with his girl. Finally, John Hester, an aging blacksmith who lived with his sister near a dusty crossroads, bought them. His shop and nearby barn rested on land that would years later be the site of a small town called Zebulon, after the adventurer Zebulon Pike. John called the man King Sam, though not to his face, because, as he told his sister, "This Negro walks around here like he's visitin' royalty, Mary. Smart, too. I'm goin' to teach him smithin', then you and me can set up the supply shop next door."

King Sam, and then Sam King to the people of the area, became the best, longest working blacksmith in the county, and enriched John Hester beyond his highest expectations. But the little girl never had to lift a hand in service. She was a kind of favored pet of John and Mary Hester. Mary tried to teach her general house management and cooking, but for a long time the little girl just played with Mary's nieces and nephews, and didn't quite realize that she was a slave. They called her Dilby, after a favorite brand of licorice that was hotter and spicier than most.

When Sam took sick one hot summer day and could not leave his bed, Dilby sat at the foot and curled her little body around his feet and legs. She never left him for two weeks, except to eat and run to the outhouse.

"The man just seemed to decide to die," confided Mary to her friends. "These Blacks can be right spooky sometimes. I swear he just put down the bellows on Saturday afternoon, went to his shed back of the store, and laid down. His poor child's half out of her mind. Seems afraid of every sound, and holds on to her Pa like all Hell was after her."

Just before his chest stopped moving, Sam King called his daughter to come close. She crawled up his side to his shoulder and bent her little head to his lips. Small beads of sweat stood out on his forehead, but his lips were dry. Carefully he moistened them with his tongue and began to whisper, "Child, never forget, you are Eka Ghassi."

"Who she, Pa?" sobbed Dilby.

Sam's face paled to gray, and his eyes looked searchingly at the ceiling as if he could discover and extract one last vision from the plaster.

"Mother of thunder, little baby; my soul and yours; she made of dirt and sky, love and fear. She our hope against evil...someday...someday."

"I no somethin' Ghassi!" she cried. "Please don't leave me, Pa!"

Sam jerked his head from side to side, and struggled to lift himself on his elbows. "Plateye, Plateye—Go! You hound, you bastard!" He grew excited and his mind wandered, but he clutched the little girl tightly to his chest, and lay back. "Never forget us, Eka Ghassi."

He didn't speak again. It took both John and Mary to pry the child from his death grip.

Dilby learned quickly from Mary after that, and became a model of hard work, diligence, and strength. Indeed she was the model slave. And yet, as the children grew up, none of them would dream of chastising, or yelling at any slave in her presence. She was becoming imperious. Her playmates drew away from her—as they had to at puberty anyway, yet also felt that something mysterious, uncomfortable had taken hold of an old friend.

Dilby thought on Eka Ghassi, and imagined herself descended from some great female spirit, although quite unsure of its nature. After all, she had never known her mother who had died in childbirth. And yet she felt stronger, braver, and ready to live the best life she possibly could until the secret worked itself out in her mind.

Eka Ghassi, Ibo mother of God
She holds the bond of Earth to Heaven
Dual nature of power and love
One being, mother of thunder
Soul of fear and comfort.

Dilby grew in strength and intelligence, and took care to search out the old slave women from around the countryside when they came to town with vegetables to sell for their masters. There was always time to sit next to them on the town square as they laid out stalls and wrapped bundles for the townswomen who carefully selected groceries, smoked goods, candles, or their choice of the caged hens and pigs. For Dilby there was magic to learn, herbs to study, and charms to pocket for a time of need.

Elizabeth ailed during the first two years of their life on Harris Creek. She believed she had an abdominal tumor. She could not escape the morbid thought. It seemed to have a power of its own she could not control, like some devil-fetus waiting to burst her belly after years of gestation, refusing to be born, and denying her womb to a real child. The year was 1789, and she was twenty-six years old by this time, practically middle-aged for those pioneer days.

Then came Dilby. She was purchased with the man called Alexander from Mary Hester. John Hester had died several years earlier, and Mary was becoming a bit senile. One of her nieces had taken over the house and business with her husband, and felt unreasonably threatened by the presence of Dilby.

Elizabeth would never forget the first day Dilby walked into the kitchen following Drew from the back porch. She stood there, a strong, muscular presence in her large, very female body. Blue-black skin over high, prominent cheekbones masked a somber, almost expressionless face. Her eyes searched the room when she entered, and then she smiled. It was a smile suggesting some delightful secret, and Elizabeth felt a vibrant warmth that encircled Dilby and expanded to include her. *She seems to think I'm humorous. I wonder where she got that idea. Surely Drew would not confide some dreadful secret to this black woman. I swear that's a bawdy wink!*

With great effort she drew herself up to her full five feet height and demanded, "Did Miz Hester teach you to care for poultry and milk a goat? It isn't just cookin' and cleanin' round here, and I've not been well, so there ain't much I can do to help you learn right now."

Dilby nodded, "Yes Ma'am. We'll do fine." She folded her hands beneath the ledge of her breasts, made an elegant little curtsey, and turned to Drew.

23

"Mistah Allen. Why don'e Miz Allen an' I just look around dis place for ourselves. I thank you for helpin' me with all my things and settin' me up in that nice shack in back." Drew chuckled. He had been dismissed! Yet he felt only a soothing sense of confidence growing that times might be changing. He hoped that by easing the work load on Elizabeth, and providing some human company for her in this lonely countryside, he could banish the fears which engulfed her and kept him at such a distance from her.

The first day, Elizabeth followed Dilby around, squeaking out instructions and feeling oddly uncomfortable about it. This was her place, wasn't it? "Now, we'll need to work at the same time on different chores. You must know that I can't tell you each thing to do all day."

Dilby nodded and continued to explore the kitchen. She progressed to the washhouse where she clucked her tongue disparagingly, then inspected the three sheds. In the last one Elizabeth continued, "Here the fires must be banked just right–especially at night–to cure the meat. We had a fire here last winter–thought we'd starve, but Mister Allen persuaded some neighbors to see us through 'til spring."

Just then a tall, dark Negro man called from the back yard, "Hey, woman! You, Dilby! Git yousef out here and carry this stuff to the cabin."

Dilby just smiled and took Elizabeth's hand. Elizabeth started to pull back, but the gentle warmth that seemed to flow through the black woman's fingertips held her in place. "You got a mamma, Missus?"

"Why no, not anymore Dilby. My mamma died of small pox a long time ago," she answered.

"Well, I got no momma, no pappy neither, Ma'am, but I know all about 'em, and I can see 'em in my mind–even talk to 'em if I want." She laughed with a little embarrassed duck of her head, and looked up and into Elizabeth's eyes.

"So I is real strong. You an me gonna fix this place up. It be the best place in Monroe County." She winked at Elizabeth, and Elizabeth couldn't help smiling and responding to Dilby's touch with a reassuring pat on her hand.

"Woman! You get out here afore I beat you silly!"

Dilby excused herself, walked out on the porch, and called to her mate,

"I guess you just musta busted that arm and leg I was worried about. You jus' try and carry that stuff to the cabin, or I make sure that arm and leg don't cause nobody no trouble ever again!"

Alexander turned and bent to grasp all the baggage, then lumbered off amidst the giggles of some black children hiding in the bushes by the back steps. "Go on, git!" He swung a foot into the bushes and almost fell to his knees. Two little boys ran laughing and jumping toward the barn.

The sick, childless mistress and the black slave woman, strong and the bearer of one child already, together forged a new health for each other. The tumor was never mentioned after Dilby came.

Drewry was pleased with his purchases. Alexander was not particularly eager to work, but he would keep Dilby pregnant, and the number of black children should prove a great asset to the value of his estate. Drew also recognized the beneficial effect Dilby was having on Elizabeth. Evenings by the fireplace, or on the swing outside on the front porch during the heat of summer, had lost the uneasy pall of two strangers forced into intimacy.

It was a straight-backed, full-bodied woman who looked directly into his eyes when she sat down beside him after the noon meal one day in late August. Lifting his hand to her lips, she kissed the gnarled knuckles, and pushed against the floor with her foot to set the swing in motion. Drew stretched an arm behind her shoulders and pulled her to him. Their first harvest of cotton was almost ready, with a few acres of sorghum cane for the hogs, a vegetable garden full of green beans, black-eyed peas, corn, potatoes, squash, pumpkins, onions and a variety of green lettuces had begun to grace their table, and the young peach trees were heavy with their first fruit.

The four oak trees across the road from the farmhouse bent lightly in the soft breeze from the west. It stirred the hair that covered Drew's neck before continuing its slow journey east toward the coastal lands, passing over the new fields with their first crop of cotton.

"I think it time to think on building up a second set of bedrooms on the house, Drew. Could you get Alexander to organize himself enough to run a pair of slaves from Mister Marshall's farm? Dilby says he's a good carpenter when he's not sleeping behind the smoke house."

"Do you want more room yet, my dear? You know I'll be busy with the cotton harvest; and then I'll have to get it bundled off to Savannah." Elizabeth gently pulled the pink and white striped handkerchief from her bodice, lifted it over his head to rest on his shoulders and around his neck. Rising from the swing, she pulled him to her.

"Come, Sweet, let's see where the stairs should rise from the hall. I think we surely will need to have another room." They walked together through the center of the house, talking softly, and continued to their sleeping quarters in the back.

As Drew turned to fold his breeches and hang them with his smock in the wardrobe, Elizabeth pulled the glass stopper from the tiny frosted bottle next to her bed and drank the potion Dilby had prepared for her. It was still bright during this latter part of the afternoon, and Drew looked a bit guilty to be climbing into bed with his wife at such an hour. When he gathered her into his arms, the faint scent of fresh cut cedar mixed with some spicy incense that rose from her lips. He felt enormously aroused as he bent to kiss his wife.

The strength of Elizabeth's response that musky afternoon seemed to have left Drew slightly dizzy. She herself felt lighter and calmer than ever before with her husband. She felt as though she could float in the air above him, but instead rested her cheek on his chest. His breaths came quickly still, and she wondered that his heart continued to beat so rapidly beneath her.

"Do you wonder still what kept me from you all those years, my love?"

Elizabeth nuzzled her chin against his shoulder in reply. "Have you seen a pack of dogs go wild in an attack? It's like the lure of battle in the midst of rifle fire. Then, of course the everlasting taunts of English soldiers, themselves encrusted with mud and blood. One cried out to me, 'Aye, can ye wipe the cow shit from yer musket and give us a fight?' He was blue-lipped from the cold, but silenced finally."

"My God, Drew! You are so gentle with me, and even with those we now own here in this wilderness! How terrifying must be your dreams!" Elizabeth raised herself to an elbow and caressed his forehead softly. Her mind turned gratingly around the question that had tormented her for months. *And was there another girl, another woman who followed the camp in Virginia? Were there nights when you rouse someone else to hot embraces before marching into battles?* She would not ask. She no longer had the need.

"I froze up north, Elizabeth, but now we are together. I have forgotten all that hatred and fear. I'm so happy we left your brother-in-law. His fever to bring in hundreds of new slaves...make money for treating them like cattle in pens. It sickened me. We'll maybe need slaves out here to work the farm, but by God they're human. We owe them Christian love and care, even though I am told they must be more like children than adults." Drewry shook his head at his own bewilderment, smiled, and arose to dress again. "Come on, Woman. We've measurements to take for the new stairway, and plans to draw for two more rooms above." He laughed and added, "The good people hereabout might think I've taken a tart to bed in the afternoon!"

Elizabeth watched him pull on his pants and smiled at his new, slightly cocky energy. "I do love you so, Drew."

That night, after all the chores were taken care of, and the animals were quiet in there coops and stalls, Elizabeth and Drew fell asleep in each other's arms, finding all the comfortable little curves where they could fit—soft, sensuous pieces of a puzzle nestling together in peace.

Four children were born to Elizabeth and Drewry, the first, named James, was born in 1790. But Dilby had only two children by Alexander, a fact that puzzled Drew. The babies had come five years apart. Her first, Joshua, was one year old when she arrived at the farm, and Nancy was born four years later.

"I swear, Elizabeth, its as though the woman turned off the tap!" He received a smart frap from the feather duster in his wife's hand. "How you do talk! Tap indeed! I just don't think Dilby likes that man. He thinks she should treat him like some great overseer with her as his alone to order around."

"Well, she surely don't tolerate that. The man seems lately to want to hide himself when she's around. She's a might scary, my dear."

Elizabeth pressed her lips together and turned away from Drew's searching look. She could never tell him of the softly murmered spells she overheard as Dilby bent to turn he soil in the kitchen garden. She only could distinguish the occasional exclamation from the black woman's mouth, spat out upon the air and around the voracious insects that gnawed at cabbages and lettuce.

"Plateye! Eat dis dirty blood!" She sat back on her heels as she said this, crushing a beetle in the palm of her hand. Yes, Dilby could be a mite scary, but not for Elizabeth.

The farm became even more productive. Additional land was purchased, and with it more slaves to work the land. They came from ships landing at the island plantations off the coast of Savannah. It was rumored that the noblest of these involuntary immigrants would come half way toward the shore through the shallow waves, and then turn and plunge back out toward the east, drowning in the deeper water. The east, and the dark earth of home, was the center and source of their being.

Eka Ghassi, Ibo mother of God
She holds the bond of Earth to Heaven.

Dilby, as one of the early survivors of the voyages from Africa, was no passive, docile servant. While efficient with housework, her labors seemed almost an afterthought. The main business of living went on in the secret part of her mind she shared only with Elizabeth, and even then it was an incomplete sharing. She was about the same age as Elizabeth, about twenty five when she first came to Harris Creek. Her husband Alexander had been selected by the widow Hester for his strong physique. Alexander hid a violent temper from white people, managing to sublimate his anger by knocking about any black female who crossed his path. Dilby soon realized that she was far more intelligent than her mate, and tended to brush him off in public like a fly. One evening after five-year-old Joshua and the new baby girl had been put to bed, Alexander decided to bring his woman sharply to heel. It was a frightening mistake on his part.

Dilby was stooped over a large black pot suspended from a hook and chain inside the opening of her brick fireplace, murmuring words that were strange to her consort who had draped himself over the nearby cot.

"What you sayin', Woman! Stop singin' them witchin' songs and git me my supper over here on the table. You been stirrin' that pot forever," Alexander growled. Dilby blinked her eyes and tensed her shoulders, but kept on singing the chant she had learned so long ago. She no longer remembered who had taught it to her. She never heard him as he quietly approached her back, but sensed his energy and anger that made her skin tingle all along her spine. Suddenly, a hand grasped the back of her neck and spun her around. She stood face to face with her husband, his head bent over hers, his other hand swung high and back in a fist.

"I could kill you now, Dilby, but you got to take care of me just like I say. I'm goin' to beat you silly...beat you till you cries like li'l Nan, and crawls to me beggin' for me to stop." He did not raise his voice, but the words were spat like acid in her face. She pulled back towards the fire, but his hand came crashing forward into her face knocking her sideways to the floor. She crawled frantically toward the door of the cabin, but Alexander now came across the room with the spade from the fire tools raised over his head. He bellowed like an enraged bull as he brought the shovel down to strike Dilby's head, but she rolled to the side in time, tripping the man as he lunged.

Swift as a cat she was on top of him, kneeling on his chest, his head held between her hands. She held a knife to his throat and growled as she lowered her face to his.

The knife! Alexander froze, his hands trembling against the floor on either side. Where had she hidden the knife? It seemed to materialize from the air around them, and now he moaned as she called on Plateye to take him into darkness.

One of the farm children, a little girl belonging to a farm hand who lived down the dirt road from Dilby's cabin, peeked in the door. She ran crying to her mother exclaiming, "Mamma, Mamma...Dilby sittin on Alexander, an' he cryin' like a baby! Josh was out back holdin' Nan and screamin'!"

None of the other slaves heard Dilby cry out, nor did they hear Alexander bellow and scream as he swung the heavy spade at his wife. The next morning Dilby showed up at the farmhouse with a cut and swollen right cheek. The spade handle had smashed against the bony frame of her eye, but the eye itself had been miraculously protected. Drewry arranged to sell Alexander immediately, and he left the next day a terrified man. Walking down the road to the gate toward the wagon sent to take him to another farm, he cringed and stepped sideways as he passed his wife. Dilby stood by the gate watching him. Her shadow in the early morning light fell across the entire road.

No one knew how she had survived the attack, for she lived in the shack a hundred yards away from the nearest house, and along the rim of the forest, and no one heard the fight during the night until the little girl repeated, "I seen Dilby lookin' in his face like she gonna pull sompin out o' him, An' Alexander he jus' lie there an' moan somethin' terrible!"

This image circulated among the other slaves for months before emerging in white gossip at Sunday afternoon teas. Mrs. Marshall whispered behind her delicate lace handkerchief to Mrs. Stokes that this just showed the kind of black African witchcraft that was loose in the land, and that "the sooner every Nigra was baptized and kept busy and away from any kind of social gatherin' the better. Let them stay for worship on Sunday and then git back to cookin and cleanin," she huffed. The word "conjurer," and then specifically, "conjure woman" slipped into the whispered conversations between ladies sitting on porches in the summer afternoons, and among the Negroes during the evenings in their cabins. Elizabeth and Drewry were appalled at the implied threat to Dilby in these superstitious rumblings, but decided to turn away from whoever began to question them about her, and rely on protecting her as their own private property. But the stories began to circulate and gestate into dire prophesies among the religious members of the white community.

Chapter 4 — Drewry

Drew stood in front of his house between two pecan trees that lined the front garden near the approach road that wove its way through his land to the farm. Now the fall of 1797, it had been eight years since he planted these trees. They were a marker which divided his home's location from the great meadow that lay to the east. It now was turned into farmland. The trees had grown rapidly and rose a foot above his head.

Drew took a deep breath, inhaling the heavy midday scents that floated languidly about him. It was late in the autumn season; the smell of apples and quince left to rot on the ground gave a rich and yeasty cider quality to the air. Off in the distance, Drew could begin to see a wavy, indeterminate shape moving at a slow pace down the road toward the farm. The good Reverend Hope came on horseback, taking his time in the noon heat. How Drew despised the man! Oozing kindly words of Christ's love and continuously smiling, Mr. Hope would shake his head at the antics of Negro children who played at the sides of the roads near his church—all while preaching that they were products of the Devil, condemned by God to lives of work. The clergyman reminded Drew of his brother-in-law, Hinton, who boasted of English titles no one had ever heard of before, and condescended to invite Drew to invest in his new importation business. "After all, my friend, you may not have risen from a family of great distinction, but you are white, har, har, even though of Scots and Irish lineage." Then with a great slap on the shoulder, Hinton would ride off in the lead as he took Drew around to meet his business acquaintances.

Aye, but I'm not new to this land as he is. My father came seventy years ago to these colonies, and we both fought the British at Guilford Court House and Cowpens. My dad's dead of it all, buried by General Greene himself in South Carolina. My brother writes that everyone in Richmond still talks about the old man. He says Virginia is proud of our family. What did Hinton ever do but hoard away his money during the war?

The heavyset Reverend Hope walked his chestnut mare to one of the pecan trees, slid from the saddle with a groan, and draped the reins loosely around its trunk. Beads of sweat stood out on his forehead. He pulled a red cloth from the saddle bag, to wipe his face.

"Good day to you, Drew," he said pleasantly. "I appreciate you takin' time to meet with me on this matter of concern." He looked around and waved a hand toward the flickering curtain at the front window. "I don't suppose Miz Allen could succor a poor sufferin' pastor with a glass of water, or perhaps some lemonade?"

Drew only smiled and shook his head. "Well now, I am sorry sir, but I do believe the women all have taken to their beds for the early afternoon, to escape this heat. Elizabeth has a might of trouble with dizziness this time of day, summer and fall. We can sit up yonder by the cedars near the porch and enjoy some shade."

The Reverend Leon Hope was pastor of the small Methodist congregation that had struggled to erect a log cabin church in the vicinity of Harris Creek. He scrutinized his flock carefully over the first three years of his ministry. Three years after Dilby's arrival in the farm community he began urging Drewry to rid his family of this evil. Drewry knew that Elizabeth would never agree to sell Dilby, so with furrowed brow and earnest voice he had taken the minister aside and confided, "Sir, I respect your views on witchcraft, and admit to some bad moments myself with the woman." He had winked and added, "In truth, she could probably pin us both to the wall!"

Once in the shade, Drew paused to scratch his chin beneath the curly beard. When his eyes searched the red dirt, he poked at ants rushing to and from their mound. "Maybe those little critters down there think I'm some kind of devil, or god or somethin'" he mused aloud, then squatted to see them more closely. "That beetle they be draggin' might be some kind of special offerin' to persuade me to move away. 'Oh please, Mister Devil, don't squash my house!'" He chuckled and looked slyly up at the preacher. "You know, I figure that if Dilby be some crazy black witch, she sure as hell ain't goin' to pack up and move on without layin' a stiff curse on the lot of us! If she's just a big, smart, nigra girl, I can sure use her around here." The Reverend's mouth fell open in shock at the thought of a really smart slave. "Lizzie finds her company. I don't figure she'd part with her anyhow. So there it is, Mister Hope." Drew cast such a guileless smile at the preacher that the man only half suspected hidden ridicule.

Dilby dropped the edge of the curtain and turned away from the kitchen window, humming a new song, finally breaking into full voice with the words.

I met my preacher the other day.
I gave him my right hand.
As soon as my backa be turned,
He scandalize my name.

Elizabeth stood at the breadboard and chuckled as she started to knead the dough. She leaned into her work in half time to Dilby's singing, her head swaying gently. Little Jim came into the kitchen to hear them and began to clap in time, as Elizabeth tapped her foot.

"See Ma dancin'!" he cried. Stopping work altogether, the women took his hand and began a small ring dance.

Walk Daniel, walk Daniel
Walk the other way.
Shout Daniel, Shout Daniel
Shout all day.
On eagle wing, Daniel
Fly Daniel, fly Daniel
On eagle wing Daniel
Fly the other way.
Fly back home, Daniel
Fly Daniel fly.

Bodies rocked and ducked, shuffled and stamped the gospel song, an old African game.

Chapter 5— James

The four children born to Drewry and Elizabeth were named and baptized early, for in those days everyone feared the early death of infants. James, born in 1790, was followed in two years by Martha, and then Stokes and Emily. Another child lived only one year and died, stricken with what the doctor called, "A rheumatism that traveled from one part of his body to another."

Since James played daily with the Negro children on the farm, he became an expert on folk remedies and all kinds of superstitions that flew around the area. He knew from experience that a cut should be wrapped in the nearest spider web to stop the bleeding.

One day during James' ninth summer, after swinging over a creek that ran through the woods behind the smoke shed, James lost his grip and fell into a thorn bush, growing at the water's edge. A large gash opened on his big toe. Josh and his little sister crowded close and gazed down at the blood gushing from the wound.

Josh exclaimed. "You gots to git Mama to wrap dat, Jimmy!"

"How he goin' git hissef over to de house, Josh? You goin' carry him?" Nancy reached down to touch the rapidly swelling toe. James rocked back and forth, clutching his foot.

"Don' touch it!" he shrieked as Nancy marveled at the bright blob of color on her finger.

"Git on over to Mama's and tell her we's comin', Girl," Josh shouted.

Truthfully, Josh was scared that he would somehow be blamed for his friend's accident. Dilby would set the switch to his legs in a minute. He helped James to his one good foot, and both of them began a hopping, staggering walk up the river bank and down the dirt road toward Dilby's cabin a quarter mile away—two little half-sized warriors returning from a great battle with Indians.

James felt rather thrilled as he anticipated special attention from Dilby and Elizabeth. "Now don' you worry, Josh. I ain't goin' to blame you," he said righteously.

"Mamma goin' to blame me no matter what. We ain't suppose to play down here You know dat." James wiped a nose that streamed along with his eyes, trying to blink away tears. "We can jus' say I cut it on one of them rocks Pappa been breakin' up for the new field of tobacco." James was just as afraid of Dilby's quick and suspicious mind. Hell, she could ruin his pitiful entrance and his mother's loving reception of her poor wounded little boy.

"Oh, Lord...der she be now, Jimmy, standin' on de porch. Now lean on me a little more."

Dilby nervously slapped a wooden spoon against her thigh as she waited for them. Then, as James seemed to be on the point of fainting against Josh's shoulder, she sprinted down the porch steps and swooped him up under her strong right arm. She went over to sit him down on the straight-backed chair that leaned against the side of the house.

"Stay right there, Baby, and don' move while I get that toe fixed." She swept into the house, returning moments after with a bowl of warm water and a towel. "Nan, you run and get a spider web from behind the table in the kitchen. Bring it right here to me." She gently washed the toe, while James and Josh winced and gritted their teeth. After Nancy returned with the sticky web wrapped around her fingers, Dilby delicately lifted it from her daughter's hand and wrapped it around the injured toe.

"Alright now, I want y'all to get on over to Miz Lizzie's. Josh, you might fetch that little wagon you all time playin' with in back, and haul little Mistah Jim on back to his Mamma." This appealed to James, and he was sure it enhanced the dramatic effect.

When they all trouped up to the farmhouse, James's two sisters were playing on the ground by the azalea bushes that bordered the front porch. Martha was mixing a bowl of mud with some daisy petals to feed her baby sister Emily, who wailed and rubbed her eyes. When they saw their brother being pulled in the toy wagon by Josh, the girls jumped up and ran to get Elizabeth.

"Mamma! Mamma! Jimmy's hurt! Josh done broke his leg!"

Elizabeth came running out of the front door, wiping her hands on an apron. She ordered Josh into the kitchen, and bent to look closely at her son's injury. The little girls bounced up and down with excitement. James tightly shut his eyes, rocked back and forth holding his knee, and tried desperately to think of a good story. "My leg ain't broke! But it sure do hurt, Mamma. Oh-oh-oh," he wailed.

"What did that boy do to you then?" she asked as she scooped him out of the wagon and carried him inside.

"You gonna beat Josh, Ma?" chimed in Martha, a bit too eagerly.

Though tempted, James shook his head and allowed as how it was he, himself who had instigated the trip to the creek. "Mamma, Josh was scared that you would blame him, but I said it was all right. Dilby gonna beat him anyway just on account of."

Elizabeth was about to pull off the spider webbing that had stopped the toe from bleeding when a long, dark shadow blocked off light from the kitchen window. Dilby warned, "You tell Mistah Jim not to touch that web round de toe, Miz Lizzie. See how de blood stop pumpin' out? It work jus' like magic, don' it?" She smiled and patted the boy on his shoulder. "Now I want to know what that rascal Josh done got him into."

Josh looked wildly from his mother to Elizabeth, but wisely kept silent. He knew these things needed tactful negotiation between black and white, and slave and mistress. Where a child was concerned, even a close relationship like the one between his mother and Mrs. Allen could rupture into classic racial friction.

Elizabeth looked at both woebegone little boys and frowned. "If I tell your Daddy about this, he's goin' to whip your legs good. Both of you! I won't this time, but I'm goin' to cut that rope at the creek. If it ever gets tied up on that tree again, it'll be whippin' time down at the smoke house!"

Martha decided she and baby Emmy had better go hide before James took after them, and sneaked out of the kitchen to play under the porch.

James and his brother were allowed to play with Negro children on the farm, but his sisters had only themselves. Girls had to be segregated from an association with any blacks, other than servants at the house. Dilby, of course, was a second mother to them. They knew she was allowed to deliver a sharp smack to them when they deserved it. Elizabeth never doubted Dilby's word when reporting bad behavior from the children.

The next summer James sneaked down to the creek again on a hot, muggy day in July. Summer in Georgia was unrelenting misery. No breeze stirred to chase away the mosquitoes that thrived in the ponds and streams. This time he went by himself, planning to rest under the trees after a good soak in the cool water. He felt anxious for some reason. His head had begun to ache right after breakfast that morning.

James did not stay in the water very long, as chills began to shake his arms and hands, and his teeth could not stop chattering against each other. He sloshed through the muddy water to the creek's edge and slumped in soft grass beneath the oak tree that dangled his favorite rope swing once again beneath its lowest branch. He sat there, clutching his knees to warm himself and wondered at the dragonflies that pulsed above the stream's surface. Expanding now, with metallic blue wings becoming long and feathered at their ends, then shriveling to tiny ant-sized creatures in a breath's time.

It was funny how hot his eyes felt, and all the skin around them. His head really hurt now, throbbing through his scalp and behind his neck. "Got to go home, now," he mumbled to himself, then dragged himself upright, holding on to the trunk of the tree.

He was a sturdy boy, with the dark curly hair and the black eyes of his black-Irish and Scotch ancestors. A bony brow hooded those eyes, like his father's, giving him a look of somber meditation. But now he could barely shuffle his legs along, and his eyelids drooped with the effort to stay open.

Step by step he marched doggedly up the red dirt road, past the Negro cabins, almost up to Dilby's house. Suddenly, his legs lost all feeling and he fell heavily to the ground in the middle of the road. He began to cry as he tried to drag himself toward Dilby's front porch. "Dilby, Dilby, I'm sick!" he wailed as loudly as he could from the bottom of the wooden stairs. "I can't stand up no more!"

The woman slave appeared abruptly, filling the doorway, white apron crisp and smooth around her waist, like an angel of strength and comfort. "Come on, now boy, you try an' stand while I hold you close." Dilby stooped, wrapped one arm around his waist, and gently lifted him to what seemed to be boneless legs. It was hopeless: James could not hold his weight at all, so Dilby carried him up the dusty road to the main house. He could smell the dryness of the browning grass that struggled to survive the long August day. He thought he saw branches move above him as he rocked up and down in Dilby's arms. A breeze perhaps, in this otherwise deathly still air. He squinted his eyes to try to make out the movement. Could a snake be twisting through those trees high above the road? When the boy turned his head to one side, he could see the road ahead and the quivering heat waves rising from its surface. It looked like an underwater vision that distorted outlines and twisted shapes.

"We almost there, Dilby?" James moaned into her soft bosom, then lost consciousness. As he drifted away from light and warmth, the sound of a breathy voice called to him before darkness took him: "You are mine, child. Lay still while your Ma cries for your poor little legs. She's still got to see your pain. Suffer, suffer, little white boy 'til you come to know me. Lay down your head. Dream the dreams that are bound to trouble souls. I'll eat your dreams! I'll take you, child, and grow strong again...grow white."

Voices sighing, crying floated around James's head. A coolness wiped across his forehead and a large hand held his wrist with fingers gently pressing to feel his pulsing heartbeats. Now, with eyes open, he began to see smudged outlines of heads bent above him.

"Lordy, Doctor, is he wakenin'?" Gradually Elizabeth's face came into focus, then her right hand, clutching a delicate linen cloth at her neck.

The doctor brought his face down closer and used a finger to gently lift an eyelid. "He's come back to us, Miz Lizzie," he said and sat back on a chair next to the bed. A small, rather portly man, Dr. Marshall relaxed for the first time in twelve hours, resting his hands on his vested belly. "Well, well my boy. You've frightened us all, but I think you'll live to try it again sometime." He turned to motion Dilby to the bed with her bowl of hot broth and bread.

James tried to push himself up, but managed only to weakly raise his head an inch or so. He was lying in his mother's bed at the back of the house, and could just make out the tops of trees outside her window. For some reason, the shifting movement of leaves and branches alarmed him. He felt he should remember something about those branches, but was too tired to think on it.

Elizabeth and Dilby, one sitting on each side of the bed, lifted him. Elizabeth took the bowl and brought the spoon to his lips. "Here, Baby, this will make you strong real soon. Dilby made it special. It's chicken and dumplins just the way you like."

James took the liquid into his mouth and felt the warm soft texture of the rounded dough on his tongue. Good. "Ma, I got to pee real bad," he whispered and tried to sit up again.

When Elizabeth tried to support him on his feet he couldn't stand. "Run get that old flat bowl, please Dilby. It sets yonder in the shed behind the door." Gently she settled her little boy back on the bed.

"Ma, I can feel my legs, but they just don't work right." The doctor reached over and began to feel along the muscle pads of each leg, prodding here and there. Finally he got up from his chair and pulled the sheet up to James' waist, smiled and smoothed the damp hair back from the child's forehead.

"Let him rest, Miz Lizzie, the doctor advised, "and I'll drop in tomorrow afternoon. He's probably just real tired and scared. I've seen people freeze right up with shock after a bad fall. Thing is, I can't find any sign of bruisin' or fracture of bones. We'll just wait a bit. He'll be fine by tomorrow." As Elizabeth walked Marshall out to his carriage, he added, "Now, Miz Lizzie, I want you to give James this purgative to clean out his system. If the poisons are still there, we can try sweatin' him. Then we can let the good Lord heal him. Jimmy's a fine, righteous lad, so we know it ain't evil livin' that's weakened his system."

The old doctor climbed into his carriage and drove off toward his own farm and workshop, five miles away. Elizabeth bit her lip and shook her head at the thought of the effects of Dr. Marshall's purgative, yet walked resolutely up the walk to the house determined to do the very best she could. When she re-entered the bedroom, James was asleep.

❧❧

John Marshall was not really a doctor at all. In fact, there were no physicians in the county in the early years of the 19th century. And fortunate it was, too, for a licensed physician, as well as issuing purgatives, would have bled the child white. No, Marshall was what was called a bonesetter and practitioner of the 'natural' herbal medicine, which encouraged emptying the digestive system of everything. Healing was not lucrative in those days, so Marshall also worked as the county carpenter and practiced some forging, to help the ferriers shoe local horses.

Days went by with no change in James' ability to stand or walk. The fever was completely gone, but the boy had to be carried everywhere. The family thought at first his weakness was the natural result of Doctor Marshall's purgatives, but by the time two weeks had passed the child still could not stand or walk.

Dilby had been a continuous antagonist to Marshall's prescription. "Miz Allen, I don' like to see that doctor suckin' all the juices out of little Jim. I swear I could fix that boy better than that ol' doctor." She urged Elizabeth to at least leave him alone and regain his strength. James listened, but only turned his head away. His dreams of voices in the trees paralyzed his will as much as his legs.

Drewry intervened at that point. "Let Dilby try her own kind of magic, my dear. Lord knows she suffers from a scandalous reputation for it here abouts. Let's see if she deserves it."

After another week in bed, without the ravages of the purge, and fed only a spicy gruel concocted by Dilby, James began to sneak out of bed by lowering his head to the floor, putting his weight on his hands, and then executing a kind of somersault. He would drag his legs behind him as he tried desperately to get out into the hall and kitchen area. Dilby would hear a bump, shuffle, shuffle, shuffle, moan, and bump again, as James collapsed on his chest in exhaustion. Each time she came into the hall, she found him quietly crying, and would pick him up to carry him back to his bed.

Finally, when all the adults in the household had given up on James ever being able to walk on his own, and were equally driven half crazy by his constant need to escape the boredom of a bedroom, Josh appeared at the back door with his little wagon.

"Miz Lizzie," he asked, "could James sit in dis here wagon and be pulled around some? Jus' so he wont be bangin' hisself on de floor?"

It was an inspired thought. James was excited by the idea, as was everybody else. yet who would pull him around all day?

An answer came quite naturally from James's sister. Martha was eight years old, with no one but baby Emily to play with all day. Her brother Stokes left each morning to do chores or play in the fields and woods.

"Mama, I could push Jimmy. We could play with dolls and build little houses for them, and all kinds of stuff."

When James was told, he vowed to himself that he'd be damned if he'd make dollhouses for whiny old Martha, and figured he could work his way around her any old time. His sister turned out to be far cleverer than he ever imagined. Martha was a little girl surrounded by boys who constantly were away from the farmhouse with their friends, mostly black children forbidden to her. She would push James up to the table in the dining room, and then surround him with all the scissors, cloth scraps, paste made from flour, pieces of wood and any remnants of wall paper she could find.

Climbing up on the high stool she had dragged in from the kitchen, Martha gave James directions for the afternoon project. Sometimes it would be puppets, and he became adept with needle and thread as he fabricated miniature people for his sister. He felt deeply ashamed that he seemed to have quite a talent with this "women's work," but became absorbed by it.

"Matty, where you gonna take me after I finish this little hat for Miz Peachy?" James asked. He had a plan that involved all the delights of a dangerous adventure. "You promised to push me wherever I said after this, remember?"

A suspicious Martha knew she could not back out of her promise, if she wanted her brother to keep on helping make dolls. Her cousins were coming for Thanksgiving, and the little girl had bragged to everyone that she was now an accomplished seamstress and puppeteer. In about two weeks they would arrive for a seven-day visit. "Where you want to go, Jimmy? We has got to be quiet, because Papa is nappin' in the rocker."

James knew very well his father always took a nap during the hot, fall afternoons, and that this was one ritual everyone in the family had to observe. "Pa done wore himself out all mornin', and nothin' is gonna wake him now."

He leaned closer to her ear anyway as he told her his plan.

Martha drew back from him in horror, both little hands flew up to cover her mouth. "Why you want to get a beatin'? You know Pa's gonna be so mad he likely will take us all down to the shed with his switch and blister our legs good."

James smiled, "Now, Matty, you know he wouldn't touch a pore little crippled boy."

"But what about ME!" she wailed, as tears filled her eyes. Martha had the most beautiful dark blue eyes, but they reddened quickly when she rubbed away the tears.

"Don't you worry none. Go on now! Push me, little cry baby! I be so fast in what I do that we be gone and up the road to Josh's place before Pa tries to move."

James giggled as he carefully threaded his needle with heavy cotton and slipped it delicately through the edge of Drew's flannel shirt at the waist. He wrapped the thread twice around the first spool of the rocker's back, and then proceeded to do the same thing with each spool, behind his father's back. Both children held their breath as long as possible before releasing a series of shallow breaths as the sewing progressed. James inched himself toward the front of his wagon as he reached higher to secure the side and shoulder on the far right side of his father, then across the upper back to the opposite shoulder.

Martha lost her initial fear as the project neared completion, edging closer and closer to James. Suddenly a loud snort sounded from the front of the rocker. Martha grabbed the handle of the wagon, pulled it around and dashed toward the door to the hall. James rocked dangerously to the side as the wagon turned the corner toward the front door. Neither one thought about the noise they were making when the wheels bumped over entryways and across the wooden porch.

"Gawd damn!" was all they heard from the parlor as they jiggled the wagon down the porch steps and rushed around the corner of the house to the shaded yard behind. Chickens scattered before them clucking loudly. Dilby turned around from the wash lines, where she hung linen to dry. Without a word, the woman turned back toward the house and walked into the kitchen. They could hear her calling, "Oh, my Lord Mista Allen! Now you just rest there and I'll cut you loose." Drew was banging around the parlor, shaking and stamping to rid himself of the load on his back. The rocking chair humped and rolled like a tortoise shell. Dust flew from the curtains at the window when he turned violently in circles next to the windowsill.

His angry howls brought Elizabeth running from her vegetable plot behind the kitchen. James and Martha disappeared. No one could find them all afternoon. It was just as well for them that they waited to appear at the kitchen door just before supper.

Elizabeth pushed open the door and sternly led them into the dining room where their father sat at the head of the table calmly slapping a hickory switch against his thigh and glaring down at them in silence.

"Leave the room, please, my dear," Drewry ordered.

Elizabeth hesitated, her arms encircling her two miscreants around the shoulders. She bit her lip in nervousness. "Now Father, I'm sure both Martha and James can tell us all about this."

Leave...the...room!" he repeated in anger.

Nothing was heard for what seemed hours to Dilby and Elizabeth, who waited in the hall. Then, the rumble of Drew's angry voice, followed by the sound of loud whacks came from behind the dining room's closed doors. Yet they heard no crying. When the children emerged, Martha stood quietly beside her brother's wagon. James sat dejectedly. Both were wide-eyed and pale in front of their mother. Elizabeth glanced furtively at Drew's stern expression, and thought she saw a slight twitch at one corner of his thin-lipped mouth.

"Dilby," he ordered, "take young James to his bedroom, please. And you, Miz Martha. I don't want to see you until tomorrow at breakfast!"

The next morning, before a late breakfast, Dilby was ready to take the cushions from the dining room chairs out in the yard to be beaten. She hesitated and traced linear indentations on Drew's cushion with her finger. Smiling, she plumped the cushion between her hands and set it back on his chair at the head of the table.

Chapter 6 — Dilby's Dream

Dilby's life seemed, by necessity, to revolve totally around the white people who both owned and protected her. She sensed that she was not only a valued piece of property on this Georgia farm, but also was part of the human glue that allowed the Allens to function as a family. She knew this, realized her power was strong, and truly loved Elizabeth Allen. The white children respected her and bowed to her authority with a minimum of resentment, much like her own children. At times she really felt a sense of being chosen, a sense of individual worth that harkened back to her days as a child with her father.

Dilby was just one generation removed from freedom in Africa. Sam had given her an idea that lay hidden most of the time; an intimation of spiritual royalty. She possessed a rich knowledge of herbal medicines, and watched the results of her doctoring and healing in the slave community. When "Doctor" Marshall had finished draining the poor crippled son of Elizabeth and Drew, she ached to be allowed to demonstrate her arts on the boy.

Her dreams became filled with dark commands to assert her skills, to cure the mysterious illness that had cut the joy out of James' young life. Finally a dream was so compelling, so demanding of action, that she began to plan a tactful, safe way to intervene in the decisions of her master and mistress. The dream pictured a naked James floating in a steaming caldron, his legs held rigidly out on top of the water. She saw herself move to hold his upper body at one end of the tub, her arms curled under his armpits and over his shoulders as she bent close to his head, pressing her cheek to his. A heavy mist cloaked the surface of the water: only delicate outlines of the boy's legs could be seen. Amazingly, the water seemed to flow through his flesh and bones, cleansing and purifying as it slid over white tissue that began to throb pink in the haze.

In the dream, James twisted his head slowly to look at Dilby. He began to smile. In that moment, his crippled legs rose from the surface, as though a gentle wave pressed them upward from below.

When Dilby awoke, she heard her son Josh singing from his special tree perch in front of the cabin. There were no words, but the sound was sad and minor—a high-pitched wail in the morning light. What would happen to this child of hers if she began to work with the white child in the way she now envisioned? Dilby swung her feet out from under the covers and sat on the edge of the bed, looking out a window at her boy. Josh stood high on a branch, gazing straight up at the clouds.

"Josh!" she called to him. "Git down here, baby, and git youse'f cleaned up for breakfast. I don' want to see any more crippled-up legs around this place."

A little later, when she placed a bowl of grits and pork slices in front of Josh, she pulled his head close to her bosom and kissed the top of his head. "I love you, Josh. You got strong bones in you face, jus' like you Grampa." Dilby always prayed that she was right about that: it was hard to raise a boy if you were black.

"Oh Ma! Let go o' me now. You know I is strong." Josh grinned and predicted, "Someday you and me and baby Nan is gonna go someplace different I heard about."

Dilby recognized the threat and promise of a dream. Running away was a flickering idea that lay hidden in her own heart, but she feared it and was determined, with all her being to keep Josh safe by her side, no matter what. "You hush that crazy talk, darlin'! I don' want t' hear it."

Josh looked at her in surprise as she pulled away from him to prepare her basket of tools to go up to the farmhouse. "But Mama—"

"Hush I said," she warned with a frown and walked out of the one room cabin and down the wooden steps of the porch toward the red dirt road.

Dilby went straight to Elizabeth, who was working in the garden to clear out old dried roots of squash and cut off pumpkins from shriveled vines. She picked up Elizabeth's basket of produce to carry in for her, and then asked, "Miz Lizzie, could I have time to talk with you about little Jim?"

Elizabeth stood up from where she stooped, to wipe her hands on an apron.

"Of course you can, Dilby. I'm a might tired of sweatin' in this heat. It sure do start early for a fall mornin'!" She wiped her forehead with the back of a hand. "Let's sit a piece over yonder under the fig tree."

After they settled on two stools under the tree, Dilby picked up one of the large, striped, turban squashes and began to polish it absently with an edge of her apron. "Miz Lizzie, I been thinkin' on those poor legs of your poor child so much that I even gets pictures in my head at night about ways to help James." She looked up at Elizabeth and concentrated on the white woman's blue eyes set in her strained and drawn face. Hairline wrinkles had begun to pucker the corners of her eyelids. "You see, Miz, I had a real conjurin' dream last night." Elizabeth looked nervously away, and caught a corner of her lip between her teeth. Dilby continued, "Yes, Miz, I did, and I knows I can fix those poor little legs."

Elizabeth bent forward to tightly grasp Dilby's arm. "There can't be any devil's magic used," she insisted in a soft voice. "People here-about will say James is bein' cursed. Maybe even losin' his soul to black magic. Well, you know the foolishness of some of these farmwomen. Go on, I'll get you all the fixin's you want. Just tell me what to find. The less anyone knows what you plan the better." She released her hold, stood up, and thought a moment before whispering, "Don't even tell Mister Allen, if you do use some of your potions, you hear?" When Dilby did not reply, Elizabeth ordered in a louder than usual voice—like a woman dictator, "Get on to those chickens now Dilby! Can't have everyone lolling about under the shade a tree."

Dilby stood as well, and began picking her way back toward the coop. "Yes Miz, I's goin' right now." Both women nodded to the peddler who stood fixing the harness on his horse in the road. He and his wagon had just arrived from a neighboring farm. The two women walked quickly to the house.

Within a week Dilby and Elizabeth had dragged an old black iron tub behind the house to set between the water pump and kitchen door. Every morning, after that they carried crocks and pots of hot boiling water from kitchen to the tub, they were joined by a parade of black and white children. As steam rose in the morning air, Drewry Allen carried James from his bed to the tub, where Dilby waited to gently ease the child into the water. She rubbed his legs under the water and made them move about with her hands as he clung to the sides of the tub.

Oftentimes James cried out from exhaustion and boredom. Sometimes he felt pain and screamed at Dilby, "Leave me alone! You just mad at me, ain't you? Oww! Don't do that now! You just a big black witch like ol' Chester says, ain't you?"

Dilby gave him a light slap, but continued pushing and pulling. The hot water kept being brought from the kitchen, and finally James would begin to cry in frustration. Then Dilby gathered him into her arms, plucked him from the tub, and sat with him tucked close to her chest as they sat on a blanket nearby. They rocked quietly together until James calmed and blew his nose with an air of affronted dignity.

A year went by. The tub was moved into the kitchen when mornings became too cold, but the treatments continued without respite. James came to accept the ritual, and even to enjoy the warmth as his legs began to move ever so slightly by themselves in the water. At the same time, he was approaching his twelfth birthday; adolescence and all of its confusing sensations were beginning. Added to all of this in such a young life, was the inescapable fact that James was very lonely. His mother and sisters spent many hours with him during the day, but he grew restless and irritable by afternoon. His brother was younger, and committed to vigorous play out of doors.

Josh came less and less to visit him. When he did, his playmate seemed more distracted and distant as the weeks wore on. Dilby was always there, bringing relief. To be truthful, James came to look forward to her touch and warm embraces after each treatment. She rocked and sang to him if he became upset and angry with long boring days, and was full of stories about imaginary animals who spoke just like she did. He treasured her touch, her voice, and the warmth of her dark skin next to his.

James lay back against her arm, his eyes closed as she rubbed his thighs and calves with her other hand. Her crisply ironed blouse smelled sweetly of sifted flour and freshly baked bread. He turned his cheek towards her breast and sighed as she finished her story.

"And then Brer Fox pulled dat sneaky rabbit away from de tar baby and threw him way up in the air and into the briar patch. When he landed he busted out laughin' and slappin his feet sayin', 'Lordy, Brer Fox, I was born in de briar patch!' Dilby chuckled and hugged James a little closer to her chest. He laughed loudly at the rabbit's cleverness and wiggled in the water. Dilby always looked sharply to see if his legs moved at all.

Chapter 7 — School

Cold rains began in late December that year. Drew drove the younger children to school each morning in the hay wagon. The Old Field School recently was set up next to the woods that bordered their neighbor's property, two miles away. The small log building sat next to a small stream that flowed through the trees and out into the cotton fields. This field, long cultivated for cotton crops by a family that had pioneered the land years before, now was abandoned, drained of its fertility by the cotton itself. This phenomenon was just beginning to appear in Georgia; farmers gradually turned the land into fallow strips, where primitive log schoolhouses were built. They were designated Old Field Schools. Traveling teachers came for a season or two; boarded with a local family; and moved on to another community.

This year, a young man named William McDowell had appeared. He received partial pay for his services, while boarding with these same neighbors. He was only twenty-three years old, yet managed to include some Greek and Latin for the older boys, along with grammar, arithmetic and penmanship. He was a recent immigrant from Scotland, eager to establish himself in the new American State of Georgia.

Each morning William stoked the iron stove in the single schoolroom with wood he had stacked outside next to the outhouse. His breath steamed in the cold air as he looked out the window near his desk and waited for the first wagonload of children to be deposited outside on the dirt road. The teacher was of medium height, about five feet eight inches tall. Curly light hair caught morning sunlight as it broke through the haze, highlighting red strands that were scattered in his short, neatly coiffed beard. Lines already appeared at the corners of his eyes. He smiled and laughed frequently with his young charges, finding them absurdly backward, yet endearingly eager and energetic. The Allen children had learned to read from their mother at home, but many of the older students had to be brought along quickly, to catch up with younger siblings and classmates.

William sighed, smoothed his mustache briskly with his hand, and turned away from a view of rolling meadows, forests, and the distant Pine Mountains. A delicate but incongruous wooden clock on the shelf at the back of the room indicated it was time to ring the bell outside and hurry his students along. He had brought this elegant timepiece from his mother's house outside Edinburgh, carefully wrapped in towels and several of his sturdier shirts. Fortunately, it had survived the long, strenuous coach ride from Savannah.

Drew heard the school bell from about a half mile away as he clucked at the two horses and flapped the reins sharply along their backsides." We're late this mornin' again! You children be ready to run inside soon as we stop, or Mister McDowell be getting' out his switches. You all hear me?" he shouted over his shoulder.

Drewry Allen insisted on driving his children to school every morning, for he seldom saw them again until late evening, after finishing chores in the barn. Before returning for supper, he visited each of his slave family's cabins himself, seeing himself as part overseer, part patriarch in a very Old Testament use of the term.

Ten-year-old Martha and nine-year-old Stokes gripped the edge of the wagon as the horses slowed to a walk. Both children jumped lithely to the ground. Six-year-old Emily tumbled after them as they ran towards William, standing resolutely by the door, tapping a hickory switch against his thigh. The teacher smiled and gently ruffled the little girl's sandy colored hair. "Good morning to you, Emily. You're very welcome here."

After Emily had moved shyly to a chair inside, Drewry gestured with his head for William to follow him outside. "Sir, my wife and I were wondering if you ever pass by our farm during the late afternoon, or perhaps on a Saturday."

William cocked his head slightly to one side. "That could indeed be arranged, I believe."

Drewry continued, "Well, you see, we have another son, his name be James, our eldest, but he's been afflicted by paralysis and must be kept safe at home." William's expressive and mobile face crinkled at the brows as he focused on the father's words.

"We were wonderin', Elizabeth and I, if you could see your way to tutorin' him." Drew held out his hand as if to stay immediate rejection of the idea. "You see, Sir, he be mighty smart. Reads all the time, now he's confined. All he's got to distract him is the wild stories of our black Dilby. She surely is a wonderful nurse to him you understand, but we don't want them getting too, well..." He paused. "Of course we'll pay you well, believe me, or perhaps you'd be interested in barterin' for a strip of land hereabouts." Drew realized he had been talking too fast and should stop and let the teacher respond.

William put his hand on Drew's shoulder and walked with him a bit further from the school door. "How old did you say he was, your boy? And what does he read these days?"

Drew sighed in relief and told William that James reluctantly was reading biblical stories supplied by the pastor. The teacher asked him, "Mister Allen, would Friday afternoons be agreeable for your household?"

"That would be just fine, Sir. We'll have James ready for you. He's goin' out of his mind with boredom right now, Mister McDowell, so I know he'll be waitin' for you all afternoon." Every Friday, during the winter months, James saw Mr. McDowell ride up to the farm to tutor him. He watched the teacher stamp his boots on the porch, then enter the hall and hand his wool scarf and long coat to Dilby. The young Scotsman always blushed when Elizabeth came down the hall to greet him. However, she always led him directly to James, who waited in the parlor in front of his mother's desk by the window.

The lonely young man, William McDowell, and the hobbled boy, James Allen, established a routine every Friday in that parlor. They included mathematical exercises based on the daily problems of running a good-sized farm, dividing labor between workers, and purchasing building materials for housing and storing animals and crops. James greedily tucked away any books William lent him by ancient Roman poets and politicians, as well as Greek plays that required a basic grounding in Greek Mythology. The boy and his tutor always found time to discuss the latest negotiations between Creek Indians and the government in Milledgeville.

Several weeks into the tutoring, William became interested in Dilby's therapy for James, and asked to be allowed to come on afternoons during the week and observe her methods. Finally, Tuesdays were set aside for afternoon sessions in the tub, with William present. James was acutely embarrassed, but his father agreed to the arrangement, even welcomed the opportunity to have someone keep an eye on what he worried was becoming too intimate a therapy with his son.

When his teacher came the first time, he sat quietly on a chair in the kitchen. James turned away from him, his face flushed, and whispered for Dilby to cover his nakedness.

She turned to William. "Mistah McDowell, please, Suh, let me get this boy finished up with his healin' today and then I'll help him dress and come into the parlor to work with you. He gets mighty embarrassed when someone is watchin' him." Dilby smiled as she spoke, yet stood to usher William out of the room. He left the kitchen, but remained out of sight nearby, listening to the conversation between James and his nursemaid.

After his teacher was gone, James turned in the water to look directly into Dilby's face. "I don't like Mister McDowell comin' in on my time with you. This is the only time it feels good to be me." Dilby looked down at the boy and slowly shook her head. Gently, she lifted him under the arms to the rim of the tub and wrapped him in a soft cotton blanket, before setting his feet on the floor and trying to urge them towards a bench against the wall.

"Let's get you dressed, Mistah Jim," she said, urging the boy to walk toward a bench against the wall. "You still got some time to talk with dat teacher before suppin'. Your daddy say Mistah McDowell's mighty interested in this here treatment, so I guess we has to help him out a little. That all right with you, Suh?" She lightly slapped James's shoulder and chuckled while pulling his pants legs up to his waist.

Covered or not, James' unmistakable pleasure in Dilby's ministrations was noted by his teacher. William did not know what to make of the relationship between the boy and his slave nurse. He put aside any immediate judgments, to contemplate later on, alone in his room and away from the Allen family.

༅

One Tuesday afternoon William came to the house with the intention of questioning Dilby about recovery prospects for her patient. On walking into the kitchen at the back of the house, he was surprised to see that the tub was full of water, but without young James in it. He called out, "Master James, Dilby, it's I, William McDowell come to visit." He sensed the presence of someone else in the room and turned quickly. Nobody! But then he felt a tug on his right trouser leg and looked down to see a tiny little girl. "And who is this tryin' to climb up my leg?"

The child stepped back and giggled. "I is Nan, and I is four years old!" When Nancy's eyes widened, William could see that she was very impressed by her own statement.

William bent down to her level. "My, my, but you surely did surprise me. Do you paddle around in that great black tub as well as Master James?"

Quickly, as agile as a kitten, Nancy jumped into his arms and held on with her hands clasped around his neck. "Jimmy be outside walkin' with Ma! I jus saw him! Look out the window. There they be now."

William turned back to the window and scanned the back yard with squinting eyes. He had left his glasses in his greatcoat pocket in the hall. Nancy was right: there stood James, supported by Dilby's strong arm, and slowly walking toward the barn.

"Does Miz Allen know James can walk yet?" he asked. Nancy shook her head.

William carefully placed Nancy down, and hurried out the door, whooping and calling to the two figures, about to disappear into the barn. James turned toward the sound and grinned happily. Dilby cautiously stepped aside. As William came up to them, he noticed that James hand slid reluctantly away from Dilby's arm in a kind of caress. What's this, James?" William slapped his forehead in amazement. "I can't believe what I see! Dilby, you...you have worked a miracle!"

Dilby looked down in embarrassment, as well a look of alarm.

James knew that she had begun to worry about rumors being passed around by the other slaves. Sometimes, he heard her murmuring under her breath as she massaged his legs. "Dumb ol' niggahs goin' to feel some of my magic on they backsides one of these days if they keep on flappin' they lips." James also had heard his mother cautioning Dilby to keep quiet about James, when the family met ladies of the church on Sundays, after the service. Since Dilby was almost always nearby to help with the children, these conscientious church women whispered behind their fans whenever the slave woman approached.

James looked up at William, his face fairly shining with excitement as sweat glistened on his forehead. "I've been getting stronger every day with Dilby's exercises, Today she said it was time to put these legs to some real work. Just look at them, Sir." James lifted one leg forward to waist height in a slow-motion kick.

Dilby frowned and wrapped her green knitted shawl more tightly around her shoulders. "Alright now, Mistah Jim, it be time to show you mamma. She be a might put out if anymore folks see you walkin' before she do."

By this time, William danced around the boy with un-masterly abandon. "Right, Right. Of course you're right Dilby. Come James, I'll go with you to give your mother the happy news!" Together they walked toward the house, William practically jumping with excitement, and James halting every few steps to reestablish his balance.

Dilby stood silently by the barn, watching them. Quietly, a figure came from inside the barn and leaned against the side of the wide door opening. Josh looked at his mother and smiled bitterly. "Ma, guess now you be havin' a lot more time to cook and clean, and hoe, and weed, and wash de Master's clothes."

Dilby scowled at her son. "What goin' on in that head of yours, boy?"

"Nothin', Ma. Jes' wonderin' if anybody goin' to notice who fixed that white boy. The one used to my friend."

"I don't remember seein' you around your 'friend' for some time, Josh." Dilby shook her head and reached to playfully swat her son on his head. He pulled away in anger, but she pulled him to her in a strong embrace. "You my best man 'round here, boy. Don't go talkin' such trash now, ya hear?" She wondered to herself if this miracle of hers could be kept secret from the rest of the community—her health might depend on it.

Back in the house, Elizabeth burst into tears as she hugged her child to her breast. "Oh Lord! Sweet Jesus answered my prayers!" she gasped. William was so moved he barely resisted putting his arms around both of them. He noticed, not for the first time, how beautiful Elizabeth was, with curling strands of red-gold hair springing from its bonds at the base of her neck. He sighed and patted both their backs nervously.

James said, "Ma, Dilby done this! I ain't got nothin' against Jesus, but you know Dilby done healed my legs."

Elizabeth drew back and wiped her eyes. "Yes, of course, James, but don't you go round sayin' that to Reverend Hope. After all, Baby, we are all just instruments of the Lord."

It was already March, but the winds whipped the tails of William McDowell's coat as he rode away from the Allen's, down a dirt trail toward his home.

After the school master left, Elizabeth sat down in the rocker by her parlor window and gazed out at the new pecan trees that flanked the boundaries of her front yard. Soon spring would be here, with the first leaf buds bursting from tree branches. She heard the wind's rather sinister moan echoing in the fireplace, and recalled that a delegation of three women from the congregation was coming the next day for afternoon tea. She thought of hiding James for the afternoon, but laughed at her cowardly reaction to this blessing.

The whole family rejoiced that evening. James sat at the head of the table for dinner. He still walked slowly and uncertainly, but there was improvement, even over the few hours since Dilby first placed him upright on his feet. After eating, Stokes and Martha tried to drag their brother outside to race down to the spring, but their father sent them off to their books with a firm smack on their behinds.

Later that evening Elizabeth confided her fears for Dilby's safety to Drewry, as they sat in front of the fireplace in the parlor. The ladies were due to arrive for tea the next day at 3:00 o'clock in the afternoon. Elizabeth knew they viewed her slave friend as 'devil's spawn.'

"These women act as though Dilby could conjure the whole countryside straight to Hell!" Drew fumed. "Damn their pryin' eyes!" He stood up to stalk back and forth in front of the mantle, a scowl shadowing his eyes in the candlelight.

Elizabeth asked timidly, "I can just say that all their Christian prayers have worked, can't I? They wouldn't dare contradict that, would they?"

"Perhaps, my dear, if you can keep James quiet about his damn fascination with our black witch." Elizabeth gasped at the word, but Drew went on, "I realize she's just an ignorant woman..."

"But Drew—"

"No, hear me out Lizzie! Dilby is kindly and skillful as well, but sometimes those airs of hers set my teeth on edge."

Elizabeth pressed her lips tightly together. She knew from experience that it was much better to wait until her husband finished a tirade and then quietly layout her arguments.

Drew fumed on, "I've seen the way our James clings to Dilby. He acts like he can't stand the thought of her even leaving the room." He reached for his wife's hand. "My dear, no matter what those church ladies try to make us do about our slave woman, I'm going to keep her out of James' way for awhile. It's just not right. I'm not blamin' her. After all, she's been James' comfortin' angel for nigh on to a year now, but for God's sake, she's still black, and a slave."

"Well then, Drew, let's just let those dear Christian women burn her at the stake! It'll solve all our problems, now won't it?" Elizabeth rose and stormed out to the hall and back to their bedroom.

Drew dropped into a chair with all his frustration and anger suddenly drained out of him. Resting his elbows on his knees, he leaned forward and stared into the fire. What was he going to do? If the church people decided to ban his family from the fellowship for harboring a witch, no one would buy from him. They probably wouldn't sell to him either. Would William McDowell let his children still come to the school? Yes, he knew he would: McDowell was no fearful gospel screamer, but an educated man—a rare thing here in Monroe County.

An idea came to him. He'd talk to the teacher, yet in the meantime, there were other things that needed to be settled with his wife concerning Dilby. He stooped down to bank the fire, then went to join Elizabeth.

Chapter 8 — Old Magic

The next morning Dilby took James and Joshua with her on her rounds to feed and milk the goats, gather eggs from the chickens, and start the water heating outside on the wood stove, to do the washing. She noticed that James walked less hesitantly with each passing minute. He hurried to catch up with Josh, when he scooted off to examine some new nest or chase hens that hovered around their eggs.

"Come here, Mistah Jim," Dilby beckoned. "You don' need to make up in jes' one day for all that layin' around sick! Set here and rest a minute with me." As James came to sit on the bench outside the chicken coop, Dilby reached in the pocket of her apron and took out a small cloth pouch that dangled from a leather thong.

"What's this, Dilby?" he asked dangling it from his fingers.

"Dat's jes' a small sweet blessin' to keep you strong and safe." Dilby smiled and took it from his hand. "Here now, let me put it 'round yo' neck like this." She bent forward and tied the thong, then tucked it down the front of his shirt. "It won't hurt nothin', Darlin', an' there be kind spirits around it tryin' to keep you safe." She almost spoke of Eka Ghassi, but bit back the words. She knew that this child could not keep a secret to save his life, and also was aware of the rumors in this small farm community that could bring harm to her and her own.

James looked down at his shirt and smelled the faint odor of lavender, pine, smoky ash, but he could not identify something sweet and musty. The boy smiled up at her. "Should I wear it when I sleep? Or swim?"

"Jes' be sure you keep it safe when you takes it off. You ain't wantin' nobody to steal it," she cautioned. "Now get on in the house and rest awhile. I got to clean up and bake fo' them ladies comin' this afternoon."

Sarah Jane Aiken and Liliane Jones clutched the sides of their two-wheeled trap that afternoon, grimly concentrating on their church appointed tasks for the upcoming confrontation with that rather odd Mrs. Allen. Liliane addressed her companion, "Sarah, I don't know how I'll keep a civil tongue in my mouth if that Nigra woman is around while we take tea with Lizzie. I swear, she scares me somethin' terrible. Why I can just feel her eyes pourin' into my head, tryin' her black spell on me!"

Liliane, or Lily-Anne as her friend called her, was truly more frightened of Dilby than she was affronted by wayward religious behavior. Her stomach already churned with anxiety, and the steady bumping of the two-wheeled buggy over a rutted spring road did not help. The woman tried to tuck a wayward strand of chestnut brown hair back behind the rim of her bonnet, but it kept escaping. Strangely, the wind whipped up and around them quite strongly as the horse jogged along. Trees seemed to bow towards them as they rode past.

"Lily-Anne Jones! I declare you don't have even an itty-bitty ounce of gumption. She's just a Nigra slave woman and you know the Lord wants her to stay in her place. Drew needs to clamp down on his black folks 'afore they get to thinkin' they can walk right alongside of white people! I don't think Dilby's got any kind of magic. She just scarin' people into thinkin' she does." Sarah smacked her folded fan sharply against her friend's shoulder in emphasis.

"My, it does look threatening up ahead, Sister! I never have seen such fast movin' storm clouds comin' from the east!" Liliane ducked as a cold gust abruptly whipped her cloak up behind her. She clutched her bonnet to her head. Finally the horse pulled up in front of the Allen's sturdy farmhouse with its two chimneys balancing at either end like sentinels.

The two ladies leaned into the wind as they walked up to the porch, grasping the short pillars to haul themselves up toward the front door. Suddenly the door blew open, slamming outward as though emanating from an internal gust in the central hall. No one stood there to welcome them; all they could hear was the sound of dishes being moved around in the nearby parlor.

Frantic, Sarah rapped her gloved fist on the doorpost and called out, "Lizzie, are you in there?"

Elizabeth rushed to the front door and was apologetic in greeting her guests. "Oh, dear, just look at that wind blowing everythin' across the yard! You all come on in right now. Dilby fixed a nice fire for us and I've got hot tea ready to warm you both up."

Liliane muttered, "You better check to see that the back is all closed in! Some kind of devilish wind just about took my nose off, blowin' your door the wrong way!"

"Really now?" Elizabeth glanced back into the hallway. "I'll just have to see about that. You all sit right here and warm yourselves while I' go check." She hurried down the hall toward the back rooms. Sarah and Liliane removed their cloaks and bonnets, smoothing back hair and snuggling into the cushioned chairs at each side of the fireplace. "Well, I can't seem to find anything open back there." Elizabeth settled herself on the high-backed bench in front of an elegant little teacart brought recently by Drew from Savannah. She began to pour the tea, asking preferences in sugar and cream.

"Did you know, my dear," Sarah confided, "that your woman was seen peddlin' her infernal superstitions around Mister Hope's place lately?"

Elizabeth looked up from pouring, with raised eyebrows, and noticed Sarah's stiff posture and nervous, darting eyes. "Why Sarah, who do you mean? There are several Nigra women workin' here."

Liliane let out a nasty snicker. "Well, I am quite sure you know very well, Lizzie, who we be talkin' of here."

Just then, Martha dashed into the room, stopping with a jerk at the sight of the trio of ladies. "Oh, 'scuse me, Mamma, but...but"– she looked at the adults–"Well, I jes' wanted to tell you all Jimmy and Josh be runnin' down the road chasin' rabbits with their sling shots!"

"You don't need to tell all of us my dear."

"What do you mean, Child?" questioned Liliane. "Your brother James surely can't be doin' nothin' like that. Why, we all seen Mister Allen carryin' him into church last Sunday mornin'."

"Oh no, Miz Jones," Martha said. "Dilby done fixed him all up! You should see what she can do." The girl stopped short when her mother stood up quickly.

"Go on now, Martha dear. We don't need to hear all your quarrels with your brother." With a small flick of her hand in the direction of the door, Elizabeth indicated her urgent need for Martha to leave as quickly as possible.

"No, don't go just yet, child. I'd like to know more about what that black creature did to your brother." Sarah turned to Liliane and murmured, "and I do mean 'black'!"

Elizabeth moved her daughter out into the hall. Martha looked over her shoulder at the two women. "You should see what she can do! Mamma says she's got real magic! Ow!" A resounding smack on the behind sent Martha on her way.

"Magic indeed!" Sara snorted. "I do declare, Lizzie, this has got to stop. If the good Lord wanted James to be runnin' around, he wouldn't send a black African witch to do his biddin'! Both ladies rose from their chairs and brushed invisible dust from their clothes. "Come Lily-Ann! We best be goin' on to Sister Borden's place. The Reverend said she's not feelin' so well these days."

Elizabeth twisted her hands together nervously. "But you haven't had your tea."

"It's time we left. Truth is, my dear, I don't care to take refreshment if that sorceress had a hand in its preparation!" With that the two women stalked out of the house and practically flew into their buggy. The wind was so strong, it practically blew them away. Rain started to pour as the driver pulled away from the front of the house.

Sarah complained, "If Drewry Allen doesn't get rid of that Dilby, and keep his son from her evil I'm personally goin' to see him banned from the fellowship! You just see if I don't!"

Liliane nodded a meek agreement with her friend. The buggy bounced along.

The creaking of the leather harness and traces seemed to expand in the air, like a repetitive chuckle, broken by a loud crash of thunder that startled the horse so badly that it veered off to one side and almost toppled the two passengers.

Chapter 9 — Church

Years later James would look back at this time, when he first was cured and able again to run down the road after his friends, as a moment of fracture in the symmetric solidity of the family's life. Like a grand oil landscape that lay too long in a dry, dusty attic, its cracked surface shifting and distorting the plane of the whole picture.

That first Sunday after the venomous tea party was bright and fresh during the early morning hours, and began like most summer Sundays that year. Families came from small and large farms, traveling in one or two horse buggies to worship in the log building that replaced the original bower. The bower, really a lean-to of leafy branches and pine logs, had been set up at the crossroads in a burst of enthusiasm for John Wesley's teachings. John Hester's forge and supply shop faced the old field where these earliest settlers had hauled the logs and branches before there were more than a handful of slaves in the area to help set up a temporary church. The first completely wooden structure was built in 1806. Negro slaves were loaned by their masters for the construction, but the church burned to the ground a year later and was replaced by the current structure.

Drewry's family led the procession of wagons and buggies along one of the dirt roads that day. He pulled into the open meadow in front of the church. Elizabeth carried a still sleepy Emily into the church while Drewry lined up the other children to follow. The boys looked moist, clean and uncomfortably hot in their tight jackets and pantaloon-style pants, buttoned at the knee. The girls were better off in their new cotton dresses and straw bonnets. Elizabeth had purchased the new cotton cloth from a peddler who landed on her porch just three weeks earlier. He had trudged for ten days westward across the wilderness from Augusta, and in exchange for a few days rest with meals, offered the family a bargain on his goods.

Once seated on the family's customary bench toward the back of the assembly, Drew checked the squirming discomfort of his children with a grim frown and shake of the head. Elizabeth had some difficulty breathing in the tightly packed space of the primitive church. Oddly, the usual soft flow of murmured conversations was absent that morning; the only sound was a sibilant flutter from dozens of straw fans. Humid air, caught and shaped by four long rectangles of sunlight from windows along a side aisle, seemed to vibrate as dozens of hands stirred and waved like a forest of antennae around her.

"Look at them, Drew, fluttering and twisting. I swear, it could be a swarm of beetles, caught in a spider web."

Drew grinned. "Darlin' we're all helpless for the next hour. Just keep on fanning like the rest and it will be over before too long."

Reverend Hope began his sermon by gazing grimly down at the open Bible, his lips moving silently. Suddenly he looked up and glared fiercely towards the back of the church. James had leaned his head against Elizabeth's shoulder and tried to imagine himself down at the creek. He smiled, thinking of Dilby, and how she restored his legs. *God, I want to do what Dilby does for people. She jes' got to be special smart. Help me get to healin' some day like she does.* Hope misquoted Genesis 9:24 in his opening remark: "And the Lord put a curse on Ham, the lustful, perverted son of Noah, just as He put a mark on the murderer Cain." He dramatically paused a moment to point with a shaking finger toward some unseen object outside the side windows. "And Ham's descendants were the black men of Cush and Egypt! They bear their dark mark today, living cursed lives as slaves." He nodded knowingly, "It is the will of the Lord." Slamming his fist on the lectern, he swept a pointed finger above the heads of his congregation. "Who among you would be seduced by the savage appetites of their slave descendants? I say, if you lighten the load, sweeten the table, welcome the lying smiles of daughters of Ham, you only open the doors of temptation both to them and to yourselves!" He smiled stiffly, "I know, we all learn to soften our hearts to these creatures who bow and cater to our wishes. Who has not a fond memory of being rocked to sleep in dusky arms? Well, Jesus Christ came to save all, some say both Black and White." He pounded the lectern once again. "Yet never, I say, never weaken, nor drop your guard! Satan slides into the heart like the slippery black serpent he is, cooing and fondling, and flattering. Beware! We have taken the children of darkness to our bosoms, but we alone must rule and control their savage desires."

Heads nodded agreement. Soft "Amens" rose from the gathered assembly. Furtive, condemning glances slid sideways at the Allen family.

After a blessing, everyone filed out of the church in silence. Mr. Hope had instructed them to refrain from song, saying he needed to stay awhile in quiet to meditate on the frightening challenges that recently had been brought to his attention.

Now alone in the church with the Reverend Hope, Drewry stood and walked toward the front where the minister remained with head bowed and arms raised dramatically as he faced the simple cross on the holy table.

"Oh Lord," he intoned, "Take this blight from your faithful people."

Drew coughed to let his presence be known. Hope ignored the sound. "Cleanse with fire from Heaven this infection."

"Mister Hope! You forget yourself!"

The minister jerked violently at the sharp rebuke. Drew had a deep, powerful voice that carried and reverberated in the hall as though Moses himself had just descended from the Mount. Hope turned, pointed his much-used finger up toward the ceiling, as though about to pronounce a prophecy, but had been interrupted.

Drew accused him. "Do you dare threaten to destroy my property? I'll have you to jail, by God! Fire, you say. And who did you come to when your barn was burning last January?" Hope lowered his arms to take several steps away from his raging parishioner, but Drew continued, "Why, 'twas to your neighbors, and mostly to me, if you will remember. My people hauled water from the spring all night to save your place."

The Reverend Mr. Hope tripped as he retreated, but caught his balance by clutching the edge of the holy table. "I speak of God's fiery wrath, sir, and you had best be rid of your black witch."

Drew turned about and stalked out of the building to join his family, grabbing James by the collar as he passed the door.

No one spoke on the way home until they drew up to the barn. Josh hurried up to the buggy, unhitched the horses and led them away to the paddock.

Elizabeth turned and whispered to Drew, "What did you say to the preacher?"

"Listen to me, now," Drew answered. "I fear Mister Hope has some ideas of bringin' down fires of Hell on us himself! And James hangin' on Dilby's neck all the time isn't helpin' one bit." He paused before stepping down from the buggy.

"Elizabeth, bring James to the parlor. No one in this family is to set foot in that church until I settle with Reverend Hope. The man's thinkin' he alone talks to the Lord. By God, it will take a bit of doin' but I'll have him out of here." Drew swung the hickory switch in his hand angrily. "Some darn fool will take him up on all that talk of fire. The Lord knows we got plenty of fools to go 'round."

.A few minutes later James stood before his mother and father, curious but nervous. Drewry told him, "My boy, Mister McDowell has found a place for you at the new academy in Augusta. You truly are fortunate. Not many young boys from these parts can go to such a fine school."

"But Papa, I can't leave you all. I don't want to live somewhere else." Tears formed in his eyes, but he wiped at them furiously. "You all goin' need me in the harvest for, you know, planting winter wheat and all." Elizabeth put her arm around his shoulders and pressed him to her side. James pulled away to insist, "I'm stronger now, and stronger still come September." His parents said nothing for a moment. James turned away to hide his tears.

Elizabeth approached him again and placed her hand on his shoulder. "You'll be home with us come next harvest, after just one year at school. Darlin' I couldn't do without you longer." She gently laid her head on top of his to say, "Just got so used to havin' my arms right here, holding such a strong little man." She pressed her cheek against his dark curls.

Drew added, "Josh can go along and help set you up in the headmaster's home."

"Josh won't want to leave his ma. And what's he goin' do while I'm learnin'? Mister Hope says slave boys can't be learnin' to read and everythin'."

Drew gestured to Elizabeth to step aside and then led James outside to sit with him on grass under the pecan trees. "Listen to me, now. You take Josh with you into classes as your boy. It sure won't hurt if he picks up some learnin' even by mistake." He placed his hands on each side of his son's face, looked directly into his eyes, then spoke softly–almost a whisper. "I want you and Josh away from here, James. I want you to meet all kinds of new people. You've been shut up all these long days with just Dilby." After James looked at him in surprise Drew said, "James, I must find a way to save–Dilby and her baby from these pious preachin' folks!"

"But Pa–"

"I know you don't understand, but I can't do this until you and Josh are safely in Augusta." Drew seemed to be groping for words, unsure himself of his arguments. James couldn't know that his warm proximity to Dilby was extremely dangerous to her right then.

Chapter 10 — Fall and Separation

A fter his father made arrangements through his teacher for James to attend the academy in Augusta, James saw Dilby only as she worked around the laundry shed or kitchen garden.

James and Josh left the farm in late August of 1804, escorted to Augusta by William McDowell. The young teacher agreed to settle the boys at the academy as Elizabeth joined her pleas with Drew's. William sensed an urgency in the mother's request that indicated a concern far beyond educational opportunities for her son.

James had marveled at the way William's eyes would follow the movements of his mother during the afternoon tutoring. He noticed that Elizabeth seemed oblivious to it all. Young William McDowell had come to idolize Elizabeth Allen, cultivating a secret passion for the older woman that fit the emotional intensity of the Romantic mood of 19th century society. She was the unreachable goal, the unattainable sexual fantasy that must remain hidden. Young James, on the other hand, only sensed a strange intensity in the man whenever his mother was present.

Now, two weeks after Drew's confrontation with Reverend Hope, a coach jostled William, James and Joshua along the rough country trails, their journey leading northeastward. They crossed the many rivers dividing "civilized" eastern Georgia from the frontier. William broke the monotony of travel by quoting lines from William Blake, his favorite poet.

Never seek to tell thy love,
Love that never told can be.
For the gentle wind doth move
Silently, invisibly.

He turned toward James to emphasize the second verse. "Listen carefully!
I told my love, I told my love,
I told her all my heart,
Trembling cold in ghastly fears,
Ah, she doth depart.

Although Joshua frowned and turned away whenever the schoolmaster's voice rose above the rattling of the carriage, James had begun to grasp the pain and ecstasy of unfulfilled, secret longing. He sensed it, physically stirring beneath his belly, and it was closely allied to the loss of Dilby's personal attention, and loneliness.

James decided to accept, for a while, the wishes of his parents and to work doggedly on his studies for a year—even as he ached with a sense of foreboding and felt the weight of impending isolation.

✌❧

Mainly to keep an ear to the ground, Drewry and Elizabeth continued to attend the worship services at the church, in spite of his earlier decision. The rains of fall kept families confined to their own homesteads, yet served as well to lessen fears of fire that always had nagged them throughout the month of August.

Long hours of constant, dripping rain and ground-hugging fog weighed heavily on isolated farm families. Late in the afternoons, the sun would emerge, suddenly and fiercely, to raise humid vapors from the fields and roads.

Dilby moved quietly about her chores, followed by little Nan, while Elizabeth grew sluggish with a now unfamiliar depression, unrelieved by the former gentle banter and relaxed affability she had shared with a slave sister. Dilby seemed to have withdrawn from her. Strangely, she communicated almost exclusively with Drewry in quiet, secretive conversations that lasted only a few minutes at a time.

Once Elizabeth asked her husband, "Drew, what were you and Dilby talkin' about this mornin' when I came out to get some eggs from those new chickens? I swear Dilby seemed downright sneaky, almost running away from us when I got near."

Drew had just smiled at her and answered, "My dear, she can be a might mysterious sometimes. You know that. I was askin' if she would worry too much with Josh gone to Augusta. Don't you worry about it."

Finally the rains ended. October arrived with an intense heat that dried the wood barns and soggy paddocks with a vengeance. Slave families were grateful at first, as their cabins leaked badly. The fierce summer had shrunk the boards of their walls and roofs, exposing them to unremitting dampness that brought on bronchial coughs and fevers.

Days were shorter and candles lit earlier in the evenings. Long shadows stretched out beside the farm house, outbuildings, and cabins. An imaginative child could envision all kinds of shapes moving beneath trees and scurrying around corners.

✌❧

Elizabeth noticed that little Stokes had begun behaving strangely. He was bothered by frightening dreams, and was overly influenced by any superstition that came to his attention.

"Ma, I heard the owl last night!"

Elizabeth reassured him, "He's got a right to call out, just like you or me, Baby,"

"But Sabrina says that means somebody gonna die!"

"Sabrina's just tryin' to scare you, honey. She needs to keep her measly little wits on her work in the gin room. I swear she'll stop to chatter with you for any excuse at all!"

But Stokes tied knots in the sheets at each corner of his bed that night to keep safe from the angel of death. Around two o'clock in the morning he woke, his eyes large with fright. All seemed to be quiet in the house, but he knew something was not right. Silently he crept out of bed, checked the knots, and went to his window to make sure nothing was hiding just outside.

A loud whinny from the barn so startled him that he threw up the window sash. He thought he saw a shadowy figure dart from the pile of hay beside the barn toward the cabins. Trembling in the chill night air, the boy pulled on his heavy shirt and climbed onto the sill. Soundlessly dropping to the ground, he moved into the darkness towards the cabins. A scream broke through the black silence, followed by a great sucking sound and a burst of fire light from the window of Dilby's cabin. Dark figures streamed out of all the cabins, accompanied by yells, curses and the sound of running feet.

"Mama! Daddy!" Stokes screamed, and ran back toward his own front porch. Drewry almost ran him down as he stumbled naked out the door with his musket. He quickly saw the cause of alarm, threw the gun in the bushes, and ran to organize a water line from the pump to the burning cabin.

Women and children were crying and screaming as their men tried to get nearer the fire to see if anyone was inside Dilby's cabin.

Drewry yelled, "Did y'all see anybody come out?"

When all heads shook from side to side, he doused himself with a bucket of water and dashed through the cabin's door. Every voice rose in a wail as he disappeared from sight. Moments later he came out alone. Elizabeth, standing with her arms around Stokes, fainted.

Two tall, bone-thin men stood at the edge of the woods, the flickering light of the dying flames highlighting their gaunt faces and scraggly beards. They blinked gray-blue eyes as the smoke drifted towards their place in the bordering bushes. Sam Aiken lowered his can of kerosene to the ground to watch the dark figures running back and forth from the blaze. Abe Jones had begun to sniffle nervously beside his friend.

Aiken chided, "Hush that noise, brother Abe! We done jes' what the Lord was orderin' us to do!"

"Who say so, that snarly ol' wife of your'n? I don' put no more store by her. She didn' say they'd be no folks in that cabin!"

"Lissen, you ol' fool. What's the point if that there witch still be walkin' around after all our trouble?" Abe wiped his eyes on his shirtsleeve and began to slink away. Sam called after him, "Don' you go whinin' to that silly woman of yours, ya hear? What we done is done. I kin blame you for the whole thing if I hear you start havin' weird thoughts and spreadin' 'em around."

The two men crept away, assured that Dilby and her children would never threaten the congregation of Hope Methodist Church again. There was no recourse to a legal system or local sheriff. A county sheriff would come by on his rounds eventually, but until then Drew had to keep his own counsel and plot the future carefully. Bones were found in the ashes, he told his slaves, and he would make arrangements for burial in a plot of land nearby, a hill behind the kitchen garden. He said nothing more to his children, but took his wife aside and asked her to accompany him to the new little cemetery and lay out a plan for it.

Two days after the fire, Elizabeth walked slowly behind Drew. He carried a small boxfull of remains under his arm up the grassy hill. As they walked, he had noticed her pallor and a dull glazed look to her eyes, but gritted his teeth and said nothing.

At the burial site, Drew said, "I want to build a low stone wall here, my dear, and place this, our first grave, at the far eastern corner. We'll have a limestone marker there with baby Nan and Dilby's names carved on it." Elizabeth broke down in sobs and fell to her knees on the ground. He lifted her up into his arms and spoke softly next to her ear, "Come, my dear, I have something to reveal. There are only the bones of an old cow and that little stillborn foal beneath this dirt."

Chapter 11 — Augusta

The carriage traveled toward Augusta almost fifty miles each day, with occasional stops to water and rest the horses. As the tiring voyage progressed, James and Joshua became silent. They looked out over the landscape; drank from canteens, and drifted into a half-waking dream state as hours of bumping along the dusty trails dragged on. They stirred with some interest when the Ocmulgee River had to be crossed on a large raft, but afterward drifted off into their own internal worlds. No one in the carriage had any idea or premonition about tragic events back on the farm.

The trip seemed divided by the many creeks and rivers that ran roughly from north to south. After the Ocmulgee, they passed the Oconee and Ogeechee rivers. All three rivers were named after their Creek Indian inhabitants, who recently had departed to the south and Florida. Friendly farmers along the way put the little group up each night. That kindness provided them a break in the desolation of farm life on the edge of wilderness forests. Finally, William was able to discern the western bank of the Savannah River as it flowed to the southeast and into the Atlantic Ocean.

Augusta, Georgia, sits on the Savannah River at the edge of the northwestern quadrant of the state, and marks the boundary with South Carolina. Commerce between the importers in Savannah and Augusta merchants flowed up and down this river, so that the wealthiest citizens of Augusta had access to china, silver ware, furniture, and fine cloth for clothing and drapery that came from England and occasionally from the northern states.

In Augusta, the carriage moved up Broad Street, along the riverbank, and then turned away from the river. A great church of red brick, with a tall steeple rising above the roof, appeared on the left of the carriage. The boys were stunned! How was such a thing possible? Mr. McDowell rapped on the window separating them from the driver and signaled for him to halt. After the horses came to a full stop, he opened the carriage door and hopped quickly to the ground and looked up at the driver.

"Wait a few minutes, my friend. I want to show these boys what's left of old Fort Augusta behind yon' church."

The old man replied from his high perch, "Young sir, there be nothin' more'n the old cross left to see. That be in the church yard yonder."

The two boys almost fell from stiffness as they tumbled from the coach. Both looked around in amazement at what indeed seemed like grand homes. Directly across the dirt road from St. Paul's stood a square-roofed, two storied neoclassical home. A front portico extended from the facade like the entrance to an ancient temple. Only this was newly built, with four, narrow white painted pillars on lower and upper levels supporting a triangular pediment. A bay window in the shape of half an octagon protruded from the left side. James and Joshua started to cross the road to see more of this marvel. Was this the new academy?

"Now boys, we have a ways yet to Telfair Street, where Headmaster Chauvin waits to greet us. Stretch your bones by runnin' around the side of that church wall." William wiped his brow with his yellowing neckerchief. It was seventy-eight degrees and even more humid than in the west at this time in October. "Come, we'll salute the Celtic cross that's been standin' there for more'n seventy years now."

The boys took off with a jolt, craving movement after the hours of immobility. Rounding the corner of the wall that contained the gravestones in a shaded grassy court yard, William reached the open gate just as the boys reached the gray stone vertical shaft. Four holes pierced the circular center stone where the cross-arm intersected. William stepped between Joshua and James to bow low from the waist in front of its base. Looking up with a grin, he cuffed the two gently on their chins. "There, maybe we've satisfied a few Scots ghosts, and of course, the good Lord, for awhile. Let's try our luck with that learned Frenchman on Telfair Street."

The academy for boys had been in existence for just a few years when James and Joshua arrived with William McDowell. It consisted of two large town homes, which sat next to each other on a wide, tree-lined street. The Chauvin house, where the headmaster lived a bachelor's life, with domestic slaves brought up from New Orleans, rose three stories from the front garden. Two flights of stairs rose to the main entrance on a curved central balcony at the second level. The staircase formed two sides of an oval that framed the lower entrance to servants' quarters and kitchen. The two halves of the house on either side of the central section of the house rose in a series of curved bays. Each had three windows looking out on the main thoroughfare of Telfair Street. Above the entrance balcony, a second balcony was supported by four slender columns. William imagined the lady of the house—if she existed—could step out on it from an upper hallway in the evenings to see the stars, or wave to carriages passing by. Augusta was beginning to look most civilized. It had changed a great deal from the rugged outpost and fort of the 1790's. William had read about those years while deciding whether or not to emigrate from Scotland. He thought, wistfully, of bringing a beautiful young wife to a house like this.

The trio removed their hats and waited on the balcony for their knock to be answered. Joshua stood well behind and carried James's small case of clothes.

Books were tied with a leather strap that draped around James's shoulders and hung on either side of his neck. He let no one carry them but himself.

Finally the door opened. All three arrivals stopped breathing for an instant, as though each was struck a simultaneous blow on the chest. Before them stood one of the most beautiful and exotic young women they had ever seen. Dark auburn curls tumbled from a headband in contrasting tropical colors of red, coral, yellow, and green. The woman looked at them with somber, slightly almond shaped eyes beneath delicate eyebrows that sprouted like butterfly wings from either side of a straight, almost Arabic nose. She smiled, bowed, and stepped to the side, ushering them in.

"*Bon après-midi*, gentlemen. My uncle has been waiting for you since early this morning. Please enter the parlor and I will tell him you have arrived." The men stood speechless for a moment, until William smiled and apologized, "Please forgive us, my dear, we expected to see a lonely bachelor greeting us. This is indeed a great pleasure." He cupped the girl's elbow in his hand as he and the boys followed her into the great parlor on the left of the hall.

James and Joshua both noticed the grace with which their guide walked. Her small slim figure was encased in a long bouffant skirt that swept the air around her ankles from side to side. A white lacy shawl covered her shoulders, but strong, well-muscled arms swung bare at her sides as she walked, belying a totally sheltered life in a luxurious home.

Tall double doors opened on a room that was obviously designed to impress parents of prospective students, as well as new members of the academy's Board of Directors. A high ceiling was bordered by a delicate frieze of sculpted flowers and what appeared to be arrows, with two-handled vases all in a row in repeated patterns. The walls were painted a soft, muted blue against which portraits of the recent governor and his wife, landscapes, and still-lives of flowers and fruit were arranged. A long, rectangular piano stood in the circle of the windowed bay where sunlight poured in slanted beams on its rich brown surface. A crystal bowl of late pink roses graced one end, while a tiny ivory miniature of a beautiful dark-haired woman was placed at the opposite side.

The young girl who brought them in couldn't have been more than fourteen years old. She perched with calm self assurance on the embroidered seat of a Queen Anne chair, indicating a love seat opposite for William and James. Then, astoundingly, she slyly winked at Joshua. "There will surely be refreshments downstairs in the kitchen for your boy." She almost giggled as she pointed to the door. Tell Maddy down there that Monsieur Chauvin's 'special niece' sent you." Joshua hesitated a moment, looked in the direction of the hall, and ducked his head to hide his confusion and the beginning of a smile.

"*Allez maintenant*, shoo!" she added with a dismissive wave of her hand. "Oh my, I am so rude! Let me introduce myself. My name is Clothilde, but everyone calls me Chloe."

James rose from his seat and bowed, "James Allen, Ma'am," he murmured.

William hardly believed his eyes. "My dear, do you always have such a good effect on the manners of young men?"

James blushed deeply, but could not take his eyes off Chloe's golden complexion, now tinted with a flush of her own.

"And you, *Monsieur*, must be school master McDowell. My uncle told me of your travels and tribulations in our west Georgia frontier." Chloe jumped up, looking suddenly distracted. "Here is Uncle now!" She ran to assume a position behind a stout, freshly shaved man who quietly had entered from the hall.

Monsieur Chauvin could have just stepped out of an elegant carriage in front of the Paris Opera. His perfectly tailored jacket was black, with a white silk cravat at his throat. Boots, rather than shoes, were the only discordant element in his immaculate presentation—a necessary bow to the realities of muddy streets in Georgia's rather wet fall season. A slight frown indicated that for some reason he was not entirely pleased with what was taking place. The frown quickly disappeared as the headmaster stepped toward his guests with a jaunty little bounce.

He grasped William's hand in welcome. "Ah, *Bonjour mon ami!* You must be exhausted. Please sit down again. We must get acquainted with your young student here, and see to his arrangements in the one remaining room upstairs." He turned to look at James. "*Alors*, I am told you wish to study and learn about the healing arts. *C'est bien*, but first we must see to your Latin, your understanding of the history of both the ancient and modern worlds, and review the basic principals of mathmatics. *N'est-ce pas?*"

This fastidious little man fascinated James. William had told him of Chauvin's career as a cavalry officer for the provincial French government in Louisiana, and of his short stint with Washington's army during the war. This peacock seemed rather incongruous to him at first. James had imagined a rigid and stoic militant in the cause of taming young men for future army careers. Was not this a military academy? Where were the parade grounds? "Yes, sir, I will do my best and—"

William interrupted. "You must know, Monsieur Chauvin, that James has been very ill for the last year with a strange paralysis. Now he is miraculously recovered and has put the long hours of confinement to good use with books. After careful examination, you may find he could use some tutoring, but he is an apt scholar and eager to explore the world of ideas."

The headmaster nodded as he looked intently at his new pupil. "I think we shall do very well. Perhaps Clothilde can help him *avec le francais* and a beginning understanding of music." He looked down for a moment, then explained, "You see, Clothilde is my ward, now that her parents are no longer *vivant*. I have educated her myself, and she can converse with most gentlemen in this town on their own level."

James looked stricken. "You mean her parents are both dead, sir?"

Chauvin shifted in his chair and paused. "*Mais oui*, it is...ah...unfortunate." Then he rose with a sigh, flicked an imaginary speck of lint from his cuff, and called out to waiting ears in the hall, "Come, please, Chloe, and bring the young servant of Monsieur James to carry him up to his room. I must confer a while privately with his teacher."

James stood, gathered his books into his arms, and walked out of the parlor to find Chloe and Joshua waiting for him in the hall. They seemed to have just finished a quite informal conversation: Josh grinned broadly when the girl turned from whispering something in his ear. This seemed strange to James, yet made it easier for him to draw them both to him in a confederacy of adolescents. With a tutor such as Clothilde. he knew that Josh could have a chance to learn at this school. The girl obviously seemed to have escaped the arbitrary isolation of white girls from association with young male slaves. Somehow, the taboos weighed very lightly with her.

Chapter 12 — Chloe

As James settled in to the elegant surroundings of the academy, he noticed that Joshua struggled with the more rigid strictures and boundaries of life for a slave in a southern city. They both found it confusing that there were almost four thousand free men of color living here, in a total population of almost eight thousand people, not counting slaves. Yet it was definitely frowned upon for Joshua to be seen talking and laughing with James or Chloe. James asked to have Joshua sleep outside his room, so they could talk late at night, but Monsieur Chauvin insisted that the boy move into the basement quarters where the rest of the slaves were quartered.

James wondered where Chloe slept? Her room was not on his floor of the large house and he knew she would not be put in the basement where Maddy, the cook, slept. After a nightly tutoring session, Chloe would give him a delicate kiss on the cheek and leave the premises, or so it seemed.

The academy was not very large. Twelve boys aged fourteen and up spent the mornings in classes next door with Monsieur Chauvin, his young assistant, Stanley Grothius, the son of an immigrant from Germany, and a one armed cavalry officer, retired, who worked diligently to graft his knowledge of world and local geography onto the narrow, circumscribed world view of his students.

Major Bob included mathematical exercises with geography by escorting his young men to the outskirts of town, where they would try to survey some of the first land grants out in the countryside. Grothius, a Latin and Greek scholar, taught the history of those ancient cultures along with the languages themselves. Often, the difficult class caused James to writhe at his desk in frustration.

Chauvin, assisted by Chloe, instructed students in both civics and the French language.

Each afternoon the boys spent hours out of doors with Monsieur Chauvin and the Major on horseback. They drilled in a little pasture adjoining the back gardens and stable while their instructors barked out commands.

This life kept James too busy to think of his family during the day, but at night he thrashed about in his bed. He missed the playful sounds of his brother and sisters; the soft melodies of Dilby's singing in the kitchen; and the rhythmic creaking of his father's rocking chair in the evenings.

⚜

Six months had passed without word from home. The two boys knew nothing of the terrible fire that demolished Dilby's cabin. James had taken to listening at his own door in hopes of hearing Josh nearby. He knew Josh had become expert in navigating the old house at night without waking the Chauvin family or their servants.

One night, after an hour of this misery, James crept to the door of his room to find out if his friend had received permission to sleep outside his room. He had badgered Monsieur for a week, saying he had terrible headaches during the nights and that Josh had been trained to care for him by Mrs. Allen herself.

Taking a cautious breath and hoping that Josh might be reinstalled outside his room, James whispered, "Josh, you there?" A low rumbling sound came through the wood panel. Josh's voice had changed quite suddenly to baritone. "Come on, now, I know you just went to bed after workin' with Chloe. How bout sharin' a bit of this here pecan sweet I got hidin' in here?"

Slowly the door creaked open. Josh's half-closed eyes appeared around one edge. "Mista Jim, I don' want no trouble with that ol' Maud. She tol' me I ain't allowed to set and talk wid you or any other white boys. So leave me be." He pulled his head back and began to close the door.

"Please Josh. Nobody goin' to know you're here. I'm so lonely an' worried 'bout Mamma and Dilby. I jus' got to talk to you."

No sound issued from the other side. Then a bare, brown foot stepped across the doorjamb, and Josh's slender body slipped sideways through the opened door. Seated on the floor beneath the window that faced on Telfair Street, the two young boys bent their heads close together and whispered, "Did you get a letter from you Mamma yet, Jimmy?" James shook his head. How come nobody wrote from home?

Now that Josh had learned his letters, he could even read articles in the local newspaper about the new naval war with England. He pulled a clipping from his back pocket to show James. "See here, Jimmy, it says they got big barges sailin' from Augusta down the canal to Savannah. I been dyin' to sneak on one and ride all the way there." James read the advertisement and began to grin. They could sneak aboard a barge and sail to Savannah and then hop aboard the next wagonload leaving for the interior with goods for the western farmers.

James urged, "If we go right before Easter, when everybody be gettin' ready to leave anyway, nobody's goin' to know we're gone until the end of April."

The boys had no way of knowing what plans might have been made for them between Drewry, Mr. McDowell, and Headmaster Chauvin.

One day late in March a horseman road up to the Acadamy's front gate, carrying a satchel of mail. In the front hall Monsieur Chauvin sorted through the delivered letters before retreating to his study across from the parlor. "Chloe!" He called from his desk. The young girl rushed to him at the strident tone of his voice. "*Va chercher Monsieur James et dits lui de venir ici a mon cabinet.*" Chauvin waved an envelope above his head. "*J'ai des mauvaises nouvelles.*" Chloe's left hand flew to cover her mouth when she leaned over his shoulder and caught sight of the words "a criminal fire demolished..."

"*Depeche-toi, ma fille!*" he hissed, shooing her toward the door.

Chloe ran out the back door and across the yard to the school building next door. What had a fire demolished? Could the poor boys have lost a loved one at home? She shook her head as she climbed the three steps to the back of the small kitchen. The young men—she thought of them as men her own size—were just beginning to accept the new life here, and they both were so much nicer than the stuffy little prigs up from Savannah!

Chloe timidly knocked on the door of Monsieur Grothius's room. She had never dared to interrupt one of his classes before.

"Enter!" rang out in the man's high tenor voice. Chloe burst into the room with "*Monsieur, il faut...pardon.* Master James *doit venire vitement chez* Monsieur Chauvin's office!"

It was a pale and trembling James Allen who stood in front of the headmaster's desk. "Sit down, please, James. I have received bad news from your family that..."

James swayed but steadied himself by catching the edge of the desk, then sitting opposite M. Chauvin.

The headmaster reassured him. "Calm yourself, James, your family is all right. I'm afraid that a fire on the farm burned one of the slave cabins and damaged the barn." James relaxed slightly and slumped back in his chair. "It seems, however, that one of your mother's most prized slave women was killed, thus we are asked in this letter from your father to keep this information from young Joshua. *Je ne comprends pas completement,* but I gather that she was the mother of..."

Chauvin never finished the sentence: James fell forward, hitting his head on the desk and collapsing to the floor. At the same moment he saw Josh appear at the door. He had followed Chloe and James from the back of the Latin room, and stood rigidly in the doorway. A high wail rose from his throat, as he clutched the doorframe as if to tear it away from the wall.

Joshua!" Chauvin exclaimed. "My...boy, let me help—"

Josh had fled. He ran out of the house where the mail rider had dismounted to gossip with the foreman of a road crew that ate lunch by the side of the road. Without a thought, or fear, he jumped on the back of the postman's horse and slapped his hand behind him, startling the beast into an instant canter. Chauvin watched without moving from the window to stop him.

⋙⋘

Joshua galloped, steering the horse at full speed toward the Augusta canal, and then west out of town. When the frightened animal tried to throw the boy several times, Josh hung on, sobbing as he clung with arms around the horse's neck.

"Mamma, Mamma," he sobbed. "Oh Jesus!" He thought he heard a sigh as he slipped past waving branches of trees along the roadside.

"Sleep, baby sleep" Dilby had sung to little Nan; somehow he could sense the melody in the air. Then, "Go on boy, if you can, but I'm always here. I'm gonna stay 'roun, baby." Yet Joshua did not believe in the voices like his mother did. Still, both he and the horse shivered at the harsh sound of thunder that came from the dark clouds in the west.

"Plateye be laughin', Ma. Maybe I's Plateye's boy now." Josh grasped the flying reins and pulled the horse's head sharply to the left, across open fields, and headed south.

⋙⋘

Groups of men on horseback searched the area for two weeks for some trace of Joshua, but then gave it up when James pleaded with them. He told them that his father would find Joshua in good time, and believed the boy would return eventually to the farm and his mother's grave. At the Academy, James did not really believe that, but feared the men with their dogs, straining to take off after a runaway. He grieved over Dilby's death to the point of refusing all food but scraps of bread and occasional dried bacon rind. Dilby could not be dead: she was too magical for that to happen. Whenever no one was looking, he compulsively gripped her soft leather bag around his neck.

Chloe watched and wondered about James' extreme mourning for a slave woman. She began to see him as a mystery.

One afternoon she questioned M. Chauvin about the rustic background of his pupil. "Could he be...?"

Monsieur quickly pressed the fingers of one hand to her lips and looked furtively toward the open door of his study. *"Tais-toi, ma fille!"* He shook his head sadly and leaned back in his chair. "This young man is just a farm boy, yet one with both intelligence and a dangerous yearning for the romance. Both are wasted on one who must survive on the frontier. I am intrigued by the possibilities of his mind, but he shows us now a weakness of spirit, languishing for his old black nurse. He needs the teat pulled from his mouth."

Chloe moved behind his chair and began to gently massage his neck and shoulders. "Now, if Monsieur will allow me, I would like to try and fill this empty moment in James' life." Chauvin pushed her hands away roughly. "Monsieur, it could not hurt to try and brighten his eyes. Perhaps distract him a bit, so he could return to his studies—" Cloe froze in place on seeing the scowl on the man's face, and the deep flush that suddenly covered his cheeks and nose.

"*Defendu!* There will be no, what you call brightening, girl, *et je sais trés bien* how you distract! *Non!* You shall keep to your tutoring, but perhaps a daily walk to the church would be in order. Be warned. I will be watching."

Soon after, Chloe sought James out, to offer extra help in French, suggesting that they prepare conversations on afternoon walks to the Celtic cross. They walked every day, whether or not cold January winds blew them along the graveled walk down Telfair Street.

Letters arrived from time to time suggesting "all is not as sad and dreary as our first letter suggested, dear James." When he wrote home asking what indeed did they mean by such a statement, he was answered with, "You see my son, I really do not believe Dilby could live safely here in this community. Papa has taken steps to see to her welfare, and that of little Nan. Do not fret. I just wish we could find poor Joshua and console him before he destroys himself."

James was even more confused by these mysterious hints. Mysterious indeed, thought Chloe as she quietly began to heal her friend, listening to his letters from home.

January passed and February saw the opening of crocus blooms. Yellow forsythia swayed as the two young people passed down the front walk on their scheduled promenade to the church and back. As March warmed the earth and air, white dogwood blossoms lit the dense woods on either side of the roads where James and Chloe walked. Huge pink azalea bushes covered the slopes of steep gardens that led up the front doors of the town's new and elegant homes. Sometimes they varied their route, crossing fields and following forested paths that led between the roads and boulevards. And sometimes, on warmer afternoons, they stopped to rest in a small clearing in the woods behind the school property.

It was on just such an afternoon when they paused to enjoy the coolness of the clearing and sat side by side beneath a redbud tree. It was here that James told Chloe about his year of suffering with paralysis and of Dilby's magical treatments.

Chloe asked, "And how did she hold you in that hot water, so that you did not kick and douse her?"

James looked puzzled. "Well, you see, I could not kick at all. If she had wanted to drown me, I truly was at her mercy." He laughed at the memory.

"Like this, do you think, James?" Chloe moved behind him and reached her arms beneath his, to clasp her hands together around his chest. She rested her cheek gently against his face. He could feel her breath against his cheek and turned his head toward her.

"Yes, just so..." His own hand rose to hold hers tightly against his breast. The sun broke through in a speckled pattern on them, standing together, dappling their slow descent to the mossy ground. A tiny ant struggled across Chloe's now bared shoulder, and was swept away by her frantic hand. The hand rested there, fingers smoothing the flesh that had already bronzed. Parasols that sheltered Southern girls seldom allowed the sun to reach their skin, but here was Chloe with a glow that stirred James to almost frightening agitation. He loved this darkish color that stirred up soothing memories.

"*Mon ami, reste calme...reste calme pour un moment!*" She cradled his head with her two hands and kissed his lips.

From the moment he and Josh had first entered the academy's hall, standing stupefied before the delicate, silk-draped body of M. Chauvin's perfect little creature, James had shamefacedly speculated each night on what textures, curves, and warmth lay beneath the many layers of lace trimmed petticoats. The rich colors of Chloe's cheeks, mirroring her sudden flairs of humor or reproach, evoked moist memories of his years in Dilby's care. James was seized now by the first passion of adolescence,—overwhelming and heightened by months of homesick yearning for the touch of loving arms. He sensed in Cloe, a warm, artless eroticism that flowed from her with natural and naïve good humor. "Chloe...Chloe," he sobbed. "Please, I can't..."

This experience was a kind of sexual baptism for both of them. Chloe considered herself precocious and wily, but never ventured beyond some teasing touches and ambivalent embraces that left her admirers gasping. James, totally stunned with what had taken place, hesitated between shame and exultation.

Later, as Chloe helped James put on his shirt, she touched the soft leather bag that lay on his chest. "*Mon Dieu,*" she murmured and quickly crossed herself. "*C'est un ju-ju!*"

James found the Catholic gesture as strange to him as any African charm. "Dilby made it," he told her. "She said it would fix me good."

Chloe shook her head and scolded, "Your papa will send you out to pick cotton if you go home talking, 'fix me good'. I declare Monsieur Chauvin would switch my legs with a hickory branch if I talked like that!"

And so the two of them walked back to Telfair Street and up the path to the academy, walking primly side by side, she with her hands folded together at her waist; he with his clasped behind his back.

Once begun, the clandestine meetings in the clearing became an obsession. Chloe's apprehension grew as her delight in James soared, creating an embarrassed tension in the presence of Chauvin that became more and more difficult to conceal.

With the onset of summer, James was needed back on the farm, but his father wrote that it would be better if he stayed in Augusta and continued his studies until local authorities settled responsibility for the deadly fire. He said there was agitation among some of the older, more established families to form a new county and with it a town, complete with a sheriff. The destruction of property, even if sanctioned by some of the openly sanctimonious, had frightened more levelheaded patriarchs in the community.

Summer passed, then autumn, with M. Chauvin becoming suspicious as the afternoon walks of Chloe and James became more and more prolonged. He began making plans to visit Paris for the purpose of seeking donations from French business connections. He wanted to expand the Academy, and perhaps establish a College of Medicine in Augusta.

As winter drew to a close he began to make his plans. In early March he called Chloe into his office to tell her of his venture.

"*Chloe, ma chere*, I want you to accompany me on my voyage to France, he said in a kindly voice. "It is time we bought you a fresh wardrobe, and the school will be closed for the spring and summer holidays. You need to get away from your kind, yet rather obsessive concerns with young James. He seems much improved as a result of your attentions."

Chloe, who had just returned from discussing the menu for the week with the cook, noticed her guardian's sly sideward glance at her as he rearranged papers on his desk. Chauvin turned away from her questioning look. "After all, his father wants him to come home now to help with farm work and comfort his mother, who is not feeling very well. I have arranged for him to depart in two weeks time."

Tears glistened in Chloe's eyes as she turned and flounced out of the room without a word.

❧

Ice storms came even before Christmas. It was the middle of March before Georgia's usually early spring warmed the ground and trees had begun to sprout their first leaf buds. In the heat of the summer, rumors of a new epidemic of yellow fever sent residents of Savannah scurrying to the countryside and delayed M. Chauvin's departure for that city. He and Chloe were to take a flat boat down the Savannah River to rendezvous with their oceangoing vessel. As it was, they had to wait until late fall.

The headmaster felt a growing need to separate James and Chloe. At the time of James' departure for the farm, M. Chauvin decided to remove a silent and scowling Chloe to a nearby plantation. She was to be on loan for a few weeks to the family of one of his students. James was carried away in a coach in spite of his beseeching questions about Chloe. Had she tired of him? Did she fear that he would embarrass her? Was she merely cowardly? It was a forlorn and angry boy who traveled through the pine forests to west Georgia.

Chapter 13 — Joshua

Three weeks after Joshua absconded with a horse and rode away from Augusta, he stood on the bank of a stream that drained the wetlands of Tybee Island. Since the Savannah River emptied nearby into the Atlantic Ocean, this portion of swampland was abandoned during hot summer months, when fever threatened white landlords, as well as their black slaves. Farther south, Ossabaw Island had a fine plantation house and a slave village, but this forlorn area was home only to giant turtles, alligators, and the sea birds who fed on tiny creatures that thrived in the mixing sweet and salty waters.

It was early evening and the mists were beginning to form that drifted each night over the land. Joshua turned away and threaded his path through thick brush covering the interior. As he subconsciously aimed toward the beach on the east, a song kept returning to plague his memories of home on the Allen farm. His mother must have sung it to him, but it echoed with a deep, masculine timbre in his head.

I had a dream last night
That's troublin' me.
Oh, I had a dream (here the voice rose to a wail)
Last night
That's troublin' me.

In the dim light of dusk, a stand of oak trees rose ahead of him, trailing veils of moss. He abruptly stopped to listen: were soft footsteps behind him falling on the damp earth?

Suddenly a dark shape slithered across the path.

"Oh, Gawd, who's comin' after me?" Joshua whispered into the darkness and backed away. His hand brushed against the rough bark of one of the oaks. When he turned to grasp its trunk, hiding his face, something cool and slightly wet caressed his cheek.

I jus' lay down in ma bed;
Somethin' jump into ma head–
I had a dream–
Last night–

Here the voice turned into husky laughter—or was it the chattering of one of the grotesque insects that came out at night in this subtropical forest? Joshua broke into a panicked run, as he crashed through trees and brush, finally breaking out onto pale, sandy dunes that shone by early moonlight. Further to the east, a strip of white beach flattened to gray as it settled beneath the incoming tidal waters. At the edge of the forest, grotesque forms stretched their black arms away from the wind, stripped of leaf and bark covering.

Joshua dropped to his knees and dug into the warm sand of the first dune with his hands. After he curled tightly into a cavity he had made, his breath came in short, panting pulses until he became warm. Slowly, he grew drowsy and drifted off into dreams that flickered from a scene of Dilby, screaming in a fire and reaching out to him, to Chloe's smiling face bending down to gently lick his ear. Chloe, the golden girl who whispered secrets of her own dusky mother.

The next day began with the faint, pearl gray of dawn. Josh was awakened by the sound of voices beyond the dunes and the scratchy brush of feet on a wet sand beach.

"Go on now, boy, and drag dat thing aroun' f'om da back. We don' want no big ol' fishes eaten our catch while it still in de water."

Josh peered over the crest of the dune and saw two black men pulling a net onto the sand from behind their beached rowboat. He ducked quickly, wishing he still had the horse. When he abandoned it behind a storage-house outside the city, his stolen mount had been ridden almost to death.

As the two men stood from their work and staggered upward on the first dune, where he was hidden, Josh tried to step back into the heavier growth of the windswept forest rim. Desperately, he looked from side to side, trying to find a new hiding spot behind the trunk of one of the overturned tree stumps that still had some dried out roots clutching the earth.

Just when he thought he was safe, darting behind one of the larger dead trees, a powerful black arm reached around his neck and dragged him out in the sunlight. "What we got here, Primus? Now don' ya move boy, 'cause I aint goin' to let you go back an tell yo' mamma 'bout Primus an' me hidin' out on dis here piece o' island."

He shook Joshua like a drowned dog before dropping him on the sand and sitting on his back. Primus, a man younger than his companion's thirty odd years, looked terrified. His lanky, adolescent body shone with sweat as his blue-black skin absorbed the full force of the sun's morning heat. "What we goin' do, Uncle? You goin' kill him so's we can get away south?"

"I aint sure what we goin' do wid 'im," replied the older man." He looked at Joshua. "What you doin' out here in de fever season, boy? Don't you know people 'roun here cut off yo' finger for runnin' away? You listen to old Solomon. You is in big trouble." Solomon scratched his straggly beard and gestured for Primus to stand close by as he arose from the sandy ground. Once up, he gave a hand to Josh and pulled him to his feet.

Josh leaned weakly against a tree to explain, "Mistah, you know the truth here. Yeah, I'm runnin', but I'm runnin' to find my ma, and I'll kill whoever done burned her up."

The two fishermen stared at the stranger in astonishment. He spoke clearly, almost like white men, yet with a more country kind of singing lilt to his words.

"Well now," said Primus as he squatted down on the sand and looked up at Joshua. "What do we got, Uncle? Why do'n' you rub his cheek a bit an' see if some paint come off."

In his defense, Josh stammered, "I...I been goin' to school with my...my young master."

"They ain't no schools for black boys," Solomon growled, thrusting his face close to Joshua's. "Who you think you foolin' boy?"

Joshua turned sharply and started walking rapidly over the crest of the dune and down the beach. The two men stared in surprise for a moment, then took off after him. When Solomon pulled him around by the shoulder, Josh swung his fist into the older man's belly. The punch could not cause any damage; Solomon's body was honed to muscular perfection. Yet he was surprised by the blow, and plopped down on the sand. As Primus tried to pull his companion to his feet, Solomon unexpectedly roared with laughter.

"Well, boy, we can't let you go, an' we sure as hell do'n' want to gut you and cook you here on the beach wid de fish! I guess you goin' to Florida wid us."

Primus was unhappy with the developing situation. "How come, Uncle? What he know about sailin' down de coast at night? How we goin'to feed him?" Primus was not happy with the developing situation.

Josh asked, "How come y'all goin' to Florida?"

"Well, boy, we heard 'bout a free black town down der called Fort Mose. The Spanish folk say dey want us, an' we runin' away to dem." Primus announced this with a lofty air. "Ain't you never heard about dat Spanish king promisin' freedom?"

Solomon looked away to clear his throat. "Well, we gon' see about it. Leastways, it's a chance we has to take now. Tonight we headin' this little bitsy boat south. You comin' wid us, boy, or goin' to roast in the sun 'til dat slave patrol gits over here tomorrow?"

Josh knew there really was no choice to be made. The three fugitives set to work cooking the fish over a wood fire, and smoking some under palmetto leaves so it would keep on their journey. After midnight, they pushed the loaded boat out into the water and began to paddle south.

Nothing ever was reported in Savannah newspaper about the capture of runaways. Fortunately, no one spotted the tiny boat when it quietly came ashore each morning along the coast. Three slaves just disappeared from Georgia. Whether or not they arrived at Fort Mose, or even if Fort Mose still existed, remained a mystery.

⁂

James arrived at the farm just as his father was clearing new land for the spring planting. Other workers were plowing and hoeing the older fields in preparation for the first crop of cotton. The slave cabins had been repaired, but the one that had housed Dilby was still a shell of black, charred beams and logs.

When James first walked into the house after the long, dusty journey, he called out from habit, "Mamma, I'm dyin' from thirst! How bout askin' Dilby to..." He stopped in the middle of the hallway and dropped his bag. *Oh God, there weren't anymore Dilby!* The house was deathly quiet, with no singing or banging around sounds from the kitchen.

Where was his mother? Where were all the children? James walked hesitantly down the hall toward the back rooms and kitchen that opened onto the back yard. There was no one about. Only a faint buzzing from a worn-out fly that struggled from shelf, to table, to stove, looking for a place to alight, die, and give way to another fly generation. Rather than bursting with activity, as it usually did in planting season, the entire place seemed to be drying up in the spring sun. Nobody cleaned, or baked, nor pressed wrinkled summer clothing that had been put away in cedar chests.

Alarmed, James wandered from room to room. His brothers and sisters were probably still in school with Mr. McDowell. But where was his mother? It seemed that everyone was busy in the fields.

James crossed the cart track in front of the house, skirted the barn, and started to run through a copse of trees that bordered the planting area. Field hands bent over their hoes, breaking up the red clods of dirt. Far in the distance he could see his father working with four men to pry up the roots of a pine tree that had been toppled nearby.

Edging around the field, James walked stealthily through bordering trees to get closer to the men, who grunted with their all-absorbing work. He didn't know why he was postponing his greeting with Drewry; distrust and anger still simmered inside, when he thought of the vague words of comfort offered him last November.

"Mistah Allen, dis stump goin' kill us all!" exclaimed one of the men.

James did not recognize any of them. Drewry sighed and pulled the long metal lever out of the hole beside the trunk. He lifted the brim of his straw hat, wiped sweat from his brow, and turned away. Looking up at the sky he asked, "Sam, anyone say where Miz Allen went this mornin'?"

"No, suh, but ma Julie sees her settin' off to de church lots o' times."

Drewry nodded. "I want you to go on back to the house, Sam, and look for Julie. She's been makin' herself scarce lately. You tell her I want her to stay close to Miz Allen right now, and even follow her if she tries to sneak off. Go on now."

James stepped out from the shadows of the trees, just as Drewry was about to turn back to his problems with the old stump. Throwing his straw hat to the ground, Drew ran with a high yelp to his son, wrapped both arms around his chest and shoulders, then lifted him in the air. "Gawd Jimmy, it's really you! Thank you, Lord! Your mamma is goin' to damn near jump and fly with joy. Sam! Sam!" he called out to the man heading toward the farm house. "Tell Miz Allen her son is home again, ya hear?" Sam looked back, and then took off running.

Elizabeth was not all that hard to find. She already had returned from her scouting trip to check on the activities of the Reverend Hope and his family. The new bay mare, a present from Drew, had carried her across the meadows toward the village church each morning. She saw that the area around the church was becoming filled with the small homes of local merchants and artisans. Four dirt streets were recently laid out. This activity made it more and more difficult to keep an eye on her nemesis without being discovered.

The pastor had become an obsession to Drewry's wife. The lonely days since Dilby had departed left hours to be filled. Elizabeth's brain never rested while she worked on the many chores of a farm wife. There was mending children's clothes, tending the kitchen garden, and supervising laundry and heavy cleaning for the house itself. Then, she always wanted to check the ten slave families each day for diseases and cleanliness, as well as seeing to the household accounts. All of this was carried on down-stage in her mind—facing the world of family life and attending to the needs of frontier survival—while the deep interior spaces contained a monologue of sorrow and revenge.

Elizabeth had spent that morning prowling in the shadow of trees that bordered the Pastor's property. By this time she knew his daily routines and could gauge what times he would be away from home, visiting parishioners or tending to his animal and human chattel. She had just conceived the idea of frightening the house servants by leaving little pictures of burning cabins and barns on the doorstep of Mr. Hope's housekeeper, a mulatto named Sarah.

James's mother had improvised a little voodoo doll from cornhusks, with a cotton boll for hair, which she pierced with a horseshoe nail. Elizabeth smiled as she examined the crude features drawn on a white face. The doll looked uncannily like old Mrs. Hope, with her fluffy white hair. Humming softly, she attached her note to the nail and slipped her little offering onto the sill of the kitchen window. Then she half-lifted her skirts, crouched low, and ran to her horse, standing quietly among the trees.

When the Pastor returned in the afternoon, Sarah was screaming from the kitchen. Mrs. Hope stood sternly over her waving a hickory switch. "I said be quiet now, or you goin' to feel my switch across your back side! Stop it and give me that fool piece of Nigra superstition!"

Sarah, hiding her face in her apron, sobbing, handed the stiff little doll to her mistress. The attached piece of paper floated to the ground. Pastor Hope, adjusting his glasses, looked over his wife's shoulder as she unfolded the note. He snatched at the paper, but not in time to prevent his wife from reading, "Beware, you all gonna burn like de baby!" It was signed "Black Witch" in wavy letters that scrawled down the paper on a diagonal.

With a moan, Mrs. Hope's slipped to the floor, her eyes rolling upward. After carrying her to the sofa in the parlor, the pastor turned furiously on a cowering Sarah.

"Who gave this thing to you, Woman! Look what you've done to Miz Hope."

"Oh Lord, I swear I jus found this *juju* on de windah. You knows I nevah could write nothin' on paypah. Please, Massa knows! I loves y'all."

Hope realized she couldn't possibly have written the note, but he was not sure someone else had not colluded with her. Fuming while fanning his hands above his wife's face, he growled over his shoulder, "Get out of here and fetch some camphor scent to bring Miz Hope around."

When Sam came running up to the farmhouse, Elizabeth had just come into the front hall, from returning the bay to his stall in the barn.

"Miz Allen, Miz Allen! Mistah Jimmy be home again!"

Elizabeth came out onto the porch. "Come on up here, Sam," she called.

Sam stopped to lean against the trunk of the pecan tree by the walkway an catch his breath. "Mistah Drew he tell me get you and say we gonna all have a party tonight 'cause Mistah Jimmy done come home from Augusta!"

Chapter 14 — Home

T hat evening the large dining room was filled with four Allen children, Elizabeth and Drew, and young William McDowell. A white lace cloth covered the table, with a much-treasured silver candelabra set in the middle. Some fresh daffodils graced the dark mahogany buffet that was against the wall, behind Drewry's chair at the far end of the long table. Elizabeth's face was flushed with excitement as she chattered about new buildings on the farm and the growing discontent among the congregation at Reverend Hope's church. Drewry smiled and nodded from time to time, but watched his wife with a cautious eye.

"Darlin'," she told him, "you wouldn't believe how twitchy that Miz Hope has become! She daren't speak to me when we pass in church, just blinks those muddy eyes of hers, scowls, and flutters her silly fan. I tell you, it just about made me laugh in her face last Sunday when..." Elizabeth abruptly stopped, lowered her eyes in bewilderment, and reached for James's hand next to hers at the table. "Oh, my, how I do chatter on. Tell me, James, how long you think you can stay before going back to the academy?"

James cleared his throat, wiped his mouth and turned towards his father. "Papa, I need to know 'bout Dilby. I need to see where she be laid to rest 'fore I can say anythin' bout goin back to school. Besides, Mister Chauvin must be well on his way to Paris by this time. Maybe there won't be no more school."

Drewry's response was harsh. "Hush, boy! Your Ma's upset enough already!" He looked anxiously at his wife: her hand had begun to tremble so badly that she lifted it from James and covered her mouth. "My dear, we'll talk later after dinner—"

But it was too late. Elizabeth rose suddenly from a chair that would have toppled to the floor had not William jumped up and caught it in time.

"Miz Allen! Are you ill?" He had unwittingly stepped behind her and grasped her shoulders with both hands, but quickly stepped away with a nervous glance in Drewry's direction.

In barely a whisper Elizabeth said, "If y'all don't mind, I think I'll lie down for a spell in my room. The evenin's are gettin' mighty warm for this early." With that, she walked from the room and down the hall. The children sat frozen in their places. All wiggling and talking had stopped.

James had lost his former angry tone, and almost whispered, "Pa, what's the matter with her? Mamma didn't do anythin' to Dilby, did she?"

Drewry ignored his son's question. "You children run along with Mister McDowell now. He promised to read you all a story before bed tonight. Hurry now!" As they all scampered from the table toward the parlor, Drewry said,

"Thank you, William. You're a true friend. I'm sorry to lay so much on a guest tonight, but you know I've got to get this straightened out with James."

"I know, I know Drew, and after I finish with the babies, I'll just look in on Miz Allen if you like." William disappeared into the dim light of the candle-lit parlor.

"James, come sit by me. This will take a while to tell." Drewry poured a fresh cup of tea for his son. James pulled out the chair next to his father's and sat down. "Son, after Reverend Hope's threats during his sermon last year, I feared that something bad was going to happen to our well-being. Women around here kept their distance from your mother, and Dilby came to me with her fears for her family. Why, even the men who always meet around old John Hestor's forge would sneak out whenever I came in with a horse to shoe. We were totally alone out here. I decided, and right on time too, to loan Dilby out to your aunt up in Carolina."

James gripped the edge of the table and leaned forward. His father spoke very softly, as though fearful of hidden ears behind the walls. He found it hard to believe that his father was not inventing this story to calm him down. "How did she get away without somebody findin' out? Who carried her up north?"

"Just the day before the fire, that ol' peddler your Mama likes was stayin' out to the barn overnight. I paid him his whole bundle's worth to take Dilby and little Nan back with him. I sent a letter to your aunt explainin' that Dilby was a healin' woman as well as a damn good worker. Then, the very next night some trash-folks crept up and tried to burn her alive." Drewry stood and bent down to his son's ear to whisper "Nobody's to know she's alive. Don't tell the other children or Mister McDowell. We want this over and done with." With a knowing wink, he added, "It's mighty gratifyin' to see all the guilt buildin' in these parts since we placed them two new stones in the graveyard."

Meanwhile, the older children had all been escorted to the large dormer upstairs where William had just settled the youngest two in the nursery. He knocked timidly on the door to Elizabeth and Drewry's room. He hoped that she would be asleep, yet also needed to comfort her in some way.

"Elizabeth," he called softly. "Are you all right?" After several moments the door opened part way. Elizabeth leaned against the frame and took his hand. "Thank you, William. I'll manage. It's just that I get so lonely without company around here. Dilby and I, we..."

"I know, my dear, her death was tragic, yet you must try to think of happier times ahead. Perhaps you would like to take James's place as student? We could set time aside to study Latin or Greek. I know you would enjoy reading some of the classics."

Elizabeth forced a sad little smile. "Yes, perhaps, William. You are too good to us."

The young teacher could hardly bear to see tears that still clung to the woman's cheek, and wanted desperately to take her in his arms. "Think on it, then. I...I would dearly love to hear your voice reading parts of the great tragedies. Yes, I dearly would."

Elizabeth nodded and closed the door as William turned to return to his host in the dining room. As he walked through the archway, William saw that James faced his father and shook with anger. Shocked, he stepped back into the hall. What was this?

"You loaned her?" James demanded "What if Aunt Candace don't want a loan? What if that ol' peddler decided he just might take some gold for sellin' her himself?" James thought of Josh roaming all over the country. "Ain't Josh goin' to ever see his Ma again, Papa?"

Drew sensed that someone else was in the room. He turned abruptly and caught a glimpse of William. "You weren't to hear this, schoolmaster. Don't breathe a word of it, or I swear, no matter how much a friend you've been, I'll see you in hell!"

William stepped forward and grasped his shoulder. "Drewry, you know better than to ask that. It won't be you or I goin' to hell over this business."

James' fury agitated his entire body. With enormous effort he forced himself to walk rigidly from the room, out the front door, and onto the porch. He stood at the wood railing and looked up at the crescent moon. The air was cool that early spring evening, with the moist smell of decayed moss roots in the freshly turned earth. *They think I'll smile and believe they really care about a slave. Dilby was just a bother to them. Get her out of here and be done with the baggage!*

Drew noticed the dark silhouette of his son through the window, sighed, and turned again to the schoolmaster. "There have been strange fires starting up around the county, Will. Nothin' big, just little outbreaks near mulch piles or in neighbors' drying sheds. Elizabeth seems to think they're a kind of minor retribution from heaven and sometimes laughs in the strangest way. There are days I hardly know her."

"She has a right, Drew, to wish some revenge. I hear the Reverend Hope is tryin' to get the sheriff from Milledgeville to come on down and check on voodoo magic." William laughed and shook his finger as he intoned with perfect mimicry, "The Lord burns the wicked and soothes the righteous. Look to the sinful fires in your hearts'! I swear he can't be burned and righteous at the same time."

Drew accompanied his friend outside, passing James in silence, and said goodnight in muted voice. William rode off towards his cottage on the Old

Field down the road. Drewry walked slowly towards the porch and stood looking up at his son. James gripped the railing and stared down at a spot of dirt in front of his father's feet.

"I'm goin' to stay through the plantin', Papa, but I don't know what to do after that."

Drew answered firmly, "Why, you're to go back to school with Mister Chauvin, James. That's understood."

"How can I? Monsieur must be on his way to France. I don't want to go to Augusta if the school has no master, and Chloe... Never mind." James felt he could not talk about Chloe to his father. Drew would realize that a lack of M. Chauvin's fine teaching in the fall was not the real reason for abandoning education at the academy."

Drew's voice softened. "And what about your plans for studyin' how to heal, boy? That won't come from sittin' around here all the time."

"I don't know. Maybe I could go north to find Dilby or somethin'."

"Dilby ain't comin' back here, James. There's no way around that, less the world turns upside down, or Mister Hope and his band of holy sinners leaves us be."

A rustling sound of skirts brushing the new grass announced the arrival of Elizabeth from around the side of the house. She moved towards them like a gray wisp in the darkness. Only a sliver of moon brightened the night. As she drew near, she asked, "What you all doin' out here?" The woman looked around in the darkness and shivered as the shadowy branches began to sway in a sudden breeze. Drew stepped closer to her, but she shied away to one side and said, "You'll go to France as well, James. Yes, Darlin', I heard your secret talkin'."

"My dear, I thought you would be sleeping. The night is damp and too cool for you to be wandering outside in your night gown." Drew took his wife's hands in his and gently rubbed them, then pulled her into his arms for warmth.

"Go to France, James!" Elizabeth repeated. There...there's just plain evil here!" She pulled away from her husband and took her son's face between her two hands. "We'll send you to Chauvin over there. I've heard tell that Doctors in Paris have set up hospitals to study and train young men like you." She released James, whirled in a circle with her hands raised to the sky and exclaimed, "I know! I'll write to him and ask that he get you a place to study in Paris. By the time you come home, sweet boy, I promise, this little world will indeed be upside down! You all will be so surprised! And that poor Mister Hope—"she made a mock sad face—"well, he'll find out about the devil." Drew grasped her in his arms once more, smothering her giggles against his chest.

"Don't you all worry about that..." Elizabeth gasped out, caught half way between a sob and a choke.

Drew shuddered. "Lord, Darlin', there just be no point at all in such talk. Hope is somethin' we can't hurry along or change. The tomorrows are in the hands of others or...or maybe the devil's for all I know. Let Him hurry the man out of here." He guided his trembling wife up the stairs of the porch and into the house; one hand held her firmly at the waist, almost lifting her off the ground.

Chapter 15 — Summer Tremors

The summer weeks passed by slowly for James. He worked all day with his father and Sam as the planting season gave way to weeding and cultivating soil around the seedlings. Most of the crop was cotton, but sorghum, corn, green beans, limas, peppers, sweet yams, and other vegetables necessary for life throughout the year were grown. The peach orchard could be counted on to provide enough fruit for domestic use through canning: Allen peaches were sought after each August by farmers throughout the county.

Days became unbearably hot, reviving James's memories of the creek and swinging out over the water there on the old rope. A constant hum of bees could be heard where they harvested nectar from the flowers that grew in front of the porch. And the smells! James would never forget the wonderful perfume of Georgia in the summer.

Sweet white jasmine and 'seven sister' roses snuggled up to the porch stairs. In the spring the whole front yard became a flower garden with spirea, flowering almond, yellow narcissus and jonquils. Now, in full bloom of summer, the crepe myrtle glowed between pink and red, depending on the light, and had grown almost as high as the pecan trees that stretched in a row now across the front of the yard outside the fence. Tiny moss roses bordered the walk from house to gate.

Elizabeth knelt beside her rose bushes at the far right of the house, singing an old song from James's childhood. It brought back the pain of memories from the kitchen days—days when the children danced with their laughing mother and a sly chuckling Dilby.

I met my preacher, the other day,

I gave him my right hand.

But as soon as my back-a be turned,

He scandalized my name!

Do you call that a preacher?

No, No.

Do you call that a preacher?

No man No

Do you call that a preacher,

No, No, he scandalized my name.

Elizabeth stopped singing and looked over her shoulder to see James staring at her from atop the front stairs. He had grown so tall over the past two years. He was slender, and still not fully muscled as a man, but his eyes looked out from under the brow with a solemn expression that brought to mind her father, who lay in a cemetery up north. She was so startled that she jumped to her feet and stepped backwards, stumbling over the basket behind her. "My, James, you just about scared me to death! You been sittin' there listenin' to me all this time?"

"No, Mama, I just remembered the time we all sang together in the kitchen when Mister Hope was talkin' so mean about Dilby. You remember how we just thought he was a darn fool, but nothin' to worry about?"

"Yes, Darlin', I remember. Oh yes I do."

"You and Papa goin' to be all right here if I go away with M. Chauvin? You think you can keep safe from whoever be settin' fires around people's mulch piles?" James looked straight into his mother's eyes with that question, and almost laughed as her eyes darted from right to left before she answered with a little smile, "Why, of course we'll be just fine."

James walked down the stairs to his mother. "How's Papa goin' to pay for me goin' on a boat, and all that schoolin'?"

"You remember when your Grand daddy died last year, and I couldn't get up to Carolina for the funeral?" James recalled that he had not been very disturbed about the death, since he had never laid eyes on his maternal grandfather. "We were tryin' to get back on our feet after that fire, and the Negroes were so frightened and worried that we had to stay here and calm things down right then. Well, my father left me some property that fetched a real good price near Durham. There's a little town there called Zebulon, a real pretty place I always wanted to raise my family in." She shook her head gently and smiled at the recollection. Putting an arm around her son's waist, she spoke like a school marm, "And so now, young man, I have money a-plenty to send you to Paris. See you use it well, and get yourself goin' to Savannah as fast as you can. Your father will go with you that far. I'll see to it."

Within a week Drewry had accepted his wife's decision—she had come alive after months of reclusive and secretive activity. Elizabeth would be absent during the middle of the day whenever he chanced to return to the house for lunch. She gave vague, wandering answers when he asked about her activities. With the urgency of packing, arranging transportation across the State to Savannah, Elizabeth whirled about the farm and rode daily into the little hamlet around the church. She needed to hire a rider to race ahead with a letter for M. Chauvin, hoping against hope to catch him before he boarded his ship for France.

Drew became more and more worried as he pondered her decision to send their first born away again. Where was her mind wandering? Why was she absent from him so often? For that was just how he saw it. He knew his wife would never physically leave their home or lock him out of their bedchamber, but he felt isolated, cut out of her mind. He was lonely. Drew began to dread his evening return to the house, especially the silence at the dinner table, after the children left for bed.

Drew and James left on a Monday morning at dawn, riding in a buggy driven by Samuel. James sat behind his father, who sat next to Sam to relieve him after several hours on the road. It was to be a somber trip, with James sitting in silence most of the way. Again rivers were crossed on flat boats, and kindly farm families took them in each night.

Hardly a word was spoken between father and son.

Chapter 16 — France

James and his father did indeed find M. Chauvin in Savannah. James was ecstatic to discover that Chloe was there as well. Their ship was scheduled to depart for France in two days, allowing time for Drewry to make arrangements for James's passage on the same voyage. Monsieur agreed to approach his business partners in Paris and intercede on the boy's behalf with directors at the restored Sorbonne. Since the school was accepting students at age thirteen, both men felt that James—a young man of fourteen years—was certainly ready for the Paris university's curriculum. Chauvin was disturbed to have James and Chloe in such close proximity of each other again, but reinforced new threats on Chloe while he waved a silver tipped walking stick close to her face.

James greatest obstacle would be the French language. Chloe would be the one to coach him and during the long sea voyage, as well as in Paris before classes began again after Christmas. He would have six weeks on board the ship, and another month after their arrival. Chauvin decided he would have to monitor them carefully.

"*Un moment, seulement un moment ma chère!*" Here the cane lightly tapped her nose to reinforce his warning. "If I see even a hint of indiscretion, you will be useless to me or any man."

Chloe stepped away from the man and bowed her head. "Monsieur, you misjudge me. I am truly grateful for your indulgence. I know who I am and must always be."

Six weeks of hell were spent floundering across the Atlantic during fall storms! Icy winds and turbulence reduced most passengers to ashen, moaning invalids who were confined to their cabins throughout most of the journey. The constant threat of piracy, or of impressing crewmen by British or French naval ships, added to the stress felt by both sailors and passengers. James, used to the relative calm of a south Georgia fall season, did not fare well. Chloe and her guardian walked the decks daily, seeming to thrive in the robust weather.

The ship docked at Nantes, sailing into the deep harbor formed by the Loire River's entrance into the Atlantic. The city lay at the confluence of the Erdre and Loire rivers, spreading from the island in the middle of the waterway to the nearby northern bank of the Loire.

As Chloe and James leaned over the railing to wave at small fishing boats that passed, M. Chauvin crossed himself and muttered, "*Mal aux malfaiteurs!*" Then he shrugged his annoyance and explained, "It was here the Revolutionary scum drowned everyone who disagreed *avec leurs Revolution.* They called their murders 'les noyades,' killing hundreds in the drownings. Can you imagine the strength of their focus? How long it takes to drown each one? Not fast and easy such as a bullet to the heart, or thrust of a sword."

An hour later, when James stepped onto the dock, the weather was fine once more. On the voyage he had lost a great deal of weight and his legs shook from the tossing of the waves at sea. He looked about him in amazement at the rows of sailing ship berths. Hundreds of sailors crowded the shore road, laughing and calling to the girls who lounged against the walls of houses bordering the wooden walkway. Horses hauled carts loaded with bales of cotton for the mills, while other wagoners waited their turn on the dock to load crates of furniture, china, silverware and fine cloth for the return journey to the west.

James and Chloe followed M. Chauvin to a dockside restaurant and settled themselves at a window table to order tea. Chloe talked excitedly about the shops along Napoleon Bonaparte's new *Rue de Rivoli*, her eyes darting back and forth at the people who ambled by. Then she stopped in mid sentence, attracted by a parade passing by their window. A score or so of men staggered past; all were linked together with a chain secured through their steel neck collars. Most of them were black-skinned, but an occasional individual of a lighter color was intermingled. She thought they might be an unfortunate Berber descendant perhaps. All shambled dejectedly toward a ship nearby that was bound for the Grenadines.

She turned away from the window to ask Chauvin, "Monsieur, I do not understand. What are slaves doing here in France? I thought the Emperor had brought freedom to all in this country." Chloe's eyes filled with tears as she touched the older man's shoulder.

"*Ah non, ma cheri.* The Emperor restored slavery in the colonies to save planters there from destitution. The wealth from those Windward Isles is necessary to the future of France." He laughed and added, "Do not worry, little one, they only take men and boys. Even a pretty girl like you would be rejected."

James was puzzled by the way M. Chauvin phrased his explanation. He was sure that only the most depraved and unruly slaves were sent to the islands. It was, after all, a punishment in America for a slave to be shipped to the Caribbean. Suddenly he could visualize Josh in chains. *Oh God, he could be on his way to some horrible life in Barbados! Of course Chloe would care.* He reached under the table to grasp her hand. For all her brash good humor, the girl was truly a tender little thing.

Chavin gulped down the dregs of his tea. "Well now, we must seek lodging for the night. Tomorrow we face a long journey and how I hate this town! *Allons `a Paris!* The city is three hundred and seventy kilometers from here, but the roads are good." Monsieur stood, helped Chloe from her chair with icy gallantry, then grabbed her elbow with one hand, snapped two fingers in the direction of the waiter with the other, and ordered that a coach be summoned.

After settling his young companions inside the coach, M. Chauvin told the driver to take them to an inn on the far eastern boundary of the city, just off an old Roman road to Angers. "*Demain nous partons tres tot.* I want to reach Angers by nightfall, and that is fifty kilometers away."

The next morning, after a breakfast of good peasant bread, some cheese, and cups of hot tea, they left before sunup. Just as they were about to depart, M. Chauvin added a dash of cognac to his tea cup.

Their journey passed along the north bank of the Loire following the curve of a rich valley. Through the wooded landscape, from time to time, they saw deserted palaces of aristocracy who had not yet been rehabilitated by the new emperor. The trees had lost their foliage, and only stands of pines hid the stone facades and courtyards of the chateaux. After Angers, their route turned in a more northerly direction, toward Le Mans. Finally, on the third day, across broad fields of wheat, they spied the towers of Chartres cathedral in the distance. Chloe leaned so far out of the carriage window that James grasped compulsively at her waist, wrapping his arms around her hips to hold her in. M. Chauvin coughed and warned him, "*Assi-toi!* Pull her in and undo your hands, *s'il te plait!*"

Chloe sought to soften his anger by pointing out the window "Oh, Monsieur, that looks like a great ship sailing across the field! What is it?"

"That, *ma fille,* is the great cathedral of Chartres. That grand, smooth, pointed tower was constructed in the Twelfth century. The taller one, there, with lacy stonework you can see through, was built much later in the Sixteenth."

That night they looked out from the third floor windows of their inn and could see the great tympanum above the cathedral's central entranceway . The bell tolled each hour all night long, but the two young people were too excited to sleep anyway. Monsieur slept in the same room with James, where he had the innkeeper place a cot for Chloe behind a screen near them.

James yearned to talk to her outside the hearing of her guardian, but the girl was kept almost like a pet, he thought, always near her 'master'. Well, tomorrow they would ask to go into the cathedral, while Monsieur made arrangements for the final leg of their journey. Perhaps then he could ask Chloe some of the questions that puzzled him about her relationship with her guardian. But the next morning was filled mostly with preparations for their departure.

As they waited for their coach to be drawn up, James noticed the statues carved in niches along the outside walls of the cathedral. "They have no heads, Monsieur!" he exclaimed, pointing at the mutilated figures just above his head.

"Ah, *c'est vrai*, the mad fools of the Revolution shot them off. Just to show how brave they are! You see, ignorant men during the great Terror of the Revolution knew only how to destroy. That is why the French cannot have a free republic! They need a strong hand to guide them." He sighed and distractedly flicked his fingers. He had been annoyed recently by this small convulsive gesture. The digits sometimes seemed to have a life of their own. "*C'est comme* the black African trying to govern himself, when he could never learn to care for his basic needs and required the guidance of a master."

"Josh could learn," James muttered. "He could read by the time he ran away."

Chauvin heard and lashed out at him. "Say no more about that boy! He has destroyed himself, that's how intelligent he was! Of course there are examples of occasional Negro individuals with some bright light, but, believe me, very few." Chloe had withdrawn to follow at a greater distance during Monsieur's short tirade. "*Viens-ici ma petite. N'inquiet-toi pas. Tu as de bon sang blanc, tu sais. Nous ne devons pas le discuter.*"

James might have caught the sense of the interchange if Monsieur had not spoken so rapidly, with his face turned away from him towards Chloe. As it was, the flow of words sped incomprehensibly past him. Telling Chloe that she had some "good white blood" would have seemed obvious anyway.

In another instant, Chloe ran between them, up the steps to the central portal of the cathedral. Turning around with a bright, almost coquettish smile she said, "*Viens*, James. Let's see what is behind these headless saints and kings!" Monsieur nodded grimly, pulled his watch fob from a vest pocket. "Very well," he agreed, "but go quickly. We must leave on the coach any minute."

The pair only had time to run down the long nave of the church when Monsieur, standing in the entrance behind them, pointed brusquely at the great rose window above. He called for them to look up at the brilliant colors that cast a blood red light on the floor below. He then walked briskly to take each by an arm, and drag them both out the south door to their carriage.

On the fourth day they rode through the little village of Versailles and gaped at the great cobblestone courtyard in front of the palace that was embraced by two vast, stone wings. Thin, ragged men lounged disconsolately on the great stairway to the central door. Scrawny dogs nuzzled bits of trash that had blown against the walls.

The coach turned east again on a newly repaired boulevard that expanded before them toward Paris. The morning was still cold. A chilling wind blew dead leaves tumbling in front of the carriage. As they were jolted along through a tree-lined avenue, James abruptly pondered the mystery of his mother's strange affliction. He had heard of women becoming hysterical at a certain age, as though possessed at times. But why would she insist that he leave all that was familiar and journey far from his family to this cold, if exotic, land? Where was the warmth, the joy of that home now that Dilby had disappeared?

In spite of the constant buffeting of the carriage, M. Chauvin dozed, his head dropping forward in sleep over the frilled collar of his shirt. James' left hand crept slowly into Chloe's muff to gently knead her cold fingers. Even more slowly, he leaned sideways until his cheek touched hers. She sat rigid with fear, her eyes riveted on the sleeping schoolmaster. Suddenly she felt a warm, moist tongue circle the outer rim of her ear. *This young man is becoming a bit more troublesome than I realized. If M. Chauvin should waken and see us like this—Oh, mon Dieu!* He might even beat her, although that had only happened once since he took her into his home almost as an equal. Where would this end? She grasped the flesh above the knuckle of James' thumb, and pinched as hard as she could.

"God A'mighty!" he shouted pulling his injured hand back.

Monsieur jerked awake and reached for a gun hidden in his vest. "*Quoi? Qui? Qu'est-ce qui se passe?*"

Chloe screamed at the sight of the gun. At the outcry, the coachman pulled back on his team to slow them to a halt.

James leaned out the window and looked forward and back along the road. Then he sat back and explained. "Monsieur, pardon me for frightening you, but I woke suddenly from a dream. I, uh...I thought I saw a monster of a head in the window, with great claws clutching at the door latch." Chloe tried to hide her smile with the muff and coughed delicately to mask a giggle.

As they rode toward the city, the three voyagers finally settled into the rhythm of the coach to gaze silently at the landscape. Buildings crowded more closely against the roadside as they drew into the outskirts of Paris. All at once the boulevard expanded on either side of a large open plaza. Carriages circled its center in an elegant promenade around an obelisk mounted on a sculpted platform.

"*Voila, mes petits.* Here Napoleon installed the great obelisk he brought from Egypt! He is truly the modern Caesar." At that moment the coach followed the other carriages around to the right, circling the *Place de la Concorde*, and then again turned right on to the refurbished *Rue de Rivoli*. The street was a wide thoroughfare bordered on one side by a long row of trees. Just beyond extended the geometric patterns of the *Tuilleries* Gardens.

When the outlines of a grand palatial building came into view at the entrance to the gardens, Monsieur exclaimed, "*Voila!* There rests Napoleon when he returns from the battlefields. It is the *Tuilleries* palace where poor King Louis was chased from his rooms by a mob of cut throats."

An arcade swept along the opposite side at street level, above which rose three floors. The first and third stories were furnished with balconies beneath tall windows.

The stormy sky turned a dark gray, obliterating all color and establishing a monochromatic film along the boulevard. Above the shops in the arcade, lights from apartment windows began to shine through a misty rain. Several low towers could be dimly seen ahead at the far end of the Gardens. They hovered like black bonnets over a large stone edifice that enclosed its arms around the southeastern end of the Gardens.

Monsieur Chauvin shook his head and clucked in disappointment, "*Quel dommage, mes cheres!* I hoped to show you both the great *Palais du Louvre* in bright sunlight, but it is there, sitting like a sodden wedding cake."

By this time they were all shivering in the cold damp air of the coach, and wished only to get to their rooms, and a warm fire. The coach finally turned towards the Seine, and clattered across a new bridge to the *Isle de la Cité* in the center of the river. They drove to the opposite side of the island. There, on their left, rose the Cathedral of Notre Dame, its doors set darkly within diminishing arches that resembled open mouths.

Chauvin wrapped his knuckles on the wooden enclosure above Chloe's head, and leaned out of the window next to her. "*Arretez ici!* Stop, *mon fou!*" he called to the coachman. "The fool has passed our *pension.* Quickly now, *mes enfants,* we must grab our luggage and walk to that corner. Madame le Clerc awaits us."

One hour later they had settled into their suite of rooms at the rear of Madame le Clerc's establishment. Now they sat around the one large table in her dining room while Madame poured tea.

"*Dites-moi, Madame, s'il vous plaît,*" asked Monsieur. "Is there not a *clinique* nearby? A place where a young man may go to study with the most learned *médecins* in Paris?"

Madame, a tall wiry woman dressed all in black, shook her head in disgust at the question, and almost cracked the saucer she slapped down in front of Chloe.

"*Grands Médecins?* Great butchers if you ask me! They consider themselves experts, even magicians of the human body now that they have hacked off arms and legs in the Russian campaign! My poor Alphonse never had a chance with these '*Grands Médecins.*"

"*Restez calme*, Madame." Monsieur gently patted her hand, which seemed poised to pitch the teapot across the room. "We only ask because this young man you see here, James Allen, wishes to study the anatomy and return to the Americas as a healer. Believe me, we have no intention of submitting to, or, *mon Dieu*, wielding surgeon's knives." Chauvin's right foot began to twitch as he spoke. "*Qu'est-ce que c'est?*" He grabbed his foot where it rested on his knee and held it firmly. *I must get more repose.*

Chapter 17 — Le Medecin Et L'amour

During the next two months James matriculated at the *Hotel Dieu* hospital, studied French, and enrolled at the newly reopened Sorbonne to continue studies in mathematics and the classics. The youthful student began reading many local treatises on surgery, anatomy, herbal medicines and the writings of Aristotle, Hippocrates, and Galen on the body's humors. He discovered that medicine indeed was a very mysterious study. At least the doctors in Paris were allowed to dissect bodies of impoverished victims of disease, war, and the many townspeople trampled down by local horsemen and coaches.

James was gaining a real understanding of how human beings were put together.

He wrote frequently to his family about life in Paris, but it took almost two months for a response to arrive from the frontiers of Georgia. Finally, he received a letter from his father just before the first buds appeared on trees in the park around Notre Dame.

March 12, 1813

Drewry Y. Allen

Monroe County, Georgia

My dear James,

> *Your mother and I were relieved to hear that you are now settled into rooms near the Hotel Dieu hospital. I understand that you have been taken in earlier than expected, because of the great need to have expanded medical care for wounded soldiers straggling in from the Russian battles. It is also rumored that the French emperor, that fake Republican, has become slightly mad. I hear that even his new wife's father, the real emperor of Austria, is turning against Napoleon. We thank the Lord that your voyage was uneventful. Americans are cooped up on our own shores for fear of English and French assaults on the seas. At least the French monster is kept busy with Spanish and Russian enemies. All of these naval blockades have the government in Washington whipped into a fury! Well, be careful, my son. Those city folks over there in Paris would just as soon tear a man to bits when they get riled.*

> *Mr. McDowell sends his best regards, and has begun to tutor your mother in Greek. We are all a little concerned that she seems so preoccupied these days. Her sister, your aunt in Carolina, writes that Dilby is in good health. We all wonder where Joshua has gone, or even if he still lives.*

> *After two slaves escaped from a plantation near Savannah last fall, it was rumored that a fisherman spied a small boat drifting towards the Florida border waters shortly afterward. Some blacks appeared to be crouching below*

the gunnels. One of the fishermen swears he saw the tops of three heads. I fear that I am one of those western farmers who hopes they managed to escape! Don't you dare mention this to Monsieur Chauvin! McDowell tells me he is not near so liberal of mind and would condemn any white man who expressed such radical opinions.

The fields are all plowed and seeded now and I am preparing to begin clearing new land in the pinewoods at the south edge. I don't expect new fields to be ready until next spring for planting. The dogwood is already glimmering brightly through the green of the forest. I do hope all the talk here about incorporating and expanding to form a town does not mean the forests will disappear. I'd rather have the Indians back.

I thank the Lord for all the rain we have had this spring. There have been so many small fires around here, and potentially serious ones. Everyone was in danger of losing their farms, were it not for the rains. I am thinking of bringing my brother Abraham and his wife down here to farm the piece of land next to William McDowell's. His Sarah could be company for your mother and help with some of the house managing chores.

Now you work hard, son, and try to come home by the end of two years. I love you, and wait to hear more about Paris, your new friend Chloe, (who is she really? I assume she must be kin to M. Chauvin), and your thoughts for the future.

Your devoted father,
Drewry Allen

James received this first letter from home in the spring of 1813, just as he and Chloe had discovered a way to hide their secret meetings from Monsieur. James was due to take examinations in Greek and mathematics the following September at the Sorbonne. M. Chauvin was preoccupied with finishing up his negotiations with local investors and planned to return to Augusta in late August to avoid rough seas. Therefore it was up to Chloe to prepare James for exams in the French language. She was technically under the rule of one *Madame Veuve Eugenie Chauvin*, a widowed cousin of Monsieur's, who lived six miles outside of Paris near Empress Josephine's *Chateau de Malmaison*. James rode out twice weekly, on Tuesdays and Thursdays, to meet with Chloe for tutoring.

On his first excursion to see Chloe in her new rooms, James rode along the *St. Germaine* road past the acres of woodland, fields, and vineyards that made up the estate of *Malmaison*. When he arrived at Eugenie's small farm, to the north of the Empress's property, he could see the Seine in the distance before it curved around the eastern boundary of *Malmaison*.

Swinging down from the saddle to a cobblestone courtyard, James walked tentatively to the large wooden doors of the house. After he tugged at the bell rope attached to the doors, he had to wait quite a while for the Madame to answer. In time, both doors swung open, framing the rotund body of the aging Madame Chauvin.

"*Bonjour, mon enfant. Entrez, entrez, donc.*" Clasping him to her in a giant embrace, she warned, "From this moment we will speak only French, you understand?"

She was insistent on that, drawing him into a large kitchen where long loaves of bread sat cooling on a wooden table. A low doorway opened on a narrow staircase to the left of a great fireplace. Madame twirled her large body on delicate, facile feet in the center of the room. "*Chloe,*" she called up, "*Le jeune homme est arrivé. Devoit-il s'assoir ici avec le pain?*" James would not have minded sitting near the bread, but Chloe came down the stairs at that moment, took his hand, and urged him towards the door.

"Come upstairs," she whispered, and to Madame, "*Il faut monter.* I have everything we need in my room."

Madame began to sputter and shake her head, "*Ce n'est pas possible, ma petite. Ma foi, non, pas de tout...*"

But Chloe seemed to have the upper hand here, and quickly she and James disappeared up the dark stairway. Once the door was closed and latched securely, they fell into each other's arms like the long lost wayfarers they were. Gone was all pretense of modesty or restraint as they fell together on the narrow bed.

"*Attention,* James! We must be very quiet, very careful. Madame will be listening below us. She must believe that you are reading aloud to me from these texts." She reached an arm to a small table beside the bed and brought over one of the books. Chloe pulled herself up to lean back against the wall at her head, opened the volume at random, and laid it beside her. Slowly she slipped back down and eased James to nestle above her. "See, you can read to me right here, with kisses for punctuation."

The punctuation became quite irregular, the text broken into gasped phrases, until no sound could be heard from the cramped attic room. Yet the lovers need not have worried: Eugenie had long since retired to her office in the stables to check accounts with her head groom and farm manager. Her cousin's use of his elegant slave girl was none of her concern. Let the boy enjoy himself!

James wrapped a dark curl around his finger, savoring the moment and yet feeling apprehensive. "Chloe, how long will you be allowed to stay here with me?"

"Oh, I think you have at least a *demi-heure, mon cher.*"

"No, don't tease me Chloe! You know what I am asking. When will M. Chauvin demand that you return with him to the school in Augusta?"

"Monsieur is not happy that I linger here, but he trusts Eugenie." Then, with a sly grin, added, "She is really quite a fool." Chloe turned to sit on the edge of the cot, pulled her chemise down over her head, and stood up to look out of the room's small dormer window. *Regarde!* We can see the black swans on the Empress's pond from here. Poor abandoned lady. Even a queen can be lost when deserted by the man she loves."

A soft breeze ruffled the delicate new leaves of the *tilleul* trees that bordered the road, wafting the subtle lemon scent of linden blossoms. James' horse snorted and strained to reach the ditch and browse the lower tree branches. James pulled sharply on the reins, but also felt his mind shift focus, as the perfume invaded and filled him with longing—a combination of returning desire and a longing for the fragrant summer evenings on the farm. This afternoon with Chloe had awakened nostalgia for the tender arms of Dilby during the many months of her loving therapy.

The sun almost rested on the horizon, sending shafts of gold, pink, and mauve light into a scattering of clouds around it. Then, in an instant, the peace of the scene was shattered. A large, bristled boar dashed across the road ahead. The beast bellowed and snorted with fear and rage, as a band of hunters on horseback broke from the brush in pursuit. James's mount skittered sideways, neighing in fright. James fell halfway off on one side, but clung to the horse's mane while the horsemen dashed past.

The last hunter shouted at him, "*Attention! Cretin, laissez le chemin pour les vrais hommes!*" Leave this path for real men, idiot.

As the sun sank lower behind trees, the breeze shifted and swept a twirling spiral of dust around the solitary figure of the youth slumped above his horse. Wisps of sand blew into his eyes. James was no coward, and no cowering believer in signs and portents, but he could not shake the feeling that he was being pursued somehow. He would indeed keep to the path of manhood, no matter that he had not yet reached his fifteenth birthday. And something bothered Chloe, something that she feared whenever he talked of her remaining with him in France.

Returning to his lodgings, James was jarred back into the present when his horse's hooves hit the cobblestone surface of the urban road with a sharp clatter. He needed to watch for the right bridge across to the city island, and his rooms at the *pension*. When a drunken older woman staggered out of a café and screamed at him with laughter, he shuddered and remembered one of Dilby's prayers. "Ekka Ghassi, come with me," he whispered and grasped Dilby's tiny leather sack that swung from his neck.

When Monsieur Chauvin finally boarded his ship for the United States, Chloe was not with him. The headmaster had listened to James' pleading for her to stay and help him catch up with his studies at the Sorbonne, but also had taken precautions. Chauvin hired Claude Bonnard, a private agent, to keep track of the young people during the following year. At the Augusta academy, he would have to take on some teaching of French in her absence. M. Bonnard, a veteran from one of Napoleon's earliest battles, would watch comings and goings, keeping track of expenses and reporting regularly to Telfair Street.

Elizabeth's inheritance was rapidly disappearing, but Chauvin had bargained with Drew to finance the final year of James' medical apprenticeship in Paris. The price was an internship at Chauvin's planned clinic in Augusta, when James returned to Georgia.

"*Alors, mon ami*," he confided to Bonnard, "keep these young fools apart, if possible. If the girl betrays me with young James, she'll suffer the roughest slave markets *dans la Nouvelle Orleans*." With that information, Monsieur Bonnard felt less than harried in pursuing his assignment. *Let it be on the head of the arrogant little quadroon*, he thought, for he detested the sight of a slave girl wearing silks and satins and parading her erudition like some aristocratic bitch of a higher breeding.

Chapter 18 — Carolina Fear

Spring weather came a little later in the Carolinas than in Georgia, and the Yarborough family land lay in the shadows of a wooded hill that also slowed its effect. Over the hill rested 500 acres of land belonging to Charles Hilton and his wife, Candace, Elizabeth Allen's older sister. Charles Hilton was an enterprising man who had done well speculating on farmland and buying cheaply from the Indians and selling dear to young men eager to acquire plantations—and the social status they implied. He had also been a partner in a shipping business that specialized in the slave trade. However, ever since the law of 1807 that fotbade the importation of slaves from Europe or Africa, his business was on the decline.

The Hilton plantation had become Dilby's new home. She was brought on as a laundress at first, then, after six months, upgraded to cook and allowed to live in the cabin closest to the main house. Little Nan followed her mother around the kitchen meekly, totally withdrawn in the new environment, and clinging to her mother's skirts whenever an adult—black or white—came near.

One day, during the spring of 1813, as Dilby moved carefully about the large dining room, gathering the silver from a mahogany sideboard to polish in the scullery, she heard Candace Yarborough crying.

Entreaties, broken by sobs, came from the library across the hall. "She's my sister, Charles! And they be sayin' she's so unsettled in her mind, bereft of reason, that Drew fears for the safety of his younger children! That cannot be. Lizzie dotes on her children, and was always the smartest one of all of us!" Here she broke down completely with wails, and Dilby could hear Charles murmuring sounds of comfort.

"Now, now, my dear. You cannot help from so far away. And as for the supposed brilliance of your sister, they say a witty woman is far more apt to drift from hysteria to dementia. Shhh...my sweet. Perhaps Elizbeth is just recovering from some devilish possession. Now that we are cursed with her favorite black witch, she will soon be her old self."

Dilby froze in place, her head turned toward the direction of these frightening words. If they believed such nonsense, why did they allow her to prepare their food?

"No, Charles! How can you say such a thing! Poor Lizzie is just mourning for her son, now shipped away across the sea to France. I couldn't stand it! And she is so isolated 'way out there in those pine forests." Candace sat up on the embroidered love seat and wiped her eyes. "Are you afraid of Dilby? Do you think her truly a witch?"

"No Candace darlin', I don't worry about the woman. Dilby won't hurt us. Oh, no, she is far too wily for that. She must know I'd send her on her way to Barbados with her brat so fast she'd never have time to breathe another curse."

Dilby gathered the silverware and dishes into her apron, and walked in silence toward the pantry, shushing Nan as she moved from the room. This could no longer be endured. She had to make plans.

Every evening, as regular as sunset, the dinner meal would be over, and the kitchen fires stoked for the night by ten o'clock. Nan would be asleep by nine, curled as usual on a soft blanket outside the back door. "Oh Lord," Dilby whispered, but she was scared! To run was never a possibility for her. She'd preached the dangers over and over to poor Josh ever since he could understand the words. But now, with no friend within hundreds of miles, she was at the mercy of this cold-hearted white man. If she could make it through the forests back to Georgia, she would throw herself on Drewry's doorstep, saying she'd heard Elizabeth needed healing. But how to make the journey without being chased down by dogs and hired slave catchers?

She planned to hide bags of food under the floorboards of her cabin. Each night she could sneak portions of salt pork, some dried beans and potatoes from the cellar. At the last minute some bread to tie in a sack on her back. Each day she must keep her eyes open, and look for an opportunity to travel in the wake of some peddler. She knew she would find a way. The Caribbean islands! No, hardly any child lived beyond a year in those evil places of death! *No m'am! No sir!* There had to be a way.

One month passed without any mention being made of anyone planning a trip south to see to Mrs. Allen's health. Dilby had hoped Candace might persuade her husband to let her hurry to her sister Elizabeth's aid, and that she might be allowed to accompany her mistress.

A frightening event happened in July, when a young field hand wandered away from his labors and disappeared for a whole week. The youth was well-known to be dimwitted; Dilby thought he probably went picking raspberries in the woods and either lost his way or just decided to keep on looking farther off.

Late one night Dilby heard dogs barking and men shouting in the driveway of the main house. "Ma!" Nan cried out on waking. "What dey doin' so late? Somebody hurt? Is they lookin' for to catch a robber outside?" The little girl ran to the door and was about to scamper outside.

Dilby caught her by the arm and pulled her back. "You just hush, baby, an' don' be talkin' so loud. We just goin' to wait an' see what all the fuss about."

Just then they heard a man's scream. Horses whinnied and men cursed loudly. A woman's voice wailed, "Charles! Who are these men? It's past midnight. Get on in here and send the ruffians away! Charles, what *are* you all doin' out there?"

At that point, Dilby recognized Candace's voice as she broke down crying. Her sobs were quickly muffled and a door slammed shut. Nan began to sob from fear, when the sound of screams followed rhythmically with the snapping of leather on flesh.

Dilby was stunned. She had heard of such brutality, but it was a rare occurrence out on the farms of western Georgia. In haste she bundled her little girl back into bed and nestled close to her with her hands pressed gently against the child's ears until the next morning. "Sleep, Baby. Hush. Mama's gonna take care of you. It's all right,"

Dilby hummed a lullaby very softly, all the while thinking that her trip south and west would have to be carefully planned. The slave woman understood the risks much better now.

In the morning she saw that blood was splashed against the trunk of a great oak tree in front of the main house. Dogs repeatedly had to be chased from around its base. The young slave who had unintentionally escaped was still alive and being cared for in his mother's cabin, while his wounds from the beating healed.

Candace disappeared into her room, and would not come down for three days.

Charles stamped around the house yelling for her to "Get yourself down here, woman! I'm not standin' for any more hysterics hereabouts!"

He was ignored by his wife. The house staff slid past him like dark spirits, although when passing by they nodded with deferential bows. Finally Charles mounted his favorite bay horse and rode off to complain to his neighbors at a plantation five miles east of his. *Let Candace sulk,* he thought, *and be damned! The nigger had to be disciplined or all of the hands might just take it into their heads to walk off the property.*

Chapter 19 — Joshua

Joshua was alone now, wandering just inland of the coast south of San Augustine. The runaway boy searched for friendly Spanish homesteaders, who might direct him to Fort Mose. His two companions had disappeared during the night, while camping in marshlands east of the great bay at San Augustine. Josh had noticed them whispering together, when he returned to the cook-fire after relieving his bowels in a thicket of mangrove-like vegetation. He realized they wanted to be free of him to explore villages along the St. John's River.

When Josh awoke the next morning, alone to the smoking remains of a camp fire and the gray, misty silence in the wet forest, he was terrified by his vulnerability. He crouched down in fear, hugging his knees and peering through the leafy branches toward the slowly moving water that flowed around and beneath the land where he was.

Wind sighed gently as watery creatures slid and sloughed their way through the bog. A bird's harsh cry startled him from his trance, and he thought he heard the sound of soft footfalls nearby.

"Who's there? Come on out, now. I jus' wanna see who's out yonder... that you Solomon?" No one responded. "Oh, Mama! I sorry I talked to Plateye! Get him away, Lord, get him gone. Please Mama!"

With again no answer, Josh realized he had to get away from the dampness and fearful swamp creatures. So here he was, tramping through a dry forest toward a freshwater lake. Watching through bordering underbrush, Joshua saw a village with houses built on stilts on the banks of a lake. What appeared to be the settlement's gardens swept up to the forest's edge. Joshua crouched in the shadows and waited.

The midday sun was high, beating down with a fury that outdid even Georgia summers—and this was only March! He had been living in the wild now for over six months. His feet were bare, toughened to leather. He clothed himself in castoff rags that gave little protection from the blood-sucking insects that thrived in this tropical climate. He felt thirsty to the point of delirium, trying to moisten his mouth with saliva sucked from inside his cheeks. Sweat pored down his face and neck, dribbling between his shoulder blades. His flanks were slippery with it. When an ant began to crawl up his thigh, Josh smacked it with the palm of a hand. The sound reverberated loudly in the woods; at the sound, Josh lurched backward to hide more securely behind a tree. But there was no reaction from the settlement. Where were they all? What kind of people lived here?

Cauiouly, he reconnoitered the village's forested circumference. Taking a deep breath, he crawled through the nearest garden toward a house. He exhaled as he paused between mounds of mature corn plants. A sound of drying tassels, rustling against the long, pointed cornstalk leaves, passed above him like a whisper. Pin pricks of apprehension spread down his back. He stopped, half-paralyzed by fear. The oppressive heat felt like a malevolent weight, a giant invisible hand pressing his body into the sandy soil.

After seemingly endless moments, Josh pulled himself up on knees and elbows and scrambled quickly to the side of the nearest house. There were no real walls enclosing the dwelling, just lowered blinds that descended from the roof and around the four sides. Someone was humming inside, a sweet sound that was broken only by a delicate smacking, as if lips relished some delicious treat.

Josh carefully shinnied up one of the corner stilts of the house, reaching hand over hand to pull himself up to the level of the floor. As he held onto his perch, the sun dipped slightly in the west, so he was protected from the full force of its heat. Still, the humid air sucked at his endurance. A different prickly sensation spread over the surface of his body, along with a ripple of nausea in his gut. He had sagged where he hung, ready to slip to the ground, when a small, strong hand reached under the blind. It grasped his wrist firmly—before semidarkness closed over his consciousness.

Strange sounds rushed at him. An unintelligible verbal cloud whirled around his head.

After his eyes opened, the first thing Josh saw was a monstrous mask hovering above his face. Dark stripes of brown flowed from cheekbones down over the jaw of the apparition, to drip lower on the wearer's neck. An owl feather protruded from black hair. This vision was replaced by the sight of a female face looking down at him, compassion written on the furrowed brow and taught lips. Josh automatically reached up a hand to touch her cheek. Immediately the two faces pulled away. Gasps reverberated around the room. Large hands grasped him under his shoulders and hauled him to his feet. He saw that the room was filled with light-brown skinned men and women, who appeared as fearful of him as he was of them. The masked figure was not really masked at all, but a shaman who wore dark paint that gave his face the eerie look of a corpse just risen from the dirt of its grave. The shaman approached, shaking a rattle made from a box turtle shell. He warily circled the black stranger. Josh weaved from side to side and began to slump toward the floor. But the hands grasped him again and people dared to come closer. Hands touched his dark skin as though to see if its black color would rub off.

"I am Josh," he murmured hoarsely. After a child screamed at the strange words, his mother quickly picked him up and held him protectively against her breast. "Help me...please...help me," Josh stammered.

A young woman stepped forward, took his hands in hers, closed her eyes, and began to chant. Amazed, Josh recognized the repetitive melody as the sound he heard while hanging from the raised floor of the house. He tried to smile at her, just before passing out again. The last thing he heard was a babble of talk from the villagers, as everyone streamed toward him.

⋙⋘

Much later, Josh learned that his last smile had been a response to the magical words sung by Walini, a granddaughter of one of the many *Yamasee* refugees from the north. These Seminole Indians had become used to harboring fugitives from the English-instigated wars of the Creeks and Cherokees in the 18th century; black and brown desperadoes fled south to Spanish lands. The Spanish had decreed two provinces in Florida, one of which was Indian, where Seminoles were free to take in whomever they pleased. And yet Josh understood their fear—he might be a frightful creature from the spirit world that had invaded their village.

The *moki*, headman of the council, ordered that he be kept isolated from the rest of the people for a probationary time. He was allowed to stay in Walini's house, to be fed and washed by her, and be carefully monitored by the *miko's* men, until he was deemed strong enough to work in the women's gardens. He was not allowed onto the ceremonial ground of the central square, but several women helped him build his own chikee hut on the outskirts of the settlement.

Both Walini and Josh were refugees, although she was two generations removed from her flight into Florida. The Seminoles had come to regard her family with respect since her grandmother had brought them news of the great happenings in the world of white men, Creeks, and Cherokees to the north. The old woman became their historical reference point and teacher. Walini, however, was told by her father of the strange loneliness he and his mother had felt for many years after their entrance into Seminole life. When she looked at Josh, she saw a strong young boy, who looked to be about her own age, lost and near starvation in an alien, frightening world.

One day Walini addressed the *miko*. "Honored uncle, let me question this boy. I can find many answers as I take care of his body. He will come to trust me."

The head of the council agreed: Walini became both spy and mentor. She took on the duty of teaching Joshua basic words in the Seminole language.

"Joswa," she would begin, trying to mimic the sound of his name. Then, with sign language, facial expressions, and object or food charades, she began his education.

One afternoon, after many weeks passed, Walini came in his *chikee*, to initiate a halting conversation. She and Josh sat on a mat in the middle of the room, facing each other. Walini began with an observation. "You so, so pretty and black for being man like ours."

Josh smiled in replying, "I think I am very beautiful, like night sky. Yes?"

This was the first time anyone, including his mother, had ever flattered him on the color of his skin. Josh looked directly into her eyes and pointed upward, to tell her in his new tongue, "You, Walini, shine." He spread his fingers at either side of his face, "Like evening sun goes down behind trees."

Walini threw her head back and laughed with delight. "You are very quick to learn, dark man." Again she took both his hands in hers.

During the lesson, Walini named the various objects and furnishing in the cramped area of his *chikee*. After she left, Joshua gathered fire from his neighbor's cooking pit, wrapped some fish in the broad leaves to cook for his dinner, and thought about Walini, treasuring the image of her slender body bending forward as she reached out to touch his cheek and hold his hands.

Months passed. The rainy season brought misery to the people of the village where Joshua became more and more a member of the community. He even gained enough skill in their language that he could teach Walini and the *moki* some words in English. He thought about sharing his newfound knowledge of written words with them, although he could think of no practical use for it.

Often, as he lay on his mat at night, he wept for his mother, Dilby, and her fiery death. He wondered if baby Nan had escaped, or if James cared at all about what had happened to them. One day he would go back, maybe with a few warriors from the village, and take care of his former white master. He would find a way. Drew had been demonized in Josh's mind. In his dreams he saw James's father sneaking into the slave area during the night, to torch his mother's cabin. For him, questions of motive were irrelevant when considering the actions of unaccountable white people. The idea that Drew might be capable of rescuing Dilby and the baby was locked out of his mind. Even memories of the warmth of his childhood friendship with James had cooled. He had learned to evaluate the world in the most straightforward, simplified terms: *No time now to think 'bout Mamma lovin' James!*

Cool nights began to merge drastically into dark, hot, soggy torments. What would be spring in Georgia, arrived in the Indian province of Guale with all the heat of July. Josh sickened with fever; pain traveled up the back of his neck and circled his head from temple to the bridge of his nose. A week passed during which he failed to appear for work in the gardens. Walini had left the village with her father, called Dark Bear in the Creek language, to visit and trade at a fort in Florida's panhandle, about 15 miles upriver from the Gulf of Mexico. They traveled by foot, leading two donkeys over-packed with bright feather work, beaded leather, and woven baskets. Walini had been intrigued by local rumors that the fort was manned by Creek Indians and a large group of strange, dark-skinned men and women from the north.

With Walini gone and the villagers busy planting new corn, no one thought to check on the newcomer who had become one of them. When she returned with her father, they walked directly to the *moki's* dwelling, next to the round council house. Excited by what they had seen in the west, they demanded to speak with him immediately.

Walini exclaimed, "We come with news of a great fort with many strong black warriors!"

Her father, Dark Bear, raised his hand to silence her, then spoke in a more temperate voice. "They say they will fight to keep the evil American leader, Jackson, and his soldiers away from our land. We must find Josu and tell him of these men! Perhaps he can speak with them and obtain guns for us to keep here to protect the people."

The old *moki*, his eyelids half closed in meditation, set aside his pipe and stared at them in astonishment. "I have not seen the Josu since seven nights. Perhaps he is hunting in the forest or building onto his *chikee*. Let us go see."

When the Walini, her father and the *moki* pushed aside a woven reed mat at Joshua's doorway, they gasped at the wretched figure stretched out on the flooring. He was covered with his own filth and insects attracted to it.

Black Bear ordered his daughter, "Walini! Bring water from the lake! We must clean Josu and bring him to the *Hadjo* for a healing ceremony."

Grunting with disgust, Dark Bear frantically brushed insects from Josh's chest and belly with his bare hands. Two other men climbed over the portal, with loops of rope vine hanging from their necks, and began to fashion a sling to lower Josh to the ground.

Walini's breath came in short pants as she hauled heavy-laden pots from the shore. One was strapped to her back, and she carefully balanced the other on her head, as she struggled up a path to the village. She wanted to run, but feared that the pot on her head would fall and break. She moved swiftly to bring water to the hut. Finally, just as she came over the brow of a grassy hill, she saw a large, heavy bundle swaying from the opening of Josh's *chikee*. Her father stood below with upraised arms, ready to receive the load. The sling was lowered slowly, when just three feet from the ground, the men dropped the bundle heavily. Walini set her pot down from her head and ran, water splashing from the pot still on her back. She threw herself over Joshua's still form. Both she and her friend were soaked in a torrent of water. All four men converged on the couple and began to untangle the two bodies. Walini weeped for him.

"Oh God," Josh gasped. Startled, he lifted his head to see strange faces peering down once again. Then he felt himself lifted from the ground by strong arms, laid on a pallet of branches, and carried away. He could hear a woman's voice keening at his side, and turned to see who it was. Walini's head was beside his own as she walked next to the litter. Her head was bowed as she chanted what Josh thought must be a prayer.

Minutes later they entered the central square, surrounded by seven long, three-sided pavilions. People arose from their benches and walked toward the small procession making its way to the seventh pavilion, where the village healer sat with his friends.

"Take him to the Council House," the old man ordered as he swung himself shakily to his feet. "Wife, bring the black drink, and my medicine bundle."

She fluttered her hands, flicking corn dust from her lap. "But husband, the bundle—"

"No questions woman, just go. The bundle has new herbs I found this morning for fevers. Hurry!"

Josh was carried inside a circular building and laid on a blanket near the central fire. The medicine man, called Amoneeta by Dark Bear, took a hide bundle from his wife, and began putting pieces of vine, elm leaves, cedar chips, sassafras root and cockleburs into the pot suspended over a fire. Water was added for the mixture to steep. Taking a large thorn in his hand, Amoneeta bent over Josh and pointed to his head.

"I must indicate pain to him. He does not yet understand well." With that warning, he began to moan, tap his forehead and roll his eyes. A sleepy Josh stared at him. Then, quick as a garter snake, Amoneeta jabbed his thorn in delicate thrusts to deliver three punctures across Josh's brow, and two more on the upper cheekbones. Josh felt the pricks, but the pain was so minimal compared to his headache, that he only grunted a weak reaction.

Amoneeta gestured for Walini to lift the patient's upper body and allow it to lean forward and let blood flow out. This was easy, for Josh felt light to her now. The medicine man took his bubbling stick and blew into the steeping mixture on the fire, to mix the brew. "This is almost ready for the dark boy. He seems conscious and able to swallow," he said, pouring from the pot into a small gourd and holding it out to Walini. "Take this and slowly feed the ill one. Your father can hold the boy upright for you."

A week passed where Josh was housed and nursed in the Council House. The fever had passed in twenty-four hours. Josh was strong enough to eat baked corn meal bread and drink a hot corn broth called *sofke*. As he was judged still too weak, Josu did not yet have to drink the black drink. That came two weeks later at a ceremony in the central plaza.

Chapter 20 — The Black Drink

The first day of summer in Georgia, though very warm, was nothing like the full-blown heat of a spring season in Florida. Guale was less tormented by the sun than areas further south, but it was steaming hot by noon. The people of Walini's village retired to their *chikees*, to rest during the sultry afternoons. Only Amoneeta and his wife moved about quietly within the area of the plaza to cleanse and purify the site for the ceremonial fire. Large pots already were filled with secret ingredients gathered that morning. Skunk cabbage had been harvested from the swamp. Fesula root from the forest had been ground to a yellow-brown paste for the black drink. All stood ready for preliminary sifting, then boiling, and a final straining process, when the liquid would be poured through woven baskets to remove all solid materials.

Shadows stretched across the earthen plaza as more and more women came to work at the side of the fire. They crushed ingredients in wooden platters and added them to pots that simmered in flaming niches. As soon as the sun dropped below the tree line that circled their lake, the villagers slowly came from their homes to assemble in the pavilions around the plaza. A still weakened Joshua was brought to Walini's pavilion and seated on the backbench. He still was recovering, but the disease had burned itself out. Now he anxiously waited for his purification and initiation into the community.

Walini leaned back to whisper in his ear, "Tonight you will become one of us, Joswa, and we may then tell you news about our fort that grows in the west." Before he could question her, she quickly turned back and walked away from him, toward the fire. Amoneeta greeted her at the center of the plaza, then walked slowly around the fire, shaking his turtle shell rattle and singing what Josh recognized as the old man's favorite blessing song. Men left their pavilions to join him. Drinking shells gathered on forays to the western beaches were filled from the bubbling pots and carried by women to the seated company. Black Bear escorted Joshua to a place beside the fire. Wahine brought her shell to him and tilted it towards his mouth. He had no choice but to drink. Bitter tasting, and smelling so rank and fetid that Josh gagged with the first sip, the black drink calmly and greedily was consumed by the others.

Singing grew softer as the people began to rock backwards and forwards. The sound of drums had joined the voices, sending out throbbing accents that seemed to echo the beats of Josh's heart. A breeze picked up and bent the flames of the fire toward the eastern Atlantic shore, and moans arose from the shadows as darkness gradually encircled the group. Amoneeta raised his arms to each side and called out a summons to the wind. Two men rose to their feet, spun around, and spewed the black drink from their mouths. They were followed by others as the drink took violent hold of each man and woman.

Walini came to Josh, seated on the ground, and urged him to have more of the drink. "Take this, friend, and become pure in the body of my people here. All evil is chased away tonight."

Josh grasped the shell, smelled it, and recalled the horrible little bags of asafetida his mother hung around his neck when he was ill. Indeed, the crushed root in the mixture came from the same source. He tightly shut his eyes and gulped the nauseating fluid. Jumping to his feet, his whole body convulsed in spasm as the black drink spouted in an arc toward the fire, which then sizzled in the night and sparkled brightly with colors. Josh gasped; a leering skeletal countenance seemed to flicker in the flames. The apparition lasted only a moment, yet Josh saw the open mouth frame the words, "Kill! Strike!" A faint rumble of distant thunder seemed to shake particles of air around his head like a guttural laugh.

Joshua staggered back to stand in his place. Other villagers began a round of vomiting from their places by the fire. In a final ritual, just as the people settled into a somnolent state, sitting slumped with their heads hanging forward, Amoneeta came to stand in front of Josh.

The medicine man raised a knife high over his head while murmuring a prayer.

"With one strike I sever the past!"

Josh, startled, fearing for his life, desperately looked for Walini. Just as the knife plunged, he fell forward on the ground.

Days, weeks, and months passed in the exotic, sultry land of Guale. Josh floated into his new existence, his new identity. He traveled west with Walini, to view the fort, but was disheartened by what he saw there. No real disciplined army of volunteer black men came to greet them. The place had disintegrated. Where were Black heroes to lead an Indian defense against the American forces led by General Andrew Jackson, who constantly threatened to return fugitive slaves to their former owners in the north? Despair, desperation, and starvation dominated inside the walls of the impoverished fort. Josh returned to the village and seemed to thrive on his new culture. Yet, deep in his heart, a fire was banked, its smoldering embers hiding behind his efforts to become newborn. He both feared and treasured a smoky image of Plateye that hovered in his dreams.

સ્વજી

Hundreds of miles to the north, the farm communities of Monroe County, Georgia, experienced a fearful outbreak of mysterious fires that demolished home after home, barn after barn. Terrified families flocked into churches to pray for deliverance from the unrelenting plague. In North Carolina, Dilby hovered over her child, carefully crafting an escape and plotting a circuitous journey to the south.

Chapter 21 — Paris

Across the Atlantic, the two young lovers came to realize that theirs was a forbidden and, therefore, excruciatingly exciting affair, rife with dangers for both of them. Over the next three years, M. Chauvin returned twice to Paris. In 1816, after Napoleon went into exile for the last time, he took Chloe back to Georgia for a few months.

James was approaching the final stages of his apprenticeship with doctors who struggled to patch mutilated soldiers together. He had come to realize how wise he had been in coming to Paris to study medicine. The unhealthy climate of the city brought thousands of patients to the hospitals, where doctors studied the symptoms of diseases in direct clinical contact. He had learned how to observe and analyze these symptoms. He was also able to recognize and describe pathological changes discovered at the autopsy table. Just this year, M. Rene Laennec had invented the stethoscope. By 1816, James knew more about his craft than any country hack in Monroe County—or in the whole of Georgia. While simple carpenters doubled as surgeons in the New World, French doctors were beginning to understand infection and its relation to cleanliness. A few thoughtful physicians questioned the use of cupping in the presence of fever.

Chloe was allowed to return to Paris, escorted by M. Bonnard. She brought letters from home to James and contracts to be signed by M. Chauvin's financial backers. A new college was planned for Augusta with a medical program that would feature the latest French treatments and medical discoveries. James had grown from a boy to a young eighteen-year-old man, mature far beyond most thirty-year-old Georgia farmers.

As Chloe stepped from her carriage in front of his *pension*, James took her in his arms. A weary Bonnard whipped the horses and drove on to his lodgings on the west bank of the Seine. Chloe shivered and drew back when James held her face in two hands and bent to kiss her forehead. She seemed to have dwindled: her shoulders and arms no longer rounded gently, but seemed delicate, elongated shadows of their former robust form. "*Mon cher*," She asked, "please take me to your rooms. I need to rest—" Glancing first from side to side, she slipped her arms around his waist and buried her head against his chest, sobbing, "I have news for you, but it will kill me to tell it!"

"What is it? Has something happened on the farm?" He almost shook her in his fear. "Tell me now, Chloe!"

"No, no nothing is wrong with your family, I swear. *C'est moi.* Just take me home."

Later that afternoon James cradled her in his arms as they lay together on the narrow bed in his apartment across from the cathedral. Only a dull murmur rose from the tailor shop below, when a few customers came and went. Chloe had been sleeping for the last hour and stirred only when James brought her a cup of tea.

"You look so pale, and your arms are so thin! Have you been ill, love?" He carefully felt around her face and neck for fever or swelling, but found nothing of alarm.

She responded weakly. "I have been very sick on the ship, yet that is expected. Before that I was vomiting everything I ate in Augusta. And now..." She stopped to hide her face in both hands.

"Gawd, Chloe..." His southern tongue was returning as he held her. "What is it? You think I'll be angry after missing you for all these months? I can hardly think or work without you here!"

"James, I...I must run away." She jumped up and began to pace back and forth before the window, glancing out each time as though to catch a spy hidden below.

He missed her tone of anxiety. "Good, let's run together! You can deliver all those papers here in Paris, and then we'll make plans to sail for Savannah. My mother..."

"*Non, je ne peut pas aller avec toi!* I can't go anywhere with you." She cringed, before his eyes as her whole body contracted. Chloe raised an arm to cover her head as though fearing a blow. Then whispered, "I...I'm going to have a baby."

James collapsed back onto the bed. Chloe had always seemed confident in her secret ways of dealing with intercourse. She always insisted that she was safe from pregnancy. He loved this girl, wanted to be with her constantly, but could only repeat, "A baby? *Mon Dieu!*

Chloe sat down next to him on the bed, then fell to her knees. "James, you see, this will be yours and my baby, but it will belong to Monsieur. He will own it, just like he owns me."

Bewildered, James grasped her shoulders and shook his head. "What are you talkin' about, Chloe? He can't own you, or me, or any baby. You're no..."

"Oh yes I am, Darlin'. Yes I am. I'm specially born and bred for Monsieur's family and I'm property. He said he'd set my mamma free if he could take me with him to Augusta, She thought he'd do right by me some day. But it hasn't come to that day yet, and I doubt I'll see it. Chloe looked up and took his hand, "So I know he acts like I'm some kind of distant relative—"

she laughed bitterly, "and I guess I am in a way. In truth, I'm really just his fancy, educated, nigger girl."

James stared at her, seeing the crisp curls that were gathered up in a ribbon that circled her head like those of a Greek goddess. Chloe's hazel green eyes sparkled with tears that on the brink of trickling down her cheeks. Her beautiful ivory skin, with its tones of gold and beige, had lost some of its luster, but he knew that the righteous Reverend Hope might read forbidden colors there.

Chloe asked in a pleading voice. "Can you help me find a place to hide here in France, or get me a secret passage to New Orleans? I promised to take care of Chauvin's business, but then I mean to disappear. Unless...unless you send me back to him." Chloe still could not quite trust this white love of hers.

James insisted forcefully, "We'll marry, right here, and then go back to the farm! Pa will..." He hesitated to finish the sentence. Just what would Drewry do in the face of slave hunters sent down from Augusta? But, God help him, he loved Chloe. He had built the fantasy of a life with her for over three years. "We'll think on it, Chloe. When...how long...do you think we have until...?" His softened voice paused as Chloe began to weep again. James lifted her off her knees and back onto the bed. He gently began to undress her to her chemise, and then pulled the cover up over her shoulders. As she closed her eyes, his fingers probed her belly with a carefully practiced lightness. There was a difference. He could feel the changes beginning there. They had about five more months to think on it. "Chloe, dearest,' he whispered, "I don't want you to go to New Orleans without me."

Chapter 22 — Georgia

It was March of 1817. Sarah and Abraham Allen settled in the west Georgia community of farm families far more quickly than Elizabeth had when she first came south from Carolina. Abraham was a quieter, wiry, and slim version of his brother, with sandy colored hair. His calm blue eyes shifted slowly when taking in his surroundings, as though carefully evaluating just the right moment to move into action.

He was content to let his wife organize the social aspects of their new life. The small yet robust Sarah, with dark hair pulled tightly in a bun at the nape of her neck, was a born church leader who fairly dove into the women's activities as set out by the Reverend Hope and his wife. She could not understand Elizabeth's surly attitude toward this good man.

It did not take long for Sarah to figure out that there was a kind of social crisis in the community. The disastrous fires had tapered off, but everyone was suspicious of their neighbors, especially it seemed of Sarah's sister-in-law. It was true that Elizabeth drew suspicion to herself as she became more and more detached from both her family and the church. Rumors circulated that she was insane, and Sarah was inclined to believe them. Not interested in any subtle probing into problems and grumbling from the children, she moved into command of the family situation immediately.

Martha, now a sulky and rebellious sixteen-year-old, was the most difficult, and insisted on checking all Sarah's orders with Elizabeth, who barely responded to anyone. When she did speak, her words rambled from present to past. "Martha, my dear, I'm sure you will help your aunt Sarah, won't you? She works very hard, you know. I just don't see why she is here all the time. Doesn't she have a house to run of her own? I feel so tired, though... Do you think I could be in a family way? I must ask James this afternoon when he comes home from the school. Where is James? I do need to ask him." Martha would turn on her heel and stalk away angrily to do Sarah's bidding.

Stokes and Emmy kept out of Sarah's way. Drew still carried them to school in the old farm wagon each day; Abraham rounded them up each afternoon to do chores. They regarded their mother with bewilderment. Sarah would never understand, but they came to believe that somehow they had caused their mother's misery. Drewry himself had withdrawn into the business of running the farm and welcomed Sarah's authoritative role in organizing household chores and child management. He lived the life of a celibate these days, but each night as he lay beside Elizabeth, prayed for her return to health. "Dear Lord, you sent us into this land and made it flourish. You gave this woman to me, and I have loved and nourished her. Why have you turned away from us? Why have you turned her away? I need her, Lord. Sometimes I don't see how to keep on goin'." When he turned his head to watch her sleeping beside him he thought, *This is a stranger, a ghost wife. I hardly know her.*

Elizabeth had aged noticeably. She spent hours sitting rigidly by the parlor window as though looking for visitors to drive up in their carriages at any moment. When letters arrived from France she sprang into energetic action for awhile, talking rapidly to anyone who was in the house at the time, and devoting hours to playing chess with a four-year-old. She also taught ten-year-old Emily to play some hymns on the harmonium.

Sarah would mutter as she bustled about the house. "At least poor Lizzie's got somethin' left of the Lord in that frazzled head of hers."

But as the days passed, Elizabeth grew lethargic again and returned to her vigil on the window seat.

With spring came the opportunity to clear more land on the southern border of the property. Drewry planned to cut down and uproot the giant oak that stood in the way of plowing new fields there. With a diameter of twelve feet, the tree would require a team of at least of four of his huskiest slaves, plus Abraham and himself. They would work in shifts to pry and lever the base, and disengage the undoubtedly deep root system.

Early one morning, the men rode out at dawn to the area, hauling tools in a wagon. By seven o'clock they had located the tree, unloaded the wagon, and paused in the cool, misty air to warm themselves with coffee and chunks of bread. By the time the oak fell to the red earth, the day had heated rapidly and all the men had stripped to their waists. It was approaching the noon hour when they finished digging a deep trench around the stump. Drewry told his men to rest in the shade of bordering woods and take lunch from baskets under the wagon. Tilting their hats over their foreheads, the black workers snoozed beneath the trees, while Drewry and Abraham walked about the land to position new fields and discuss angles to the sun for future plantings.

Three dark figures moved in the rich undergrowth at the edge of the copse of trees, silently creeping behind the sleeping men. Their shadows fell across Damon, the farthest from the group. A bronzed hand suddenly shot forward to cover Damon's mouth while two men grabbed his feet and dragged him deeper into the woods. A blow to the head from a wooden club sent Damon into temporary darkness.

Drewry returned with Abraham, satisfied with what they had discussed to increase the yield on the new land. He roused his men from their nap. At the trench he gave out directions. "All right, now...y'all get over here and lean on this bar. We want to get home by sundown and this is one great ol' elephant that don't want dyin'." Drewry climbed to the top of the stump that rose a good six feet from the ground. "John," he ordered, "you get down in the trench there. Sam can help Toby leanin' on the bar. Abe, I'll just get down near John and dig for this side root." Drewry shaded his eyes, looked toward the woods, and called over his shoulder, "Damon, get your lazy self over here! Abe, you can help these men set the bar when I'm ready to change the angle."

Quietly, with his head bowed beneath a broad-brimmed straw hat, the last black man came out from the trees to stand behind Drewry, in the trench.

Two sets of black eyes watched from the forest rim.

No one spoke as they grunted from the exertion of the work. Only an occasional order from Abraham to shift the position of the bar broke the silence.

Drew had reached the tip of a root that was as thick as a man's leg and seven feet long. "Damon! Are you with me now, Boy?" He looked back over his shoulder. "I want you to hold on to this thing and pull it back as far as you can, while I saw it off. Can you do that for me?"

The man called Damon nodded and mumbled, "Yessah."

Flies swarmed about the sweating flesh; even birds were quiet, too indolent to sing in the oppressive weight of the humid air.

Nobody could remember exactly what happened next; they all were intent on holding the base of the tree up at one end and leaning on the great iron bar. Unexpectedly, a loud slap brought all the heads up from their downward focus, to see that the root had been released. It struck Drewry in the neck and severed what was a major artery. Blood pulsed from the wound; Drew lay unconscious in the trench, his arms thrown to the side as though falling backward through the air.

"My God...Drew!" Abraham lunged toward his brother to clap a hand over the gaping wound. "You men help me!"

Startled at first, the workers glanced at each other, then ran to the wagon for a blanket and spare rags from the tool box.

John shouted, "Mistah Abe! Where be Damon?"

"Damned if I can worry about him right now," he said without looking up. "Help me tie up Drew's wound!"

The help of Drew's brother's was futile: James's father died before the bloody rag could be tightened as a tourniquet to staunch the gush of scarlet blood.

After wrapping Drew's body in a blanket and placing it in the wagon, two of the men spread out in the woods and searched for the missing Damon. They found him with his arms and legs tied behind him. His mouth was stuffed with rags. He looked at them with wide frightened eyes as they released him and pulled the gag from his mouth. For weeks Damon could talk of nothing else but the monsters with green, black and red stripes who had attacked him as he slept!

As Abe raced the wagon across the rutted farmland, Drew bled out his life on the boards of the bed. John held Drew's head in a cushioning embrace all the way to the house. His hands dripped with his blood. The two men carried Drew's body onto the porch, just as the door was flung open: Elizabeth saw her husband then raised her arms above her head in horror, eyes wide in disbelief. She was finally awake to the world, only to scream away from it, as she collapsed on top of her husband's body.

The black men backed away as she fell between them. Abraham tried to pull her up from Drew's chest. She could not be drawn away. Sobbing now, her arms circled his chest, hands gripping his hair at the back of his neck. She rocked from her knees above him and began to murmur strange sounds. It became a kind of chant that frightened the superstitious workers. Abraham stepped away and turned to see men, women and children running towards the house from fields, and barn.

Oh Lordy!" moaned Sarah from the doorway, her hands held at either side of her cheeks. "Abe, get Elizabeth up off the poor man! She's gonna lose her mind for sure now." Bustling about, flailing her arms, Sarah shooed away the gathering of farm hands and children.

Elizabeth fell sideways to lie unconscious next to her husband.

Moving south, three tall shadows slipped silently through the piney woods. They paused by a creek to wash away stripes of facial paint, then hurried on. It would take them a couple of weeks to reach the languid breezes that curled onto the coast of northern Florida, then they could cut sharply westward to their inland lake. The men traveled only at night, giving wide berth to the small farm settlements along the way.

Josh staggered between the two Creek warriors throughout the first night of travel, incoherent as he mumbled strange sounds that alarmed his companions. He stumbled from time to time, whenever he seemed about to lose consciousness.

"He gone now. Oh, Lord, Mamma. I's so tired." Seeming ready to fall, he was grasped by the Indians and dragged to a gulley next to the path. They bent protectively over him as he retched convulsively. The air was still: not even the tiny scratching noises of invisible night creatures could be heard. It was still cool in early spring, after the sun went down. Abruptly, the temperature dropped. The men crouched low as a damp wind swept over them. Josh rocked back on his heels and clutched his temples moaning, "So much blood! Lord, how come so much blood from that white man? Please, no more...it be all done now, Lord!" All three clung together, shivering in the chilling wave of air that washed over them.

The next morning found them sleeping where they had crawled into the brush, hidden by rocks from any who might happen to pass along the forest path.

Josh grew stronger as he progressed southeastward toward the sea, shedding layers of hate and guilt as he went, until he arrived at the coast to see the crescent moon shining on the water. The waves rolled onto the beach in lazy curling mounds, stretching wet fingers toward the men. Slowly, reverently they walked into the flow and washed themselves by moonlight.

Drewry was buried on the farm, his granite stone marking the first of the family's graves in the little cemetery. Dilby's mock grave had settled into the earth at the other side of the enclosure. Two portions of the plot of land were separated by an invisible line that marked black and white deaths for the future.

There had been quite a large group of people who walked through the muddy pasture and up the gentle rise of hill to bury Drewry Allen. The Reverend Mr. Hope followed the immediate family, led by Abraham and Sarah Allen. Stokes held his mother's arm to guide her over the ruts and clods of dirt in the unused path to the cemetery. Martha walked on her other side with an arm around Elizabeth's waist. Emily grasped her sister's other hand, looking up in fear at Martha's frowning face. Jonathan Aiken and Jacob Jones helped William McDowell and one of his students, Cecil McCurdy, carry the coffin. Liliane Jones walked with Sarah Jane Aiken and a large group of ladies from the Guild, at the rear of the procession.

The grave had been dug the night before by Sam and Toby, since Damon was still recuperating, his head bandaged and eyes swollen shut. Elizabeth, her gray shirtwaist buttoned crookedly under a black shawl, began to visibly tremble as the coffin was lowered onto ropes that stretched across the gaping cavity in the ground. Wisps of gold-gray hair clung to her face in the moist heat of the afternoon.

As the preacher began to pray in the deep "stained-glass voice" he especially reserved for funerals, soft responses of "Amen" rose from the chorus of ladies. Sarah Allen raised her hands as the words droned on, as though bestowing a blessing from on high. She was dressed in proper black silk, with a cameo broach at her neck depicting a soulful, praying female bust with clasped hands beneath the chin. A black bonnet shaded her grim face from the hot sun beating down on the group. Martha reached her arms around Elizabeth's shoulders, turning deliberately away from her aunt's performance.

"We are here to celebrate the new life of our brother Drewry who has gone to meet his true Father in heaven!" Mr. Hope's voice rose with the last word as his hands reached above his head, one finger pointing high to poke at the sky.

"Hallelujah!" came the echo from Lilianne.

Elizabeth abruptly pushed Martha away and strode toward the preacher, silencing him in mid sentence. "Mister Hope! Ask God who killed my husband! Ask him who burned my servant Dilby and her baby!" This last she said with a sly look around at those gathered there, and winked horribly at Hope.

Abraham quickly stood up to pull her into a protective embrace. "Stay calm, Elizabeth…"

She sobbed, "Please tell him to send my son home to me."

After Drew's coffin was hurriedly lowered into the ground, the agitated crowd dispersed. Martha dropped a handful of red dirt on top of the lid, and then followed her siblings out of the enclosure, toward the farm house below. Sarah Allen was left to apologize to her pastor with sharp exclamations of horror at her sister-in-law's behavior.

Hope patted her hand. "Now, now, Miz Allen, you mustn't fret." He turned toward the group and raised his voice dramatically. "We must all pray that Sister Lizzie comes to see that Jesus is the great comforter. He will heal her and lead her back to the good people of His church."

Jonathan leaned toward Abraham to murmur, "We're goin' to keep on lookin' 'til we find somebody might 'a seen strangers roamin' round here. God knows they got to be stickin' 'way out in this country."

The Allen children seemed to adhere more closely to each other now in their loss of both father and mother. Elizabeth slipped farther away from them each day. Martha began to look around for options, a way to save her siblings from being taken over by righteous neighbors, and a way to save herself. She saw Sarah and Abraham as greedy opportunists eager to take over both family and farm.

Sarah assigned the younger children their chores for the summer. Martha was asked to follow her mother during the daytime hours, making sure she stayed on the property. Mr. McDowell visited twice a week ,during the summer. He brought books for Elizabeth to read and tried to engage her in conversation over tea.

"Have you been able to make sense of any of the Latin poems I brought last week, my dear?" William leaned forward in his chair to make eye contact with Elizabeth. Martha sat beside her mother, but turned slightly away from their conversation. Elizabeth held the book of Ovid's poetry open in her lap.

"Why do you task me so hard, William? I have barely made out the poem's title to be 'Myself.'" She leaned back in the rocking chair and raised a hand to smooth her hair. William noticed how gray the red-gold strands had become, as though singed in a fire. He nodded and opened his book to translate aloud,

"Take me, and I your slave will be

As long as life endure:

Constant," here he sighed, *"in my fidelity*

And in your service sure."

Elizabeth smiled wanly at him. "Ah yes, you are my constant friend, dear William. These days I feel as though I just float among my children. I see them, yet seem to pass through them, unaware of who they really are."

Martha turned toward her mother, frowning with impatience. "Mister McDowell, I have found another poem to my liking. It is also by a Latin poet." She stood and moved to the window seat next to his chair, sitting slightly behind him and leaning to hold her book where he could read with her. "See here it says,

Curious to learn

how many kisses

of your lips

might satisfy

my– What is this word, sir? Oh, yes, could it be lust? *My lust for you...*"

Shocked, McDowell chided, "Why, you have Catallus there! I never assigned anything by him. He's a scurrilous Roman! Stop my dear, he is unfit!"

"Why then do you have his books? Are you so incorruptible?" At this Elizabeth reached forward and slapped her daughter's hand, resting on William's shoulder. William blushed and took the book that had fallen from Martha's hand, tucking it into the pocket of his jacket.

Martha stood up from the window seat with a smile. "Well, here is a bit of Ovid then for both of you. 'You bid me write to amuse the tedious hours, and save from withering my poetic powers. Hard is the task, my friend, for verse

139

should flow from free mind, not fettered down by woe.' That last is especially for you, Mother." Martha straightened her skirts and left the room with a rigid spine. Her coiled braids bounced with indignation.

How like she is to her mother, thought William McDowell, *yet so much harsher... with such sharp angles to her mind!*

After that lesson, Mother and daughter avoided each other, although it would be hard to see any contrast in Elizabeth's demeanor between annoyance and indifference. In her present state, she had no way of knowing that Martha might have a plan of her own for the future. Her daughter looked forward to the fall. She knew William McDowell would be overwhelmed at the school this year. Settlers from the northern states of Virginia and the Carolinas were swarming into the area with their children, to farm the rich, red dirt of western Georgia.

Sarah had a plan as well. She had promised the ladies of the church women's brigade that she would control her sister-in-law and make sure that she no longer roamed the woods and town by herself. She assigned Martha as guardian, but did not trust her reliability in that regard. Martha was not Sarah's idea of a model older sister for her siblings.

Sitting at dinner one Sunday afternoon, Sarah signaled little Emmy to pass her uncle some warm buttermilk biscuits. As each child helped himself from a basket that was passed, Sarah asked, "Abraham, when can you get the men started on a new cabin?" Abraham looked up at his wife, then slid his glance quickly around the table.

"Sarah, we'll talk of this at a later time."

Martha noticed that Sarah had waited to speak until Elizabeth had complained of a headache and left the room. "Children, you need to rest and read your Bible lessons after this big meal. Go on now, and push your chairs in to the table as you leave,' she called after them. Martha sat, looking calmly at Abraham as though waiting for him to continue a conversation.

"Go along, girl. Your uncle and I have some business to discuss without you children eavesdropping on everthin' we say!"

"Auntie Sarah, I'll be pleased to be discreet for y'all, but I want you to be sure in your mind about somethin'. I am not a child in this house anymore, and I'll not be treated as such!" With that Martha rose with an almost serene dignity and left the room. *Tomorrow I meet with William McDowell, and we'll just see how much of a child they can push around I'll be!*

Abraham threw his napkin on the table and stood so abruptly that his chair toppled behind him. "I'll get to it tomorrow, Sarah, and you may lock poor Lizzie away by the end of the summer! Gawd knows why we have to cotton up to those bitches in the church guild. Drew would have me horse-whipped if he were here!"

Sarah reached up to grasp his arm. "Darlin', you know that's why Elizabeth's been allowed free rein all over this county to do her mischief. She could make Drew do anythin' she wanted to, even half crazy like she is. It's our duty to the community..."

"Quiet, Woman...just shut—"

Sarah's eyes blazed with fury. She jumped to her feet and slammed her fork down on the plate with such force that the china cracked. "Just you take care of buildin' that cabin, Abraham, and I'll see to it that we don't all get run off of our own land."

He retorted, "It's not ours yet, my dear, and don't you forget that little fact!" Both left the room to attend to evening chores at opposite ends of the house.

Chapter 23 — Dilby's Treck

Dilby set her tired little girl down next to her, then leaned against the tall pine bordering the Ocmulgee River. It was getting dark, yet she did not dare build a fire here by the shore. There was a small settlement just south of the river's bend, and she could see the soft glow of candlelight from some of the farmhouses. Slowly. she slid back down the side of the tree to sit beside Nan. The child was heavy now, almost eight years old, but had reached her limit of endurance a mile back. Dilby had carried her since then. She wrapped her arms around her child and hummed softly, as they rocked together in the approaching darkness. Finally Nan's eyes closed and she drifted into sleep. Dilby gazed at her daughter lying curled against her hip. *She is goin' to be tall, and please, Lord, strong.* Nan had inherited a long Arabic nose from her father. Her eyelashes curled over the high cheekbones that she took from her mother.

And what about her son, Joshua? Was he still following James around Augusta? When she left over four years ago, Mr. Allen had told her that was his plan. She longed to see Josh, to know he was alive and well. What must he have thought when Elizabeth wrote James about the fire? Dilby closed her eyes and began the ancient chant to Eka Ghassi, holding in her hand the magical purse that rested always between her breasts. She whispered, "Find my boy, Mother, and help him find some peace and love."

Soon they would be in Monroe County and then Dilby knew she would have to be especially careful to move only after dark, until reaching the Allen farm. Her only hope lay in finding Elizabeth and begging her for protection against the absurd charges of witchcraft. She knew that, in any event, Drew would not tolerate any interference from his righteous neighbors.

Right at the midpoint of August, when the trees spoke the rhythmic hum and buzz of summer nights, Martha heard a soft tapping at the back door. She left her bed wrapped in a thin cotton robe and tiptoed barefoot to the back of the house. She lit a candle in the pantry and took it to the door.

Solid shadows waited there outside the doorframe: a dark hand reached in and grasped the wrist that held the candle. Martha gasped, then stifled her scream as a familiar face followed the brown hand into the candlelight.

"Miz Martha, please hush now! It's your old Dilby here with my girl Nan."

"But you're dead...ain't you?" Martha hissed the question, her whole body trembling. "We buried you, up in the new field!" She stepped back into the kitchen. Dilby and Nan followed her. Dilby sank to the floor, sitting slumped in the puddle of her skirts. Nan stood next to her with arms wrapped tightly around her mother's neck.

Martha slowly settled onto her knees in front of Dilby, peering into her face all the while. After a moment she reached out a tentative hand to touch Dilby's cheek.

"Well, you sure are real." With a little cry, Martha threw her arms around both mother and child, sobbing out two years of pain on Dilby's breast. "Where've you been all this time, Dilby? We thought you was buried up on the hill after the fire!"

Dilby drew back from Martha's embrace to look her sharply in the eyes. "Darlin', I's too tired to tell it all right now. Your Papa knows all about it. So does your Ma."

Martha covered her streaming eyes with shaking hands and sobbed, "Dilby, I...I can't stand any more! Daddy's gone, his head almost ripped off by a tree root. Mama's just plain gone crazy! And now we got ol' Aunt Sarah takin' everythin' over..." She looked up and stared at Dilby with new fear rounding her eyes. "My Gawd, what's Mama goin' to do when she sees you?"

Dilby and Nan slept in Martha's room that night. Against Dilby's protests, Martha insisted on tucking them both in her bed, noting that Nan would be too frightened to sleep alone on the chaise in the corner. She took that place herself and dropped immediately into a deep slumber. Somehow the very presence of Dilby in the house restored needed comfort.

The next morning Martha slipped quietly from the room and tiptoed to Elizabeth's door. She knocked softly, leaning her ear against the wood to hear any sound of activity inside. She heard a rustle of bedclothes and a low moan. "Mama," she called in a loud stage whisper. "It's me, Martha. Let me in. I got to tell you somethin' real important before Aunt Sarah gets up!"

Shuffling steps approached the other side of the door. "Just a minute, girl, and keep quiet. I have to slide my own key under the door to let you in. Sarah doesn't know I have it." Martha watched as a page from an old letter appeared from under the door with a key lying in the middle of it. She looked furtively over her shoulder while twisting the key in the lock. The sun had not risen as yet and a soft pearl gray light filtered into the long central hall. All she could hear was the occasional soft call of a mourning dove in cedar trees outside.

When Martha slowly slipped through the open door, a wave of scents floated from her mother. Sweet lavender, with a hint of gardenia, blended with a slightly acrid odor of sweat. Elizabeth stood with arms clutched around her belly, her bare feet under a wrinkled white muslin gown curled against the cool floor. Her hair hung over her face, no longer neatly plaited for the night as in the past.

Martha softly closed the door and stepped up close to whisper in her ear. "Listen Ma, and don't say anythin' for a minute. Dilby's alive!" Her mother opened her mouth but Martha clamped a hand over it. "Hush now!" Elizabeth's eyes grew wide, and she grabbed Martha's shoulders as though to shake her. "She's here, Ma, with little Nan. They're in my room right now sleepin'." She lowered her hand and waited for her mother to respond to the news. Instead of shock and tears, Elizabeth slowly transformed herself in front of her daughter's eyes.

She dropped her grip on Martha's shoulders, straightened her back, and walked purposefully to the window, murmuring to herself, "I must take over this place now, get that woman back to her own house." She squinted her eyes to see the almost-finished structure at the rear of the property.

Martha joined her at the window. "That's Uncle Abe's cabin he's been buildin'. I think you had better—"

"That's it!" Elizabeth exclaimed. "We'll hide Dilby there! Then I'll just tell Sarah I'm feelin' so strong now that we won't be needin' her any longer here at the house." Drew's widow was excited now. She turned to the wardrobe and pulled out her long gingham work dress and petticoat.

Martha touched her arm. "Mama, I'm not so sure Aunt Sarah's goin' to want to believe you are all better now. She seems to kind of be takin' an interest in this place for herself. You got to be careful. That woman means harm here. Even Uncle Abe is a little afraid of her."

Elizabeth ignored the warning. She hurried to finish dressing, then began combing out the tangles in her long hair. "First thing, I want you to get Damon to saddle up one of the horses and you ride over to Mister McDowell's. We'll get him to talk to Abe and let him know I can take care of this place. Maybe he would help hide Dilby until that cabin is finished."

Amazed, Martha shook her head. What was happening here? Her mother seemed to hold a totally optimistic view of the domestic situation now that she knew Dilby was nearby. Why was she completely unsurprised that Dilby was alive?

"I know..." Elizabeth stopped in the midst of twisting her hair into a bun at the base of her neck. "I'll keep Dilby and Nan in here until you bring William back. You tell everybody I'm feelin' better all of a sudden, but want to stay in my room undisturbed all mornin'. Bring in some of the farm account books from your Daddy's desk. Tell them I'll be busy getting' back to normal and organizin' the work around here."

Martha hardly believed her eyes and ears as she watched her mother bustle about the room and heard her say, "This time I'm lockin' my room myself, from inside. You tell 'em I don't want nobody comin' in here to bother me right now."

After Martha awakened the mother and child, cautioning Dilby to keep a hand over Nan's mouth, she led them to Elizabeth's room. Afterward, she walked quickly to the barn. Five minutes later she fairly flew down the dirt road on her gray pony, past the cluster of buildings near the church, and out toward William McDowell's farm. The Old Field with the school house bordered William's new land at the base of a pine-covered hill. She noted how well his peach trees were growing, their branches pink with spring blossoms. His orchards promised to rival Drewry's as the finest in the County.

The girl knocked frantically on the door, calling out, "Mister McDowell! Please open the door! It's Martha Allen."

When he finally opened the door, shirttails only partially tucked in and curly red hair standing out from his head like turkey feathers, Martha had to clap a hand over her mouth to stifle a laugh.

He frowned at her intrusion. "What in the world's got into you, girl?"

"Please, Sir, may I just come in before someone gets all curious about my bein' here so early in the mornin'?" He stepped aside as she hurried in with a rustle of long skirts. Once in the hall she turned toward him and heaved a great sigh before beginning her story of Dilby's return.

One hour later William rode up to the Allen farm. Martha followed on her pony. Abraham was just coming out of the barn. William tied his horse at the porch railing, helped Martha dismount, and led her pony toward Abraham.

"Thought I'd return your horse, and your niece, Abe, before you set a group out after them."

"That's mighty thoughtful, William. Now just what were they doin' over to your place this time of day, Sir?"

"Abe, I wonder if you and I could have a bit of talk by ourselves, while I get this pony settled back home. Somethin's happenin' here that concerned Drewry very deeply before he died. It's kind of private, you see, so I think it would be best if you and I spoke while no one else is around."

Abraham followed William into the barn, frowning as he closed the heavy double doors behind them.

Meanwhile, Sarah pounded on her sister-in-law's bedroom door, demanding to be admitted and threatening to get Samuel to force the lock. "Lizzie, you open up, ya 'hear? I'm good and tired of your craziness!" She banged with two fists while asking, "What's all that noise I hear in there?"

Running to the front door, Sarah stamped out onto the porch and shrieked, "Abraham, you get over here! I'm tryin to get breakfast on the table for you all, and Elizabeth Allen's locked herself in her room!"

146

When no one answered she whirled around and went back to the attack on the bedroom door.

In moments it opened. Elizabeth stood tall and immaculately dressed, as though prepared to set out for a church meeting. Sarah stared in astonishment, speechless at last.

"Calm yourself, Sarah. You must not carry on so. The slaves will hear you and think you're possessed! Why don't you just go set awhile in the parlor and rest. Why, I seem to be completely recovered now, and it's only been three weeks since..." she paused, then shook her head slightly as though dispersing a shadowy internal spider web. "Thank you, Sister, for all your help after the funeral." Elizabeth closed the door behind, brushed past Sarah, and proceeded toward the kitchen. Her sister-in-law fluttered after her.

A young black woman, slicing bacon at the center table, dropped her knife at the sight of a rather regal-looking woman entering the kitchen. Elizabeth greeted her.

"Good mornin' my dear. Now who, Child, would you be? I seem to have been drowsing or maybe dreaming these past weeks." She lifted a hand to her forehead as if to wipe away webbed strands of dreams. "I'm afraid I don't remember your name."

"It's Callie, Ma'am."

"Thank you, Callie, I'll not forget now. Let's get this kitchen hustlin'. After breakfast I want to sit down with you and see what problems need our attention. I think I have found some help for you here."

Sarah had finally collected herself. "Lizzie! I want Abraham to talk with you about some of these problems. My dear, I'm afraid you are not goin' to like our solutions."

The two women faced each other in the dining room. Elizabeth fought to control an inner trembling that threatened to take over her outward posture of serene composure. She felt as though she were trapped between two worlds; one of dreams in which she had seemingly sleep-walked for months; the other was a demanding world of fierce combatants, fighting, pulling at each other, trying to push her out of the way. Invisible fingers were beckoning and reaching to draw her to the sleeping world. She began a slow, almost imperceptible, rocking from foot to foot.

Abraham appeared in the arched opening from the hall and smiled. "Lizzie, my dear, how good to see you up and about. William here has been tellin' me all about your news."

William stood at his shoulder while Martha scurried behind him down the hall. Elizabeth turned to face them looking slightly dazed, William thought.

Sarah demanded, "It's time, Abe, right now! Lizzie's becomin' a wild woman! Just look at her. Why, she even told me to leave! We all know she can't even take care of her children, much less run this farm!" Sarah brought her face so close to her husband's that flecks of saliva fell on his beard.

At that moment, William tore his attention away from the scene to look down the hall. Martha reappeared and walked to his side, placing one hand on his shoulder and beckoning toward a tall figure following behind her.

Dilby bowed her head to the group, then straightened and looked calmly at Elizabeth.

Sarah staggered backwards, one hand darting to her cheek. "Who is this creature, Abraham?" He gestured to William, who nodded for him to reply. "William McDowell told me of Drew's plan to get those witch huntin' white trash folks to leave this family alone. This here is Dilby, Lizzie's woman, who some wanted to burn 'cause they thought she was conjurin' spells and curses."

William took up the story. "She's been up north in Carolina ever since young James went to school in Augusta. That was some five years ago now, and Elizabeth's been mournin' the loss of both James and her Dilby ever since. Ain't that right Ma'am?"

Elizabeth responded softly, "More like six years it was, William, with James studyin' to be a doctor over there in France." She turned to Dilby. "You see, I couldn't take the loneliness." After Dilby shook her head in warning , Elizabeth added with renewed vigor, "I must have this woman with me now. She's a most valuable asset to runnin' house and farm. Abe, I'm sure that new cabin you all been workin' on in the back can house her and her child." With that she beckoned Dilby with a hand to follow her. Both turned to leave. As the back door was heard closing, Elizabeth and Dilby walked across the grassy field toward the cabin.

Sarah muttered, "Oh, she'll use that cabin all right."

Abraham walked to the front of the house with McDowell and shook his hand at the door. "Thank you, William. We'll just have to work on this."

Sarah called after them, "I'll just be goin' to talk to the pastor about what's goin' on here! We can't be harborin' black magic in this community! We'll just see about Miz Lizzie Allen takin' over the farm!"

Abraham started to reply, then shook his head and walked out with William to the barn.

Chapter 24 — Chauvin

The Emperor Napoleon's grand plan for Paris transformed the gardens of the aristocracy into glorious public parks. The most popular was the grounds of the *Elysée*. Nature was recreated in "Antique" form with artificial cascades, Greek temples made of stucco, and statues looted from Napoleon's conquests and set on pedestals. The bronze horses from St. Mark's in Venice were dismantled and placed in the gardens of the *Tuilleries*.

By early spring, most citizens were intoxicated at the renovations. Social life flourished out of doors, with dancing, music, and tea under the trees. Young couples sat at tables, transported by the music as they enjoyed elegant flavored ices that were shaped like fruits. No one paid much attention to the somber gentleman stalking the flower-bordered paths. Deep in thought, M. Chauvin glowered at the brightly clad women and bewhiskered men he passed. When he reached the park boundary at the Seine, he signaled the hansom cab waiting there. The man hopped inside with all the urgent energy of a dedicated gendarme. "*Au Pont Neuf, mon homme, et vitement s'il vous plaît!*" "I'll walk across from there and find the little beggar," he muttered to himself. "James has to have her. Why was I so blind! He never even asked to buy her from me...not that I would have given her up to a red-dirt farmer like him, no matter how brilliant they say he is!"

The cab rattled past the *Palais du Louvre* and toward the *Hotel de Ville* just visible in the distance. At the destination, the horse was reined to a stop. To Chauvin's right extended the arched bridge that crossed to the *Ile de la Cité* and *Notre Dame* cathedral. Stepping down to the cobbled street, he reached up to pay the driver, and stumbled slightly to the side before regaining his balance. "*Merde*," he grumbled as he began his walk into the maze of buildings that housed so many of the students at the new Sorbonne.

Languidly, the river drifted beneath him as he crossed. He could see fishermen seated on its banks under softly shivering chestnut trees. He stopped for a moment and leaned over the side rail. "*Incroyable!*" he murmured. "I never would have thought such peace could come to Paris after the last horrible years of conflict." For just a few moments he let the perfumed breeze dry beads of sweat on his brow, and looked up at the buttresses that rose to support the northwestern facade of the cathedral. Lowering his gaze, he saw men and women working with bent backs to sweep the steps and husband planting around the grounds.

"Little gray moles," he commented with a smirk.

Two women passing by looked at him sharply, then stepped quickly around the dark little man.

After glancing at his pocket watch, Chauvin turned back toward the cathedral and his search. He was lost in the narrow, curving streets almost as soon as he entered *La Cité*, yet knew how to orient himself with the help of shopkeepers. The headmaster stopped first at a bakery, sniffing appreciatively at *les petits pains* on display outside.

"*Bonjour, Madame.*" He tipped his hat to the female baker seated next to the doorway. "I would like six of these delicious works of your art, *et un petit pot de marmalade, s'il vous plaît.*" He fanned his face with his hat as she counted the breads. Noticing that she offered no bag for the bread, Chauvin requested, "Ah, *Madame* I do not have a net bag to carry these. I wished them to be a small gift for my nephew who lives nearby. Perhaps you could direct me to his *pension*. He is a young doctor, or almost a doctor, for he studies at the *Hotel de Dieu* nearby. If you could direct me there, I will pay you now and order a *petit gateau* as well. Then I will return with a *panier* to retrieve them later."

The *boulanger* stopped what she was doing and looked up at him sharply. "*Monsieur*, you do not know where your own nephew lives? That is a bit strange, *n'est-ce pas?*"

"*Mais oui, Madame.* I...I am getting old, I fear. I have come from America for a visit and put the address paper in my vest pocket, right here. *Maintenant il est disparu! Madame*, what am I to do?" He smiled at her with a charming tilt of his head, holding out his hands helplessly to the side.

The woman dumped all but two of the breads back in their bin and held out her palm for payment. "Take these two for your pockets. I do not know any young American doctor who shops at this *boulangerie.*"

Chauvin took the buns, bowed politely, and moved on down the street.

James no longer lived in the rooms he rented from Madame Le Clerc. Right after Chloe had come to him in December, with news of her pregnancy, he moved them both closer to the *Hotel Dieu*. It was farther from the cathedral.

On the morning of M. Chauvin's arrival at the *Pont Neuf*, Chloe awoke to a pain that gripped her abdomen in a tight vise. A bit uncertain in the practice of obstetrics, since a midwife—*sage-femme*—was still the primary expert in this field of medicine, James ran down two flights of stairs to ask that his landlady summon the local *sage-femme*. He paid the woman in advance and asked her to bring a basin of hot water to his rooms as soon as she could.

Medical books lay open on the large table in the center of the small *salon* as James pulled a pile of fresh linen from the cupboard. *She is early! I should have had everything ready otherwise!* Just then, Chloe cried out from the small bedroom, "*Mon Dieu!*"

Chloe saw James's face hovering over her as though through a veil of mist drifted between them. His mouth moved but she could not understand his words. The pain had faded again. She felt a warm, moist flow between her legs that spread beneath her thighs onto the bed sheet. It soothed her, and she turned her head toward the window. The green, lacy crest of a linden tree swayed lazily outside. A subtle fragrance of lemon drifted into the room. The scent seemed to surround her, caressing her mind and body, enfolding her in a new space. Her eyes slowly closed.

The walls of the room dissolved and many more trees swayed at the far end of a tropical garden. Chloe seemed to lie in a swinging bed that hung from wooden pillars at the edge of a patio. Flowering azalea and rhododendron glowed in pink, lavender, and white banks to the right. The left side led back to a vine covered brick wall. Voices of a man and woman sounded nearby. She could not see the couple, yet thought she must know them. Who were they? *Maman? Papa?*

A young man approached her bed and began to rock her gently. "She's so beautiful, Thérèse. I love her already, just as I do you, Cherie. She has my mother's eyes, you know." His face was so fair that the flesh seemed opaque, the suggestion of tiny blue veins pulsing underneath at the temples. Dark, almost black eyes gazed at her half-sleeping form. "She looks very French already, and only two years old! What a *coquette pour les cotillions* in another fifteen years! She should be able to enchant any of the fine young New Orleans rakes..."

At this moment the woman came into view and slid comfortably under his arm to snuggle against his chest. As he bent to kiss her mother's lips, little Chloe opened wide her eyes to see the caramel cheeks of the woman next to the white of his brow. Her long brown curls draped low against the white muslin of her dressing gown. When they parted, Thérèse drew back, her arms extended with hands resting on the man's chest. "Remember his promise when he learned I was going to have your child."

"I remember he made you a free woman at once, and said we could set up this house for you and me to live in." The man looked worried, his forehead ridged as he confronted her mother.

"Yes, and I am very comfortable here. Even when you are home with Mme. Chauvin, I am so happy, *trés enchanté dans mon jardin.* I love you to distraction... you know that, *mon amour.*" She turned toward the child then and bent to gather her into her arms. "Look at her. She is as white as your mother, *n'est-ce pas?* Could she not pass for that outside of New Orleans?" He shook his head. "She would never pass here, as you know, because everyone will know who she is. Uncle will not let her out of his sight."

"But that is what he promised! Monsieur Chauvin said he would see that she was educated if she proves to be intelligent, and that someday he would set her free as well!" Thèrese rocked little Chloe from side to side more vigorously, causing the little girl to wail and twist in her mother's arms. The man took her to his shoulder and gently caressed her hair crooning, "There, there, *ma petite. Mama* will not put you out in the nasty old world. Uncle Georges will keep you safe." Addressing Thèrese he added, "He said 'someday,' and I will talk to him about it. But do not count on his generosity. He gets enthusiastic one moment and then turns all his attention to some new project or person and forgets all his promises." Placing the child down again in her rocking crib, Chloe's father lifted his hand to silence her mother's protests before they even began.

"Please, Thèrese, this is not like you! These conversations become very distressing. I'll leave you to compose yourself." With that he started to walk away, leaving Chloe's realm of vision. But she heard her mother's cries as she ran after him. "No, André, please do not be angry! I am just so happy here that I want our baby to be this happy someday! I am so sorry to upset you... you are my life, *Cheri*. Please stay to eat with us at noon." Their voices faded, and the garden wall rushed toward the patio and the swinging bed.

A pulsing drum beat loudly in Chloe's ears. She was suddenly lifted from her dream and in a tight embrace.

James tears fell on her face as he called to her, "Chloe, Chloe, don't leave me now, Darlin'!" When she opened her eyes and smiled at him James lowered her to the bed again. He took her pulse, then placed the end of the cylindrical stethoscope on the swollen mound of her abdomen. He was interrupted moments later: a large woman steamed into the room, carrying an enormous sack that clanked alarmingly with each of her steps.

"*Alors, Monsieur*, I am Madame Girardin, *Sage-femme*. 'Midwife' you say in Anglish." She shook hands vigorously with James and placed the bag on the floor. "I know you are *le docteur* here, but if I am to be of service, you must step aside, *s'il vous plait*, and let me observe the landscape."

"*Pardon, Madame...?*" James frowned, then nodded, "Of course, but may I look through your implements while you examine my wife? Her water has broken and she is in some pain, so I hope we can proceed quickly." He bent down to kiss Chloe's cheek. "Her name is Chloe, Madame. She is very dear to me."

Mme. Girardin murmured soothingly as she lifted the light blanket, raised Chloe's gown, and squatted her stout body at the foot of the bed. James pulled two metal basins from her sack, as well as knotted ropes twined neatly as sailors' sheets. He inspected a large bottle of olive oil, sea sponges, bandages to wrap an infant, a pillow that the newborn might be placed upon, and a fillet full of things to smell. He recognized pennyroyal, barley groats, a lemon, apple and cucumber. Last of all he pulled out a fearsome pair of forceps, and large cake of soap.

A small gate-leg table stood against one wall of the tiny room which James brought closer to the bed and extended its leaves. Methodically, measuring his movements with care to disguise the inner quaking that shook him, the young doctor spread one of the towels across the top and lay each of Madame's instruments on it. Each gesture was performed like a ritual.

Outside, a vendor's voice rose from the street. "Knives! Scissors! Knives and scissors! Bring your weapons to me, my dears, and let me set them straight!" James could smell freshly baked bread from the baker's oven below. He closed his eyes and prayed, "Dear God, let all this set Chloe straight and our hands be steady in this work!"

Chloe moaned and tried to sit up as the midwife probed her vagina.

The old woman clucked in disapproval. "*Mais non, ma petite!* You must lie back and be calm." She turned to James and whispered, "*Docteur!* You did not say the baby must be turned!" James answered feebly, "I...I hoped it would arrange itself before her time had come. As you see, she is too early. You are right. I will massage and work the uterus from outside." He moved to Chloe's side and began to press carefully on the mound of her belly. He believed the baby lay sideways and could be gently maneuvered to a safe birth position, with the head facing the cervical opening. The midwife washed her hands in the oil, then reached with two fingers of her left hand into Chloe's vagina.

Chloe's eyes grew large with fear. She gripped James' arm as he worked.

"I will die, James! I feel my spirit drifting now...dreams want to take me away. I think I will faint!"

"You will not die, Chloe! Madame, I must stop to give her a few drops of tincture of opium." With that he stood and hurried to a cupboard next to the bedroom door.

Madame said, "Ah, the orifice is beginning to open. I can feel the birth sac, it is the size of an egg. *Eh bien!*" The midwife smiled satisfaction, then quickly withdrew her hand. "*Venez!* Chloe has swooned and will need no drug for awhile. *Attention*, I fear her heart is not strong. See if you can feel a pulse. It is so faint!" Madame Girardin began to rub Chloe's hands and delicately slap her cheeks. James adjusted the stethoscope's earpiece and leaned close to Chloe's left chest. He could hear a slow, hesitant beat that gradually became stronger. "*Madame*, She just lost consciousness. He held up a small open flask to place a few drops of the tincture on her tongue. "Here Chloe, take just a sip of this magic."

"But you must stay with us now, *cherie*, and work as we bring your baby out." Madame began to demonstrate deep breaths and grimaced pushing until her face grew red. Chloe even began to smile as she watched, but was gripped with a contraction that arched her back and drew a sharp scream from deep in her chest. It was a hoarse cry that led to a frantic series of spasmodic grunts.

Chloe grew weaker as the sun slowly worked its way to the west. As day drifted toward night, a cooler breeze came through the bedroom window. Her cries diminished into moans as the hours dragged on. Finally, with the first gray light of dawn, a tiny baby boy was eased from the birth canal.

The newborn was quiet, yet seemed healthy enough for his 2.5 kilograms of weight. Mme Girardin admitted that he could have used another month in the womb, yet his color was rosy, with a hint of gold, as though brushed gently by the sun.

"This one will never suffer from sunburn, I warrant," predicted the midwife as she carefully wrapped the baby in white strips of cloth. James washed Chloe with sponges, then covered her in clean linen sheets as she finally slept.

Watching Girardin, James whispered over his shoulder, "*Madame*, he should be crying, *non?*"

"*N'inquietez vous pas, Monsieur le Docteur.* He breathes and his mama lives. We are fortunate indeed."

Shortly after, when Chloe awakened, the newborn tried to suckle, but she was unable to hold him. James held the baby close to her breast.

The new mother drifted from sleep to waking, yet never seemed wholly aware of the tiny creature next to her. By noon she had fully regained consciousness and sipped water from a cup. Madame Girardin began to pack away her supplies in the burlap bag in preparation for her departure.

"*Docteur,* I will return tomorrow if you wish, just to see how the little one is doing. You may pay me then. We have been too hurried along by your young friend here. Be sure the baby suckles regularly. Try these clean cotton tits soaked in barley water if he refuses her breast. The midwife reached down to touch the baby's bare arm, and flick her finger on his flesh. A sharp little cry ensued.

James swept the baby into his arms in alarm. "What do you think you are doing! Are you insane?"

Madame shook with laughter. *Docteur,* you thought he was too weak to cry, so I have proved him a full-chested little male, *n'est-ce pas?*" With that she walked from the room and called out, "Á *demain,*" as she opened the apartment door and left. Chloe reached to caress her baby's cheek as he lay in James' arms.

"À *demain,* indeed! She is too rough for my sweet. I thank her for my life, but do not let her touch this *bebe* again!"

James rocked the infant in his arms, until, gradually, the baby's tiny clenched fist crept shakily towards his mouth. *How amazing,* thought James. He gently unwrapped the linen cloths and checked the little body from delicate ears to miniature toenails. He was beautiful. His head was slightly elongated from the birthing, and was covered with a moist down of dark wavy hair. The button nose poked pertly above a Cupid's bow mouth. His cheeks had begun to glow from the exertion of his cries.

James leaned close to Chloe, resting his head beside hers on the pillow. "Our baby is perfect. He is you and me together."

Chloe gently eased the infant from his arms and nestled him against her breast. He seemed to smell the colostum that seeped there; the tiny mouth began to work in a faint sucking motion. Chloe guided him towards a nipple, and finally, with much twitching and frustrated groping with his mouth, the child latched on firmly and began to suck.

"What shall we call him, James?"

"Let's think of some names. My family—"

Just then a loud crashing sound came from below, as the door at the entry to the *pension* slammed shut. The baby jerked free of the nipple and waved his hands wildly. Chloe tried to sit up at the sound of footsteps coming up the stairs. They stopped outside the main door to the apartment. Chauvin's pounding on the portal was followed by, "*C'est moi, ma petite.* Open this door immediately! Have you gone mad? *Ouvre* I say!"

James lept from his chair and ran toward the outer room. The door burst open. Monsieur Chauvin, his red face sweating profusely, stalked heavily into the outer room and demanded, "Ah ha, what are you up to *mon salaud?* Where is my girl Chloe?" He shook his fist in James face, then tried to push him out of his way to look into the bedroom. He saw Chloe and screamed, "Get out of there, *crétine,* and be ready for a thrashing like you've never had before!"

Angered, James drew back his forearm to strike Chauvin across his chest with enough force to push him against the wall. Quickly closing on him, James wrapped his arms around Chauvin and lifted him, kicking, into the air. The little man was completely startled. When James lowered him to the sofa, Chauvin realized that this boy now towered over him. His pupil had filled out as well, outweighing him by at least thirty pounds.

"This is where I live, Monsieur. You must control yourself!" James breathed heavily and withdrew a few feet from the little man. "Chloe gave birth to a boy just a few hours ago, and I will not let her be disturbed! *Vous me comprenez?*"

Chauvin folded his arms and grasped his elbows—a hulk of quivering, frustrated fury. "You have deceived and betrayed me, flitting about Paris with this baggage! I have trained Chloe throughout her life to become my assistant, my prize possession!" He struggled to his feet and walked toward the woman's bed, body bent forward in accusation as he neared Chloe's side.

"This is the way you behave! How nice to give me a physical return on my investment!" Then suddenly he pulled aside the binding cloth that covered the baby. "*C'est dommage* that the child is male." He turned his head to look at James and added with a smirk, "He'll be the whitest looking field hand I own."

Chloe pulled herself as far away from Chauvin as she could on the narrow bed, covering her tiny son as best she could to shield him from the man.

At that moment, James, exhausted after twenty-four hours with out sleep, felt a great surge of energy that shot upward from the center of his body to his brain. It was an instantaneous hatred that burned in his mind, clouding all restraint. He was a savage, leaping to the kill, dropping layers of church-inspired gentility and family nurtured sweetness in a moment.

Chloe screamed as James hurled her guardian-master to the floor and straddled his chest with hands that squeezed the old man's throat.

"*Pardon, Monsieur Docteur, mais...*" A rumpled Madame Girardin stood at the door, her hands raised in horror. "*Mon Dieu, qu'est-ce que vous faites!*"

James climbed to his feet and dragged Chauvin up with him. The older man massaged his throat, but he couldn't speak for a moment. He flinched as James stepped up and pretended to dust off his vest, searching for a reasonable explanation to appease the midwife's probable suspicions.

Chloe intervened. "*Il est un voleur*, a kidnapper, *Madame*. He is trying to take my baby!"

"I will fetch *un gendarme* immediately!" Then shaking her fist at Chauvin, the midwife turned and ran out of the apartment and down the stairs, calling for the police.

Chauvin stepped toward the doorway and pointed a shaky finger at James. "You wait! I'll have the child and you in prison. Oh, and don't threaten me with action from your father. Perhaps you haven't been informed. There will be no action from your family. Your father is..." Then he left, still physically quaking, but laughing nervously at the expression on James' face.

Chauvin managed to slip past the uniformed men as they entered the front of the pension, tipping his hat gallantly as he turned and walked rapidly up the street to round the corner.

Madame Girardin had followed behind the men a short distance. Now she stood, leaning against a lamp post to catch her breath. She saw Chauvin and pointed down the street. "*Alors, le voila!*" she called to the officers. "*Vitement, messieurs!* The monster escapes."

Exhausted by her all-night vigil, the midwife staggered on toward the *pension.*

Chapter 25 — Mother and Child

The *Gendarmes* left after questioning James about the alleged threat of abduction, and soothing Chloe with promises to pursue the strange intruder. When Chloe backed off her original charges during Madame Girardin's later visit, the midwife shook her head in disgust. She insisted on checking Chloe one last time and looked approvingly at the baby, who vigorously clamored for his mother's nipple. "*Eh bien*, I'll leave you alone, but *Monsieur*, you must promise to lock this door after I go. I will complain to your landlady about the security of this house! "*Mon Dieu!* I cannot believe she allowed such a ruffian to invade your privacy!" With a few more grumbled exclamations to "*Le Bon Dieu*," she left.

Chloe confided to James, "*Les agents de police* must not talk to 'Uncle Georges'! He will claim his rights of property and has papers to prove them. *Merci aux bon Dieu*, you did not tell them his name." Anxious, Chloe leaned back against her pillows. James placed the baby next to her for a feeding. She looked at him, the muscles of her face taught. "Chauvin will return. What are we to do?"

James walked to the window to scan the street outside. "When he comes, I will apologize and take him outside to the cathedral for a talk. There must be a way to satisfy his greed. The man must want something. I know he helped my father with expenses, and now needs something from me in return."

Chloe said, "At first, he will be frightened of you. Let me talk to him. You must take the baby into the front room then. I don't want him nearby should Monsieur become violent." Chloe's eyes drooped shut, and her voice sank to a whisper. "*Viens, Cheri*. Lie next to us while I sleep."

James lay down, cradling her head against his chest while the baby slept between them, his mouth puckering gently in rhythmic pulsations, as dreams of warm milk filled his head.

Two days passed, with the baby they had decided to name "Young Drewry" growing stronger with every hour. Chloe remained weak, and James noticed that she had become feverish over the last twelve hours. Whenever he left the *pension*, he checked with the landlady to be sure she watched out for any unknown visitors asking admittance to the building.

At eleven o'clock on the morning of the second day James returned from the *epicerie* carrying a full sack of fresh fruit for Chloe. He juggled the net sack in one arm and tried to pull the bell cord to summon Madame Fouquet to main entrance. The door opened before he had grasped the cord. A grim-faced landlady told him, "*Docteur,* You have a visitor. I have kept him here in my parlor, but he is making a true storm of anger. I want you to get him out of here!"

At that moment a red-faced Chauvin appeared behind Madame Fouquet. James noticed that the man appeared to be both angry and fearful at the same time. His hands quivered as he shielded himself behind the landlady's stout frame.

James stepped into the foyer and set his bag on the floor next to the stairs. "All right, Monsieur, let's be civilized. We both need time to talk. You have said some deeply disturbing things to both Chloe and me. I am sure you have many questions to be answered as well. Before disturbing Chloe, come with me now. Let's take a stroll in the *Parc de Notre Dame* and talk." He turned to Madame Fouquet. "Would you be so kind, *Madame,* as to look in on my wife while we are gone? Tell her we will return shortly."

Hesitating a moment, Monsieur Chauvin nevertheless followed James down the stairs to the street. They walked in silence toward a central area fronting the cathedral. It was a good fifteen minutes walk away; Georges Chauvin gradually lengthened his steps to keep abreast of James. Rounding the last corner, the two men came to a broad path that led through trees and plantings, to the eastern facade of the cathedral. Benches had been placed at intervals along the path, where a few laborers had stopped to rest and eat before returning to work in the nearby gardens. James led Chauvin to a spot as far from the workers as possible. After the older man seated himself, James slumped down with his head held forward between his hands.

Seemingly encouraged by James' resigned demeanor, Chauvin sat up straight, puffed out his chest, and began his tirade. "You seem amazingly ignorant of the very basic virtues and lawful rights of every American citizen. My property rights go back further than yours, to French laws set down by the king, before Napoleon arrived. They are continued to this day in the Territory of Louisiana."

James remained silent, his hands still covering his face, so that any reaction to the man's words could not be discerned.

Chauvin continued, "We French in New Orleans have developed a far more humane system than you roughnecks to the north. We breed a superior group of slaves and create as well a pool of quite beautiful women of color, to service our young men. These women are pampered and cared for as are the valued mistresses of Paris. Their children have opportunities far beyond those of base field hands. But the key to all of this is the separation of blood. No matter how beautiful or intelligent seem our new class of slaves and free people of color, they are forever tainted with impurity. The blood of a savage race cannot be completely purged! This can never change!" He paused to control a tremble in one hand, then continued, "You see, my young friend, we owe a duty to the white race. We must not deceive our brothers by letting even one mask of purity bring the disease of mixed blood into our pure society." Chauvin slapped both hands against his thighs to emphasize his point. "Just imagine! What if a young American woman of Georgia entered into marriage with a man of unknown breeding!"

James half-smiled at the intense little man, then leaned back and stretched his arms above his head. "Don't you think, *Monsieur*, that an awful lot's been going on since Adam and Eve? Hundreds of years ago, Romans were running through here with troops of barbarians, Jews, and a good many legionaries from Africa, too. Those soldiers surely didn't have the manners of King Louis's court, and it just may be that a lot of babies right here in France have great grandpapas related to Moroccans."

Chauvin's voice softened to a plea. "So you would bring back that tainted blood, would you? Don't you see that I truly care for Chloe? She is a part of my household. I would protect her with everything that I have, yet she can only be the best of her kind, not ours. I will always take care of her *if* she behaves herself. But if you interfere, James, she will be an outcast. I will see to it that she is sold to work in the fields or the scullery of one of my sisters. Her child is an octoroon *batard*, and always will be!"

James flushed, but controlled his anger, "No, *Monsieur*, he is not a bastard. Three months ago, Chloe and I were married in a side chapel of this very cathedral. Our baby is not even the octoroon you mention. He has so much Scot-Irish in him there's not much room left to count his Negro blood."

Chauvin burst out laughing. "What if there were more? Tell me. If Chloe were a few shades darker, would you still marry her?"

"My son is named after my father. Do you think I'd do that if I had doubts about his mother?"

Chauvin frowned at these words, then shook his head while silently realizing, *So no one from home has contacted the boy about his father's death.*

Images of Dilby hovering over him in the giant metal tub swarmed in James' mind. He savored the memory of her strong hands caressing his legs and holding him tightly to her breast. Yes, perhaps he had been aware all along, at the deepest visceral core of his being, that Chloe was associated with Dilby. A strong passion for color, a rich earthy humor, and a sense of security that both Chloe and Dilby radiated—a confidence in their own female competence.

James rose slowly to his feet. "Chauvin, what do you really want from us? Why have you spent so much time, even your own money, to have me learn the latest skills and treatments at *Hotel Dieu*. The hospital?"

It was Chauvin's turn to lean gracefully against the back of the bench and smile. "*Mon ami*, you will head my new school of medicine in Augusta. All the finances are in place and the building is being prepared as we speak. It is designed in the classic Greek style, with pillared porticos on two levels and a grand oak tree-bordered entrance drive that will impress the local bourgeois." Chauvin leaned forward and warned James. "To head this academy you may not bring a mixed blood wife with you."

"If I fill your expectations, *Monsieur*, it will only be with my wife and child next to me. If I come, and if you ever betray us, you won't live for long afterward. Believe me." James leaned down to put both hands on either side of Chauvin, casually seated beneath him. "You call us ruffian farmers from west Georgia. Oh, yes, we are. We are descended from violent, warrior Celts. I will surely kill you in a minute, if killing needs to be done."

James turned and walked away, leaving a momentarily flustered and frightened Chauvin behind him. The man recovered quickly, his fear overcome by offended dignity and called out in spite, "You are safe from your father *mon ami*," he called out in spite. "I forgot to tell you that a renegade Indian murdered him two months ago!"

James stopped to face his new enemy. Chauvin spread his arms high and wide above his head in jubilation, and burst out laughing.

A gardener who knelt by the park's flowerbeds across from the cathedral looked over his shoulder at the voices that disturbed the warm spring morning. Even the birds had ceased their busy twittering, as though shocked at the bitter sound of Chauvin's laughter. Other visitors to the park had disappeared as well. The gardener pulled himself painfully to his feet, leaning on his hoe, stiff knees creaking, and rotated his aching shoulders like an old, retired street fighter. When he looked to see who had harshly broken the tranquility of the morning, he saw Chauvin's back as he walked with a slightly crooked gait along the central path toward the Seine River. A swirling spiral of dust and dry grass followed the departing figure—an invisible but monstrous pet growing in stature as it drew nearer the man to envelope him, weaving with his lilting gait.

A soft sighing wind swept through the trees above. The gardener shivered, despite the warmth of the morning sun, and hobbled away to take an early glass of *calvados* at the nearby café. The three large doors on the facade of *Notre Dame* were closed, and the decapitated figures of saints and prophets stood there blind, desecrated during the early days of the revolution. Chauvin and his whirlwind disappeared from Our Lady's Park.

As James watched Chauvin disappear, he had trouble breathing. His spine seemed to liquefy, the muscles unable to hold him upright. He staggered to the corner building and leaned against a stone wall. *His father! Nothing ever touched his father.* He was the source of total strength. Everyone one else in the family could falter, cry, scream in frustration, but his father sustained everyone through any hardship Drewry always maintained a wry, earth-warmed humor as he eyed the daily struggles of men and women in his frontier farm community. At least, James thought Drewry always maintained his good-humored balance. *If some liquored-up farm hand, or God-crazed fanatic from the church had attacked Drewry, well... But out of nowhere? A renegade Indian? My God....*

James rushed back to the pension, tears streaming down his face. When he reached the third floor and stood in the door to his rooms, he paused a moment and tried to calm his thoughts before going in to Chloe.

A loud cry from the baby jolted him into action. James smiled as he entered the bedroom. Chloe was out of the bed and walking back and forth with the infant in her arms, humming a soft lullaby that he faintly remembered from his own childhood. She looked at him, smiled, and placed a finger to her lips for silence. James went to her and the baby to embrace them from behind and join in the gentle rocking of the song's rhythm. Finally, Chloe placed the baby in his wicker basket cradle, covered him with a light blanket, and walked with James to the outer room.

"Why are you out of bed, darling?" he asked. "*Madame* Girardin asked us to be very cautious and spare your strength."

"I feel so warm and happy today, my love. Even *Monsieur* no longer seems such a fearful ogre. You have made me calm and safe here. I believe in you now..." Chloe buried her face against James' chest and wrapped her arms around his waist.

James wanted desperately to tell her about his encounter with her uncle, but hesitated. *Finally, she seems at peace.* He wanted to vent out his pain with the news of Drewry's death, but knew he must wait. "What was that song you were humming to Young Drewry, Chloe? I feel that I heard it long ago."

"My Mama used to sing it, James, when I was little. I don't remember many of the words, but she said it was from her mother and grandmother. Some of the words were French, but mostly a mixture with English and Gullah. It comes from my grandmother in New Orleans." Gently she lay the baby in his little bed.

The words were not French when he heard them. Now he remembered that it was Dilby who sang them to him as a small child. James gently eased Chloe's arms away.

"I'm taking you both to Georgia in a few weeks, Cherie. Humming is fine and I love your voice, but let's not sing the words in front of anyone else. You're going to be a free, well-born white lady from now on, so we must be careful." *I sound so pompous, even to myself.*

Chloe pulled back from him. She was still very weak and her husband's words had frightened her into a fitful agitation. "James! I think I know more about the history of the world than anyone in your part of Georgia! And I read both Latin and Greek, and of course French. Are you telling me to watch my words and songs to hide something you don't like? I need you to love me, James. Just me and all that I am." She walked unsteadily toward the bed, and collapsed forward the pillow to stifle her sobs. Her body shook. She felt an increase in the flow between her legs that resumed after the midwife's last visit. Chloe turned to draw her knees up and pulled the cotton wading tighter against her pubis as she lay face down again.

James followed and bent to caress her shoulders. "Look here, Chloe. Look at me! You know I love you. Look at me now..." His eyebrows drew together in a frown as he ran his fingers through the curls at the base of her neck. And what would his wife do when she lived where a slave would be expected to help her with a house in the country? Lord, look what happened when his mother and Dilby formed a friendship! Could Chloe sell off an unruly slave someday? Would she come to hate him and his family? James dropped to his knees by the bed and gently turned her over to face him. Tears flowed down her cheeks. He began to caress her still swollen abdomen.

Young Drewry thrived over the next few weeks, but needed to nurse every one to two hours. Since he seemed to gain weight daily, James and Chloe rejoiced in his good health. They planned to leave France as soon as possible and return to the farm in Georgia. James told Chloe of Drewry's death, but did not share his worries over the effect this all must be having on his rather frail mother. Who was overseeing the property, the planting, and the younger children? Would William McDowell have stepped in to help? And what kind of people were his Aunt Sarah and Uncle Abraham? James decided to return as soon as Chloe and the baby were strong enough.

When Georges Chauvin left his card with the concierge, Young Dewry was two weeks old. Chauvin demanded a meeting to set conditions for James' residency with the new hospital in Augusta. He claimed the building phase would be completed in one year. No mention was made of Chloe or the baby. Chauvin insisted that passage was to be arranged on a ship bound for Savannah as soon as possible.

Chloe still complained of fatigue, yet could not bring herself to tell James about a slow but constant drainage of blood. Still, she was no longer as haggard and pale about the face. She was able to accompany James on short walks to the Cathedral park each day, while Madame Fouquet watched Young Drewry.

Thursday afternoons became the time for set appointments with Chauvin. James met him at precisely three o'clock at a table at the dark rear of the café bordering the park. It was the same café that had welcomed the agitated gardener on the morning of James' and Chauvin's original confrontation. As the weeks crept by, these meetings developed a peculiar pattern: Chauvin always arrived first and James had the opportunity to stand quietly at the café's entrance to observe the man. Chauvin looked more diminished each time. He would sit hunched in his chair, a ceramic goblet clutched in one hand, the other hand abstractedly roaming the surface of the table as though searching for errant crumbs of bread. His fingers tapped erratically in the process. Once Chauvin noticed James' arrival he would stop immediately.

∾ั๏

One afternoon James stepped boldly toward the table to ask, "*Qu'est-ce que vous cherchez, Monsieur?* Are you besieged by ants, or perhaps tiny black invaders from the south?

Chauvin looked quickly to the right and left, then gulped from his goblet. There were only three other customers nearby, and the room was steeped in shadows by blinds that above the two front windows. The proprietor tended the bar at one side; now he sat quietly by the front door sipping a small cup of sweet, black coffee.

"*Assis-toi, mon fou*," Chauvin hissed through his teeth, as though contemplating some criminal conspiracy. After James pulled out the chair opposite the older man and sat down, the Headmaster demanded, "What are you talking about? I sit here quietly trying to arrange a contract for you, and you speak rubbish to me. What invaders from what south?"

"Oh, you know. All those insidious African particles of blood that threaten us white gentlemen." James called to the proprietor to bring him wine, regretting that he had upset Chauvin this early in the conversation.

He held up a folio. "Here are the papers. When I reach Augusta, I will hire a Georgian lawyer to clear up any details that need attention, but these paragraphs are the essentials of our agreement." Chauvin jabbed his index finger nervously on the papers, then pushed them toward James, who read silently.

Georges Chauvin

Director, Telfair Institute for the Study and Practice of Medicine

56 Telfair Avenue

Augusta, Georgia

Dr. James Allen, of Monroe County, Georgia, agrees to assume supervision of medical training, and supervision of medical students and interns, as well as overseeing treatment of patients admitted to this institution. He will live on the hospital premises, but may also maintain a separate residence of his choice in the city of Augusta

James looked up and frowned as he folded the paper and returned it to Chauvin. "This is not a contract that anyone should sign, especially without witnesses and a private consultation. At any rate, I must return to the farm first. After I have seen what must be done there, I will talk with you over a proper contract, signed by your lawyer. First, I'll need some guarantee that you will be silent about everything that has taken place here in Paris during the past few months. One word from you about Chloe, other than that she was your assistant in administering the school, and I promise you'll regret it for the short number of your remaining days." James leaned forward across the table as he spoke these last words, but could not tell their effect on Chauvin. He had looked away, a small muscle in his face twitching slightly. *What is ailing the man?* "Are you well, Monsieur?"

Chauvin focused again on this man who persisted in threatening him. "Of course I am well! As well as can be expected while being betrayed, abused, and threatened by my own student and his black wife."

James smiled and shook his head. This old man was going to be manageable after all. But there was something very wrong with him; something he had seen before in the hospital perhaps, yet he couldn't quite match what he saw before him with a particular diagnosis. "*Monsieur*, you probably will not listen to me, yet before leaving Paris, you should be seen by Doctor Duran. You tremble from time to time, you know, without any visible cause, and I notice that you seem to have an occasional limp. Have you injured yourself recently?"

Chauvin jumped to his feet, knocking his chair sideways to the floor. "Impudence! There is nothing the matter with this body that you have not caused. You shall see how strong I am, when we have returned to Georgia!" With that he turned abruptly and fairly ran from the café.

James watched the man's gait as he halted at the street before crossing the cobblestones. Returning to the table, James recalled Dr. Duran's lecture on the subject of a disease that emerged in certain families in each generation. He would have to ask Chloe about her father's family, but if Chauvin had a disease from his own "pure" family, why had he never shown symptoms before now? The man was at least fifty years old, but there might have been symptoms there before James became aware of such things. Shrugging his shoulders, he left several *francs* on the table and began the short walk to the *pension*.

Chapter 26 — Death at Sea

Young Drewry snuggled closely against his mother's belly as the ship's bunk rocked violently from side to side. One week at sea out of the harbor from Nantes, a violent storm hit the packet vessel *Rhone*. During the night wind tore at the ship's sails as they were frantically lowered. Chloe squeezed her eyes shut, fearful about a poor seaman who, a few hours earlier, had been washed overboard into the dark, monstrous waves. After vomiting some of his mother's milk, the baby drifted into a fitful sleep.

James rose from his bunk to check the bindings that held Chloe and the baby secure to the bed. After, he staggered into the ship's narrow corridor and up the steep laddered steps toward the still-dark deck. When he cautiously poked his head above the hatched opening, a high, shrieking sound assailed him. Wind whipped his hair straight up from the scalp. He saw two pairs of bare feet run past his face, as sailors dashed from one side of the deck to the other, tying down everything that could move. Even from the level of the deck, James could see huge, flickering tips of waves as they tumbled high above the port rail and spread long fingers of water across the planks toward the hatch where he looked out. The packet's three masts tilted drunkenly at a forty-five degree angle, as they rocked forward and aft. Just that evening at dinner, the ship's captain had warned of such a storm yet had seemed encouraged that the direction of the wind would hasten his vessel's journey. The *Rhone* was one of the newer, faster packet passenger ships, designed not only for cargo, but also to reasonably accommodate passengers. They offered speedier voyages than the older packets. Three weeks was a normal travel time, but now the ship seemed to be turning around on itself in the whirling waters.

"Three weeks is not very damn likely," James muttered. He carefully stepped back down to the level of the corridor once again. Bracing himself from wall to wall, he crept toward their cabin.

There was no sleep for the rest of the night. James marveled that Chloe remained quiet and still throughout the remaining hours of darkness. He must have fallen into a short nap at dawn, when the baby's sharp screams awoke him. He slid from the bunk and staggered toward Chloe and her frightened infant. His wife's eyes were open, her lips slightly parted. When he touched her cheek, it felt cold.

"Chloe!" He called her name aloud, panic-stricken. Unbelieving, he dropped to his knees, pressing an ear against her chest. Holding her head with two hands he brought his cheek close to her mouth to feel any breath. Nothing, no pulse, no breath escaped the graying lips. With shaking hands he untied linen bindings that held the child to his mother and placed him on the adjoining bunk. James gently laid his body over Chloe's, rubbing her arms and face in desperation, breathing into her mouth. After she did not respond, he lifted her in his arms, thinking to carry her up on deck. He knew better: he had seen so many dead young women brought in the hospital from the streets of Paris, yet his mind could not accept this vision of his wife. After lifting her, James he saw the deep-red stain on the bed beneath her legs. The realization of his final loss struck him like a dagger through the brain. *How has she kept this from me? That's too much blood! Damn that midwife! She'd botched extraction of the afterbirth But this night, why hadn't Chloe called out to me?* Moaning, he gently placed Chloe back down on the bunk, and held her left hand up to his lips. The dainty fingernails had begun to turn blue. A slight tear of skin at the corner of her right thumb was ashen white, where she had nervously picked at it when she thought no one was looking.

The baby's cries diminished to gasps and whimpers. When James turned his head from Chloe, he saw a tiny crease on his son's forehead. His jet-blue eyes stared at him, as though at a stranger. One little fist reached, index finger extended, toward the mother. James eased up Young Drewry, held him tightly to his shoulder, and began to rock his son. He tried to hum the little tune that Chloe liked so much from her childhood. It wouldn't come. With closed eyes he whispered, "Your mama had to go, baby. I guess she just couldn't figure how to live with us. You're just mine now." He kissed the child's wet cheek. "We're goin' home to Georgia to find your Grandmother."

Chloe was buried at sea later in the afternoon after the night she died. The waves settled into long gentle rises as her shroud-wrapped body slipped over the side. *Monsieur* Chauvin stood hunched beside James, who clutched Young Drery tightly to his chest. After some final words by the captain commending Chloe's soul to God, Chauvin abruptly turned from the rail and walked to his cabin. As he stepped over the sill of his cabin door, he shouted over his shoulder, "Now, James, I am doubly cheated! You owe me. It's the hospital or that child!"

James looked toward the man through his tears. By God, he was unrecognizable! Such inhumanity seemed demented. *He wants my soul or this baby boy!* A bedtime story his mother used to tell came suddenly to mind. *Rumpelstiltskin is his name!*

When the ship docked in Savannah two weeks later, Chauvin and James took separate paths, Chauvin traveling inland by river boat to Augusta. James desperately searched in the city for a milk-nurse to feed Young Drewry. The baby had survived on shipboard by sharing the breast of a nursing mother, whose baby died during the voyage. Once they landed, the woman departed with her husband for points north toward the Carolinas. James checked the notices of upcoming slave auctions posted in the dockmaster's office. After assessing each name he murmured "I'm sorry, Chloe, forgive me."

Two days later, when he boarded the westbound coach, a matronly black woman followed him, carrying his baby snuggled between her pendulous breasts. Her name was Clemma, and she brought along her own small boy by the hand—who toddled awkwardly by her side. The child was much lighter skinned than his mother. It seems that they both had become an embarrassment to a prominent family in Savannah society. James was saved the ordeal of watching the horrors of a human auction; he found Clemma through a posted notice in the dockmaster's office advertising the private sale of a milk nurse.

Clemma was not happy at being sent away into the wilderness of western Georgia, but she was pleased to have the least demanding job of all slave labor.

She adjusted the infant to her breast and smiled down on him. "Mistah Allen, dis de smallest chile I evah did see..." With a nervous glance at James, she hurried to add, "But he strong, he suckin' real hard. An' he mighty, mighty pretty." Her own son, Julio, watched her with wide eyes as he sucked a forlorn thumb. When James nodded acceptance, a thin smile creased the drawn and haggard cast of his features. He caressed the tight curls on top of Julio's head and turned his face to gaze out the window. The carriage passed through Savannah's park squares, which were surrounded by handsome town homes. Yet with his mind focused on Chloe's tragic death, he noticed little of the local scene.

Chapter 27 — Locked In

Elizabeth lay quietly on her bed and listened to the soft, slow breathing of Dilby from the darkness near the cabin's door. Outside the small, barred window, leaves whispered in the early morning air. The slave woman had been here now for several weeks. A dream had soothed and dulled the pain of that first day, but they had locked Elizabeth in, clucking and shaking their heads as she struggled to escape from Abe and Sarah. *How dare they! The Reverend and pious Mrs. Hope, lifting their hands and voices, crying out to God to heal her soul as they supervised her jailors. Dear God, why didn't you smite them, the hypocrites?* Only Dilby stayed to comfort her, and now she slept behind the locked door as well.

The dream returned with images of love. They wove a pattern, shimmering in the night air, quivering like some hidden song and evoking echoes of her life with Drew: There was a house with many rooms that seemed to grow organically, forming turrets, columns, wings, and arms of apse-like cells. Everything was bright with sunshine and warm with smells of apples baking. She moved, bustling through the spaces there, finding places for all the people she loved. She held everyone within, folding them into her giant hive. Then the dream shifted to a different time, with Drewry still alive. She told it to him in the darkness with soft whispers. *We were very old, you and I, thin and small and wrinkled. Your face was creased with smiles, with crinkled eyes, as we sat by the fire at Christmas time. A door would fling open, and our children entered laughing. We drew them in to our warm-lighted room, with soft-kissed cheeks and warm embraces. All our friends were there, smiling out of old, smoke-dried faces to see us so blessed by time.*

Elizabeth pushed herself up on her elbows to breathe spicy air coming through the bars. "We always wove our lives with care," she whispered to herself. "I have broken with it all. It's my doin'. Forgive me Drewry, darlin'." She twisted to her side and gazed at Dilby. *What will you do if something happens to me? And what of little Nan?*

⋙⋘

Early the next morning Sam came to unlock the cabin door and release Dilby for her daily chores.

Dilby thanked him, and turned to Elizabeth. "Miz Allen, you jes' rest awhile and I'll fetch you some biscuits and fruit. I heard you jes' tossed aroun' last night." With that she turned and walked toward the farm's kitchen in front of the cabin. Sam sighed many times as he went to relock the door again.

"So sorry, Miz Allen, you surely know that," he mumbled as he closed the door on her.

Elizabeth dressed lethargically in an old blue gown that hung loosely on her body. She had lost weight over the last few weeks, even though Dilby tried to coax her with all kinds of tempting dishes from the family table. This dress had become a kind of prison uniform—Elizabeth had lost interest in presenting herself as anything other than the family lunatic. Her younger children had departed with Martha and William. Even William seemed to have sadly resigned himself to her "sad and incurable melancholy," as dear Sarah forever was lamenting. Elizabeth no longer cared. Drew was gone forever, and James seemed to have disappeared from everyone's life. Monsieur Chauvin had written from Paris that James was no longer enrolled at *l'Hotel Dieu*, and he, Georges Chauvin refused to take responsibility for the young man's defection.

Elizabeth fell back on the small bed and closed her eyes. "Sleep, dear Lord, just let me sleep again."

The early chill had worn off by eleven o'clock that October morning, and by lunchtime, the day was warm as summer. Abraham stayed in the fields at midday to take his lunch with the hands under the trees. Sarah had the whole house to herself at that time of day, having directed the canning of fruits and vegetables and supervising the cleaning and polishing of just about everything in the house. The farm never looked so good; everyone commented on that at church.

By afternoon, just like all the afternoons since Sarah had forced Abe to lock Elizabeth away in the cabin, the house was totally silent. No children, no slaves, not even a cat could be found lounging in the windows or on top of the tall pine *chiffrobes* that stood guarding linen and clothes in the bedrooms.

Sarah grew restless as the autumn months passed. Domestic chores, such as canning fruits and legumes in the kitchen, and the preparation of meats to winter in the smokehouse, were almost completed. Where was that girl Martha? It was scandalous the way she had stepped into Willliam McDowell's home, keeping the children there as late in the day as she could before sending them back to Sarah and Abe. And with no chaperone in place on the McDowell farm! What was she thinking? Everyone knew that William still mourned for crazy Elizabeth, though, Lord knows, Martha would be a more suitable mate for the man. Still, something had to be settled there. A marriage could be forced, if necessary, but that would strengthen Martha's legal standing. She would be in line to inherit. Sarah would get after Abe tonight at dinner. At least there would be something to talk about: Abe was downright sullen these days.

Sarah fanned herself as she rocked on the front porch. No breezes stirred the cedar trees by the road, and the pecans by the side yard sporadically dropped their fruit in the shade. Her eyelids drooping, Sarah's head dipped forward as the rocking chair drifted to a tilted stillness. The fan hung from her fingers at her side. The rhythmic clicks of tree frogs gently broke the silence, repeating over and over their ancient songs.

As time and space whirled inside the bony shell of her brain, Sarah wonders at the darkness. She sees only flickering lights in a distant space. Then night chants hum and shout. Frantic feet seem to attack the ground, thumping like some earthbound heart beat. Misty exhalations whisper through invisible trees. Drawn from her chair along a flowing wave of damp air, leading out into the night, Sarah clutches her elbows tightly and bends her head forward.

Suddenly she is standing in the light of a bonfire. A small, dark man prances there, twists and leaps as his black fingers flick at the darkness, summoning...summoning, something. "Come closer, Woman. See the fire and use it. All of your wishes can be God's wishes too. All this should belong to you. Rest in the comfort of the chosen few." With that, his dancing feet stamped faster as he shifted from foot to foot, then leaped high into the air. Screaming laughter scratched her ears and pricked her skin.

Sarah jerked awake to see Abraham standing in front of her chair. *It must be getting dark early already,* she thought, for the sun had already set.

"Oh, you startled me, Abe! What time is it? I must have slept for hours."

"Didn't you hear the scream from back yonder? It came from beyond the smokehouse, probably poor Elizabeth crying out." Abe turned to leave the porch and circle to the back of the property.

His wife raised her hand toward him. "Now wait, my dear. Let Dilby take care of it. That's why we let her stay, 'stead of turning her over to that church rabble.

"Oh, I thought those were your blessed compatriots, Sarah. Now they're rabble?" Abe shook his head, his smile grim. "You've got me afraid of them now."

Sarah rose briskly from her rocker and held out the hand to him. "Come now, Abraham. Callie must have dinner ready by now...at least she'd better have it. Let's just go on in and enjoy some time together."

There was a hint of the aging coquette in her manner that astounded her husband. It was not a flattering pose for his wife. Abe pulled a grimy kerchief from his pocket to wipe his forehead. How had he become so easily manipulated by Sarah? She had fallen in with the worst scandalmongers at the church, and was turning the whole country side against his brother's family, even threatening him.

When they were seated at the table, silently eating Callie's chicken stew, Sarah asked, "Abe, when is Judge Gilpin comin' round the circuit to read Drewry's will?"

He slowly laid his fork and spoon on either side of the bowl in front of him. *What is the woman thinking? It will be weeks before the judge finishes working north of Mr. Grishams's land and he is high up stream on the Flynt River. She knows that Drew left everything to Elizabeth. If Lizzie is incapable, then James or Martha would be in line. If somethin' happened to Lizzie...and if James really has disappeared... then perhaps. Martha is unmarried, so she's no threat. Yessir, my Sarah's got brains for sure.* "There be plenty of time for the readin' of wills, Sarah. I'm more concerned about what happens if James comes home to see his mother locked away. Have you thought of that, my dear?"

"You know, Abe, I don't rightly think he'll be comin' home for a long time. He's gallivantin' all over the continent, I reckon. No Judge would consider him responsible for all this land holdin', do you think? Martha? Well, as you say, she's still a child. I'll make sure nothin' changes in that direction."

On the other side of Elkins Creek, where the McDowell farm nestled, Martha had other ideas. She had taken the austere household of bachelor William McDowell and brought order to his kitchen and laundry. During daylight hours, her sister and brother were settled back in the schoolhouse nearby, and she was well on her way to intriguing her benefactor with the truly astute nature of her intellect. William was amazed to see such a vigorous mind in a young woman. She was also becoming a clever seductress, with quite an agenda of her own: when William sat at his desk in the evenings, correcting the papers of his young students, Martha sat nearby on a horsehair sofa with Latin texts spread out on the table beside her. If William would lean back in his chair and remove his glasses to rub his aching temples, she was alongside.

One evening she offered, "Mister McDowell, can I bring you some fresh cider? I baked ginger cakes this mornin' and I just know you'd enjoy one before you go to bed." She smiled at him as she went to bring the treats, and gently touched his shoulder as she passed by his chair.

William returned her smile and covered her hand with his own before she withdrew herself to the pantry. While she was gone, he arranged the papers in a cardboard folder and tied it closed, then stood to stretch his arms and back. As he heard Martha's steps coming from the hall outside his parlor, he moved to the sofa and sat with elbows resting on his knees, his head held between his hands. He noted Martha's feet laced tightly in high black shoes, looked up at her, and patted a space on the sofa beside him. She sat, lowering her tray on her lap, began to cut a slice of brown, pungent ginger cake and handed it to him.

She asked as she handed the cake to him, "How was Stokes today, Mister McDowell? Has he found enough manners yet to answer you in school? I'm mighty embarrassed that he just sits there when you question him."

William leaned back to enjoy the treat. "He's mournin', Martha. It's his way. He's only fourteen, yet has grown big as a man now. I think he feels he should be able to take care of Elizabeth, get her out of that cabin and save her from whatever demons are out there. But Stokes just can't. He's frightened 'cause he's lost without his pa holdin' everything together."

Martha held the knife tightly in her hand and squeezed it against the dish. She shut her eyes and tried to hold back a shudder of apprehension. "Stokes is a baby! I'm scared as he is, but I know what I have to do about it."

After he took a sip of cider from the clay goblet, William looked at her with curiosity. "What is it that you think you have to do, Martha?"

As a reply she passed another slice of cake to William's plate. "This has just a might too much ginger spice. Ma says I tend to overdue the flavorin', but then I just may have a different way of tastin' life in general." When the girl rose to take their plates away, she bent down, kissed William's forehead and coyly murmured, "What do *you* think, Sir?"

Martha never stayed overnight at McDowell's for more than four days in the week, sleeping next door in an old storehouse shed that William had hastily made up for her. She had escaped the constant turmoil of the Allen homestead, yet needed to return to check the house with Dilby, and see to little Nan every few days. When would James come home? She felt helpless to protect her mother on her own. That was why she first ran to William—to escape Sarah's domination!

Dilby moved from the house to the locked cabin like a lost spirit, always watching for some way to turn Sarah's mind, some way to steer her greed in another direction. She prayed to her father's spirit more than ever before, and waited for an answer.

Chapter 28 — Home

James was first delayed in Savannah, while searching for a wet nurse. He was further hindered by the flooded rivers that crossed his path to the west. Thus, the overland trip to Monroe County extended longer than the sea voyage itself. It was the second week of October, on a chilly Thursday evening, when James' carriage drew up to William McDowell's front porch. He told the driver to stay put.

"I must fetch Mister McDowell and arrange a bed for you this night. Wait here while I take the children and this woman inside." James jumped down from the carriage door and called out, "William McDowell! Are you here about? It's me, Sir, James Allen, and I need your assistance." Clemma shivered in her seat as she rocked a whimpering Young Drewry and kept Julio tightly at her side.

There was no response. The house was dark; only a dim, flickering light shone from inside the parlor. Clouds blew swiftly across the sky, dimming the full moon and finally blocking it out altogether. James was about to call out again, when the front door was pushed open: a dark silhouette with fluttering outlines dashed toward him.

Martha flung herself into his arms and screamed, "Thank you dear God!"

After a moment in her tight embrace, James pulled back his cheek from soft curls that blew wildly on the crown of Martha's head. "What are you doin' here, little girl? I can't believe Mama would let you stay so late at an old bachelor's house."

Martha smiled as she wiped the tears from her cheek. "Now James, William ain't old, and I'm no longer a little girl. Come on, let's get him up. He's been so tired lately with the school growin' so fast and nobody but me to help him with teachin'."

James cocked his head as he looked at Martha more intently. "Well, I guess you've got to be grown up, 'cause look here..." He motioned to Clemma and took her elbow to help the woman step down from the carriage with her child and the infant. "This is Clemma with my baby son. You're an 'Aunt Martha' now."

His sister stared at him in astonishment, then plucked aside a corner of the little blanket to look at the sleeping babe. Martha's right hand clapped over her mouth. She stepped back to look in horror at her brother. "What are you talkin' about, James? You mean this woman is the mother of your son?"

James beckoned for Clemma to follow him, and turned Martha back towards the house with the other. "Let's go in and get William. We need to talk, and no, Clemma is not my baby's mama." James paused to identify the little boy by the black woman's side. "This here is Julio, Martha, and yes, Clemma *is* his mama." Her son yawned and rubbed his eyes. After Clemma gave a robust tap to the top of his head, Julio threw a startled look at his mother, then bowed his head and murmured to Martha, "I's Julio, Ma'me."

She did not acknowledge his greeting. The group followed Martha into the house, where they were met by William in his nightshirt, carrying a candle. The musket he had in his other hand shook, He stared in disbelief a moment at the people who had arrived, then set the gun against the wall.

"Gawd almighty, James Allen!" he exclaimed. "How...how in Heaven's name—"

James's eyes began to tear as he grasped his old friend's arm, then turned his head toward the milk nurse. "Clemma, give me the baby. I'll let Martha take you and Julio to a bed, while William and I set for a while in the parlor. Sister, you come back, too. Now Young Drewry is goin' to meet some family!. Clemma, I"ll come get you when he cries to be fed." James recalled the waiting carriage owner. "William, come back to the door a moment. Do you have a place our driver can sleep tonight?" William peered out at a man standing beside his horses. "Driver, you can take your trap and horses into the barn yonder. The loft is warm for sleeping, and there are blankets in the cupboard at the right side of the doors. Come on, James." William led the way into the parlor, where he poked the banked fire back into life and added kindling wood to a nascent blaze.

James sat in a big rocker near the fire, where he nestled the baby close against his shoulder. Martha returned and stood with arms held at her sides. She awkwardly reached forward, but pulled her hand back from the tiny fist curled on its father's chest. William took the bench opposite James and leaned forward. James thought he looked tired and older by more than the few years that had passed since the two had seen each other. Dark circles below William's eyes and furrows that creased his forehead hinted at the emotionally strenuous weeks that had preceded this late night reunion. James noticed a patch of white hair that grew amid his auburn coloring. It sprang above the left side of William's prominent brow, as though one section of his brain had received a terrible shock of some sort.

"What have you done, James?" whispered Martha so as not to wake the child. William raised a hand to his chin. "Let James tell us, Martha."

James began to rock the baby slowly, while he told his tale of Chloe's pregnancy and tragic death. He left out Monsieur Chauvin's accusations and threats, saying only that he had pledged to set the Augusta clinic in motion, yet feared that Chauvin was strangely demented and could not be trusted with anything. "I'm countin' on Mama to take care of Young Drewry while I take care of things in Augusta."

William said, "That's not goin' to happen, James, until we settle your pa's estate." He leaned back and shook his head. Martha began to weep quietly.

Puzzled, James asked, "What do you mean?

As gently as possible, William told of the terrors and grief of the last few years. He began with Dilby's recent return from Carolina. Martha added her observations of their mother's gradual decline, and her dive into total depression and irrationality after the murder of Drewry. James questioned about the mysterious intruders, and was told the rumors about Creek Indians returning to avenge some wrong.

William stood to rummage in his desk and take out his notes on Drewry's will. Sarah had waved it triumphantly in his face, after she had arranged for the church wardens to incarcerate Elizabeth. The wardens had readily agreed that Elizabeth was a mad woman dangerous to herself and entire family.

By this time James, energized by his anger, had gotten up to pace the floor with Young Drewry. The baby began to whimper.

Martha reached her arms towards her brother. "Give him to me, James. I'll take him in to that Clemma for the rest of the night."

When Martha cradled the child against her chest and took him to the back of the house, James marveled at her calm efficiency. She was indeed a young woman now.

William commented, "Sarah has complete control of poor Abe. She fancies herself a grand lady by joining Drewry's lands with her husband's in a frontier version of an east coast plantation, *and* with herself as leading a new aristocracy on the frontier!" William lowered his voice. "James, I think she is the one who is slightly mad. She plans to have the circuit magistrate declare her and Abe as guardians for the children and heirs to Drew's property."

"What the Hell did she think I would have to say about that?" James fumed.

"She has a letter from Chauvin, declaring that you had escaped from your responsibilities at the medical school, defaulted on repayment of what you owed him for your education, and disappeared completely." After a pause, William rose to tend the fire again and continue. "I swear I don't know what has happened to the headmaster. He's either a scoundrel beyond imagination, or something very bad has taken hold of him—"

James interposed, "Chauvin is not well, William. I meant to research his family to find out if any of them had strange behaviors or similar nervous symptoms in their later years. I just haven't had...you see, William...I married Chloe in Paris. Do you recall how she was? Just as light and delicate as a butterfly, and smarter than anyone Josh and I had ever known. Josh and I... well...I loved her..." James turned away as tears formed in his eyes.

William walked to him and grasped the back of his head to pull him into an embrace. "Aye, Chloe's a special one. Do you not love her anymore then?"

"She's dead, William! We took the earliest ship from France at Chauvin's bidding. A few nights out, on board she...she began to internally bleed. I fear the midwife she had left some of the afterbirth. I...I had trusted she was the best." James shuddered. "Oh, I probably caused Chloe's death, William! I...I feared that Chauvin would ruin us if we didn't leave as early as he insisted."

"Then Chloe is the mother of your babe?" James nodded and tore at the top buttons of his shirt, gasping for air and trying to control the despair that always hid behind the vision of a pale Chloe lying in his arms.

Realization of what had happened slowly began to smooth the features William's face. "James, leave it all until tomorrow," he advised softly. "Come with me. You'll have to share my bed tonight, since Martha has privacy in my shed next door. She stays there when it's too late to return to the farm. We will talk in the mornin' and plan."

Both men slept heavily. Even disturbing dreams were unable to keep them awake after the emotional turmoil of the night before. Martha, however, was restless and left her bed several times to look at the sleeping baby nestled in a basket next to Clemma and Julio. Who else's child was this, besides being James' son? He was too young to look like anyone in the family as yet, but Martha stared at him intently, as if to catch an emerging tremble of lip, a frown on the tiny brow that might remind her of someone.

When Young Drewry woke at dawn, crying to be fed, Martha sat and watched in fascination as Clemma took him to her breast. Julio slept on, curled against his mother's back while she nursed the infant.

William rose at his usual early hour to begin home chores and open the schoolhouse before the children arrived. He let both Allen's sleep, even Martha whom he needed desperately with his students. Somehow the day would pass, and then he would need every bit of craftiness at his disposal, to help a family that gradually had become his own. William was a gentle soul, intelligent in a scholarly way, working to bring as much of his love of classics to this wild community as they could handle. He was also a true Scotsman: no one ever hoodwinked a McDowell in shrewd dealing! William relished the opportunity to venture forth into the field of legal mayhem. He chuckled as he fanned the flames in the schoolhouse stove. He sensed that Martha would turn out to be a crafty ally. She wept from grief, but he saw that she was no delicate, faint-hearted girl who let life sweep her along at will. Yes indeed, Martha was a caution!

James was awakened later that morning by the cries of the baby. It was unusual for Young Drewry to sleep so late, but Clemma had nursed him twice during the night and he was beginning to feel satisfied once again, after several days of minimal nourishment during the transition from ship to Clemma. When Martha knocked on his door to announce breakfast, James clothed himself and joined her in the large kitchen.

Over breakfast Martha described the cabin jail where Elizabeth lived in ever increasing despair. "The preacher, Mister Hope, says she's mad, settin' fires all over the community. I don't know. Maybe she did do that, but she blamed everyone here for the loss of Dilby, so fire must have seemed like a just revenge. She was gettin' much better once Dilby came home from Carolina, but Aunt Sarah just kept at her, screamin' and threatenin' to have her up for witchcraft."

"That's a far fetched accusation by a lot of stupid people," James said.

"I know!" Martha clashed the china plates together in anger as she cleared the table. "Uncle Abe's just about useless exceptin' when he's in the fields or barn. I swear the man's lost himself to the real witch over there."

When William returned late that afternoon, he retreated with James to the barn. They talked as they forked hay from the floor up to a platform above. James told him that he had determined to throw his aunt and uncle off the land.

"That's quite drastic," William remarked, unsure of his friend's action.

"Will you come with me tonight? If there's trouble we'll need two strong backs to set them both in a wagon and pack them off to their own land."

William stopped to lean against the handle of his pitchfork and outline the situation as he saw it. "You'll have to get to your mother before Sarah hears that you've come home to claim the farm. Sarah shouldn't have a chance to gather round all those church folk. And Dilby and her girl will need protection, once Sarah gets desperate and even meaner. Witchcraft is a hard charge to fight in this congregation, and Dilby is the prime witch as far as Mister Hope is concerned."

"He's a damn fool—"

Now listen, James. There's talk of formin' a town here. Monroe County is being split into two parts over the next few years. I've been busy buyin' land right where Judge Gilpin says the new town ought to be. When he gets down here from the Flynt River I'm goin' to open his eyes to some profit with land for the new courthouse. He can either give in to the wishes of Sarah Allen, or he can have a good chunk of my land in the middle of the new town. John

Gilpin knows he'll be around to benefit from that. If you can hold out for your mama, while I ride north and hurry the greedy old man on his rounds, we'll work this out safely."

James rested his chin on the handle of his fork and closed his eyes to imagine a night raid on his own home. "May I have a couple of your men here? You best be off while I sneak up on that nest of snakes over yonder."

Chapter 29 — Arson

William left the next day on horseback, carrying saddle bags full of salt pork, corn meal, a few fresh apples, a water canteen. He brought along as many documents and copies of documents as he could scrape together—with the help of Martha's nimble fingers. She had searched for them, scouring the drawers of the main desk in the Allen parlor ever since Elizabeth had been moved to the cabin. William realized it would be a long ride upriver to intercept the magistrate, but he should catch up with the man within eight hours. He hoped to be lucky in his choice of farm gossips along the way. Martha promised to keep working with the youngest students at the school while he was gone, and during school hours, have his older ones write a long essay on one of the Latin poets. He hoped she could cope with that; in any case he planned to return within a few days.

James and Martha began to plan a course of action as soon as William's mount had disappeared around the first curve in the dirt road. They decided to go straight to the prison cabin, after dark, and break down the door to reach Elizabeth and Dilby. With the expected surprise to help them, they would confront Sarah and Abe before there was time for the couple to summon help from Hope or his group of church elders.

"Take William's man John, with you," Martha cautioned. "He knows many of Mama's slaves, and has kept up with the daily routines on the farm. He fancied Callie's sister, but Aunt Sarah sold her last month to a passing brandy merchant. Yessir," she added with a chuckle. "I think John can be relied on to help us tonight."

After the storm on the night of James' arrival, an uncommon body of cold air swept through western Georgia. The temperature rose during the day, but colder air returned, and winds from the north pushed black clouds before them. There was little chance of a visible moon that night. James prayed that any rain would hold off until the early morning hours.

At ten o'clock James, John, and even Martha, wearing dark pants, sweaters, and black cloaks, rode in single file across the open land toward the Allen farm. James and John carried short-handled axes and wedge bars strapped to their saddles. Martha insisted on being in charge of a leather sack of gunpowder sealed with beeswax. If the need arose, she planned on setting off a small but distracting explosion.

With only occasional light from a thin wedge of moon above them, the three rode silently along the wagon ruts of the forest road, looking for the turn to the south where they would come to the creek that bordered William's land. Tall pines stood close together on either side, standing straight some seventy-five feet into the night sky. Just before the group reached the banks of the creek, a round, furry shape scuttled past the horses' feet. Huddled by the roadside, the animal's bright yellow eyes gleamed at the group as they passed.

John leaned from his horse toward Martha to murmur, "Mistah 'Coon out huntin' tonight too, Miz Martha." He laughed softly. "Tonight we needs to move fast and quiet jes' like him."

Once turned at the creek, they found themselves on a road that circled a large meadow. Toward the middle of the field, the giant form of a White Oak spread its branches over a broad circumference of laurel and sour bush.

James reined in his horse and beckoned the others to him. "If we cut across the meadow here we'll save a good fifteen minutes. I used to play in that high oak yonder. I reckon the ground's level and safe for the horses."

John and Martha agreed and turned their mounts off the road to follow James across the open space. The still air was cold around them. The only sounds came from the soft thuds of hooves on damp ground, and the distant call of an owl somewhere in front of them. Steam from the horses' breath drifted to either side of the riders in thin wisps.

After about thirty minutes, James stopped to point ahead toward a glow of light behind the trees at the other side of the meadow.

"Sweet Jesus! Martha cried out. "Ain't that where the new cabin's settin'?"

John kicked the sides of his horse and led the way across and into the trees. James came close behind, swearing at his horse as he flicked its neck with the reins and leaned far forward.

They drew up behind the cabin, yet distant enough to be able to tie the horses to trees bordering the truck garden and dismounted. Only a glow shone from the front of the cabin. The horses could not be allowed to alert any of the family or slaves. Steam from their muzzles misted the air, as they restlessly stamped their hooves.

John peered nervously into the darkness, toward the farmhouse, then raised a hand in warning. James leaned toward the black man to hear his whisper. "All the windows be dark, Mistah Jim, but I see's shadows over yonder movin' to the little house where Miz Lizzie liyin'."

To see better, James crept forward between the old rows of the garden. Martha came behind him, her cloak pulled tight to keep out the cold. Abruptly, John and James halted simultaneously to sniff the air. A faint reek of scorched wood—especially the well-known smell of pine pitch burning— drifted toward them. Without warning, a great burst of flames shot up from the front of the cabin and almost immediately spread around one side and over the pitched roof.

James bolted across the last few yards of old plantings dividing him from the cabin, crying out to the others, "Run! They'll be burnin' inside! Oh, Christ Jesus!"

John rushed behind him, his axe raised high over his head. At the cabin he slammed it into the door. Screams rose above the crackling of flames igniting dry wood.

James hurled his shoulder into the weakened portal, shouting, "Mama, Dilby, get up now! We're goin' to get you out of there." No further sounds came from the interior until the night air was split by a sharp, agonized yell, and a rhythmic muttering that rose finally as a shout in Dilby' deep voice, "Oh. Lord, help us!"

Martha ran to circle the cabin in panic. She braved the heat and slipped over to the window and laid her sack of gunpowder on the ground beneath it. The front door had not given in to James' and John's efforts. Martha reached into the mouth of the sack to grasp a handful of powder, then stepped backward, dribbling a black line away from the wall about fifty feet long. Her whole body shook violently, causing the line to wobble from side to side. Striking a long wooden matche against a stone, she lit the end of her line and watched it fizzle towards the wall.

Voices rose in keening wails from inside the cabin as John and James continued to force the door, their grunts and gasps a percussive ostinato.

The explosion under the window knocked Martha backwards. She fell against a small boulder and stared over in a half-daze at the disintegrating wall before her. All sound had ceased, but a large, smoking figure seemed to float out of the blaze, pushing a smaller one with slowly flailing arms before it. The arms glowed with tiny flames, like candles, licking up from the sleeves. Martha could not move or call out. She felt as heavy and solid as the stone behind her head. The dark figure wrapped its arms around its flaming companion. Both dropped to the ground and rolled away, just as the cabin's roof collapsed. Martha could see her brother and John stumble back from the inferno.

After a few moments, Martha was able to hear again. She recognized Dilby as the dark figure shielding a smoking bundle on the ground. The black woman coughed and staggered to her feet, lifting the limp shape up in her arms. In the chilly air, smoke and steam rose from them both as Dilby fled across the garden.

Martha finally was able to call out, as though from a nightmare that had deadened her vocal chords, "James! Come help!" She pushed her weight up from the ground with trembling arms and moved in the direction taken by Dilby across the hardened planted rows of the garden.

The noise had roused sleepers in the farmhouse. The back door crashed open when Abraham dashed out. Negro men were running down the road from their cabins, carrying blankets and pails of water.

"Who the Hell is out there?" Abe yelled. He slid to a halt on seeing flames that exploded from the side of the cabin, and three figures silhouetted in the firelight.

"My God, she's gone and burned her own place down!" he exclaimed, then ran to the huddled group. When he saw John standing close by the other two figures, he exclaimed, "That's it, you crazy Nigger! You couldn't stay out of trouble even when we let you go to Mister William's place! I hope you like cuttin' sugar cane!"

James turned, tears streaming down his soot-blackened face. Abe stepped back in astonishment.

"Shut up, Sir!" James said, glancing around. "And where's my dear lovin' Aunt Sarah...Uncle?"

Before Abe could respond, James bolted after Martha, whose back was disappearing in gloom behind the burning rubble. She almost stumbled on the stooped figure of Dilby, who had paused in her flight with Elizabeth.

"Help me, chile'! We got to get mama to the cold water in the creek! Take her legs now." They both staggered forward again with the gray, smoking figure of Elizabeth between them. They tumbled down the bank of the creek, Dilby dragging Elizabeth like a large rag doll into the water. She lay down with her, supporting her head with the crook of an arm as the water rose around both. Martha stood near them in shallower water. Her feet could have been freezing in the flow, but she felt nothing.

A wedge of moon appeared in a break between stormy clouds just as James arrived at the scene, his eyes darting wildly from Dilby to the almost submerged Elizabeth. Martha beckoned him with one hand to come closer. He waded carefully up to the dark tableau and bent to look at his mother. Kneeling in the water, he pressed two fingers to her neck, and bent his head to listen for breath from her cracked lips. The acrid, sweet odor of burning hair rose from her head. Elizabetrh's face was horribly burned, but her eyes looked up at him with clarity of recognition.

Dilby leaned closer to the one undamaged ear and whispered, "Dis cool take away you pain, Lizzie."

Elizabeth opened her mouth, now a lipless gap. Her hand lifted from the surface of the water to try to touch James' face. Then she turned her gaze toward Dilby and gasped with a rasping hiss of sound, "He'll make it... all right, Sister." Her eyes rolled back as James fell to his knees in the water, wrapped his arms around the two women and wept, holding them both in a final embrace.

Martha poked frantically at Dilby's shoulder, "Come on, we got to get her up to the house so James can do his doctorin'!" Dilby just kept cradling Elizabeth like a large doll. James again pressed a finger to his mother's throat to feel for a pulse, and shook his head. Martha looked up, sensing a vibration in the air that swirled about them. It strummed against the hidden membranes of her ears. She felt faint. It was as if she, Dilby, and her brother were being bound together by an invisible force that threatened them with extinction, as sure as the fire that had burned the life out of her mother. It was a fearful, evil force, yet impossible to grasp.

Dilby threw her head back to wail, "Plateye...You think you won now!"

"Plateye?" James repeated. Oh, good Lord, Dilby. Not that now!" He looked down the course of the creek's flow to see where it disappeared in a sharp curve into the dark trees of the pine forest. This was the same creek he had so loved when a boy. He wondered if the rope still hung from the tall oak that grew beside the water's edge. That time, too, had been cursed finally with pain and the sense of some secret evil.

Abraham and John arrived in a wagon pulled by the same horse that had carried John earlier in the night. With James they lifted the body of Elizabeth carefully into the cart and headed back to the farmhouse. As the wagon passed by, the Negro men still beat the remaining flames with blankets, or hauled water to douse the embers.

On arrival, the three men carried Elizabeth into the farmhouse and lay her on blankets in the main bedroom. Martha spoke softly, almost in a whisper. "Mama, You're lyin' there just like before Daddy died."

Dilby knelt by the bed to pray. Finally giving in to exhaustion and her smoke clogged lungs, she fell sideways to the floor.

It was only then that Abraham really looked around to see where Sarah might be. Leaving James, Martha, and Dilby to mourn in privacy, he went quietly and began a search for his wife that lasted until daybreak.

When Abe returned, the sun had just topped the pecan trees to the east of the house. Exhausted and cold, his coat and trousers still were wet from the night before. He went immediately to the front parlor and fell on the horse-hair couch, pulling his wife's patchwork quilt to his chin. Abe slept sporadically, dreaming of death by fire, hearing all over again the sobs of Dilby and Martha, and seeing the angry figure of James swinging an axe from side to side as he came toward him like an angel of death out of the Old Testament.

"Abraham!" He awoke to his name being hissed close to his ear. It issued from the mouth of a wild-eyed stranger who looked uncannily like his wife, Sarah. She was bent over him as he lay on the couch, the skin stretched tight over her cheeks as if she had been fasting. A deep furrow between her eyes accented the sense of manic energy that hovered around her upper body like a quivering halo. Abraham pushed himself up onto an elbow. Of course it was Sarah, but her mouth twitched at one corner. Her apron was torn at one side as though it had caught on a nail or branch. Her lace-up shoes were dirtied with blackened mud.

When she took a step back from him, she thrust her hands behind her back. "I've been to the church, Abe, to ask the Lord's help with Elizabeth and the black witchery of that slave of hers."

Abe looked at her in disbelief. "You've been gone all night, then Sarah? You didn't hear nothin' of the fire last night?"

Sarah backed further away as he walked toward her. "I seen aplenty! That fool woman finally set fire to herself. Maybe the Lord heard me after all!"

Abe looked at her in horror, grabbed both her shoulders, and shook her angrily. "More like the devil, Woman!" Sarah jerked her hands out from behind to steady herself. Abraham had backed her up against the wall dividing the parlor from the hall. With a scream of agony she brought both hands forward, her body bent to shield them.

"Let me see your hands," Abe ordered, and grasped her wrists. Red, swollen, and blistered, Sarah's hands were terribly burned, oozing fluid at his touch. Tears streamed down her face. For the first time in months Sarah looked to her husband for compassion. He turned away, flinging his arms out to the side to refute her claim. "You weren't at no church last night!"

Chapter 30 — Judge Gilpin

By the time William reached the Flynt River, heading for the home of a farmer called Silas Baker, he had questioned and pondered on the images of young Martha Allen that had begun to plague his dreams. She really wasn't at all like Elizabeth, either in looks or temperament, the woman who had ruled his imagination for years.

Lizzie, with her delicate, porcelain skin, her blue-gray eyes, and Titian-colored curls now flecked with silver. Lizzie, whose mind would suddenly sweep into poetic images whenever she looked out a window at the golden summer scenes around the farm. Or burst into song with Dilby and her children, when they were younger. Now all of that had been twisted and crippled by the stunted, self-righteous hypocrisy of a frontier church and the people who filled its pews. Not just that, but the loneliness and sorrow of widowhood had drained all Elizabeth's former vitality.

And here was Martha, tall and strong like her father, but with gray eyes and light brown curly hair. Her sharp intellect and persistent refusal to accept any defeat had finally spurred him to action . She possessed a wit and wicked sense of humor that was very much like Drewry's. William laughed aloud, remembering Martha's mimicry of Sarah one afternoon as they were straightening up after school hours. He had slumped at his desk in front of the classroom, muttering, "Goddamn Marshall twins got the brains of a turnip!"

"Ohhh! The Lord goin' smite ya, Mister McDowell! An' if he don't, I'll be his messenger. I surely will." With this, Martha had swung her dust cloth in the air like a whip. Then she stamped up to him, still swinging the cloth, until she gasped and stooped in front of his legs and began to wipe the floor with rapid strokes. "My Gawd, jes' look at all these little demons tryin' to creep up your legs! The devil's goin' to get ya!"

William burst out laughing at the memory.

In spite of William's plan to return to the Allen farm in a couple of days, he was delayed by the peripatetic travels of the judge. George Gilpin, despite his rather stout, heavily muscled body, managed to run through legal hearings and pronounce judgment in record time. He generally left each location after two days and moved on to new territory. Oftentimes he neglected to tell anyone where his next court would be held. A week had passed by the time William had located him, and succeeded in convincing him to shortcut his pre-arranged circuit.

The judge was relaxing after a noon dinner with his most recent plaintiff, when William rode up to the yellow farmhouse about a quarter mile east of the river.

William was tired and breathless as he walked into the dining room to confront Gilpin.

He turned the rim of his hat nervously in his hands, while looking into the judge's eyes. "Sir, my name is William McDowell from south of here in Monroe County. I'm the schoolmaster at the Field School near Reverend Hope's Baptist church, and a good friend of the Allen family."

"I know the church and I've heard of your school as well. What's drivin' you so hard and so far from home?" Judge Gilpin hated to be disturbed after a heavy meal, but sensed some desperation in the man before him.

"Judge, Elizabeth Allen's been feelin' poorly since her husband was killed, and her relatives have taken to shuttin' her up like some demented idiot. She's a prisoner on her own land. These same relatives aim to take her farm and disinherit her children through plain greed. Truly, I fear for her life right now." William opened the leather sack that was bound crosswise over his shoulder and chest, and drew out a thin envelope.

"What have you got there, son?" Gilpin asked, interested now

"These papers be the first section of Drewry Allen's will that his daughter managed to find. I think you should read them aloud to the family as soon as possible. James, their oldest boy, has returned from studyin' to be a doctor in France. He wants to settle this right now, before his mother dies."

The judge took the papers and glanced at the opening paragraphs. William rocked nervously from foot to foot as the older man read.

"Please, Your Honor. I truly am afraid we must hurry."

As William and Judge Gilpin rode along the southeastern trail, they could glimpse the brown waters of the Flynt River, just visible from time to time through the thick undergrowth of evergreen laurels and creeping ivy. The waterway meandered calmly nearby, shadowed by tall dark pines, red oaks, hickories and sycamores. The path itself was almost choked by laurel and sumac bushes that reached hampering branches across their way. This was a scarcely traveled short cut south that badly needed clearing. The two men finally neared the forest's edge and kicked their horses into a canter.

A half hour later, stopping to give the animals a brief rest after a long gallop to the southeast, William leaned forward to pat his mare's neck. He breathed in deeply of the fresh, pine-scented air, before revealing his strategic plan.

William had to present both the problem and the opportunity to the judge. First, he would present the picture of the greedy relatives, highly respected by the Reverend Hope and his congregation, who were trying to disinherit the distraught widow Allen and her children. Then would come the subtle promise of future gain.

William began, "Judge, I know you to be a fair man, and you know I have the papers with me to prove Drewry Allen's intentions from his unfinished will. You know he was murdered on his own land last spring." After Judge Gilpin nodded his head solemnly, William continued, "I believe a judge as upright and fair as you are needs to set these things straight. In fact, it would only be in the best interests of everyone if you had a proper, dignified place to work out such disputes in the future."

Judge Gilpin glanced warily over his shoulder at what McDowell might suggest.

"Yes, Your Honor, "I have invested in property to receive just such a judicial building nearby my school."

Gilpin studied William through narrowed eyes. "Now that's mighty interestin' son. Why would you be buyin' land right now?"

"Well, I'm willin' to help set up a proper courthouse when the new town and county seat are established. And I hear that should be happenin' right soon. There should be a legal, decent place for you to hold court."

The judge nodded once more, folds of flesh pressing down against his chest. He glanced sideways at his companion and chuckled: his belly responded with gentle waves over his belt. "Just how do you intend to help me with that, William? You goin' to cut down your forests and bend your back buildin' a courthouse for me?" George Gilpin did not believe much in the generosity of frontier folk that rested under his jurisdiction.

"Well, Sir, I got the land. Yes I do, and I would dearly like to give it to help bring law and justice to this part of the county. You think you've got the fortitude to handle the holy Mister Hope and his friends?"

Gilpin smiled. "Mister McDowell, I do indeed honor these holy men, but nobody evah claimed to scare the bejesus out of this old man. Don't you worry."

It had been a week since the burial. Sarah had been moved to the Reverend Hope's house for safe keeping until the magistrate's arrival. Mr. Hope had insisted that he could not allow a good Christian woman in his congregation to be incarcerated by the sheriff in some drafty jail cell—even if the community had one. James had been required to dress Sarah's burns, which he did, washing the injured area carefully with cold water before spreading on a layer of lard as Sarah screamed in pain.

"God damn you, Auntie," he chided between her loud wails. "Can you now think on the pain of our Mama, with burns like these all over her body?"

Sarah turned her head away from him toward Reverend Hope. "You see what I have to deal with here? This whole family is mad. This man is as crazy as his ma. Right now I'm even a bit worried about the state of my Abe."

James leaned forward and spoke softly into her ear, "Ever hear of a haunt called Plateye, Ma'me? Watch out, 'cause he loves to burn up murderin' women and bury them in cold swamps!"

This provoked loud wails and shouts of righteous indignation from his patient. Sarah began to wear even on the nerves of the good preacher himself.

"When did you say William McDowell was bringin' that judge, Mister Allen?" James noticed that the preacher usually looked at some spot to either side when addressing him. This time he scratched nervously behind his ear while asking his question.

"Soon, soon, Mister Hope. He's comin' to settle Papa's will, but I'll be sure he sees to Aunt Sarah. Don't you worry."

The sun had come out after a cold, misty morning, as James made his way across the road and down toward the barn. His mind reeled with all the conflicting issues that circled each other and waited to be addressed. How could the farm be maintained if he had to take his baby to Augusta and deal with the deceptive Frenchman he once admired so much? How was he to be fair to Abraham and yet banish Sarah from their lives?

Where were William and the magistrate? It had been almost two weeks since McDowell left. Would the property be settled in his and the other children's favor? Would Dilby and baby Young be safe here, if he left to set up a clinic for Chauvin? James took a deep breath and smelled the damp hay and steaming manure that lay in piles outside the barn, waiting to be hauled off to cover the fields for the winter months. The mixture of odors had a sweetness to it: decay, fertility and nurture all together.

James found Dilby in the barn seated on a stool, holding a tiny kitten wrapped in a piece of flannel. Nan was standing beside her, anxiously twisting her hands while her mother tried to feed the kitten drops of milk from a cotton nub. After Dilby handed the kitten to her daughter, she smiled at James and began to stand. Instead, James sat on the floor next to her.

"Go on out with your kitty, Nan," he urged. Nan walked to the double doors and turned when he called out to her, "See if Miz Martha can find a place to keep it for you."

Dilby said, "I don' believe my eyes, seein' you so tall and straight, Mistah Jim! My Lord, you be a man now for sure."

James touched her arm. "You know I wouldn't even be walkin' around if it hadn't been for you. You're the one set me on healin', Dilby, and I thank you with all my heart." He dropped his chin to his chest to hide tears that flooded his darkly circled eyes without warning.

"You need some time to mourn, I know. You done lost wife and mama all at once, it seem. I swear that little bit o' magic I gave you don't want to be doin' its job, do it?"

James looked up at her to recall, "I put it round Chloe's neck after she died, Dilby. To...to take care of my wife when they slipped her body into the ocean. I guess it had done all it could for me."

Dilby nodded slowly, "Where yo' wife come from, Mistah Jim? Was she a French lady? Or was she someone you met at de school up north?"

James rose to his feet and extended a hand to help Dilby up. "Could we take a short walk down yonder? I'd like to see what's left of your old cabin, and we could talk there by ourselves. I got a lot to tell you. Now Elizabeth's gone, I feel like you're the only mama I've got."

"You hush now, Mistah! That ain't no good kind o' talk aroun' here, you know!" She followed James out of the barn and down the road toward the old swimming section of the creek. The burnt-out remains of her cabin lay along the way.

As they walked, the sun disappeared behind clouds that swept by, and the day was cold. Ground fog still dissipated above the treetops, and left a frosty silvering on the grasses beside the road. Their breath steamed before them. Dilby pulled her shawl more tightly around her shoulders, sheltering her hands in its folds. James thrust his fingers into the narrow pockets of his jacket and stamped his feet, before they moved toward the blackened chimney at the side of the road. He was shocked at the desolate skeleton. Bare vines twined around rocky stumps of the old walls and crept over a few dark planks fallen from the cabin's roof.

Dilby stooped to pick up a shard of crockery. "I used to wash Josh in this bowl when he was just a bitty baby." With a shake of her head, she added, "I sure miss my boy. You think he still be livin'?"

James leaned against the base of the chimney and looked up at the tree that rose at least twenty feet above what used to be the window frame of the cabin's main room. "I saw him ridin' off like all hell was chasin' him. Josh must've thought you and Nan were burned alive in this fire. I thought so too, until I got home that summer and Pa told me what he had done. I heard nobody ever caught Josh, so maybe he's just bidin' his time somewhere. I sure hope so."

He looked at Dilby. "Josh sure was fond of Chloe, too. Chloe's the sweet lady I married. She lived with the headmaster at the academy in Augusta. Taught me French and helped Josh get real good at readin'."

"That's mighty strange in a young white woman. Where she from, Mistah Jim?"

James glanced sideways at her and hesitated before answering, "Chloe came from New Orleans, Dilby. She was sort of kin to Monsieur Chauvin, who ran the school."

"Mistah Jim, how come she died so young? I know she must a' been lookin' forward to meetin' Miz Allen and seein' the farm." Dilby stepped closer to James to look into his eyes. "I heard from Clemma that her birthin' didn't go right. Was that what killed her?"

James explained to her, "Chloe had bleedin' that she didn't want to tell me about. And she really was scared to come here. She hated the idea of runnin' slaves on the farm. Didn't believe it was right somehow, I guess."

Dilby nodded and turned away to recall, "You still remember the day you cut yo' toe and walked up to this porch crying yo' heart out?"

"I never forgot the spider web bandage you fixed for me, Dilby. It was the first time I started thinkin' about you as some kind of magic doctor."

"Yes. Lord, my Pa started teachin' me when I was jes' a tiny girl like Nan." She tucked the pottery shard inside her shawl. "Mistah Jim, I'd sure like to help some with dat baby of yours. Do he favor da family, you think?"

"Yes, but he has his mama's hazel eyes, and I think his hair will have some red to it, like hers. He's mostly bald right now. I'm bringin' him from the McDowell place this afternoon. Pretty soon, Clemma's goin' to need a place for herself and her boy."

"She can stay with me jes' as soon as I got a cabin again. I suppose she be in the main house, near de baby until then. My Nan would love to watch over Clemma's boy for her. I'll jes' come on over tomorrow an' see how li'l Young Drewry's doin'."

James smiled at her. "I'd like that very much, Dilby."

Chapter 31— Plans and Plans

W hen Dilby came to the back door of the farmhouse the next day with
Nan, Martha welcomed her into the family kitchen, where she was
working with Callie to sort out the pantry for the winter. Each crock of grain
needed to be checked to see how full it was, and Martha had to write out
orders for refilling their stores from the mill. Sacks of dried beans were placed
on the higher shelves. They had pulled up the trap door to the cold cellar to
place sacks and barrels of root vegetables beneath the floor. Martha welcomed
the work. Any quiet moment allowed memories of the night Elizabeth died
to sweep over her; the thought weighed her down with a heavy grief, and
brought a flood of tears to her eyes.

"Dilby, bring that little gal of yours over here please," Martha asked. "She
can help Callie while I'm introducin' you to our new baby boy." She turned
to Callie. "I think little Nan could sample some of those cookies you fixed
this mornin' if she works real hard, don't you?" Wiping her hands on her
apron, Martha led Dilby into the hall and back toward the small bedroom
she herself had used when still a very little girl. The room was across the hall
from her mother's and father's old bedroom, where James had settled over
the past week.

Clemma was bent over a cradle that had been salvaged from the attic and
cleaned for Young Drewry. Dilby walked over to stand next to Clemma and
look down at the squirming baby.

"Clemma, this here's Dilby," Martha said. "She raised all us Allens with
Mama, and she's just dyin' to see my nephew."

Clemma stepped back. "I's heard of you, ma'me. This here is my boy Julio."
Dilby was startled to see a pair of eyes peeking from behind Clemma's skirts.

"Come out, now, boy. Come on and shake hands with old Dilby. Don't
you know I loves a little boy more'n anythin'? When Julio dared to step out
from behind his mother, Dilby grabbed him up in a great hug, lifting him off
his feet and pressing him to her bosom. Clemma smiled and relaxed. She had
feared being subjected to the older black woman, losing some of the benefits
of a primary nurse to the new baby.

When Dilby finally lifted Young Drewry to rest his head on her shoulder,
she sat down in the rocking chair next to the cradle. Martha leaned down
to her. "James wants you to meet him down by the barn when you finish
here. There's plenty of time, though. He's busy workin' out plans with Abe
to rebuild the cabin."

Dilby rocked the baby, stroking his soft head with the palm of one hand.
He was not content to go back to sleep, however, and jerked his head back to

look up at her face. She laughed and set him facing her on her knees, gently bouncing him up and down.

"Will you look at this little boy, Miz Martha! He minds me of Stokes a bit when he was first born. Couldn't wait to hop down on his feet and start runnin' aroun' with his big brother. Learnin' to walk first was jes' too much trouble! And, my, he's got the prettiest golden shine to his li'l face." She paused, and tilted her head to examine the baby's fingers and toes, murmuring softly, "Yes sir, you come a long way li'l man. Longer than you'll ever know, Baby. We'll make sure of that."

❧

Dilby found James talking with Samuel in front of the barn. She waited quietly until Samuel ducked his head and went into the barn, carrying a thick role of papers under his arm. James turned and beckoned her forward with a smile. "Do you think my son will do, Miz Dilby?"

"He's mighty pretty, Mistah Jim." She chuckled wickedly. "Almost too good lookin' for this family, I swear."

James nodded agreement. "His mama was as beautiful. She was so frightened for him, Dilby."

Dilby nodded and took his hand in both of hers, then leaned close to whisper in his ear. "We'll take care...She wouldn't ever have to worry. I knows when a secret keeps a life safe in this world, Chile."

James put his arms around the old slave and pulled her to him, resting his head on top of her graying one. When he stood back, he gazed at her for a moment before suggesting, "Dilby, how would you like to help me set up a clinic in Augusta? We'd bring Nan along, of course, and I have a debt to pay to my wife's guardian there. Chauvin claims I owe him for my education. I owe you more, and need you. I'll train Nan in nursin' too. Might be she could be a free woman one of these days and it would come in mighty handy for her to have healin' skills."

"You'd leave your baby with Clemma?"

"Only for the first few months. When he's bigger I'll ask you to come back here and get him for me. I 'spect Martha and William can keep an eye out on things while we're gone. William still has to get back here with that magistrate first, and I have to deal with Abe and Sarah.

❧

The skies were pouring down rain as two men rode up to the fence that bordered the front garden of the Allen farmhouse. Their wide-brimmed hats drooped over their heads, front and back, giving the impression of two headless horsemen with long necks.

Judge George Gilpin had been muttering curses for the last few miles as he rode, the seat of his pants making a sloshing suction against the saddle that aggravated him tremendously. William had taken to leaning far forward in the saddle to ease the burden on his horse's back, and thereby eliminated the percussive saddle smacks on his posterior.

The travelers climbed wearily down from their saddles and immediately sank ankle-deep into the red mud of the road in front of the house.

The judge's voice rose loud in complaining, "This sure as hell better be worth it, Mister McDowell! I could be settin' right now at the widow Brooks's front parlor in front of a warm fire and sippin' a cordial. I still don't see why you're in such a hurry."

William grimaced and shook his head as he put a sheltering arm across the old man's shoulders. As they stumbled up the path, James heard the two men and came out on the porch to welcome them. A waterfall cascaded from the roof that overhung the front steps, pouring down the collar of the judge before he could scurry through and into the house. Inside a fire smoked in the fireplace as its flames tried in vain to catch an updraft.

"You thinkin' of buildin' an ark, Mister Allen?" Gilpin jested as he shook out his hat.

James ignored his remark to call out, "Martha, will you fetch the children please, and ask your uncle Abraham to join us here in the parlor. Tell him Judge Gilpin is here to talk about Papa's will."

Martha disappeared to the back of the house.

Gilpin looked around the dark room, then asked, "Mister Allen where be Elizabeth Allen? We'll need her here to verify papers that Mister McDowell showed me."

"Mamma's dead, Judge. She...she died when the cabin back yonder burned during the night a few days ago."

"Dead?"

"She'd been forced to sleep there ever since the good people hereabouts decided she was demented."

Judge Gilpin slumped into a large chair next to the fireplace. "Dead, you say! Good Lord, how did this happen?"

William staggered backward as though struck by some invisible force. His face paled, and he threw one arm up to cover his eyes. James went to his friend and laid a hand on his shoulder.

"Sit down, William. We buried Elizabeth several days ago up on the hill next to Pa. This was no accident, Judge. If anyone will listen to her woman, Dilby, it will all come out. Poor Abe is half out of his mind with all this, but I'll let him tell you."

Martha came in the room with Stokes and Emily. She motioned the children to the long bench that rested along a wall by the fireplace. They took their seats silently, looking up at the new arrivals from bowed heads, and hunching their backs as though fearing new horrors to be revealed. Emily shivered in the cool room and wrapped her arms around her chest. Stokes pulled himself up to a rigid posture, his arms folded in front of him, gritting his teeth so tightly that the muscles in his jaw visibly twitched.

William McDowell stood, his head lowered, and spoke in a scratchy voice. "I...I'm goin' out back." He left the room and disappeared down the center hall.

Martha said, "William, it's still rainin'! I'll take you up to her grave tomorrow..

"Leave him be for awhile, Martha," James urged. "He's already wet through and through, and needs to grasp what's happened."

Martha remained at the arched entry to the parlor and gazed down the hall.

Judge Gilpin cleared his throat, picked up his brief case. "Could we all go into the dinin' room, Martha, and lay out these papers on the table there? And where's that Abraham Allen got to? He needs to be here as well."

Everyone moved to the dining room across the hall, taking seats around the table. Just then the front door crashed open, as though from a blast of wind. Abraham stumbled into the hall. He wore no coat, and his hair was plastered down across his forehead. Turning his head to the left, his glance roamed the table, fixing on the judge at its head.

"You all can do what you want to," he muttered. "I'm through here. I'll never build on the land I agreed to buy from Drewry. Just let me take my Sarah home to Carolina. I'll do anythin' to get her out of here." His words were slurred a bit and he rocked from foot to foot as he stood in a muddy puddle he had made on the floor.

"Set with us awhile, Mister Allen," growled Gilpin, gesturing toward a chair next to him and across from James. "There's more here to talk about than the disposition of land adjoining your brother's. We may have a murder here, so you'll have to convince me your wife is not involved, or at least so damn crazy that she didn't know what the hell she was doin'. Abraham joined the group at the table, then lowered his head. The judge spread out papers in several piles.

"I've looked at these already, and the only way Abraham and Sarah could claim ownership or guardianship over this estate would be if James was still in Europe, unavailable to his younger brothers and sisters and unreachable by legal authorities. Since he's sittin' right here and has reached majority age, with a child of his own, and is recognized by his mentors to be qualified to treat the sick and infirm, I don't think anybody really needs another guardian."

James nodded, and glanced at the still rigid Stokes, who sat next to him. What could he do for this normally quiet boy who looked ready to kill someone at a moment's notice? Stokes trembled slightly from the tension in his body.

James looked across the table. "Abe, you kept this farm together after Papa died. I thank you for that, and I'll see you get back any money you invested in the land next to us. But you let Aunt Sarah take away our mother. You let her run wild here. Drewry always said a man's got to take responsibility for an unruly wife, even when she's gone crazy like yours. I tell you, it makes me damn mad that you all convinced everybody around here that my mother was the crazy one. I'm not thinkin' about payin' any more for your time here."

Emily wiggled in her chair and wailed, "I want Mama back. Get Aunt Sarah to bring her back if she took her away!" Martha pushed back her chair and drew Emily close, almost in her lap.

"Hush, Baby. Mamma's with Jesus now."

The little girl sobbed, "No, no Sissy I don't want Jesus to keep Mama!" Martha left the room with Emily and passed William coming in from the kitchen area. She reached up to caress his cheek as he went by.

Abraham leaned back in his chair. "James, I don't want none of your money. Just let me take care of Sarah and get out of here."

Judge Gilpin nodded and passed a sheet of paper for Abe to sign, relinquishing all claim to the Allen property. "Where is Sarah bein' kept now," he asked James.

"Reverend Hope's keepin' her locked up at his place, Judge Gilpin. He says he'll be mighty pleased to see you over there."

"All right then..." Gilpin pushed back his chair to stand up. "If you all can give me a blanket and a place to lay my head, I'll stay the night here and visit your good Mister Hope tomorrow."

That night the rain stopped pouring and diminished to a misty drizzle. By dawn the skies had cleared. Chickens in their coop waddled out to search for worms and insects caught drying in the early light. Inside the house, Martha wakened to the cries of Young Drewry, wanting Clemma to put him to her breast. Dilby came out of the barn, where she and Nan still slept until their cabin was built. She carried a bag of corn seed for the chickens and tossed it through the fence, where the fowl eagerly clucked and scrambled. A rooster crowed in delight and flapped his green and red-feathered wings.

Dilby leaned against a post to rub her lower back. *Lord! I sure don't want to go up to Augusta draggin' my poor little girl across this country again! I'm jes' tired out with moving around, even if I don't have to slog through forests and swamps on foot this time. Someday I'll take James up on his offer to give Nan her freedom, but not right now.* The slave still breathed with difficulty. Smoke from the fire had left Dilby gasping; now she began to feel herself an old woman. *James could get Mistah. William to teach Nan here, couldn't he? Who would have to know beyond people livin' on this farm? What if Josh comes back?* Dilby half hoped he wouldn't, but if he did she wanted to be here. She nodded as she thought, and resolved to talk to James again after this nasty business with Sarah Allen was finished. *If James has to settle with that old Frenchman in Augusta, he should leave the baby here.* She would see to Young Drewry just as she had cared for James himself. Maybe someday she could help him set up a healing place here-about, not so far from the farm. She would think on it while he was up north.

Chapter 32— The Trial

When the Reverend Hope tried to escort Sarah from the back bedroom of his home, she cowered on the side of the bed, rocking back and forth as she clasped her knees.

"Now, Miz Allen, it's time to meet with your nephew and the good Judge. They've come to hear what you have to say about the fire in that cabin behind the farm."

Sarah pulled herself up by holding on to one of the bedposts. She seemed to transform herself in front of the Reverend, straightening her skirt and standing tall. She walked to a chest of drawers, took up a comb and hand mirror, and began to assemble her wild, gray locks into a bun at the back of her neck. Pinching her cheeks, she turned to walk past Reverend Hope with regal dignity. As she entered the pastor's office, she noted that two men stood facing her from the fireplace to her right. A dark-cushioned chair was placed in front of a desk that backed up against a heavily covered window. The drapes were pulled aside to allow some light to filter into the room from the clear morning outside. This was a place she knew well from previous chats with her pastor, but it looked darker to her now—more forbidding.

"Good mornin' gentlemen." Sarah smiled. "I'm so happy to see you, Judge. I swear it seemed like forever waitin' for you. I'm sure all this tragic misunderstandin' will be cleared up with your fine legal mind here to help." With that she motioned the men to sit down on straight-backed chairs at each side of the fireplace. She would show them that she could command here, as though she were the lady of the house.

"Madam, please sit yourself down," Gilpin ordered, then continued with solemn dignity, "You must realize that you are under suspicion for arson and murder. If there be a misunderstandin', it will be my job to find out about it."

Sarah glanced over at James, wondering what she could discover from his face and stance. She sat on the edge of the pastor's brocaded couch and tucked her hands under her arms. James remained standing. Judge Gilpin sat opposite Sarah on a straight-backed chair with elaborately carved legs.

Gilpin asked in a low yet firm voice, "Miz Allen, I would like to see your hands if you please."

She shook her head vigorously from side to side. "You...you can't! They're all bandaged up from the burns I received tryin' to help that crazy Elizabeth."

"Hell, Woman..." James half stood to take a threatening step towards her.

Sarah drew herself back, "Don't let him touch me! He's as crazy as his mother!" She turned toward the sofa's curved arm and tucked one knee up on the cushioned surface.

"Now, Miz Allen, your nephew is a doctor and can safely remove the bandages to let me see where your burns are. I can discover what caused them. It's a mite curious that you have no other damage from the fire, besides on your hands."

Sarah glared at both men and twisted further away.

"Sarah..." Mr. Hope intervened, stepping up behind her and gently grasping both of her wrists. "Sarah, the Lord will protect you and reveal his truth. I must insist that you let James remove your bandages. No one will let him harm you."

Amidst reluctant sobs and bitter curses called down on the men, Sarah held out her hands. The process of healing had begun, but her burns still oozed clear fluid from a large area of infection above reddened scar tissue.

James withdrew a small metal container from his pocket. "Mister Hope, does your wife have a bit of lard for us? I'd like to mix this paste of rhubarb root with it to spread on Aunt Sarah's hands, before we bind them up again." James gently traced a pattern of the burned skin with his index finger. "See here, and here? A fluid carried the fire. The burned area flows down her wrists. Papa wrote me that he found an empty crock of coal oil after the first fire that burned our Dilby's cabin to the ground. I can see flowin' oil doing this to these hands and wrists. Is that what you used, Aunt Sarah?"

"Get away from me, James!" Sarah shrieked. "Who do think you are, talkin' to me like this? Abe and I saved the farm while Elizabeth whined and poked around. And you! You so smart and all, runnin' round with French hussies, and pretendin' to learn about doctorin'! Why, you should be down on your knees thankin' me and Abe!"

James whirled away from her in fury and pressed his hands against each side of the doorframe leading out of the parlor.

George Gilpin scratched his beard thoughtfully and confronted Mr. Hope. "Reverend, why in the world would Sarah Allen, with the help of members from your congregation, I'm told, take it on herself to lock up a free widow lady in a little old shed? It's all mighty, mighty confusin' to me."

Sarah answered while standing and backing away behind the sofa. "We did lock Lizzie up, Judge, on account of she was crazy and dangerous! She might of been under a curse from that black witch, Dilby.."

James retorted, "That 'black witch' you so all fired scared of was another state away, at my aunt Candace's place."

Judge Gilpin continued his questions. "Reverend, were you knowin' what was goin' on?"

Hope first stuttered in denying any connection with the events on the Allen farm. "Lord, Judge, I...I been prayin' on that myself for...for months now! It seems like...like the very devil himself been...been twistin' people's minds." He paused to add a crafty disclaimer, "Why, I do believe some people started thinkin' real strangely after Sarah Allen took over handlin' the farm!" The pastor clasped his hands and closed his eyes. "God of us all, save us from the cruel doin's of women who scheme to divert Thy holy will in this congregation!"

"Judge, the fires on our farm began long before Sarah came down to Georgia," James recalled, as he packed up his bandaging cloths in a carpetbag. "Whatever my aunt did, it was from pure greed. The church folk have to answer for what goes on in their hate-filled minds. Take Sarah out of here. I don't care if she goes to prison, a mad house, or just poisons the rest of Abe's life in Carolina. But you, Mister Hope, you owe this family a lot. Next time you need help with somebody dyin' of fever in the church, and want some doctorin', think very carefully about your meanful preachin'!"

Gilpin rose from his chair and announced, "I'll be callin' court in session for all of these questions and the possible guilt of any parties involved. Let's try to start before this week is out."

The judge set about laying the plan for a hearing that same day. Within two more days he had convinced Reverend Hope to let him use his church to hear evidence and pleas from each side of the family.

The congregation of farm families eagerly waited for the opening day of legal events: this was a dreary time of year with little to distract people from late fall doldrums. When the day arrived, the yard in front of the church filled up with wagons and carriages. Some had come the night before, camping out in their wagons to be sure of securing a seat in the pews.

With the early morning light, people stepped out and started cook fires alongside their wagons. A light mist rose from the ground, well before the sun peaked above the surrounding trees. It then highlighted the whitewashed boards of the church's façade and a slightly crooked steeple above. Crows descended from the pines with loud caws and circled above family fires to scavenge scraps of bread or bacon. Gradually, soft conversations could be heard as men and women came fully awake and began to discuss the upcoming affair in court.

When the double doors opened, everyone hurried inside to settle in seats close to the pulpit. Judge Gilpin had ordered a desk be brought to the front of the middle aisle, where he laid out his books and papers. Two smaller tables facing each other were set up at each side. Sarah sat at the one on the right of the judge, next to her preacher. William sat at the other table opposite them. Abraham was in the front pew on the right side, sitting by himself. James and Martha sat with Stokes and Emily in the pew on the left. Dilby and John slipped in quietly and climbed the rough-hewn stairs to the low loft at the back of the church. Negroes were allowed to sit there, and a few others had come with their owners out of curiosity—wondering about the strange goings on with these white folks.

Gilpin banged his favorite gavel on the table and rapidly rattled off a legal prologue. It was not nearly as high-flown a speech as heard in the Savannah courts, but served its purpose.

"All right now. I'm callin' this court in session on the...what the hell day is this Walter?" He turned to his newly appointed clerk, who whispered the date in his ear. The judge turned back to the assembled audience. "Yessir, on this sixteenth day of November, in Monroe County, of the sovereign State of Georgia. Now, I propose to hear witnesses and arguments from both parties in this trial of Sarah Lynn Allen concerning the death by fire of the deceased Elizabeth Yarborough Allen." He looked toward Abraham and inquired, "I believe you have given me documents covering the most recent pages of Drewry Allen's will as well. Is that true?"

Abe and James nodded, then replied, "Yes, your Honor."

Gilbin went on, "And I assume Miz Elizabeth Allen died intestate, Mister McDowell?"

William rose to reply. "To the best of our knowledge, Sir. She was grievin' and not really well durin' the last year of her life. That's accordin' to her daughter, Martha Allen."

"We'll hear from Miz Allen at a later time. As I have appointed you the prosecutin' official durin' the time of this trial, you will be able to call her as a state witness."

William glanced nervously at the crowd from whom a jury had to be chosen; all were loyal congregants of Reverend Hope's church. Their faces seemed to shine with innocent amazement at the entire event. Perhaps the violence of Elizabeth's death would dim what he feared would be a religious bias in favor of Sarah. The pale and drawn faces of the Allen children in the front row did seem to affect many of the ladies present; they shook their heads and pursed their lips. Two or three even wiped a tear from their cheeks with white muslin handkerchiefs.

"Well then," Gilpin announced, "I need the nine gentlemen who volunteered to sit on this jury to come up here and be examined by Mister McDowell for the Drewry Allen family. Mister Hope is representin' and defendin' Sarah Allen."

James noted with satisfaction that neither the Aikens nor the Jones families were among the volunteer jury members. The nine men sat primly on a line of chairs set temporarily beneath the two windows behind the defense table. Judge Gilpin had followed through on his word to choose from the original group only volunteers who were the least familiar with the family, to sit and evaluate the evidence.

As the trial date had drawn near, James noticed that Abe became more and more distraught. When he finally refused to testify, James was disappointed, yet not really surprised. Dilby, as a slave, was considered an unreliable witness. It was the common belief that a slave either would say anything her master ordered her to say, or in any case, was lacking in moral reliability, due to her inferior status. William consoled his friend, saying they would do very well with Martha's testimony and his own verification of the events.

William looked over the names of the jurors opposite and jotted down their ages and occupations beside each man's name. They slowly came into focus in his memory; being a schoolmaster had its benefits.

When he stood and approached their table he smiled. "Mister Barnes, I believe your Chancy is workin' out real well with his new smithin' business. I'm not a bit surprised." Here he nodded his head and tapped his nose. "Always was a fast worker in school, and he could move mighty quick, too, when the bell rang."

Barnes began to chuckle, then sat up straighter and tried to wipe all amusement from his face. Mrs. Barnes smiled from the pews and fingered ribbons on her dark brown bonnet, folding the brim back from her face.

William addressed each juror in much the same manner, carefully assessing their responses to geniality, while he drew out connections with their children. Finally he nodded, smiled at the judge, and sat down, beckoning with an open hand to Mr. Hope to carry on.

The Reverend stood and walked to the center of the aisle, rested his thumbs under black suspenders, and would speak loud enough to address the entire room. Realizing he had a new audience, he turned toward the jurors' table.

"Now my friends, I say friends 'cause I think we are all friends in Jesus, are we not?" The jury as a whole nodded in unison. "Well, I don't know if you all are from close enough around here to have met this fine church lovin' woman. I mean Miz Sarah Allen sittin' right there." The group leaned forward to look at Sarah. Obviously they were not too sure about recognizing her from the few times they had come to church since the accused had arrived. The pastor shook his head and turned to Judge Gilpin.

"Your Honor, I don't think it's right to have complete strangers sittin' in judgment on Miz Allen."

"Mister Hope, that is just the point of their bein' chosen by me. This is supposed to be a fair examination of the facts by an unbiased group of Miz Allen's peers. No, indeed, I'll not allow a group of her own choosin' to settle this matter. Now have you any other objections to tell me about, Mister Hope?" The Reverend frowned and looked around at the gathering in the church to assess their reaction. He paused too long, and the judge slammed his gavel on the table exclaiming,

"This court is in session! Mister Hope you may proceed to tell the jury what Miz Allen claims happened on the night in question when Elizabeth Allen died."

Hope rose and turned his eyes upwards as though communing with his Lord for a moment. He then began to pace slowly, staring down at the floor. He stopped suddenly and looked over at the jury. "Miz Sarah Allen and her husband Abraham were summoned by Drewry Allen to come from up north to help with his poor wife, who had become spiritually weak, mentally confused, and unable to take care of her farm duties. When Drewry himself was killed, there were some who wondered if his poor wife might not have had somethin' to do with that herself—"

James jumped to his feet yelling, "How dare you, Sir! What the Hell do you..."

Judge Gilpin banged his gavel. "Sit down, James Allen, or I'll be forced to have you removed from this court! Never address these proceedings again without askin' my permission. Do you understand, Sir?" James sat and clenched his hands on the table.

"And you, Mister McDowell. You keep your client in line." The judge turned to a now-smiling Reverend Hope. "You, Sir, may not attack the victim in my court, unless you have witnesses to agree that Elizabeth Allen was ever suspected of hurtin' her husband. Do you have such witnesses?"

The smile faded. Mr. Hope answered, "Well no, not at this time Your Honor, but there have been rumors in this church about—"

Gilpin interrupted, "This court does not accept rumors, Mister Hope. This is not a ladies social for the bandyin' about of titillatin' gossip." Jury members chuckled. Gilpin banged his gavel for order. "Now, Mister Hope, proceed with your presentation."

I'm sorry Sir, it's just that I care very much about this Christian woman's good name and innocence." Hope turned back to his audience. "I just want you to know that Sarah was invited to come here. When she heard the complaints of the godly members of this congregation that Elizabeth Allen was becoming a threat, maybe even layin' curses and conjurin' black magic with her Dilby witch slave."

James began to tremble with anger, but remained silent, only whispering to Martha.

William stood and protested, I must object, your Honor, to Mister Hope's continuing to attack the victim with rumors."

Judge Gilpin nodded agreement. "I think, Reverend, that you had better leave off this now and bring witnesses to the stand when it is your time. We'll let the jury decide if there is any basis to these rumors. Now, do you have something to say about the night in question, when Miz Elizabeth Allen burned to death?" The jury gasped; expiring by fire was the most feared cause of death in this part of Georgia.

"I would just like to call Sarah's husband, Abraham Allen, to testify, your Honor." Hope ducked his head and raised a hand to fend off objections. "I know Mister Allen has stated he does not want to testify, but he is the only one who can say where his wife was during that night."

Abraham sat shaking his head and studying the floor.

"Mister Allen"—the judge leaned toward the man as he spoke—"you may not be compelled to testify against your own wife, but if you have information that you believe would be helpful to her, by all means you must step forward and share it with this court." Sarah turned to face her husband, rapped sharply on the table in front of her with a fan, and glared in his direction.

Abraham raised his head at the sound, and took a deep breath. "Your Honor, I...I...believe she was beside me in bed the whole night." He quickly dropped his gaze to nervously pick at his fingernails.

"Please step forward, Sir, to be sworn in by Walter Brooks here. We can't accept your testimony without you puttin' your hand on the Bible and swearin' you're tellin' the truth." Judge Gilpin gestured for a chair to be drawn up beside him next to his table. Abe rose, shuffled to the chair, and sat down, his shoulders hunched forward. Walter walked to Abraham's side with a Bible and asked him to place his right hand on the cover, swearing that everything he said would be the truth, the whole truth, so help him God. After Abe complied, Walter moved back to his place on the other side of the judge, laying the Bible down on the table to the judge's right side.

Mr. Hope approached his witness, hands clasped behind his back. "Mister Abraham Allen, you are the brother-in-law of the deceased Elizabeth Allen? Is that correct?"

"Yes, Sir, I am."

"Where was your wife Sarah sleeping the night of the fire? Was she beside you during the whole night?"

William stood to object. "Your Honor, if Abe Allen was asleep himself all night, he wouldn't be able to swear that his wife was next to him all of the time. Reverend Hope is asking for a conjecture, now isn't he?"

The judge nodded assent. "Yes, but you can clarify that when it is your turn to question Mister Allen. Go on, Reverend, but be more careful with your questions."

"All right now, was Sarah Allen next to you whenever you awoke during the night?"

Abe relaxed a bit and looked straight at the preacher. "Yes, she was next to me whenever I looked, but when I woke up, uh...I mean in the mornin', she was gone, of course, to take care of her duties before breakfast. That was normal for her, you see. I think she probably was there until the roosters started crowin'. I jus can't..."

"Mister Allen," Hope interrupted with a new line of questioning, "since we are all talkin' about fire here, hasn't everybody been talkin' about a whole lot of fires set around the county over the past few years? And isn't it pretty much accepted that poor Miz Lizzie Allen has been the one settin' them?"

Gilpin banged his gavel hard and warned, "That's just about enough of that, Mister Hope! I'll not have any more rumors and conjecturin' in this court. The jury folks have got to ignore what you're insinuatin.'" The Judge's face had become quite red as he spoke. He shook his finger at the jurors for emphasis.

Chastised, Hope explained as calmly as possible; "All in good time, friends. You will get to hear my wife's story of findin' a voodoo curse—"

"Sit down, Mister Hope!" Judge Gilpin actually rose from his chair and pointed to the defense table. "It's time to give Mister McDowell a turn here."

William stood and addressed Abe from behind the table. "Abraham Allen, when did you see your wife that morning? Didn't you have to search all over the farm to find her?"

"Uh...uh, yes sir, I did. I mean I did find her, but it was about nine o'clock in the morning by then." Abe glanced at Sarah and winced at the frown on her face. "She was probably tryin' to figure out what was goin' on, what with so many people hangin' around the burnt-out cabin and all."

"All right, so she wasn't around the house with you after you rose from bed, and she didn't appear until nine o'clock that morning. That's all I need from Mister Allen, Your Honor. Sir, I'd like to call the victim's son James to testify if I may."

James was sworn in next and sat on the same chair his uncle had left. "You are a medical doctor, James Allen, are you not?" William asked. "And you have recently finished three years in France studyin' all kinds of injuries and wounds. Is that not true?"

"Yes, I just returned to the farm a couple of weeks ago. I have had the privilege of workin' with the finest doctors in France, who treated wounded soldiers from Napoleon's army." James felt comfortable now, and thought he could guess where William was going with the next few questions.

"Were you asked to treat severe burns on Sarah Allen's hands after the cabin was destroyed by fire?"

James looked at the jury when he replied. "Yes, Sir. I did indeed see and treat my aunt Sarah's hands. The burns there looked to follow a flow pattern, as if a liquid had caught fire on the flesh."

McDowell continued, "And did you find traces of such an incendiary fluid near the sight of the burnt down cabin?"

James's pointed along with his reply. "That crock my sister is holdin' up over there. We found it tossed in the bushes a week after the fire. Look at the markin' on the top that states its contents."

Martha carried the crock over to the jury table and set it down before the men. A cloth tag, marked witha skull and crossbones was attached to a wooden handle, now almost obscured by brown and black scorching that had turned the pot itself black. One of the jurors sniffed the surface and shook his head before passing the container on.

Mr. Hope jumped to his feet to yell an objection, "Judge, how dare you talk of speculatin' and rumorin'! Who knows where this crock was really found! I object to McDowell usin' such tricks here."

Judge Gilpin flushed, yet held his temper and turned to James. "Doctor, you have sworn to tell all the truth here. Do you know this fire to be set by the use of coal oil? Could your mother have set it herself?"

James breathed in and out slowly to control the anger that threatened to turn his testimony into an attack on the judge himself. "Your Honor, the smell of coal oil was strong all around the ruined boards and the burned brush outside of the cabin. But my mother's burned body showed no traces of fluid-shaped burns like Aunt Sarah's did. We didn't smell any of that fluid on the interior wood remains."

Judge Gilpin was silent for a few moments, then consulted a pocket watch that lay beside the Bible. "I think we all need a recess at this point. I am going to ask you all to come back this afternoon to question Miz Martha Allen and a member of the congregation requested by Mister Hope. If you wish, Reverend, you may call Sarah Allen to the stand at that time as well." The gavel came down again. "Court's adjourned until two o'clock this afternoon!"

Walter Brooks looked at the judge with confusion for a moment, then shouted, "All Rise. Y'all come back after lunch like the judge here says."

❧

After eating a kind of winter picnic from baskets brought from home, people straggled in to the church a few minutes before two o'clock. Some had sat around the fires of the forge across the road from the church. Others visited friends at some of the near-by farms. Judge Gilpin decided to stay in the church building, munching on sandwiches that Martha had provided that morning. He did not want to appear to obviously accept the hospitality of either of the contestants by going to their homes.

When all appeared to have settled down on the benches, Gilpin called the court in session—banging his gavel on the table when the clerk seemed totally at a loss about what to do. He looked at both William and the Reverend Hope as he lectured the court

"This court is now in session and I want to hear from Miz Martha Allen about the night Elizabeth Allen died. I'm callin' her to speak and I don't want either of you men representin' the State and Sarah Allen to interrupt until I ask you. Is that understood? Martha Allen, please come up here and swear yourself in with clerk Brooks."

Martha handed her cloth satchel that held any papers she might need, her purse, and a small box of biscuits to Stokes, then rose from the bench and walked with measured steps to the judge's table. Her lips were pressed tightly together, her jaw clenched. When Martha placed her hand on the Bible and repeated her oath to the clerk, her voice quavered. She began to stammer, but quickly swallowed and gathered herself together. "I do swear to tell only the truth, your Honor, so help me God." The judge smiled at Martha and indicated that she should sit beside his table.

"My dear, I just want you to tell me exactly what you did on the night in question, what you saw and heard. I will allow Mister McDowell and Mister Hope to ask questions later."

Martha sat down, took a breath, closed her eyes for a moment, then began to tell her story: the agonizing approach to the glowing cabin window; her brother frantically beating on the cabin door with the axe; screams from the cabin; the final explosion she had set that broke open the wall.

"Just then, as I was tryin' to focus my eyes, I saw Dilby draggin' Mama out through the hole in the wall. Smoke was streamin' out from them both. She saw me and called out for help takin' Mama to the creek behind the garden lot."

Martha shivered, and clutched her shoulders with her arms. Down in front, Emily covered her face with her hands and began to sob, turning convulsively toward Stokes' shoulder.

"It's all right, Baby," a voice called out from the back of the room. All heads turned to find the speaker. Dilby strode forward down the aisle, her head swathed in a black turban and shoulders wrapped in a plaid shawl. She walked with a steady dignified stride to Emily's side in the front pew. Stokes had risen to his feet, shaking with a futile anger at the scene, furiously wiping tears from his cheeks. Dilby stepped between them both, drew them to her breast and sat quietly down with a crisp nod to the judge that she would keep order there. A wave of murmuring voices rolled up the lines of benches, then drifted into silence.

Gilpin tapped his gavel, but did not challenge Dilby's entrance. "Go on my dear."

Martha continued, "Dilby, there, tried to save my mother, but she was locked into the fire too. I wish you all could have seen her carryin' mama in the darkness to the creek. James and I followed. We...we heard mama's last words as she lay in the water."

Judge Gilpin asked, "Miz Allen, did you smell fluid, the coal oil kerosene at that time on your mama?"

"No, Sir, not on mama's clothes or skin, but the next day I smelled it for sure around the smoking boards. We found the crock the next day, when we were pourin' water on any hot embers around the cabin."

"And did you see Abraham and Sarah that night?" The judge scowled and held up his hands in a wide gesture of restraint; both Hope and McDowell had started to rise.

Martha responded, "We all saw uncle Abe, because he helped get mama inside the house and laid out on the bed." The young woman stood, swaying from one foot to the other for a moment, then stepped toward Sarah's table. Her body bent at the waist, as she shook a fist at the accused. "But I never saw you, Aunt Sarah! Not until you wandered in like some beat up old harpy that..."

Judge Gilpin stopped her with a clack of his gavel. "That's enough now, Martha. I want you to keep from addressin' Miz Sarah. Just talk to me or to one of these two gentlemen here." He motioned toward William and Hope. "Martha, I'm goin' to let you sit down now." While Martha returned to her place in the front pew, Gilpin glanced over at a pale and wild-eyed Sarah. He paused to wipe perspiration off his brow with a handkerchief, then summoned the pastor. "Mister Hope, you may call your witness now. I think it would be best to let Miz Allen calm down a bit before you do any examinin'."

"Thank you, your Honor. I want to call Miz Jones to testify."

There was a rustle of many petticoats as the petite figure of Lily-Anne Jones hurried from her seat down the center of the aisle. Her head bobbed as she walked and her bonnet slid forward, threatening to cover her eyes. Hope gallantly extended a hand to help her up the step to the podium and held the chair as she sat down. Mr. Brooks brought out the Bible again and swore her into the proceedings. Lily-Anne simpered and covered her mouth with one hand before adjusting her skirt hem and sitting up straight in her chair.

"Miz Jones," Hope began as he leaned over her. "I'd like you to tell this court about some of your first hand observations of the relationship between Miz Sarah and Miz Elizabeth Allen. Also you may, if you wish, describe the feelin's among the people of this church towards some of Miz Elizabeth's actions over the last few years."

William was quickly on his feet. "I have to take exception to this line of questionin', your Honor!"

"All right, calm down, Mister McDowell. I let Miz Martha speak freely, so I'd best let the Reverend have some leeway here for the moment. You can cross examine her yourself, after she speaks. Miz Jones..."

Lily-Anne complained, "Oh dear, I do wish I had Miz Aiken here beside me. She's so much better informed you know. I just will have to do my best, your Honor, and I do hope you will be understandin.'" The petite parishioner looked coyly at the judge and smiled, revealing a truly fetching dimple in one cheek.

When there was no response from Gilpin, besides a nod and cough, Lily-Anne proceeded. "Well, we didn't see much of Elizabeth after her black woman disappeared. Everyone thought ol' Dilby was kind of a witch, on account of her healin' young James's paralyzed legs an' all. You see, she hardly ever prayed with any of the black folks at church, I'm told, and mumbled somethin' fierce about some heathen spirits she called Plat-somethin' or other, and another called Gassi Gas I think. Anyway, when some fool set fire to Dilby's cabin she wasn't seen for years." Lily-Anne turned to face the judge as she continued, "We all thought she was all burned up and gone to Hell, Judge, and Mister and Miz Allen even made a grave for her up in their graveyard. Now, that's a might suspicious in itself, don't you think?"

"Go on, please Ma'am, and try to focus on your observations of Miz Allen after her sister-in-law came to live with her."

"Right, your Honor. Well, after Dilby done left, and Drewry was killed by some wanderin' Injuns, Elizabeth just went to pieces. If Sarah hadn't been there, that farm would have just fallen apart. Abe was good too, but Sarah joined right in with us all at church, joined every committee she could, and made sure the children and slaves minded themselves and their duties. Finally, she told us that Elizabeth was gettin' a mite strange in the head. She convinced us all that Lizzie seemed kind of dangerous, and that she herself was afraid to have her wanderin' around the property unwatched. She asked us to help her get Lizzie into that new cabin she had built. Lizzie wasn't too hard to fool as it turned out. When she saw us tyin' up Dilby to keep her away from interferin', she quieted down and walked right meek like into the cabin and let us lock the door."

"But I thought you said Dilby had disappeared, Miz Jones?"

"Well, yes she had, but by some trickery she returned a few months ago and almost drove poor Sarah out of her mind!"

At this moment Stokes pulled himself to his feet and yelled, "Aunt Sarah sure is out of her mind. She's been that way ever since Papa died. She went out of her head tryin' to get all Papa's land away." There was a grumbling from the group around him and some nodding heads.

A visibly annoyed Judge Gilpin tapped his gavel. "Sit down young man and control yourself! This jury's goin' to hear all sides of this story before makin' any decision. You ain't helpin' your brother and sister by yellin' out like this." After quiet was reestablished, Judge Gilpin turned to the witness again. "Can you give me anythin' else here, Ma'me? I mean, did Elizabeth Allen ever talk to you about her sister-in-law? Tell you how she felt bein' locked up?"

"Well no, you see none of us went to that cabin to see her. We was that afraid from what Sarah said."

"I plainly see that as well," Gilpin sympathized. "Poor woman was completely isolated and alone with no one to talk to exceptin' her servant Dilby. You may go back to your seat." Lily-Anne started to speak again, but the judge banged his gavel hard this time and dismissed her. She walked stiffly back to her pew and sat down, slamming her purse on the seat next to her."

"Did you need to cross examine this witness, Mister McDowell?"

William shook his head. "No, Sir. I think her words speak for themselves."

Judge Gilpin sat moodily quiet before glaring at Sarah and rising, "Do you want Miz Sarah Allen to take the stand, Mister Hope?"

Before he could respond, Sarah stood and lifted her hands above her head. Her low moan rose in pitch and volume to a shout. "God take the Allen family and burn them all in Hell! I am the just and righteous one here!" Flecks of foam appeared at the corners of her mouth as she ranted.

The judge leaned back, his mouth open in astonishment. "Mister Hope, I need to know your decision? Do you think it wise to put your client on the stand?"

The Reverend stared at Sarah for a moment of thought, then gave a slight shake of his head. "I think not, your Honor."

Gilpin's gavel came down. "That's all the proceedin's for today. Walter, you may dismiss this here crowd, but I want to see the jury bright and early tomorrow. I have a few words for them myself." With that he stalked down the center aisle and out the front door.

During the night there was a lot of commotion around the Reverend Hope's house. Lights glimmered from room to room; a neighbor complained the next morning that she was wakened several times; the pastor's wife fell ill with a stomach ailment after supper, and Hope was afraid to call James. Instead, he took her to the home of one of the older women in the congregation who claimed knowledge of healing herbs. In fact, the woman had picked up all she knew from Dilby, but hid that information with a fierce self-protective fervor. When Mr. Hope returned to his house, there was no sign of Sarah. Both she and Abraham had disappeared.

When the jury returned the next morning they faced an angry judge. The room was colder than the previous morning's session; Gilpin's breath steamed as he spoke. Clerk Walter Brooks hurriedly began stoking the pot bellied stove and blowing on the nascent flames.

After opening the court, Gilpin did not immediately sit, but faced the defense table to demand, "Mister Hope! Where the hell is your client? I trusted you to keep her safe after you declined havin' a deputy assigned to watch your house all night." The judge stalked back and forth as he spoke, his clenched fists fairly trembling.

The Reverend Hope swayed on his feet behind his table. "Y...your Honor, I...I just don't know what could have happened. Abraham stayed with her when my wife became ill after supper. I had to fetch a herbal woman at the last minute. The wife was givin' out blood and faintin'! It was almost like she'd been poisoned!"

The judge resorted to feigned sarcasm. "You mean you left the house and the defendant in the lovin' care of her husband?" By this time Gilpin's complexion was splotched with bright patches of red. He had started back to his seat when the doors at the rear of the church abruptly flew open.

James strode forward from outside, holding up a restraining hand. "Stop, please! Hold up your Honor!" James was winded as he reached the judge and leaned sideways against one of the benches to catch his breath. "This... mornin'...we found two of...of the wagons gone. Our two best mules with them."

Gilpin continued on to his table, where he sat scowling, arms extended sideways across its surface. "Looks to me as though these good people on the jury been cheated. But no sir! I'm deputisin' every man in this congregation now assembled to sweep out and find these two fugitives. The jurymen and male spectators muttered among themselves. A few started to rise. "Wait!" Gilpin waved his gavel. "Not before the jury meets and reaches a verdict. If the verdict is 'Innocent' then why did the defendant run away, I ask? No, that's not proper. But if you find Sarah Allen guilty of murder, I want her brought here to face this community."

"Your Honor..." Hope bowed to the judge with a certain elegance, to suggest, "If the jury finds Miz Allen guilty of murder, perhaps the sentence could be adjusted. That is, if she is found to be under the power of witchcraft, possessed, as it were. by some evil black spirit." Hope glanced slyly about the room as he added, "The court could bring compassion to its sentencing."

"Mister Hope, it's a bit late to be callin' a witch trial!" Gilpin slammed the gavel down and called out, "All stand! Walter, please escort the jurymen into the vestry room next door. I want you to stay right there, outside the room, until they say they have reached a decision on this case."

People milled about outside the church, talking quietly and casting glances from time to time at the huddled Allen family group waiting by the steps to the front doors. It had been cold, but the early December day was warming in the sunshine. Georgia days before Christmas were not balmy, but still held on to an autumn mildness.

The jury met for about an hour before returning to their seats in the main body of the church. When Walter rang the church bell, everyone filed back inside to hear the verdict. All eyes focused on a tall, thin man who stood to reveal the jury's verdict.

Judge Gilpin motioned for the man to step forward. "Mister Marshall, have you reached a decision on the guilt or innocence of Miz Sarah Allen?"

"We have, Sir. We find Miz Allen guilty of murder and likewise an instrument of the devil!"

Hope rose to protest, but the entire congregation began to clap and call out, "Oh yes, Lord!" He sat back quickly and waited until the uproar died down before standing again to address Gilpin. "And what sentence, Judge, would you and this jury wish to impose, if Miz Allen were indeed present?"

Before the judge could respond, Marshall exclaimed, "We want that woman hanged, your Honor.! In fact, we'd as likely see her burned alive, but don't hold out any hope from this court for that time-honored remedy."

Judge Gilpin struck the table with his gavel for a final time, "There'll be no Northern-style burnin' in this county, but hangin' the defendant is just. First I want to see all you men gather here in this room, first thing tomorrow mornin'. Bring horses and pack mules ready for a week-long search."

"What time, Judge?" a man called out.

"Seven o'clock sharp, y'all!"

As the families left for their wagons and buggies, Martha whispered to James, "I'd be willin' to venture a full wagon load of cotton that Aunt Sarah's taken off for the Aiken farm. She'll be hidin' there under the lovin' care of Miz Aiken and her husband! And they won't be lettin' anybody search their land without a real fight."

James surmised, "If they can hide out until March, when ice storms are over, they might make it north to the Carolinas. You know, I'd just as soon have that happen as see a hangin' in the family...even if it is a murderin' auntie." James noted a shocked expression on his sister's face. "Well, they'll probably find Sarah and then we'll have to take care of poor old Abe. Let's just wait and see."

Judge Gilpin's search party rode all over the county, but were unable to force their way onto private property without permission from the owners. Most of the farm people willingly let the men look wherever they wanted, yet some stood firmly on the principle that their land was sacrosanct and could not be forced open to the posse without proof that the owners were breaking the law. It was an argument that was not ready to be made by Judge Gilpin at that time.

By the last week in February the volunteers were tired of the hunt; a search was called off until possibly the late spring. Judge Gilpin swore to "keep the varmints out of Georgia," and promised to carry out a swift execution, whenever Sarah and Abe set foot in his district.

In March, James began to think about making peace with Chauvin, and to try to fill his obligations to the man. Before making final arrangements for a carriage to take him to Augusta, he composed a carefully worded letter to the man.

Dear Monsieur,

You must have been a bit anxious over the last few months, wondering about the outcome of my travel home to my family in Monroe County. We arrived safely, and my son fared well, in spite of the deprivation of not having a loving mother to care for and feed him. I am sure you will be relieved to hear of his health and well-being. Tragically, my mother was quite horribly killed in a cabin fire after we arrived, and there were countless issues to arrange for the upkeep of the farm and my sisters and brothers.

James decided that Chauvin would not care in the slightest about his family's troubles, so he continued to write in the cold-blooded fashion he would expect from his former headmaster.

All has been worked out in spite of our grief and mourning, so I am now ready to plan a visit to Augusta and help you prepare for the opening of your medical school and clinic. I will leave within the week and hope my trip will be uneventful, missing the river floods that sometimes hinder travel eastward, crossing the numerous waterways that can block passage. Hopefully I will arrive by the end of April.

How is your health these days? Have you had a recurrence of those symptoms I noted before we left Paris? I believe I have information concerning these matters and will discuss this with you when I arrive.

Please try to secure the names of local medical personnel for us, as well as the names and introductions to possible benefactors of the clinic. You once mentioned your affiliation and favorable contacts with the Catholic Church in Augusta. I gathered at the time that the Church was small there, but that there might be possible interest from the main diocese in Maryland, to sponsor a hospital, and by this good work spread the influence of the Catholic religion in the area.

I shall help you in the selection of beds and medical equipment, and will interview any personnel to service doctors and patients. This all will involve at least a year of preparation. I will be able to return for short visits to the city during that time, but, after this initial visit, will need to return to the farm and my family by June.

In my absence, my sister and my good friend, Mr. William McDowell, have agreed to supervise the spring planting season. Mr. McDowell's school duties will be suspended briefly during the spring, to release students to help with their family farm duties. He usually has them return to their studies for a final examination in June.

Until April, I will remain your obedient servant,

James Allen

❧❧

James immediately began preparations for his journey. After breakfast, one morning, he was surprised to find Dilby herself clearing the table. The children were getting ready for the wagon ride to school and had already left the dining room. Dilby stood beside his chair, with her hands clasped together at her waist.

"Did you want to talk to me, Dilby?"

"Yessir, please..." She tried to take a deep breath, but began to cough. The woman finally was able to breath evenly and began again. "Please, Mistah Jim. I'm not feelin' too strong yet, and my little Nan is beginnin' to feel comforted by bein' back here after our trek from Carolina. It jus' so hard to be packin' up again right now." She lowered her eyes to await his response.

"Lord, Dilby, I guess I'm only thinkin' of my own problems right now. But I really need you to help collect herbals for the clinic. You know more about what the forest holds than anyone I can think of."

Dilby smiled. "Come on down to the barn, cause I has a whole pile of things for you to take along to Augusta. And I sure mean to see dat Clemma knows how to take real good care of li'l Young Drewry. He gonna need somethin' more den dat silly woman knows how to do for him."

James sighed and stood away from the table. "Guess I'm still expectin' you to take care of me too. I'll come down and look through your magic bag of medicines before Friday. Guess I'll only need a horse for the trip now."

Dilby bent to gather up the tablecloth, folding in crumbs from the meal, and walked back towards the kitchen. Her back straightened as she realized at least one burden had been lifted.

"Mistah James, mebbe I can keep an eye out on Miz Martha and that ol' school teacher what seems to like hangin aroun' lately."

"You mean William McDowell? Well, I guess he's not so old, you know. I mean, fifteen years of advance trainin' might be just about right to take on our Martha."

Dilby muffled a laugh and left the room, "I know dat's de truth!"

❧❧

As Martha was to supervise management of the farm while James was gone, she told William that she would be unable to help him at the school. He once assured James that he would keep an eye on the orphaned family, and hoped to persuade Martha to help him correct lessons during some of the winter evenings, after the children were in bed.

James had replied at the time, "That's mighty kind of you, Sir." He suppressed a smile, adding "You surely will be dog tired after workin' with those children all day. I imagine you'd feel more like goin' right to bed after your supper."

William had looked sharply at his friend. "No, Sir, I tend to find your sister a right invigoratin' challenge. She's said she'd like to keep her hand in with the school work."

Chapter 33 — Angel of Death

Georges Chauvin looked like a very old man as he sat twisted in his high backed chair. The fingers of his right hand flicked aimlessly at his side, and he swung his head in spastic arcs from side to side, like a spider scanning its web. Monsieur waited for something, or someone, but it took tremendous effort to remember much about his immediate plans for James Allen.

The young doctor was pledged to appear in Augusta. A Greek Revival building had been constructed to house a medical clinic, but stood as a shell, with empty rooms and cubicles branching from the center hall like cells in a deserted hive. Furnished only with a chair and a desk, the room where Chauvin sat ensconced looked out a vast bay window onto a broad avenue leading into the center of town. Books for his entertainment were stacked on the desk.

Servants darted across the road from the school to check on the old man every half hour, and to bring him home after he gave up watching for new arrivals. The school itself had closed: rumors about the invalid in charge had circulated from plantation to plantation along the Savannah River.

Chauvin was only fifty-five years old, yet looked and felt like a very decrepit octogenarian. Two canes rested against his chair. Pillows puffed out behind his back. His trembling legs were covered by a wool afghan and silken quilt, even though a fire burned brightly in the hearth. He grimaced as he thought of James. It was less an attempt at a smile than a distorted leer.

A black woman entered the room, carrying a large basket on a stool. "M'seer, please. Cook sends hot tea and nice warm *petits pains.*" She bowed formally to the figure in the chair and called quietly over her shoulder, "Come on, now Sally. Don't you spill nothin' *depuis le croque!*"

A young girl followed, carrying a tray with silver tea service and copper pot. Her face, while a deep shade of *café au lait*, looked startlingly like Chloe's. Hazel eyes and tight auburn curls completed the resemblance. *Comes from some of my best breed stock*, Chauvin thought.

Both women set their tea services on the desk and began to fidget with Chauvin's pillows and covers. Afterward, they folded their hands and stood mutely before him. They both had been brought up from New Orleans along with a large crew of house slaves, to care for the man huddled in the chair.

"What...hour...is it...now, Jeanette?" Chauvin's voice was strong, although he spoke more slowly than months earlier, when he had stormed against James' marriage in Paris.

"It is eleven o'clock, Monsieur."

"Eleven, already? Ah, Jeanette, time passes and I am a poor shadow of myself, *un pauvre malheureux, comme mon père.*" The women stood silently, hands clasped in front of them, gazing out the window as their master continued, "*Oui,* Papa slipped from the step of a carriage. *C'etait terrible!* I remember his feet jerking and trembling. Ah...ah...ah...He struck his head against an iron hitching post. *Il était meme plus jeune que moi...*even younger than I...but mean... so withdrawn, always making enemies, even of his relatives."

Jeanette's glance slid towards the younger woman as she whispered, "De magrums. I tol' you 'bout dat."

Chauvin looked back at the slave woman and chuckled softly. "Jeanette, how *mon Papa* would have punished you after you spilled the sugar yesterday. That soft skin on your back would be striped today." He shook his head in remembrance. "*Ah non.* Papa was not mourned excessively."

Chauvin's health had taken a sudden decline into the same kind of invalidism he remembered from years ago in his father. Now the son moaned at the memory.

"*Allez vous en!* Get on with you! I wish to be alone now." The slave women silently giggled, turned, and scurried out of the door. *What might young James know of this illness? Surely, with all the training I provided for him in France he will know how to aid me with this terror.* "Alors, il faut garder cet homme." *I must keep a tight hold on him when he comes.* Chauvin tilted his head to gaze at the high ceiling above him. *This building hangs like a great rock over me,* he thought as his feet began to tremble once more, tapping the floor erratically. He refused to feel like an enfeebled Sisyphus, finally overcome. No! Now James would be his personal savior, healing his body and mind. The hospital could wait until he was cured. At this moment he felt the end of his life was imminent. A dark depression hovered over his former ambitions. Yet at other times he felt sure that he could be cured. Chauvin turned to look once more through the window, waiting in weakened impatience for James to arrive.

The Savannah River rushed by on James's right as he paused just south of the Augusta city boundaries. It was cold yet windless in the fading afternoon light. His horse blew out steam with a vibrating sneeze and a shake of its head from side to side.

James shivered at the thought that he could be facing the Frenchman in a couple of hours. Plans and strategies had occupied his mind throughout the long journey, yet the possibility of violence hid behind a lifelong training in gentility. He realized Chauvin had become a monster over the last couple of years, perhaps even slightly mad, but he also was a product of something

James had come to realize was evil at its core. No amount of doctoring could cure it. Fear and contempt for the weak and other different unfortunates, who became caught in a slave society invaded his mind. Slavery had been accepted in the world for hundreds of years; the status had blossomed in his own society in a new and colorful form. Beauty, love, loyalty, religion, and patriotism all coexisted with this evil, outwardly unaffected by it. James chuckled. *Dilby would close her eyes and curse Plateye.* He saw it more concretely for the demon it was—threatening to destroy the rest of his family, his child, and his life in the only home he really cared about.

Fog and rain began to creep over the riverbanks. A freezing gust, like a breath from an icy cave, swept around James and down the collar of his coat. He shivered from the wind, but also in remembering whispers in the trees from years ago, when he came down with a paralysis—the slithering presence in the trees that had threatened him as a boy. A seductive thought grew and pushed up from his fear of that distant time. *Join us, leave it alone, this is the way life was meant to be. You will become physician to the richest landowners. Just take care of the old man and lead the life your fathers set for you.*

What *had* he heard those long years ago as he lay immobile in bed? "You're mine, white boy." And who was it chased that voice away, bathed his twisted legs every day for a year? Leave it alone? Accept it and the likes of the Reverend Hope? Thrive on the power of hate and fear? He tightened the reins and kicked the horse's flanks to gallop towards the city of Augusta and Chauvin's new hospital on Telfair Road.

The following morning two strong men carried M. Chauvin across the broad avenue from the house to the entrance of his hospital. They hired out from a small community of free blacks in town, since his own slaves all were female and unable to carry his weight over even that short distance. The two women from the evening before followed, carrying pewter canteens of tea, a *panier* of fresh breads, and a brass seat warmer. The old man would need the warmth while they rekindled a fire in the hearth from the previous day.

The April sun shone brightly after the dismal rain that had poured all night long. With their eyes focused on the rough terrain in front of the building, neither the slaves nor Chauvin noticed a horse tied to the iron railing, nor the man standing in the portico.

James made a slight bow. "Good morning, Sir. You look in need of my attention, I fear."

Startled, Chauvin looked up from his hunched pose in the arms of the men.

"Put me down!" he ordered. "Wait awhile. I will see what this gentleman wants of me." He stood shakily at the bottom of the stairs squinting as he watched the newcomer slowly descend to him. James wore tight black trousers and boots. As he stepped down, he pulled a dark cape from his shoulders, revealing a brown homespun shirt belted at his waist. A wide brimmed black hat shaded his face from the morning sun.

"*Monsieur*, don't you recognize me? You've followed me across the ocean many times, and now I am here for you." Perhaps James resembled the Angel of Death to the old man, for he cried out in fear as the man rested a hand on his shoulder.

"It's me, James Allen. Surely you are pleased to see me. We need to discuss this...this mausoleum" James waved a hand behind him at the giant building behind him. "Let's go in. It seems you are prepared to do some work here."

"*Cak–cak...Qu'est-ce que vous cherchez?*" Chauvin crossed himself with a trembling right hand. "*Allez vous en, Prince du mort!*" he screamed in a high-pitched nasal scream.

James leaned forward to assure the old man that he was flesh and blood, not the Prince of Darkness and death. "Now, now, calm yourself *Monsieur*. Your eyes are deceiving you. *C'est vraiment moi*, James Allen."

"*Mon Dieu!*" Chauvin exclaimed. "Finally you come!"

As he was helped up the stone steps, the headmaster was forced to lean against the young man. His eyes darted furtively about as he ascended, as though looking for a possible escape. Chauvin remembered with sudden clarity the look of hatred in James eyes after Chloe was buried at sea, and the way he had clutched his baby tightly—to hold him protectively away from his great uncle.

Once inside the building, James assisted Chauvin into the library, or office, and settled the frail man into a cushioned chair. A fire already burned in the fireplace, and condensation on the windowpane had almost completely evaporated. Chauvin reached a shaky hand toward the silver tray beside him, but could not grasp the crystal stopper on the liquor decanter.

James moved quickly to the bottle, sniffed its contents, and filled a small goblet. 'It's early, *Monsieur*, for cognac, but, here, drink your potion if you must." He placed the goblet carefully in the man's hand. Sitting on the edge of a straight-backed chair opposite, James bent forward and looked intently at the quivering face before him.

Chauvin took a sip of cognac, then admitted. "I'm not well, James. Have the quakes." He laughed without mirth, while holding up one leg that wavered erratically. "I'll need your healing skills. After all, I paid for most of them."

James leaned back in his chair. "I believe my poor mother paid you a handsome fee for your efforts. Alas, she has died and left no proof of this. All right, you do deserve my help, but what of this supposed new clinic? This hospital?"

"We'll deal with that after I have recovered and can supervise your work here. First, what is this damnable disease of mine?"

"I frankly don't know. From talks with some of my professors, doctors at the hospital said that something like what you suffer occurs in some families. You'll have to tell me a great deal more about yourself and your family in New Orleans. I'll need to know all the symptoms and when each first appeared. And, of course, I'll need to thoroughly examine you, *Monsieur*. You seemed to have had a milder affliction when we met in Paris some months ago now."

Chauvin clenched his teeth in pain, then stared in anger at James for a few moments. Finally, he nodded his head, sighed, and drew a crocheted afghan off the arm of the chair and up to his chin. "*Oui, oui, c'est vrai.* I have been having minor problems for more than a year. *Mon père* had some kind of seizures, the same shakiness, but never so badly. That was before he fell from his carriage. Soon after, he died from a head wound received in the fall." Chauvin rolled his head from side to side. "Papa was much younger than I am now. Perhaps he was lucky to leave this life before this...this curse could get a hold on him."

James had pulled a tablet of paper from his vest pocket and begun to write. "*Monsieur*, did you know your grandfather? I assume he has gone to his Maker by this time, yet did you have the opportunity to witness his passing?"

"*Mon Dieu, tu es fou!* Fool, wha...what has this to do with me? Do you suggest that the whole family...that the family was poisoned by some hidden assassin?" James stood and walked to the window, tapping the edge of the tablet against his chin as he looked out at leafless trees on the boulevard.

"An assassin indeed. Before I left Paris, I talked with one of the finest doctors at *l' Hotel Dieu*. Back then Chloe was still confined in bed for most of the day. I sought his advice on many things, and indicated a special interest about inheritance of characteristics. Chloe and I were anxious about our son." James remembered his difficulty in broaching these subjects to the *mèdecin*. He was ashamed and embarrassed, yet felt driven to know if his child would show negroid features as he matured. He could never discuss this with Chloe. At that time he mentioned the strange symptoms he had observed in Chauvin at the café.

"*Monsieur*, You walked with a slight stagger in Paris. That was new to me, but I remember from school here in Savannah, your habit of tapping and flicking your fingers. That peculiarity had increased when we visited at the café."

Chauvin snorted his disapproval, "So, you mocked me. Mocked my personal gestures to your medical friends! Those were as nothing compared to my dis...disease! Is this what you call treatment? Ridiculing the ill?"

James moved to the old man's chair and gripped him by the shoulders. "Your disease, *Monsieur*, is passed on through the blood of families. Elegant, white, aristocratic families and destitute families in the slums of Paris, who have no way to hide their affliction. The good doctor did not know how, or why, or really what it is that strikes down its victims. But yes. You may indeed have had an assassin stalking you. Tell me, what happened to your grandfather?"

Chauvin tried to rise from his chair, but fell back under the barrage of frightening words. "Be Damned! *Mon Grandpère* . . .he was a brilliant man, a man of culture. *Distingué!* No one understood his passions. His own wife accused him of cruelty and dementia, only because of his methods of discipline. Yes, I knew him and emulated him! When he fell from his bedroom balcony, I knew it was her doing. *Grandmère* resented his great potency. But no one would listen to me! Dementia! How dare they, and how dare you? What are you saying? Do you pretend to treat me only to drive me insane?" Exhausted, a crooked smile slipped past Chauvin's lips. "If you are so sure about my family," he whispered, "take heed and think of your little black... your little...little bastard of a son. Even if he passes as white in your primitive society, he also has our blood. I laugh to think of the time when he swaggers with white friends and falls twitching to the ground!"

James flinched, wondering if Chloe's father, Chauvin's nephew, had also carried this disease. He reached for the absent leather bag that used to hang about his neck, but now rested at the bottom of the Atlantic. Chauvin's hoarse laughter obliterated any compassion he might have felt on first seeing the old man.

James insisted, "Young Drewry is Scots-Irish. Chloe brought good, strong blood to her son from her mother. Yes,"—James could not resist a jest—"she was part Chauvin, but African daughters seem to have survived even *les Chauvins.*"

By this time Chauvin had managed to get to his feet and stumble toward the fireplace. He grabbed a brass-handled poker and held it above his head. As he charged toward James, a high-pitched howl reverberated off the walls. The scream ended abruptly; saliva flew from his mouth when he landed a glancing blow on James' shoulder. The old man fell sideways, knocked off his already precarious balance by the force of his strike. His head hit the edge of the desk. Georges Chauvin fell unconscious to the floor.

James knelt beside his assailant and called out for help. Hearing no reply, he sprang to his feet and turned toward the door. Two silent, brown faces looked back at him. The women remained just outside the room, staring impassively at the scene.

"Quickly," James ordered, "fetch some men to help carry *Monsieur* to his home. Bring towels and strips of linen from there. Take my medical bag in here from the hall."

The shorter girl, who reminded James of Chloe, stepped forward and bent to examine Chauvin's face. Blood flowed from his left temple and across his eyes, trickling to the floor. James had both hands pressing to close the wound.

"Dis man goin' die, Suh. It's de magrums got him. *N'y a pas une raison* for livin' like dat." Then she half smiled. "We know some about you, Suh. *Monsieur* he talk wild-like when he think he alone. Time now for be happy, we t'ink."

James was stunned at her revelation, but repeated, "Go. Do what I ask. It's only proper for now."

The taller Negro woman entered again with his medical bag and set it down beside him. After James thanked them, both women left the building, not in too much of a hurry, and crossed the boulevard to the old school.

"You poor old bastard," James murmured as he cleaned the wound at Chauvin's temple. *Magrums.* He'd heard that term once or read about it. *Dutch, I believe.* He remembered Dilby's old stories of the good and evil spirits. "*Monsieur*, I think ol' Plateye's got you now!"

During the weeks that passed through the Easter season and after the first of May, when dogwood trees began to blossom, Georges Chauvin was confined to his bed. He drifted in and out of consciousness and the ability to speak. He did, however, write down for James to summon *Père* Jean Renaud. The French priest came often with two nuns to confer and pray with the old man. When Chauvin became well enough to speak slurred words with James, he asked only two things: first, he commanded James to outfit the main floor of the hospital.

"Use the slaves, James. They will do what they are told to do, or face the auctioneer. White scum around the city," he complained, "are hopeless for your work," "After I die, the hospital will go on. I leave it and this house, to God." Chauvin crossed himself shakily and closed his eyes. "I mean, *Garçon...* Boy...it goes to the Church. The Holy Catholic Church." He opened one eye and fixed James with a stern look. "But you must see that everything is established by then. It is part of our agreement, *non?*"

Unfamiliar as James was with the Catholic Church and final bequests, he nevertheless nodded, and bid the old man *adieu*.

By the last week of June, Georges Chauvin was dead; his tremulous body had finally stilled with a last exhalation of breath. The old headmaster had hoped that his gift of the hospital would pave a 'Golden road to Heaven,' but he had become apathetic in the last days, unaware of his surroundings, and looking quite lost as he twitched and thrashed his arms on the coverlet. Only in sleep was his body quiet—and it was in sleep that he died.

James had met with several local doctors during the final weeks, and began training Chauvin's recruited women in basic hygiene for clinical work. The late headmaster's estate furnished funds for the bare essentials, but *Père* Jean was granted enough seed money from Baltimore to purchase most of the additional equipment that James wanted. In addition, the diocese in Maryland donated the services of five nuns to work with him.

One afternoon, as James sorted through linen supplies on the second floor of the hospital, Sister Marie Clare, one of two nuns who had attended Chauvin during his last days, beckoned him to follow her. She stepped into a small vestibule behind the main desk and turned to whisper, "*Monsieur* Allen, please do not tell *Père* Jean that I am speaking to you about this." James nodded agreement and looked around to see if anyone was nearby. The nun advised, "You will be needing many more women to nurse the ill. You will need white women, who agree to work with slaves." James opened his mouth started to object, but Marie Clare touched a finger to his lips. "Listen first. I should not be recommending this, but I know of several Quaker ladies who would feel it a blessed duty to work here. They even accepted former slaves into their community north of town. If you wish, I will send them to you and let you decide if they are suitable."

James gently took her hand to reply, "Rest assured, Sister. I would be honored to meet with these ladies."

Sister Clare squeezed his hand. 'Then, doctor, I am delighted to have asked."

They both returned to complete a supply inventory. Each looked forward to an upturn in the hospital's fortunes.

The weather became unbearably hot by the middle of July, and heavy rains had left shimmering marshes around wooded areas, where mosquito nymphs flourished. When the insects took flight through town, people fell ill with a strange fever. Some thought it was the yellow fever, like an infection that besieged New Orleans every year. Even the horses sickened and died. A kind of encephalitis accompanied this new scourge.

The first patients had been admitted on the first day of July. They were greeted by new, white volunteers, who admitted them and installed them in the inspection area at the rear of the first floor. James and one of two other doctors waited to examine them and arrange treatment. These volunteers were members of a small Quaker sect, those left after a major emigration northwest to land that bordered a great lake north of the Ohio River. They worked alongside the black nursing staff with a calm respect that James noted with especial interest.

"Friend, you work well with my staff," James commented to Clarice Burridge, who sat at the admissions desk. "I especially admire the way you read my instructions to them without any hint of disdain for their ignorance." She blushed and acknowledged the compliment with a simple nod. "Is it true that your faith forbids owning slaves?"

"Dear Mister Allen...Oh, I am sorry. Thou would be Doctor Allen. We Quakers refraineth from formal titles, but thou certainly deserveth my respect."

James smiled and gave a slight shrug of acknowledgement. "It's kind of you, but please, Mister Allen will surely do for now." James sat on a chair next to Burridge's desk. "But do tell me about your faith and how you live with former slaves."

"Well, thou art correct, Sir, when thou sayest we accepteth not the local concept of slavery. Quakers believe that no man may own another. My group, or I should say our Meeting, have settled in northern Georgia, about ten miles northwest of Augusta. We taketh in new members from the free African community nearby." Clarice exhaled a breath and set one elbow on the desk top. "I confesseth, however, that more and more of the Friends succumbeth to the benefits of free black labor, to compete with other Georgian farmers and craftsmen around town. We see new black faces working on the Quaker farms, and we knoweth they are not free laborers." Clarice turned her head to look out the front entrance, past the thick Doric columns of the porch.

"Some thinketh now of splitting the community so that Friends who believe strongly in the dignity of all men can move to new lands northwest of here and set up another town above the Ohio River."

"You mean you may not be here very long to help us?" James tried not to reveal disappointment, or to seem to put pressure on his new Quaker "Friend." When do think you might depart?"

Clarice laughed as she stood to stretch her arms and back. After sitting for any length of time, she lately noticed stiffness in her back. *Ah well, at my age I need to keep these bones moving.* She approached her fiftieth birthday. Some strands of dark brown hair had sprung loose from the wrapped bun at the back of her neck, and she gently pushed them back from her temples. "Never fear, Sir, it taketh at least two to three years for all the arrangements. Some of our male Friends have traveled west to look at land, and work with lawyers and county officials there."

James nodded his head, pleased at what he had been told. "You have given me some ideas here. I need to think on them for a while, but I may have a proposition for you at a later time." After rising to leave, he turned and walked out on the covered porch to breathe the air and rest a few minutes.

When Monsieur Chauvin died, the hospital had ten patients filling beds at all times. More and more of Augusta's poor were beginning to show up at the clinic doors. Cholera from tainted water took away large numbers of the poverty-stricken residents of the city. Typhus was endemic. Diphtheria spread among children and adults as well, from tiny droplets expelled from lungs. Victims suffered a partial paralysis that frequently disappeared during the healing process. Heart damage from the disease would be revealed in later years.

With the recent Yellow Fever epidemic, James' staff was exhausted from the long hours of backbreaking work. Were it not for the nuns and Quaker volunteers, the new hospital would have turned into a crowded morgue. As it was, tents had to be set up in back of the building to take the temporary overflow of patients suffering from Yellow Fever. Summer in the South was a nightmare of pestilence this year.

James had convinced many of the city's doctors to donate one day a week to make rounds and tend emergency patients. Chauvin had left a large amount of financial aid to help the doctors feel more generous with their time. The local bishop had begun to take notice and started making plans for final acquisition of the hospital; James felt he could perhaps return to the farm in September.

He dreamed every night of his baby. Often times the dreams were frightening, as a demonic figure of Chauvin cackled, while leaning over the baby's crib. Other dreams included Dilby holding Young Drewry in her arms as she paced the floor and sang the song Chloe had loved so much. Usually the dream ended with Dilby standing still and looking straight at him to whisper, "Come, Mistah Jim. Ever'thin's holdin' and waitin' on you. Oh, come on home now!"

Martha wrote that the baby was thriving on Clemma's nursing, and that Dilby had taken over the rest of his care, "spoiling the child with constant attention and picking him up at the slightest sign of a whimper! I do declare, I don't remember her treating any of us like that. She acts like a grandmama!"

James chaffed at any delay in departing, but eventually found a wagoner willing to brave the journey west. Wooden bridges had been completed over most of the rivers along the way, making the trip less daunting for the travellers and their horses. Freight wagon companies had formed in Augusta by 1812, ferrying goods between the interior of the State and Philadelphia. They took in substantial profits from the beginning, and acquired an immediate monopoly. James took advantage of one of these. He packed two barrels of supplies from the hospital to take home, focusing again on a future clinic in the farm country.

Doctor James Allen passed the outskirts of Augusta as the wagon drove south along the Savannah River. The trip usually would take many days longer by wagon than on horseback, but with the new roads, a wheeled vehicle could make about eighteen miles each day. He planned to arrive at the farm in twelve or thirteen days or two weeks at the most.

On the journey, as the hours passed, James clung to a rope binding a heavy carton. It eased the side-to-side thrusts of the carriage on each turn in the rough road. His trip was a lonely. Riding in the wagon bed behind the driver, the heat of late summer beat James into an almost comatose state. His mind wandered through fragmented images of his life and loved ones. For the first time he wondered how little Nan was adjusting to her distracted mother, then remembered that Nan was not so little now. He also worried that his aunt and uncle might be agitating for legal redress to their imagined woes. James yearned to hear that they had somehow departed for the Carolinas. And what was developing with his friend William's hesitant courtship of his sister? Would the quiet scholar be able to handle the vigorous and slightly shifty Martha Allen?

James smiled to himself and thought that these problems were really minuscule compared to the storms of his life up until then. Young Drewry was safe, his future unthreatened now that Chauvin was dead. At least he hoped the tainted blood of the Chauvins hid no physical threat for him. The old man never had acknowledged the impurity that came from his white ancestry, and his family freely had mingled with healthy bodies of Africans and African Creoles.

As the doctor rode across rivers and through marshy woods around them, a caravan moved in the opposite direction, going northeast towards the Carolinas. Two wagons, pulled by one mule each, traveled only at night. During daylight hours the three occupants camped out in obscure valleys of the Blue Ridge Mountains. It was rough going as the trails winding through dense forests were undeveloped.

Abraham and Sarah were escaping north, aided by Aaron, an old black man lent them by the Aiken family. They hoped to set up some kind of home once more among people who knew nothing of the Allen family. Abraham was adept at surviving in the wild; he caught their dinners in the swift rivers that flowed from the Blue Ridge Divide.

Once out of Georgia they left the mountains and came down to the flat piedmont plateau in South Carolina. There, Abraham decided it would be safe to change the pattern of their journey and begin traveling during the day. That night, after a meager repast of rabbit, and fresh watercress from a nearby stream, he and Sarah bedded down in the back of the largest wagon. Old Aaron curled up in the smaller one. Their campsite rested not far from a swamp that was surrounded by a wooded area. There was no moon that night; the only light came from glowing embers of a dying cook-fire. Aaron pleaded with Abe not to douse the fire with water. He feared the area and wanted to keep any wild animals at bay.

"Lord," Aaron prayed, eyes closed. "Keep them haunts from us all. An' don't let poor Miz Allen wander off like she wants to do all de time." He fingered a sharp pole beside him that he kept hidden in an old potato sack.

Abraham tried to sleep, Sarah lying beside him. When she twitched violently, he reached an arm across her stomach to whisper, "Sleep now, my dear. Perhaps we may find a friendly homestead tomorrow and spend a night indoors for a change. But please rest here next to me this night."

Sarah said nothing for a while, then sat up with a frantic gasp. "Abe, Do you see yonder light in the trees?"

He supported his upper body on one elbow to look. "No, Darlin', there ain't a light anyplace but a dim one in the camp fire. Lie back down."

Sarah lowered herself on the bed of sacking, but lay rigid beside her husband. As Abe drifted into sleep, his wife watched and waited. When his breaths became even and she heard light snoring begin, she crept on all fours to the back of the wagon and lowered herself to the ground. She walked completely around the camp, peering intently into the woods beyond. *Where is it? I saw it last night like a lantern signal to come to it. I knew it would appear again. There it is! 'Way beyond those trees, gleamin' like a small moon, and blinkin'! It's a sign for me. Callin' me! It's the sign from God come to deliver me from all the evil everyone been conspirin' to bring down on me.*

When Sarah reached the first tree in the copse, she fell on her knees and mumbled, "I'm comin' Lord. Whatever you tell me to do, I'll do it. Just like after that dream you sent me. I knew you wanted Lizzie and that black witch burnin' in Hell, so I did what had to be done, just like you told me to. There weren't no reward for me there on the farm, but I know you got somethin' for me now. I'm comin', Lord!"

If Drewry were still alive and present he could have warned her. This was almost the exact spot where he had been bewitched by a deadly light from the swamp on his journey to claim his lands in Georgia. Now Sarah stepped carefully through the trees; the light grew stronger, yet seemed to move across sparkling water beneath it. It was like following a rainbow to find its source. The frantic woman kept walking toward the light. Her steps grew slower. Both feet seemed drawn into the sandy earth. Each step sank further into moist terrain. The light seemed very near now. She reached out an arm to touch the flickering edge of it, then took one more step.

Sarah screamed as the sandy forest floor sank below her. When she tried to pull her feet away, out of the suction of the grip, she sank more quickly. She whipped her head from side to side, trying to find a branch she could hold on to, but there was nothing there. She tripped and fell forward, but caught herself with her hands in the mud. They sank as well. She saw clearly that the light had gone, gradually disappearing into mist at the other end of the swamp.

Sinking into the mire, Sarah screamed out. "Abe! Abraham! God damn you, man! Get me out of here!" Her husband was just stirring awake. He cocked an ear to listen to a noise in the distance that sounded like the muffled cry of a fox. When he rolled to one side he discovered that Sarah was gone.

"Just like the night this all began. What kind of trouble now?"

At a heart-rending scream that drifted through the woods, he scrambled up and sprang off the wagon, then ran into the woods—toward a thrashing sound beyond the trees.

When Abraham arrived beside the edge of the swamp, he found only a scrap of white cloth torn from Sarah's dress. It had caught on a half-submerged root from a tree that long ago sank beneath the quicksand. He fell to his knees and reached an arm into the mire, groping for his wife. He touched nothing. Struggling to his feet, he rushed through the woods to the camp, hollering for Aaron.

The next morning the two wagons pulled away from the campsite, with only one figure on each driving north. A grieving Abraham had marked the site with a small pile of rocks at the edge of the swamp; he hoped to find a community with a preacher nearby to pray at the deadly site. There still were no inhabitants in the area. Farmers were not yet eager to try to drain swamps. Besides, there were stories of mysterious happenings near the tree line bordering the wetlands. Strange lights that some said were caused by swamp gas, frightened even the sturdiest farmer from approaching the area.

Abe lived the life of a widower for quite a while in North Carolina, finally writing to his family in Georgia several years later about the loss of his wife. He never explained anything more about her disappearance than to say, "The dratted woman just had to chase after any will-o'-the-wisp, long as it sparkled enough!"

Chapter 34 — Freedoms?

No one heard the coach drive up, nor James' heavily stamping feet on the porch. He stood in the central hall and whistled. A small, black face peeped out at him from the back archway into the kitchen. Julio stepped into the hall and waved shyly.

James said, "Go on, boy, and tell Mis Martha that her brother's here from Augusta."

After Julio hurried into the kitchen, a high-pitched scream of joy ensued. Dilby whirled into the hallway carrying Young Drewry in her arms. She stopped suddenly and held the baby out in front of her. "Lord, it's you're daddy, chile. Hold out your arms now."

James moved to take his son from her and swung him around in a happy dance, singing, "Shout Daniel, shout Daniel, shout all day! Fly Daniel, fly the other way..." He hugged the child closely and whispered, "We're free, Baby! You and me!"

Dilby overheard and laughed out loud, then sobered down with a shudder. She lowered her head and covered her face with her apron. James went to her, shifting the baby to one arm, and putting his other arm around her shoulders.

"I'm sorry, Dilby. The song you and Mama used to sing just jumped into my head. Forgot you might still be grievin' for her."

Dilby glanced up and shook her head, wiping a tear from her cheek. "Mistah Jim, it be more'n that. I'm real happy for you an' de baby, but I'm thinkin', what goin' to happen to my chile Nancy when I gone?" She collapsed slowly to the floor in front of him, guiding herself painfully on one knee at a time, and holding on to the edge of the dining table.

"Get up, now!" James ordered. "Don't you kneel to me, Dilby...why... it's like havin' Mama on her knees. Get up, damn it!" She looked up at him and sank back on her heels. "Lord, I don't want to be free. What would I do with it, Chile? I's tired...been livin' so long. I jes' soon be buried here. But Oh, sweet Jesus, I sure would like to get some learnin' for Nan, and get her somewhere she could breathe and live free. Poor Josh prob'ly dead by now, but I think he did run free for awhile."

James lay Young Drewry down in front of the old slave woman, and went down on his knees as well. "I been thinkin' on it, Dilby. There's some nice folks up near Augusta movin' out to new country in the west. They're takin' some Negros with them as free men and women. Call themselves Quakers, or Friends. I'll have to be goin' back up there from time to time. One day, about three years from now, after Martha and William McDowell finish teachin' my sister Emily and your Nan, you and me can just go to Augusta and see what we might arrange with the these new Friends." He took her hands in his and ordered with mock sternness, "Come on, Woman! Get up now and see what you can do with this soakin' wet baby. I swear he just about smells like a stable!"

Dilby climbed slowly to her feet, and bent to pick up the baby. She smiled at James before saying, "Mistah James, I wont be goin' to no more new places. No Lord. I'll need to be here waitin' for..." She did not continue, but James nodded. He knew she would always hope to see or hear something, somehow from Joshua.

❧

The winter months remained damp and windy, with ice layering the pecan trees in front of the house. William worked at the schoolhouse without Martha's help, for she was now the domestic manager at the farm. James handled livestock and maintenance of all the outbuildings on their land. He also began meeting with Judge Gilpin, William McDowell, and several local landowners about plans for a new county and town. Monroe County was being split to form the new Pike County, in honor of the late General Zebulon Pike. McDowell assured Gilpin that he remembered the promise of land for a new courthouse.

Young Drewry thrived in the care of his aunts and Uncle Stokes. Aunt Emily, at age ten, was allowed to rock the baby in his cradle every night, though sometimes she fell asleep herself in the process, and hung over the top rail of the cradle like a rag doll.

Clemma and Dilby managed to control their jealous tutelage without angry outbursts of possessive energy.

❧

Several hundred miles further south, across Georgia's boundary with Spanish Florida, thousands of Creek warriors and their families had migrated to the peninsula to escape the brutal repression; the disastrous treaty of 1813, signed in Europe after the war.was forced on them by victorious General Andrew Jackson. They joined members of tribes who had lived all across the forests of Florida for hundreds of years, assuming the name of the ancient dwellers who called themselves Yatsiminoli, or "free people." These people so cherished freedom that African slaves had been protected in their communities for over a century. The migrating Creeks sometimes brought their own slaves with them. Many were not happy with the attitude of the Yatsiminoli, but as immigrants, dependant on the native culture, they learned to change their ways, or migrate west to the Arkansas Territory.

Joshua was one of these "free people," who learned to fight with them in the first Seminole War that ended in 1818. They were never defeated, and Seminoles refused to bow to the American demands that they return runaway slaves to their "rightful owners." Joshua loved these natives with a burning passion, and scorned those who gradually acquiesced in removing themselves. As the years of violence progressed, the United States was ceded Florida by Spain in 1821.

༺༻

Joshua stopped to wipe the sweat from his forehead. He turned to check that his wife was keeping close behind him. Walini had fallen back, her steps slowing as the weight of a new infant pressed her back forward. Josh raised his hand to halt, in a signal to her and the rest of the village survivors. Dark Bear was gone now, killed in a battle with the white soldiers a few months earlier, and Josh had gradually assumed leadership of the small remnants of the village.

"Sit now and feed the child, Walini. We are so deep in this swamp today that enemy soldiers will die of heat before they find us." Josh lifted the reed cradle as Walini lowered herself to a fallen tree trunk bordering a path they cut through to brush.

"White skin does poorly here at mid day," she agreed. "Amoneeta was wise to advise this path." Walini took her son from his open weave carrier and pressed his mouth to her breast. Her head dropped forward while the baby nursed. She half-dozed, sitting and rocking back and forth on the log. Josh sat beside her to blow cooling breath on her face. When she looked up to smile at him, he marveled once again at the strength and serenity in her face. Black hair looped low over her forehead from a central parting above, revealing an elegant, straight nose that flared slightly at the nostrils. Josh thought her eyebrows were shaped like wings of a sea gull, where the arch of her nose met the skull. Beneath these wings her eyes glowed darkly, like burning coals from her lost village. *How did you come to love me? You, a chief's daughter, full of compassion for a poor black boy like me.*

After the baby slipped from Walini's breast, asleep and calm in her lap, Josh pulled a clay flask from his belt and raised its open neck to her lips. It was filled with juice from berries and palm fronds, water was dangerously fetid in the nearby swamp.

Walini held herself in a quiet inner space during the day as she stumbled through the humid heat, lashed by sharp branches. Only at night did fear creep into her consciousness as she and her infant hid high within the confines of tree branches. The cries of dying warriors, the screams of children as they were carried away from the dead into the southern wilderness; all these sounds returned at night, echoed by the nocturnal screams of birds and beasts around her.

Within the hour the group began their slow march again, the men hacking with sharp, curved swords stolen over the last few years from both Spanish and American invaders. By nightfall Amoneeta hoped they would find an island he remembered from a long ago hunt. He knew it would sit darkly within a forested swamp. He could see it in his dreams. Sometimes even during the day an image of it would float in front of his eyes as he walked with his people along the freshly slashed path. He pictured the island rising above water on ground that was a good bit higher than the low, insect-infested land they had been traveling across for the last few weeks. Amoneeta cast his auguries every evening with tiny shells found beside the dank waters, chanting and singing to the spirits of this damp land.

Josh prayed silently to the loving Eka Ghassi.

Walini followed her husband closely. She once more quelled her fear of reptiles that lay hidden in the ferns nearby, slipping back into her private, hypnotic sanctuary. Although Josh tied her and the child securely in the crotch of a tree each night, she knew there were monsters who could slither up to her nest. She banished the thought, yet resolved that this would end, must end for her very soon. They must stop, she swore to herself, and build a safe refuge where they could stay and keep watch. If the soldiers came, well, she was tired of running. It was time to settle, perhaps die, but she would find a final resting place with her child.

By dusk they had cut through a thick tangle of vines to find a fresh-running river that flowed into a swamp. A sigh of pleasure rose from those assembled on its banks: the water was clear and clean and flowed swiftly! It did indeed border a small island that rose about fifteen feet above its watery base. They discovered that the stream was about neck deep for most of the women struggling through it to the island. After dragging themselves ashore, they built a large community fire and camped around it for the night. It was too late in the day to hunt for food, so hungry children wept themselves to sleep, dreaming of fresh fish from the stream the next morning. Josh cradled Walini and his baby near the fire. He wrapped his body around them both, one arm beneath Walini's head as she slept.

The next morning the new camp whirled with activity. Mist hovered above the river as the campfire was revived and men cast bamboo spears into the water for fish. Breakfast was soon ready. Afterward, while the sun broke through the forested ceiling above the stream and sucked the moisture from the surface of the water, work began on a community lodge. Amoneeta sat on the bank and directed the laborers. He knew they must build the lodge on stilts above the water. It would house everyone at first, thus a lodge had to be large enough for twenty-five adults and ten children.

Warrior sentries were sent out to the north and east, where they were to hide in trees above the trail and scan the countryside for intruders.

By the third evening, the poles had been found, cut, and rooted deep in the mud of the steam. A platform was built above them with a vine-rope net woven to circle the platform and prevent children from falling off during the night. The women collected palm fronds and wove them together to form a roof. More poles, this time slender and lighter in weight, were cut to hold up the roof. These were secured by vines stretched from the tops of the poles to the netting that formed the circumference of the lodge. It was a beautiful house in the eyes of these Yatsiminoli survivors. Now any feared reptiles could no longer steal their babes away during the night.

Even during this frightening passage south, new migrants from the north kept joining them. New, smaller lodges appeared along the river. If one or two newcomers despaired of living in the tropical wetlands, they left for the north again, hoping to sneak back into the former lands of the Oconee people.

In the summer of 1821, one of the newcomers, a Maskoki warrior, approached Josh during the night. By this time the people had built many *chikees* over the water, up and down the path of the stream. They had carved slender boats from tree trunks to ply canals between the dwellings.

The leaders of the tribe met each night in the original round lodge. There they reminisced, planned the future, and prayed. Afterward, some of the men slept in the lodge until dawn, but most left to join their families. It was on such a night that Josh decided to leave the assembled sleepers around midnight and return to his small family. As he rose from his mat, the Maskoki approached him with some trepidation.

"Josiah, I leave tonight for the woods of Georgia."

"Hush!" Josh raised a hand to cover the man's mouth. He replied in the Yatsiminole tongue, "You're a fool to speak to me here of such a thing. None of us can afford to have a man captured on the trail out and reveal where we live. We'd have to kill you tonight to keep our village safe."

The man jerked Josh's hand from his face. "I go now, and pray you will not betray me." He drew Josh out of earshot, toward the far rim of the room. "I heard you have family people in Georgia. I can get there, don't you fear, and I'll take a message to anyone you wish."

"What if you're captured by the whites? What if you are forced to lead them to us? Maybe I had better kill you now."

The Maskoki nervously fingered a dagger at his waist. He did not want to start a fight that awakened sleeping men around them. He asked Josh, "Can

I take news of you to your mother? I know the land of western Georgia as if it were my own village. I can find anyone and never be seen there. If I'm taken, I swear I will die before betraying this place. I have taken herbs from Amoneeta's wife. She promised they would kill me in seconds."

The fire at the center of the lodge had gone out, and insects began to swarm in the fresh, smokeless air. No bird sounds broke the silence of the night, mostly grunts and croaks of amphibian life rose from the muddy shore.

Josh smelled the rank perfume of decaying vegetation mixed with the seminal odors of night mammals hunting mates and prey. He wanted to slip away on the tepid waters to wrap Walini and their newest child in his arms as they slept. He listened quietly, thinking about the white family who had sent him to Augusta, and who had suffered from his revenge. He wanted some one to know that Drew had died for the death of Dilby. "Friend, I have no family in the north." Josh looked into the man's eyes in a stare that forced them to flicker back and forth nervously. Stripping a piece of smooth bark from a pole at the entrance to the lodge, Josh carved his name on it with a sharp arrow point and inscribed "JOSH LIVES AND DREW ALLEN DEAD" beneath the names. He gave the bark to the Muskoki. "If you take this to the Allen Farm, south of the Flynt River, give it to one of the black women there. Tell her to give it to a James Allen It will keep you safe from our people here. They will think you are going further south to find more of your own tribe."

The man tucked the bark in a leather sack tied around his waist before climbing down to one of the wooden boats in the water below. He raised his hand in parting, then turned forward. As the craft slipped smoothly away in the darkness, Josh could hear the soft splash of a paddle. He waited to see if any of the sleeping men stirred, then stepped out of the lodge entrance and climbed down the supporting lodge poles into his own craft. It was now really over. James would know what he had done. An evil Plateye would be satisfied. It was time to seek Eka Ghassi, the goddess of kindness and love.

During the years that followed, soldiers of the U.S. Army fought doggedly to defeat the Seminoles, but never could probe deeply into the damp and fetid landscape where their enemy struck at them from the darkness. Life for the refugees was a constant struggle in the swamps, yet Josh and his survivors never despaired. They knew finally that they and their brothers, who had refused to be removed to the west, were the one faction of the Creek and Seminole peoples who would never surrender to the whites.

One Saturday morning in the spring of 1822, William McDowell rode through the pinewoods separating his homestead from the Allen property and tied his horse to the front porch railing of James Allen's home. All of Elizabeth's spring flowers were in bloom on either side of the walkway up from the road. Warming air was pungent with the scent of hyacinth and apple blossoms. Crimson and white azalea bushes crowded around the base of the house that seemed to float on a flowery carpet, as the last mists of the night dissipated in the morning heat.

William breathed deeply, looked up at the promising blue sky, and straightened his shoulders before pounding on the front door. Martha opened it for him and turned away with a slight smile.

"James," she called out. "I do believe Mister McDowell is here to talk with you." Taking William's hand, she led him to the dining room, where James sat drinking coffee.

"What's this, brother William?" he jested. "A mite early isn't it for this fine Saturday mornin'? Come set with me and have some breakfast. Martha, see if you can find somethin' left in the kitchen for Mister McDowell, please."

William held on to Martha's hand tightly. "James...I'd like Martha to stay here as we speak together. If you are pleased with what I have to ask, we'll drink coffee afterward. Or perhaps something more...ah...celebratory."

Martha blushed by this time. The woman swatted William's shoulder before pulling away and dashing out to the kitchen.

"It seems my sister is a bit flustered by you, William, or else she is afraid to hear what is about to be said. Sit down now and tell me what you have in mind."

William remained standing. "Martha and I wish to be married, James. I may be almost twenty years her senior, but she is a wise and fully-grown woman. I love her dearly. Thank the dear Lord, she is willin' to be my wife."

James smiled, arose from his chair and drew William into a warm embrace. "Now, Friend, will you sit here with me?" Martha reappeared in the doorway from the kitchen, hands on hips and her head cocked to the side. James beckoned to her. "Martha, I'm real pleased. Come over here now."

As she approached both men, her comely face broke out in a broad smile at what she knew the schoolmaster had proposed. She abruptly stopped near them, as though she had just found an impediment.

"William, we need to talk about Stokes. If I move to your home, I know James will have his hands full with all these children. Dilby and Clemma can take care of the little ones, but Stokes needs a firm hand and mighty big load of learnin' to take into his head before he's really grown up." Martha paced as she pondered the problems. "And of course there's the baby—"

William cleared his throat and stopped Martha in mid-sentence. He came to draw her to him and held her small hand for a moment. He had always marveled at a delicateness that belied the heavy work she insisted on carrying out. "You see, James, we want to help with the raisin' of this family. You've been away while Stokes was tryin' to handle losin' his pa, and now Elizabeth is gone as well. The boy's mighty prickly these days, fallin' into all kinds of sulks and dark moods. I'd like to set him up with so much hard work at the school, with a promise of gettin' paid legal time in the new courthouse with Judge Gilpin, that he won't have much time to brood. Martha's got a good strong hand with him, too."

James considered William's words and nodded his head. "Well now, how can I object? Between you all, everythin' seems to have been fixed and settled." He pushed back his chair and patted the one next to him. "Martha, you come here and set with us awhile. We have a wedding to prepare!" James fairly burst with pride. He felt for the first time that he was truly the new "patriarch" of his family. He laughed and kissed his sister as she pulled a notebook from her apron pocket to begin setting down her plans.

⛌

Martha and William both wanted the wedding in the fall, before the rains began and while the weather was warm.

"I won't go down the aisle of Mister Hope's church though, James! The wedding will have to be here in the front garden. And I don't want any of those church people comin'!" While William agreed whole-heartedly, James cautioned them and proposed a different plan.

"Let's have everyone here. Let's put on such a feast they won't be able to stay away! I want to set up Dilby as head manager, standing, Martha, in the greeting line with you and William. And let's have her dressed in a fine black silk gown with a white apron and turban! We'll just knock them all over with Judge Gilpin's plans for the new town. They won't know what to do first, so's they can get in on the best deals comin' down in the next few years. William, I think we can have a real good time with this."

MacDowell frowned at the plan. "I don't know, James. These people know we don't care much for their society...or their church. Martha won't have that preacher around at all."

"That's all right. You have to count on greed and ambition here. Now Martha, the wedding can be in the garden, just as you said. We don't have to go hat in hand to the pastor to use his church. I'll ask the good judge to preside. Reverend and Miz Hope will be invited though. That should curdle their skimpy blood."

As plans began to take shape for the wedding, James began to put together a notion with Dilby about setting up a rural clinic. It would start out there on the farm itself, but he would move it to the future town, in a few years time.

Dilby asked, "Who's goin' to come to this clinic, Mistah Jim? You goin' to treat black and white folks the same ain't you? How you goin' to do that in one place?"

James knew she was right in her not-too-subtle questioning. Farm owners treated most of their sick slaves, or did not bother to help them at all. The idea of a real doctor, taking both black and white patients in the same building .would be frightening to both clients—and downright unacceptable to most whites. He pondered the problem for weeks, planning strategies right up until the week before the wedding in October.

By the end of September the worst of the summer heat had passed. Invitations had been meticulously hand-lettered by Martha and Emily. Stokes carried them in a leather satchel to each farm and store in the area, riding his favorite sorrel mare and imagining himself a military courier on some important mission.

The wedding day arrived, bright and clear, with late autumn asters and every color of chrysanthemum in bloom around the borders of the front garden. A bower of saplings, still resplendent in red and yellow leaves, bent over the walkway in front of the porch. The bride and groom would stand there in front of the local church pastor. In the end, William and Martha relented on the subject of Reverend Hope, since James had need of a docile church leader to further his plan for a clinic.

Tables covered with white linen ranged across the grassy lawn to the right and left of the house. Women and girls of both races moved back and forth from the kitchen, carrying bowls of fruit and flowers to decorate each table. Others tied white ribbons on all the chairs.

At three o'clock on this Saturday afternoon, the carriages began to arrive, depositing guests from miles around. They were greeted by James with Stokes at his side. Dilby, dressed in a long, black silk dress, her hair covered by a cleverly wound white turban, stood slightly behind the two men.

Guests were directed to stand in front of tables set at either side of the pebbled path. Everyone became quiet when music from the parlor harmonium was heard. For two months, Emily had been practicing music for the wedding, and played a respectable march. James hurried around by the back entrance to meet a nervously waiting Martha and escort her around the house and behind the guests. She would make a grand entrance down the garden path. Stokes accompanied William to the bower, clutching his vest pocket and the ring it held, while they waited for James and Martha to appear. The Reverend Hope edged his way to the center of the bower from a hidden spot on the porch.

After a great deal of coaxing, Martha had given in to James' further arguments for a long, drawn-out revenge on the preacher. It would commence after the new town was firmly established. The Reverend Mr. Hope would soon find competition from a new source of spiritual guidance: James hoped and planned for a rival Baptist group to come out from Augusta and build a new church.

"Martha, these Baptist preachers are so wild, poor Mister Hope won't have a chance in hell of outperforming them," James had confided to her with a chuckle.

A gentle breeze stirred fall leaves decorating the bower above the preacher, and lifting his thinning gray hair enough to reveal a vulnerable bare spot on top of his head as he bent forward in prayer. With a Bible open in one hand, Mr. Hope raised his other hand when William stepped beside his bride-to-be. James stood back a step or two. Hope paused for several long minutes, as though communing privately with God.

"Let's move along now, Mister Hope," William whispered through gritted teeth, and a curt bow toward the man.

"Dearly beloved, we are gathered here..." The Reverend began with a start and ran through the opening of the Solemnization of Matrimony at a most irreverent pace. The two men standing before him had come to be intimidating forces in his tight congregational community; he felt a bit unbalanced compared to his usual self-confident pomposity. Gradually he slowed and began to repeat the well-known, traditional sentences with deep, resonant tones. "Forasmuch as William and Martha have consented together in holy wedlock, and have witnessed the same before God and this company, and they have given and pledged their troth to each other, I pronounce they are Man and Wife..."

William pulled Martha to him in a tight hug, shutting his eyes as tears blurred his vision. Martha burst into laughter and called out, "Emily, come on out here Darlin' and catch these flowers I'm about to throw!"

Everyone clapped and started to laugh, forgetting for a few moments the bitterness of the last few years. Emily burst through the front door, skipped around her sister and ran down the path in front of her. She did indeed catch the bride's bouquet.

∞∞

Later in the afternoon—after the feast of smoked hams, turkeys, yams, beans, and breads made from corn meal— just before William and Martha were to leave for the McDowell place, James stood at the head of his table and called for quiet, to make an announcement. He waved his arms above his head and called out, "Good friends, as you know William McDowell owns a large parcel of land where our new town is planned. He has said that he will donate not only the land for the courthouse, but also for a clinic to be built on the outskirts of the town. That way I can look out for the health and care of the sick in this community." He paused as whoops and exclamations of "Yes, Lord!" rang out from the tables. "You all know that I came home from France after several years of training with the best doctors in Europe. Why did I do this?" Everyone sat still and quiet. "Because I almost died once, and was paralyzed for a whole year. There was no properly trained doctor hereabouts. My nurse, Dilby, probably saved my life."

An expected silence pervaded among the guests. Most of the local people questioned the presence of the old slave woman who had a grave with her name on it in the family cemetery nearby. Mrs. Hope frowned and crossed her arms on her ample bosom.

James continued, "I have learned that her treatment is now highly respected among the newest practitioners of healing in France..." He paused as the sound of murmuring grew from those seated at tables. "It seems that it was some other poor folks, who died in that mysterious fire seven years ago. My daddy, God rest his soul, feared for the life of his loyal slave, Dilby. He sent her and her baby girl north to his sister-in-law for a while. He told me he planned to see who showed up looking guilty at the funeral we held for Dilby." Muttering renewed at the tables. James spread documents on the table in front of him. "Now, Judge Gilpin has some papers signed by Drew Allen explaining what he found out at that funeral." James rested a moment, absorbing the lie he had just put out, and looked around the gathering before adding, "There will be a proper time to go into that after the clinic's set up here. It will be mighty interesting to see who makes the biggest fuss about that."

"Doctor Allen," a young man called out from the farthest table. "What's this town of ours goin' to be called? You goin' decide that too?"

James was about to respond, but was interrupted by a growling voice from the back of the assembled guests. "You be sure an' keep likes to likes when it comes down to treatin' people, won't you?" The speaker, a lanky, bearded fellow from the road, leaned against a tree near a few men who had found no place at the tables.

James turned to his brother and said in a loud voice, "Stokes, please get the name of that gentleman over there and write it in my journal of farm expenses. I want to be sure and remember who he is." When the man turned and left, James continued calmly, "My mother, God rest her soul in heaven, remembered a beautiful little town in North Carolina she hoped our town would look like someday. I hear it was called Zebulon, named after a great explorer in the western territories. I would like to see our town with that name in memory of Elizabeth Allen, and her dreams for us. She died in great suffering not so long ago." He paused and looked down to remember "She sent me to learn to doctor you all, with great love in her heart."

Not a word was spoken after James sat down. A sense of collective shame had gradually risen over the fate of their Sister in Christ, Elizabeth Allen. Gradually, the guests rose from their seats and went to shake James hand, and congratulate the bride and groom. Most agreed that Zebulon had a nice Old Testament ring to it.

Stokes was kept busy on the Allen farm for the first two weeks of Martha's marriage to William. By that time James felt it was time to get the boy settled in the new household. Stokes packed his clothing, books, and tack for his new black gelding without much enthusiasm. James helped him load his things into an open wagon, and tied the gelding behind. Climbing up next to his brother, he clucked for the mule to pull away from the front of the barn.

"Now, Brother, don't you go an' shame us at Mister McDowell's place. You can either do well, and show Mama and Daddy you're going to be a strong man and make them proud, Or you can sit around like some sissy boy who wants everybody to cry for him."

"I ain't no sissy boy, James! What do you know about me and what's been goin' on here for the last five years? Leave go of me!" Stokes pushed James hard on the shoulder, slid sideways on the driver's bench and grabbed the reins yelling, "Gee-up!"

He reached behind him for the whip and gave a good crack with it over the mule's head.

James pulled his hat lower over his brow and slumped back in his seat.

The trip to the McDowell piece of land was short, but long enough for James to assess the immediate future of his diminished family. Martha and William should have had plenty of privacy by now; the haste and urgency of his own passion with Chloe having gradually dimmed into a romantic haze of the past. He wanted to settle himself with his baby and younger siblings, and find time during the weekends for building a temporary set of rooms for seeing patients on the site of the burned-out cabin where Elizabeth had died.

Dilby's Nan was still mighty shy and fearful of what she perceived as a violent white world, so he hoped he could start training her at the new clinic and letting her see some pretty sorry white folks coming in for treatment. *Yes sir, in a few years I'm going to see if Dilby'll let me take Nan to Miz Burridge up in Augusta.*

Chapter 35 — Stokes

Plateye seemed to be sleeping in some dark cave, leaving the white man free of his insinuating ways, calculating wiles, and grasping fingers. Yet he never left the nightmares of slaves at the end of a hard day. Peddlers of human flesh walked chains of men behind a lead mule over the countryside of Pike County, calling out their human merchandise from the roads in front of farmhouses.

Life on the Allen farm seemed peaceful. James brought several indentured servants to work the farm alongside the older black workers, trying to appease his conscience by renouncing the purchase of new slaves.

One evening in 1827, during an exceptionally cold spring, Stokes Allen was seventeen years old and spending some time working for James during the harvest. He walked out behind the Allen's house to lay muslin sheets over newly sprouted seedlings in the kitchen garden. Dilby had predicted a late frost that night, and the air was crisp and clear, with stars sharply visible in the early evening sky. He could hear the waters of the creek in the distance and felt an urge to walk over to it in the quiet of the night. The creek was about a hundred yards away. After he arrived he saw that the water had swollen over its banks and rushed noisily over rocks. He didn't hear a man who sneaked up behind him. One moment he was gazing at Venus in the darkening sky, and the next he was stretched out on the ground, his hand holding a folded flap of bark. The message from Josh had arrived.

Dilby arose from her bed with a low moan, lit a candle, and hurried to answer the knocking at her door. She felt the cold more than usual this year. Her bones seemed to grind and crunch against each other when she sat or lay down for any length of time. She touched the graying bush of hair that sprang from her head before opening the door.

"Don't worry, Dilby, it's just me, Stokes Allen," a voice called out from the other side. She opened the door and rushed him into the room, to quickly close the door against the cold.

"What you want so late, Mistah Stokes? My Lord, what happened to you face? Let me get some water to wash off dried blood on yo' forehead!"

"Don't you worry, Dilby, it just seems someone had to deliver a message without bein' seen. I showed this to James and he said to tell you." Stokes unfolded the flaking bark and held it close to the candle for her to see.

"This here is a note, James thinks it's for you and him. It says, "Josh lives and Drew Allen is dead.""

Stokes caught Dilby in his arms as she fell sideways. The candle tumbled across the floor. He eased her down before stamping on the flame that had already begun to singe the hem of a quilted bedspread. He waited until she had revived, before leaving as she urged, "Gwan now, I be fine...jus' gettin' old."

The next day Dilby sat in her cabin and meditated on the scrap of bark in her lap. Josh was alive, but now she knew he could never return to her. He would never know that she was really alive. She clasped the small leather pouch that rested between her breasts and began to rock as she hummed the mournful tune.

I had a dream, last night, that's troublin' me—
Her voice rose higher:
I had a dream, last night, that's troublin' me.
I lay down in my bed,
Somethin' jump into my head—
I had a dream, last night—

Her voice broke. She fell silent, her shoulders shaking as a tear trickled slowly down her cheek. "Oh God! Why you don't free us all from dis evil spirit? Plateye done won, and You just sleepin' through it all."

Chapter 36 — Plateye Lives

Young Drewry grew up to be a leader in the new and prospering Pike County. He had a vivacity and charm about him that attracted people, but James wouldn't let him rest on that easy road of life. Young had to perform every evening for his father, translating classics from Greek and Latin, and discussing with him the latest political events out of the new capitol building in Milledgeville. James smiled to himself as he watched his first-born son develop. *He has Chloe's sparkle and eager mind. Yes, Darlin', your son can charm the pants off these farmers, but he's smart too, with just a tad of cunning that might make ol' Monsieur proud.*

Mr. Young D. Allen was elected to the State legislature for two terms in 1845. He had married a bright young woman named Clara Brooks, whose mother had died in childbirth. She had suffered Young's same deprivation of maternal love. They raised three sons together, who reached maturity in 1861—just in time for the tragedy of the Civil War.

Robert, the eldest of the three, took after his grandfather, James, with curly dark hair and hooded brown eyes. He was as tall as great grandfather Drewry, but tended to be a bully in school until cousin Willy McDowell knocked him into the creek one day and stole the shoes off his feet as he crawled to the side of the stream. Poor Robert stumbled home on bare feet, much humbled by his humiliation.

A large group of young men, including Robert, went out with the Confederate Guards, Company A of the 13th Georgia Regiment, in 1861. It was the first of seven companies in Georgia, and was placed in Gordon's Brigade of the Army of Northern Virginia.

Six months later, after a disastrous battle, Robert found himself alone at dawn, stumbling through a woods. Morning mists swirled about the trunks of the surrounding trees. He had become separated during the night, after the soldiers in his platoon fled in panic from a barrage of canon fire. They had disappeared into the brush, each flailing desperately at branches that blocked their way and totally unaware of direction as they ran, then fell, got up and ran again.

Then all was quiet. The air seemed to tremble with the last vibration of gunfire. Something disturbed the leaves on the forest floor—the wind perhaps. As the sun began to rise, trees were brightly backlit in the mist. Swirls of vapor were picked up like wraiths, will-o'-the-wisps, curling around the young man's body.

A high-pitched scream broke the silence. Robert saw a long, low shape lope by, a twitching rabbit caught in its jaws. His heart beat so fast, *like a kettle drum*, that he felt it would burst from his chest.

The trees gained a halo as the sun burned through the morning haze; Robert brought a hand up to shade his eyes. Another dark shape emerged from behind one of the trees and started to come towards him. Cold fear gripped his gut and a strange aching pain swept upwards from his belly. A musky smell seeped from the ground. He choked violently, spitting phlegm on the earth. *Not a moment to lose.* He turned and ran again, this time sure that the creature was breathing hard on his neck. He called out in desperation, screaming for help from anywhere. Stumbling, whirling, he gasped for air as he fought his way once more through the forest.

The breath on his neck came closer. Then he was on the ground, curled into a fetal position, waiting for whatever horror was behind him. He felt a wetness under his ear that flowed down his neck and onto the ground beneath. All tension released his body, and the thud of his pulse vibrated against the bones of his skull.

"You almost be mine, boy. But somethin' sweet and dark inside you, keepin' me away. Ah, Ah, there's some love holdin' here, she's comin' from the salt sea, from long ago." The whispered words drifted away, soft as a sigh, and Robert saw and felt nothing more.

ॐ

He awoke in a hospital tent three days later. A pretty, round face leaned over him, and broke into a smile as he opened his eyes.

"There you are! Back at last. Doctor, he's with us now." The young woman hurried away, then returned. Two faces leaned over to look into his eyes. One belonged to a stern-eyed older man who took his wrist and felt for the pulse.

The doctor shook his head in wonderment. "You are a truly amazing boy. Your jugular was severed by a piece of shrapnel on the field, and somehow someone must have been right there to tie off the vein. You could have fallen right next to an army surgeon, 'cause this was done real pretty."

For several generations of Allens and McDowells the story of the amazing wound to Robert's neck was told over and over again, and of course compared with the strange coincidence it had with the wound of his great grandfather Drewry Allen. The tree branch, or the iron rod used to uproot the tree, had whipped against his jugular vein and severed it; he had bled to death quickly. Robert never told anyone of his delusional encounter with the dark figure in the woods. It must have been a phantasm, a figure from his imagination arising out of the stress of battle. Still, he had strange dreams afterwards that recurred every few years: A golden-fleshed young woman with auburn curls sang a song to an infant in her arms, then turned and smiled at him before disappearing.

When Robert told his grandfather about the dream, James sat back in his rocking chair and looked off into another space. He was a very old man by that time, and had buried a second wife, after siring seven more children. Yet Chloe was the spirit who haunted him. He had cherished their short time together all his life. When he closed his eyes at night, Chloe's image floated there. He saw the same vision as his grandson over and over. He and Chloe had watched through the years as Young Drewry grew to manhood, searching yet fearing to find signs of the Chauvin disease. He had been right; Chloe's strong heritage had defeated "the Magrums."

This time, when he closed his eyes, after Robert left, Chloe was there again. She placed her ghostly infant in the crib and turned to look at James with a slight frown.

"Tell the boy, James. He should know." But James could never tell Robert the truth. It was, finally, his betrayal of love. Plateye still hid, waiting to beguile once more, while love waited for a day when fears of African roots would dim and gradually blink out.

Ekka Ghassi also waited, alive as a great possibility in the hearts of each generation.

Epilogue

James had acquired several hundred more acres for the farm near Zebulon, Georgia. before he died, and left a substantial inheritance. Martha bore nine children to William, yet still managed to assist him in the schoolroom in between pregnancies. Her brother Stokes became a partner in the new sawmill that was built in 1834. He became quite wealthy for that area, and moved into a large home in Zebulon.

Emily made up for a lack of intellectual vigor by becoming an energetic flirt, charming young men for miles around with her long, red-gold hair and wickedly teasing personality. She married at age sixteen, under slightly suspicious circumstances, a new baby arriving after seven and a half months. James proudly escorted his youngest sister down the aisle of the new Baptist Church across from the Courthouse. Even the oldest ladies of the congregation beamed benignly from their pews as the couple passed by.

Three years later, when James made one of his annual visits to Augusta, to review the operations at what was then called the Telfair Hospital, he took Dilby's daughter Nan with him. They spent a month in the city, during which time James visited the remnants of the Quaker communities to the north west of town. He Introduced Nan to Clarice Burridge and several of the families planning to move to a new Quaker village in Ohio. Clarice worked out arrangements for Nan to travel to Ohio as companion and free house servant to an aging matriarch. Nan was by this time both literate and gifted with numbers. Dilby mourned the loss of her daughter, but urged her to "get goin' north, Baby. Do it for me an' my love for you."

Nan wrote to James years later, telling of the school where she became assistant teacher, and eventually head mistress.

Dilby lived to be an old woman of eighty years. She worked for most of those years with James, treating the slave population outwardly, but seeing some white women secretly, who came to her late at night seeking help with unwanted pregnancies, or hoping for magical potions to attract a bored husband or indifferent lover.

The clinic was divided in two sections, with a door for Dilby's patients at one end and another door for James's appointments at the other. James worked both sides, entering each from an inner door. It was an elaborate strategy that fooled nobody, but enabled both healers to see patients and discuss treatments.

It was discovered in the late 1800s that the disease afflicting families like the Chauvin's was indeed hereditary. Each child of an affected parent had a fifty percent chance of inheriting it. The disease was not generally recognized until the classic description of it by George Huntington, in 1872. Genealogical studies now suggest that the disease had existed in America since at least the seventeenth century.

Georges Chauvin exhibited almost every symptom of Huntington's disease, with a midlife onset that gradually worsened. Whole muscle groups acted involuntarily, with flicking of fingers, tapping of feet, leg vibrations, and facial grimacing. He became more and more irritable, was wildly maniacal at times, and was easily provoked to anger towards the end.

Dr. Huntington noted in a paper presented in Ohio, in 1872, that if children of affected parents went through life without the onset of the disease, "The thread is broken and the grandchildren and great-grandchildren of the original "shakers" may rest assured that they are free from the disease." Thus Plateye, ever resourceful, had to find other means of destroying his victims.

The descendants of Drewry Allen survived in the socially crippled society of the Old South, most of them decent, caring human beings living in a centuries-old web of human exploitation. They thrived and suffered in each generation, finally struggling through the horrors of a cruel civil war that brought them all into decades of mind-numbing poverty.

Only Joshua and Nan succeeded in escaping the invasive power of Plateye. Nan and her offspring lived in a strict Quaker community, one that abhorred both slavery and violence. She married a hard-working farmer and built a reputation as an educator, devising teaching skills that were far ahead of their time and incorporated a curriculum with the teachings of the Society of Friends. Her school grew from a one-room building to a large establishment for children from kindergarten through twelfth grade.

Joshua lived a dangerous and strenuous life in the steamy forests of southern Florida with Walini and their many children. Yet he was surrounded by a people who respected and honored him for his courage, strength and quick wits. He felt truly reborn as a Yatsiminoli; the killing of Drewry Allen was, for him, a cleansing of the shame of his old life.

His new people never surrendered to the Americans, and his grandsons became powerful in the political struggles of their time, representing the Seminoles in State and Federal courtrooms.

About the Author

B orn in New York City, Jennifer Allen Noyer has been both a contemporary dance choreographer and an author. Her graduate studies in dance at the University of Michigan, the humanities at Detroit's Wayne State University focused on the complementary crossovers between dance, the arts and history. She was given the 2002 Arts Achievement Award by Wayne State University, and has become an award winning sculptor in New Mexico.

Ms. Noyer has written *The Legacy*, a comprehensive video/text overview of the career and choreography of Bill Evens and the history of his company. *The Albuquerque Journal* employed her as dance critic for twenty-six years. Her lifetime concerns for the destructive effects of racism and slavery in America led to the writing of the novel *Plateye*.

Ms. Noyer lives with her husband Albert in the Sandia Mountains of New Mexico.

CPSIA information can be obtained at www.ICGtesting.com
Printed in the USA
LVOW10s0457051114

411665LV00004B/1/P